Also By

DREA DAMARA

The Blinney Lane Series

The Weeping Books Of Blinney Lane

The Trinity Missions

Chasing Vengeance

No Death For The Wicked

Contributing Author

In Creeps The Night

featuring "The Blessing"

A Winter's Romance

featuring "Lighting The Darkness"

A BLINNEY LANE NOVEL

BEYOND FARWIN WOOD

DREA DAMARA

INDIGO
Livonia, Michigan

BEYOND FARWIN WOOD

Published by BHC Press
under the Indigo imprint

Library of Congress Control Number: 2016954229

ISBN: 978-1-948540-43-8 (Hardcover)
ISBN: 978-1-948540-71-1 (Softcover)
ISBN: 978-1-948540-44-5 (Ebook)

Visit the publisher:
www.bhcpress.com

ACKNOWLEDGMENTS

I'd like to thank BHC Press for their talent and tireless dedication to my projects. I am humbled to say I now have fans. Without your interest, I would not have created this addition to Blinney Lane—this story truly is for you—*a place far beyond, but forever yours and near.*

for all the misfits

BEYOND FARWIN WOOD

A BLINNEY LANE NOVEL

CHAPTER ONE

FARWIN WOOD

A WARRIOR with nothing to do is a troubled warrior."

This was the response Varmeer gave to Lord Vasimus Daundecort when asked why Ranthrop Groslivo, Lord of the Southlands, continued to train so intensely even though peace now reigned in the land.

"That explains nothing, Varmeer. I consider myself a warrior, and I have plenty to do as should Ranthrop," Lord Vasimus groused as they sat on a bench in the training area that abutted Daundecort Hall.

Varmeer touched his bloodied lower lip, wincing. Ranthrop had taken turns jousting with them until they had been forced to forfeit. Waiting on the sidelines, they watched as Ranthrop clambered mighty blows against the sword and shield of one of Lord Vasimus's men. Angry growls and grunts escaped the sandy-haired giant with each bash and thrust. As the opponent slumped to his knees, Varmeer's hope fizzled, wondering if Ranthrop would call for a new opponent. "Lord Vasimus, not all men are as easily satisfied with their daily obligations as you, I fear."

Vasimus snorted, standing with evident rigidity that wasn't his norm. His swollen fingers rubbed a knot on his knee, a gift from his joust. "*All* men? Or just our friend Ranthrop here?"

Varmeer thumped his head against the wall and closed his tired eyes. *A visit*, that's what Ranthrop had told him when they'd ventured from Groslivo Stronghold three days ago. He listened as Vasimus strode over to congratulate Ranthrop on yet another win and that the pummeling of his men was over for today. Thank the stars!

The clank of metal shin guards and squeak of rustling leather grew closer. He could sense Ranthrop's imposing presence before he heard the familiar gruff voice.

"Am I boring you, old man?" Ranthrop asked with exuberance. Varmeer took comfort in the sound of heavy breathing between the man's words.

Varmeer cracked a lazy eye open as Ranthrop gave his foot a swift kick. "What's to bore when you so gracelessly bash each man in such a uniquely different way, my lord?"

Ranthrop threw his head back and laughed. He brought his fist down and mock punched Varmeer in the lip. "Graceless, was I? Sounds more like you are a graceless loser!"

The three men rallied and walked down the patio that wrapped around Daundecort Hall. The men hobbled, casting their torsos in different angles; a motley crew of disheveled warriors—two in red Southland tunics, one in Northland blue. Past the thick shale stones of the lofty fortress walls, they trudged through a side entrance, leg and arm bracers squeaking over their strained muscles.

Vasimus led them to a thick wooden table at the end of his great room where a pitcher and goblets awaited. The men let their swords clatter to the floor, discarded, and each collapsed into a seat.

Ranthrop held out his cup to Vasimus who poured a lime-green colored liquid from the pitcher. He waited for the other two men to have their goblets filled and then raised his for an expectant toast.

"To peace in the land," Vasimus declared.

"We can't drink to peace every time," Ranthrop stated. Vasimus cast him a bland look as though he were awaiting an alternate suggestion. "To Farwin Wood," Ranthrop finally added. The two lords looked at Ranthrop's trusty guard for his contribution.

"To no longer dueling," Varmeer said wearily.

"Almost like peace...I'll drink to that." Vasimus clanked his goblet against Varmeer's, leaving Ranthrop to stare at them dumbfounded with his own glass held out like a neglected friend.

"What's the matter with you two? You sound like old women!"

Vasimus wiped his brow with his sleeve. "And thanks to you, Lord Ranthrop, me and half my personal guard have *felt* like old women these past few days. If I didn't know better, I'd think you merely paid me a visit just to use us as jousting dummies. What say you, Varmeer? Is the guard at Groslivo Stronghold as battered as mine?"

Varmeer glanced at Ranthrop who scowled at both of them. "I cannot lie. There has been a lot of unnecessary training these past few weeks."

"Ah, I see." Vasimus pinned his light blue eyes on Ranthrop. "Are you sure you're not planning to go to war with me again?"

Ranthrop sucked in a sharp breath, nostrils flaring. "I am restless, not stupid."

Vasimus leaned forward and clasped his goblet, his wavy black hair settling just above the silver-floral cloak clasps on his shoulders. "What have you to be restless about? There is much to be done. Why, there isn't a day that goes by I don't find something on my lands that needs repair or someone who needs assistance."

Ranthrop slumped back in his chair. His head hit the high back with a thump, legs sprawling lazily out before him. Taking long gulps of beetleburry ale with unkempt slurps, he frowned. "I have repaired nearly everything I can throw a stone at."

"Sire, there is much to be done in Naublock Village. The stable at the stronghold needs a new roof and the barracks are still in need of repairs," Varmeer reminded him.

"We are not at war any longer, Varmeer," Ranthrop complained, pointing a finger toward Vasimus. "There's no need to give him a report."

Vasimus gawked at Ranthrop, and then shifted his eyes to Varmeer. "My word, how long has he been like this?"

Varmeer sighed. "Weeks."

Ranthrop sucked down another chug of ale. He slammed his goblet down and glared at it, his mouth twisting in a sour line. When he realized it had grown quiet, he looked up and found both men watching him. He could no longer escape their scrutiny or make excuses. "I have…grown bored."

Vasimus splayed open his free hand as though he were pleading. "But you wanted peace! You confided to me afterward that you had grown tired of our war and wanted life to get back to normal."

"I did! I still do, but something...is not right within me. I cannot help but feel something is missing."

Vasimus and Varmeer caught each other's astonishment. "Perhaps you are ready for a wife?" Vasimus asked.

Ranthrop's face flashed from somber to disgust. "Did I hit you in the head out there? Whatever gave you that idea?"

"You said something is missing. Maybe what you're craving is companionship. It might do you good to settle down."

"Feel free to clip your own wings, Vasimus, but I have no desire to chain myself down just yet," Ranthrop snapped and refilled his goblet to the brim.

Varmeer didn't miss the look that Vasimus gave him as his lord pouted like an overgrown child. He had lost count of how many times he had already tried to assuage Ranthrop's restlessness over the past few weeks. He dug down deep to muster more patience and enthusiasm. "If not settled then, my lord, why not seek out some new wenches while we're here in the north? Perhaps a pretty new face will do the trick?"

Ranthrop resumed his dejected pose and stared at his feet. "I've grown tired of wenches."

Vasimus and Varmeer snapped their eyes to each other. They turned in unison and stared at the unhappy man.

"Ranthrop, are you feeling unwell?" Varmeer spoke so hastily he didn't even think to add the man's title, although he could get away with it. He had served him for the last twenty years. Their relationship was closer to friendship than one of lord and personal guard.

Ranthrop's wide chest heaved. The golden embroidered crest on his tunic bulged. "Don't worry yourself, Varmeer. I've not gone mad. I simply cannot seem to find joy in anything anymore. Nothing excites me. I have this craving...for adventure."

"Adventure?" Vasimus asked. He eyed the man strangely as he brought his goblet to his lips. "Be careful what you wish for."

CHAPTER TWO

BLINNEY LANE, SALEM, MASSACHUSETTS

NO MATTER how much you are willing to give or accept, love can be a downright selfish bastard. There was no denying it, Franci Doltman acknowledged, as fat tears streamed down her porcelain face. Famed film actress Lorna DuClaire graced the screen of her television set as she watched one of Lorna's classic romance movies for the fourth time in a week.

The tissue flapped as she blew her nose violently. She sat curled up on her floral sofa under the reassuring comfort of one of her mother's old afghans. She watched as Lorna strutted in a silky gown. The actress's shapely legs took each step like she was born to wear the strappy high heels fastened around her trim ankles. Lorna stopped at a garden railing and gazed out into the distance, a forlorn look on her face and tears in her eyes.

The handsome Archie Hamlin with his combed-back black hair looked dapper in his black suit as he inched up behind Lorna and grasped her shoulders. Franci held her breath, waiting for the words she knew he would speak.

"What do you want me to say, Melody?" Archie leaned in and whispered by Lorna's ear, his chin grazing the side of her cheek. "That I've loved you from the moment I met you? That I would have waited on you hand and foot until the day I died if I knew there was a chance you could have ever been mine?"

"Ricardo, don't! Don't do this...not after all that's happened. It's too much!" Lorna said as her voice caught in her throat.

Franci clenched the wadded tissue in her hand closer to her chest. Her lower lip trembled as she watched, holding back the urge to sob.

"No! I have to say it." Archie jerked Lorna around and into his arms. "I loved you then, and I love you now. I've loved you so much it hurt in ways I didn't know were possible!"

"Ricardo, no! Don't make me hear anymore."

"I won't." Archie traced Lorna's jaw with his thumb as she turned her head away. "That's why I've come to say good-bye. I knew you could never be mine; now you finally know it too."

Franci let out an anguished wail and sobbed just as Lorna did on the screen. She hated this part. For the life of her, she couldn't understand why she continually watched it. Melody, Lorna's character in *The Lady and the Doorman*, had scorned Ricardo when he was her butler. Now, nearly destitute, Melody runs into Ricardo years later and finds the tables have turned. Ricardo, polished from head to toe, is now a wealthy business owner...and married.

"Don't cry," Archie whispered to Lorna. Franci sniffled to silence as though he commanded her as well. "I'm a married man. We can't change that, but kiss me good-bye...as old friends."

"We were never even friends, were we? I treated you terribly," Lorna warbled, and Franci tearfully mouthed the words along with her.

"Then kiss me like the friends we could have been. Kiss me like the lover I wanted to be, like the man you want now, like the woman I can't have. Kiss me good-bye, Melody. It's the only thing I've ever asked of you. Just kiss me, damn it!"

Franci let out a wistful breath as she watched Archie embrace Lorna. She blew her nose, dabbed at her eyes, and then clicked the remote to silence her pain. She got up and grabbed the wadded tissues that tumbled from her lap. Collecting her teacup, she went into the kitchen and made her way to the window.

The hole in her heart intensified each day since her mother had passed away two weeks ago. She'd closed her store the week after the funeral but reopened once her friends began to worry about her. She hadn't told them that she'd spent each night watching her favorite sappy love movies, dreaming of a different life.

With her mother gone, no one helped to occupy her days or nights. Without her mother to wait on, she realized she wasn't happy with herself. Since that revelation, she hadn't been able to break free from her emotional slump.

I'm too old to find someone now, she thought as she stared at the soft glow of light from her greenhouse below. I don't have any children. No one will be here for me like I was for Mother. I'm going to die alone.

All was quiet tonight from her view through the apartment window above her shop. The expanse of yard between the back of the shops and the stretch of houses, inhabited by some of the other Blinney shopkeepers, was void of life.

This space had been unanimously combined by the residents to serve as a community courtyard. There were benches and picnic tables on a patio in the center of the strip where the shop owners had their weekly cookouts. Pumpkins and corn shocks encircled four gaslights at its corners for the upcoming Halloween holiday. The sight of the dormant common area only made her feel more alone. She stirred her tea and walked the length of her kitchen to the front of her apartment, hoping for a more promising view.

From the window that overlooked Blinney Lane, she noticed a light on in Sarah Allister's apartment above the bookstore. When Henry Teager passed by one of the windows she let out a wistful breath. At least Sarah was no longer alone.

Sarah had been dating Henry, Blinney Lane's deliveryman, ever since he rescued her from a misadventure into one of the cursed "weeping books." How Franci would love to venture into one of those books. Maybe there, no one would care that she was a bit eccentric or plain in appearance.

Raised on Blinney Lane, she didn't find it unusual to dress in old-fashioned clothing. The scars of the Agatha Blinney curse appeared upon her neck when she was seventeen. The high-collared dresses she wore to hide the ugly marks had been a saving grace. Looking out the window at Sarah's newfound happiness, she wondered if dressing more modern like Sarah would have helped her in the "love department."

Franci had never put much stock in her appearance. She was a romantic. She had always assumed that "Mr. Right" would find her like he did the heroines in the old movies she watched. Lorna DuClaire certainly wouldn't have had to worry about tempting a man into falling for her. No, when Lorna waltzed into a room, heads turned.

She looked down at her dated furry house robe. "I'm no Lorna DuClaire. I need to stop feeling sorry myself."

Turning away from the window, an idea bloomed. She would take advantage of the Halloween season by exploring what it felt like to be someone else.

Her spirits lifted as she returned to the living room and put on another Lorna DuClaire movie, *The Singer and the Suit,* featuring Lorna in one of her feistiest, most glamorous roles. It had the added bonus of Franci's favorite leading man, Archie Hamlin! Nothing would be better motivation. After all, Lorna and Archie had been married in real life. Maybe Franci would finally meet her own Archie.

When the movie started, Franci sat down to her laptop at the living room table and searched the internet for Lorna DuClaire costumes. The shop owners on Blinney Lane always dressed up in costume for the entire two weeks prior to Halloween. She'd already missed a few days due to her sulking. Her friends usually dressed like a different character each day, but she didn't care. This year...she was going to be Lorna DuClaire every day of the Halloween season.

Lorna had starred in enough roles that technically Franci could be a different character each day. She knew all of Lorna's parts by heart. It was Halloween, and no one would bat an eye if she tried on different personalities. By the end of the week, maybe she would feel like a different person. And then she could transform into the woman she knew lurked within her.

She found a site with a few costumes that replicated some outfits Lorna had worn in her films but wasn't satisfied with the selection. She picked up her phone and called Genie Mathers's who ran a dress shop at the end of the street. Genie actually had one Lorna DuClaire costume she'd made several years ago that a customer had never picked up. Sold!

After that, Franci went through her old dresses to see what she could alter herself. She gave up scouring through her wardrobe and went into her mother's old room. In the back of her mother's closet, she found some long vintage slips and a few elegant mid-century gowns. With a few adjustments and creativity, she could turn them into Lorna DuClaire costumes. The thought made her giddy and the nostalgia of wearing some of her mother's clothes warmed her heart.

Franci sat down at her mother's sewing machine and began the alterations. She thought about Genie's warning not to wear the costume more than once, which made her want to laugh. She knew about the power of the clothing Genie made well-enough already.

The costumes made in Genie's shop, particularly ones that were modeled after people who had actually existed, could cause the wearer to act like that person if they donned them for too long. Luckily, the effect wasn't strong on outsiders, especially if they wore the costume elsewhere than Blinney Lane.

Franci didn't care if she did get a little boost of charisma from the "Lorna costume." After all, she didn't need trick costumes with the loot she'd just discovered in the closet.

Franci reached for a new spool of thread, her seasoned fingers threading the spool without a glance. If she had looked, she would have noticed the label on the bottom that read: Handmade. Mathers's Dress Shop, Blinney Lane, Salem, MA.

Franci hummed as she looked at her progress on the dress. "Look out, Archie! Here comes Lorna."

CHAPTER THREE

FRANCI WASN'T the only one whose life had never known a happily ever after. Valerie Millville was walking proof that love was, in fact, selfish. If not love, at least, Dexter Haynes.

Ugh. How can someone you found so attractive one day become so revolting the next? she wondered.

"Why the hell are you still following me?" she screamed over her shoulder as she pushed through the gate to the passage between Franci's and her mother's shops.

"Val, come on! You got it all wrong. What are you going off about? Would you let me explain?" Dexter pleaded. The gate ricocheted back and smashed into his arm.

Valerie stopped just as she reached Franci's greenhouse. She spun around, pinning him with her eyes. She watched him fumble through the gate and hurry toward her. His narrow frame lumbered clumsily under his bulky, black leather jacket. His combat boots thudded against the cobblestones. Ripped jeans, a silver earring, a wallet-chain dangling from his jeans pocket—all the things she'd once found cool about him.

"Explain? Why would I want to hear you explain that you cancelled our plans to go shag some other chick?" She spun around and proceeded to march toward the back of her house.

She'd accidentally answered his phone when they were in the car, thinking it was hers. The purring voice of someone named Charlene greeted her, cooing that she was waiting impatiently and promising it would be better than last time.

"Val, wait up!"

She tromped up the deck stairs to the back of her house and clamped a hand on the screen door. When she heard his steps approaching, she turned back, halting him with her icy glare.

"Look, she's…she's…"

"That's one too many 'she's.' Just save it."

He ran up the steps when she jerked the door open. "No, wait! She's auditioning for the band. I was just going to meet her to see if she's any good."

"You expect me to believe she's auditioning for your band...your *all-male* band…called Man Cave?"

"Yeah. We're thinking about diversifying to appeal to a bigger audience."

Both Valerie and Dexter turned their attention to a noise inside. Mary Millville appeared on the other side of the door, pulling on a silky lavender robe, her mess of gray curls strewn about her shoulders.

"Valerie," Mary whispered sharply. "What's going on? You're going to wake up the whole neighborhood." Mary's features took on a different countenance when she noticed Dexter standing on the deck. She tugged her robe tighter over her pajamas.

Dexter held up a hand. "Hello, Mrs. Millville."

"Hello, Dexter." Mary turned and whispered to Valerie, "Why don't you invite him inside? At least then not all the neighbors will hear."

"No, Mom. Dexter was just leaving. This won't take long." Valerie gave her mother a feigned smile before turning back to Dexter. She walked up to him slowly as she spoke. "Dexter, I'm sure Charlene will be very good. But *you*, on the other hand..." She swung her leg and brought the toe of her shoe hard into his groin. "...won't be!"

Dexter let out a grunt and doubled-over, dropping to his knees.

"My goodness!" Mary gasped. Her eyes darted from Dexter to Valerie, who walked inside and let the door slam behind her. "I...should we do something for him?"

Valerie shut the inside door to block her mother's view of Dexter. "What? Like ice his balls for him?"

Valerie tugged off her brown leather jacket and hung it up on a peg in the hallway. She could feel her mother eying her outfit disapprovingly as she often did. She was a half-foot taller than Mary, having taken after her father. She also had his straight pitch-black hair, while her mother had been blonde before graying. Mary usually wore long, frumpy dresses made of linen. Valerie opted for short skirts, tight tops, and preferred leather and acrylic.

"You don't have to be so crude."

"*Crude* is what Dexter did, not me. I just had to listen to some hussy purr in my ear about how excited she was that he was meeting up with her for a rendezvous."

"So...this one's over now too, I presume?"

"Ma, you didn't even like Dexter. Don't try to make me feel like you're disappointed." She rolled her eyes and started for the stairs that led up to her room. She wasn't in the mood to hear her mother's latest opinion on her love life.

"But I am disappointed. How are you ever going to meet a nice man when you go through them so fast I can barely learn their names?"

She was really going to go there? Valerie spun around on the steps. Her mother always turned her nose up at how she dressed, her hair. Even the small diamond stud in her nose. And now this! Couldn't she make up her mind? Talk about being a hypocrite. Her mother had no idea how hard she tried. How could she find someone and commit, which her mother insisted upon, if she didn't date? She might as well just have called her "loose." Her mother acted as if she were intimate with every man she dated. She'd never know the pain of how many "Prince Charmings" had deceived her and let her down, or were just plain unacceptable. The woman never gave her any credit.

Valerie tried not to raise her voice. "What do you want from me? Do you think lowering my standards means I'll meet someone decent? Or am I supposed to stay at home like a nun and pray some knight in shining armor will just burst through the door one day?"

Mary set her hands on her wide hips. "I don't know if it's possible to lower your standards any further, but maybe if you were a little more pleasant and actually took some pride in your appearance you'd meet the kind of person who'd burst through a door after you and sticks around."

Her words hit like a blow to the stomach. Of course her mother expected her to be just like she was—proper manners, dress in pastels, plaster a fake smile on her face. And where had that gotten her mother? Valerie's father had left when she was only thirteen.

"Someone just like Dad, you mean? A lot of good that did *you*!"

Her words might as well have been a bucket of water because they doused the angry lines in Mary's face instantly. Her hands dropped from her hips and her shoulders sagged. Valerie swallowed a lump in her throat, realizing what she'd just said as Mary stared at her with evident hurt.

When she thought the uncomfortable silence couldn't get any worse, Mary's back straightened. She turned, without a word, and walked down the hallway to her bedroom.

Valerie collapsed onto her backside and leaned against the banister railing. She felt sick. How could she have said that to her own mother?

Why was it so difficult to connect with her? She knew they were different but wasn't love enough? Couldn't Mary see that she loved her in spite of all their differences?

She hated that her father had abandoned them. Although Mary would never admit it, it had also hurt her deeply. Her mother acted as if nothing had happened and never spoke of him again.

Valerie's father had left because he couldn't handle the cloistered life on Blinney Lane. He lived in fear of the unusual things, which occurred on the cursed dead-end street where they lived and ran their shop, Scents and Suds. She remembered him screaming and hollering whenever he stumbled across anything strange.

Shortly before he left, her mother had been mixing a new type of soap. Her father tried it and the following day he awoke to find his entire body covered in what resembled raccoon fur. His screams had filled the morning as he frantically shaved his hands. She remembered telling him, "At least you didn't grow a tail." But he only slammed the door in her face.

The sight hadn't shocked Valerie, even at the age of thirteen. Nothing on Blinney Lane ever surprised or worried her like it did the other residents. She knew there was always a way to resolve any issue that the curse of Agatha Blinney caused—the woman whom the ancestors of the Blinney Lane shop owners had condemned as a witch years ago.

She wished her mother didn't harbor the pain of being abandoned by her father. Now that she was older and could put things into perspective, she knew he wasn't worth it. Her father had always been humorless and boring. Maybe that's why her mother had married him. He probably seemed like a safe bet for someone who was stuck on Blinney Lane. Her mother was one of the unlucky who bore the scars of Agatha Blinney and couldn't wander more than three blocks from the peculiar street. Perhaps Mary had just taken what she could get when she'd met her father.

As much as Mary fretted about things, Valerie could now see that her mother had been the stronger of her parents. Whenever something had gone amiss in their shop, or on Blinney Lane, Mary never went into hysterics like her father had. The older Valerie got, the less she respected him. How could he give up his family and not tolerate life on Blinney Lane for them? She accepted their life was difficult living there. But what kind of man didn't face his fears for the ones he loved? It had taught her never to be like him. She would never make anyone feel like they were abandoned. That's why she'd told her mother she had the scars of Agatha Blinney, even though she hadn't.

When she was seventeen, her mother began making comments about her going off to college or being able to start a new life outside of Blinney Lane. The curse of Agatha Blinney chose who it wanted to keep captive. It did so by the appearance of scars forming on the inhabitant by their eighteenth birthday. Once the person had the scars, they could never venture far from Blinney Lane without enduring unbearable pain.

Two months before her eighteenth birthday, Valerie still hadn't gotten any scars that resembled the wounds Agatha had received when she was tortured by the villagers so long ago. Mary had been relieved and hopeful, even a little forlorn, that her daughter would soon be able to leave. Valerie made a decision one night and came downstairs the next day with sweatbands around her wrists.

She explained to her mother that scars had formed on her wrists during the night, just like the marks Agatha Blinney had gotten from the rope binding her hands when she was dragged to her place of execution. Mary had been distraught, but Valerie never let on that it was a ruse. Valerie was an only child, and she had no intention of leaving Mary all alone to run their shop as her father had.

She'd probably be furious I never told her. Maybe she'd have preferred I left after what I just said to her tonight, she thought.

Hugging her arms tightly against herself, she tried to suppress the sensation of not feeling welcome in her own home. She didn't belong anywhere. People in town viewed her as eccentric. Fortunately, Mary had never caught on that she'd ventured much farther than three blocks away over the years.

Valerie was different from the outsiders. How could she not be after the life she had lived on Blinney Lane? In truth, she often felt she didn't even belong on Blinney Lane. Mary made sure to reinforce this notion, whether she meant to or not. She was too hip and easy-going for Blinney Lane, and too spooky and knowledgeable of all things holistic and occult for the outside world.

As she mulled over her mother's words, she realized it didn't matter if she tried to act or dress in a more pleasing manner. The kind of man that would be right for her simply didn't exist. She was as weary of not being taken seriously by men as her mother was of her relationships ending in shambles.

Valerie trudged up the steps and reminded herself of the decision she'd made when she was seventeen. She was still committed to not abandoning her mother. She would work on repairing and improving their relationship, although it would be an uphill battle after tonight. She decided to officially give up on men, leaving her nights free to get back into Mary's good graces—a win-win situation. No more dating meant no more complaints from Mary about her choice in men.

Jackal poked his head around the door to her room. The long black fur on his erect tail was bushier than normal. He looked at her with his yellow eyes as though asking if the battle was over. She scooped him up and hugged him to her chest.

"I'm done, mister. You're it for me. Maybe I'll end up like Franci—a crazy, single coot. I'm not wearing those damned dresses though."

CHAPTER
FOUR

ALLISTER'S BOOKS

RICKY ALLISTER walked into his Aunt Sarah's bookstore with a smile on his face, dumping his backpack on the floor by the counter. Filled with heavy textbooks, it landed with a thud. He adjusted his Salem State Vikings hoodie, which had ridden up on his narrow hips. Glancing around the shop, he noticed no customers were ready to check out so he took the opportunity to work on his homework. Perching on the stool behind the counter, he opened his economics textbook.

Five months ago, this wouldn't have been the case. Now, eager to study and learn, he'd enrolled in Salem State University just in time to be accepted for the fall semester; an officially proud freshmen and a member of the men's soccer team. Go Vikings!

A college student with a full-time job, he'd come a long way since the beginning of the summer when he'd been sent to stay with his aunt. Last June he would have fled Salem. Now, there was no place on earth he'd rather be.

His Aunt Sarah walked over and set a book with a crinkled cover jacket on top of the bureau behind him. Eyeing his textbook, she smiled.

Ricky nodded to her. "How was your morning?"

"Oh, pretty good. I had to restock the horror and supernatural books you put on the main display last week. We nearly sold out of everything. People really get in the mood for gore and the occult around Halloween."

"See, I told you they'd do well there." He wriggled his eyebrows. "I can pull some more from the genre shelves after I get this done."

Sarah canted her head. "Well, aren't you the devoted little marketing wiz. How are classes going?"

"Good. I actually still understand everything so far, and my teachers love me. Let's hope it stays that way."

"You're still planning on staying here for the whole semester?"

Ricky frowned and set his pen down on his book. "Do you really not want me here? I thought we were done talking about this?"

"Of course I want you here. You're welcome to stay as long as you want." Sarah shrugged and straightened a bookmark display.

"Why doesn't it feel like that? Is it Henry? Do you guys need more privacy or something? Are you not happy with me working in the shop anymore?"

"No, it's not that at all." Sarah laid a hand on his forearm. "I love you. Henry loves you, and you've helped me here more than I ever could have imagined. I'd trust you with the shop all by yourself if I wasn't here. It's just that...I worry that..."

Ricky gave the customers in the shop a cursory glance before steadying her in his sights. "You're worried the curse will still get me."

Sarah's face was a wall of strained concern as she squeezed his arm. "Yes. You have to see that's still a possibility with you staying here. If you're committed to staying in Salem, why don't you at least rent an apartment outside of Blinney Lane? I talked to Henry last night. He said you could stay with him if you like. Plus, if you still want to work full-time he can get you a job with his company so you don't have to work in the shop."

"Aunt Sarah," he let out a sigh and turned to her in his chair, "I'm not afraid of the curse."

Making a face that was half-doubtful and half-incredulous, she hooked her thumbs into the thin black suspenders fastened to her gray dress slacks. The position indicated she expected a reasonable explanation.

"Okay. I'm not as afraid of the curse as I was a few months ago, but it doesn't bother me as much as it bothers you and the others. I don't care if I end up with the scars. So what if it claims me? What's the big deal?"

"Big deal?" Sarah sputtered, her eyes growing so wide they looked as if they could pop out of her head. "You can't mean that. Are you telling me you're prepared to be stuck here for the rest of your life? You'd have to give up going to college. Salem State is over two miles away. Why would you sacrifice that? Is this…about Shelby?"

"No, it's not about Shelby. I like her. I like her a lot, but believe me, I have enough sense to not make a decision based on my relationship with her even if some of my past indiscretions might still be making you think otherwise."

Sarah withdrew from her stance and added with more delicacy, "No, I don't think that. I trust your judgment. Just not when it comes to this harebrained idea about staying here."

"Look, believe it or not, I have thought about everything. You took distance-learning courses for college. So could I. And I have to work and live somewhere for the rest of my life. Why not here? I like it here. Everyone's really friendly. It's peaceful and private. I grew up in New York City. It's nice being somewhere less crowded without horns honking all night long. I could see myself being happy here. Even if some of you guys don't like it, you have to admit, it is possible to live and work on Blinney Lane."

"But if you get the scars...you'd never get to leave. You'd never get to see the rest of the world. There wouldn't be any vacations. Have you considered that?"

"Aunt Sarah, I've been to more places than you ever have. No offense. Mom took me to France and England, and Dad and I went to South Africa, remember?"

"Yes, of course I remember. That's my point. You'd never be able to do that again! Don't you think you'd ever want to see anything else? Believe me, no matter how much you might think you love Blinney Lane, after a while, *everyone* wants to leave," Sarah said, folding her arms across her chest.

"Oh?" He arched a brow. "Where would you go?"

Sarah shrugged. "I'd go visit your father in New York City."

"And?"

"And...I'd probably tour Europe."

"Visit...tour... Are you seeing the pattern I'm seeing?"

Sarah planted her hands on her hips and shook her head. "No. What pattern?"

"You'd come right back here, wouldn't you? Because this," he motioned to the store with his hands, "is *home,* isn't it?"

"What's your point?" she asked in annoyance.

"I'm at the time in my life where I have to decide where I want home to be. I'm glad me and Dad have patched things up and get along better now, but I can't see myself living in his penthouse or some apartment there. Isn't it all right if I pick a home that's at least near some of my family, what little I have?"

Sarah made a flabbergasted sound. "What if you're lucky enough to get married someday? You'd be crammed in the apartment upstairs with me. I appreciate the devotion, Ricky, I really do, but if you get married and have kids that's a lot to put on a spouse. You're not going to be a teenager forever, Peter Pan."

He patted her arm. "Well, my dearest aunt, I promise I'll grow up someday, and I promise I'll never grow sick of you even though I can't promise the same will be true of you for me." Sarah shot him a sour look and he chuckled. "*And*...if I get married, I hope it's not to some high-maintenance chick who can't handle my responsibilities, but since you brought it up... I hate to think of outsiders ever running the shops around here. There's three empty shops on the street. I was thinking...I could open one of them."

"*You* want to open a shop *here*?"

"You don't *think* I could run a business?"

She looked up in thought, a tactic he hated that always kept him on the edge of his seat. Finally, she gave an unconvinced, "I suppose you could."

Green light! Now was his chance to go in for the kill. "Great! So who owns the old public house between Alex's blacksmith shop and Genie's place?"

"All the empty shops are owned by the Blinney Council as a trust. Why?"

He pumped his fist into the air, unable to hold back his relief. "Awesome! I'd much rather deal with the council than worry about getting a loan from the bank. Do you think they'd rent or lease it to me?"

"I don't know. Slow down, Ricky." She held her hands up like his energy made her nervous. "I'm still trying to absorb the fact that you want to stay here. What kind of business are you thinking of putting in there?"

"I'd like to keep it traditional and run it as an old-fashioned pub. I could live upstairs so that takes care of your spouse worries for me. I wouldn't rent out any rooms, though," he pointed out, before she could object. "I remember you said the council forbids having lodgers on Blinney Lane again."

A woman about Sarah's age walked up to the counter and set a stack of children's books down. She held onto a little girl's hand at her side. Ricky smiled at her and the little blonde head that stuck up just over the counter. Her curious eyes peered over it at him.

"Hello," the woman started, "I was wondering if I could pay for these now and have you hold them for me while we do some more shopping down the street. We're coming back for story time."

"When are you gonna have the stories?" the girl inquired. Her little fingers clung to the counter so she could maintain eye contact.

"Shh, Karen. I already told you, honey. We'll be back in a little bit," the woman whispered, smoothing a hand over the girl's hair.

Sarah came around the counter and crouched down next to Karen. She looked up to address the girl's mother. "Of course. Ricky will ring you up, and you can just pick them up on your way out later." She directed her attention to Karen and took on a sweet voice. "I have to get into my special story-telling outfit first. It helps me tell the stories better. Do you have an outfit for Halloween yet?"

Karen fingered her lip and smiled. "Mm-hmm. I'm gonna be a princess."

"I thought so! You look like a princess," Sarah cooed.

Once the woman and Karen had left, Sarah rested her elbows on the front of the counter like she was ready to pounce. Apparently, the distraction hadn't soothed her ruffled feathers. "So, let's just...speculate here...nothing certain. Let's say the council unanimously approves leasing you the old public house. What about school? How are you going to run the place and handle school? If you're not open for very many hours of the day, you might not make enough money for it to be profitable."

Ricky raised his index finger in the air. She had no idea how prepared he was. "That's not true. There's a steady flow of tourists and locals who come to Blinney Lane. My classes are all in the morning, so I'd open when I got back from school. And…" he raised his voice when it looked like she was about to interrupt, "I already work more than full-time here and can handle school. Why would it be any different?"

"Well...well," Sarah stammered. "People can get rowdy when they drink. Can you handle that?"

"I'll serve some food too and won't stay open past ten," he said with confidence.

"And what about a 'pouring' license?"

"I'll be eighteen in a month and then I can legally serve alcohol according to Massachusetts's law."

"And? That still doesn't let me know how you're going to get a liquor license. I don't think I'd feel right signing for you."

Damn it. She'd found the loophole. Now the hard part. "I thought you might say that so…"

"So...what?"

"So...I found someone who's willing to be partners with me." He tried to sound nonchalant and directed his attention back to his homework as though the subject didn't merit further discussion.

"Who?"

Ricky set his pen back down and studied her. He already didn't like the look on her face. "Listen...it was my idea, so don't go overreacting."

"*Who*?" She straightened up and demanded.

"Look, I didn't want to bring this up for a while. I don't want this hurting your relationship or anything. He planned to mention it to you first…before we decided on anything."

"*Henry*?"

"Uh...yeah." His palms started sweating. "He didn't do anything behind your back. I swear! I approached him about it. Come on, now. Don't do that thing women do. You know, get all silent and draw crazy conclusions like you're on another planet that we don't have access to."

Sarah's mouth hung open. She stared at the floor as if she were in a trance.

"Um...hello? Earth to Aunt Sarah." Ricky waved a hand in front of her.

"What?" Sarah muttered, bringing her attention back to him.

"Sheesh, I thought your head was going to start spinning around." He chuckled until he saw "that look" on her face.

"Look, I have over eight grand saved up since I started working here. Thanks for all the overtime by the way." He gave her a cheeky flash of his teeth. "I thought I'd need to find a partner, not just to help run the place and get the license but to help with the loan in case I needed to buy the building. Since the council owns the building and I can lease it from them, I can just use what I have saved to get a small business loan to get it started myself. I'd still love it if Henry were the license owner and worked there with me, but that's totally up to you guys. I'd rather not speak for him. That's something you two should discuss."

"Oh, I intend to," she shot back and walked away.

"Shit," he muttered as he watched her stalk up the stairs to the apartment.

He remembered seeing that same look on her face when she'd found out he'd taken one of the "weeping books," *The*

Lands of Farwin Wood, and given it to Shelby. She had been justified then to have such a reaction. He never would have imagined a book could pull someone into its world. His aunt was right to have panicked when she found out Shelby had been drawn into Farwin Wood. He didn't understand, however, how his attempt to lay a foundation for his future life was reason enough for her to look like she wanted to commit murder. Henry was an adult. Henry could make his own decisions even if he was in a relationship with his aunt. Sarah always had to overreact when it came to anything with Blinney Lane.

He turned back to his homework. Hopefully, the pleasantness of her storytelling persona would rub off on her mood and calm her down before Henry got off work.

CHAPTER FIVE

HENRY TEAGER held the door to Allister's open for Shelby. She was dressed in black from head to toe, a cat-ear headband atop her head. Her ensemble was complete with a long black tail pinned to the back of her pants, black face paint on her nose, and a few streaks across her cheeks for whiskers.

They both tiptoed over to the counter where Ricky sat. Sarah's voice floated over the silent shop. She was perched on a short stool, dressed in one of the gowns she used to wear in Farwin Wood, complete with a cone-shaped princess hat that had a long taffeta tail suspended from the tip. The dozen or so children sitting in front of her on the floor were immersed in the story she read aloud to them. Several mothers looked on the scene with loving smiles and snapped photos from their spots on the couch and chairs at the front of the shop.

"Hello, kitty cat," Ricky whispered as Shelby came around the counter to greet him. She threw her arms around his neck and rubbed her nose against his, purposely leaving a black smudge.

"Meow," she whispered and gave him a quick kiss.

Ricky sighed and wrapped his arms around her. He buried his face in her neck and pleaded in a desperate whisper, "Hold me."

"I thought you were going to dress up?" she scolded and leaned back to remove his face from her neck.

"I did. I'm a dog. Can't you tell?" He peered up at her, refusing to let go of his only source of comfort since his aunt's mood had changed.

"I'm not convinced," Shelby replied sassily and arched a brow at him.

He motioned his head toward his aunt and let out another exasperated breath. "I'm in the doghouse."

Shelby scrunched up her face and looked over at Sarah. After a few moments of narrating, Sarah glanced up at Henry. Someone who didn't know the woman might not detect anything. Shelby, however, could easily see it wasn't the look of loving adoration Sarah usually had when she looked at Henry. Sarah's eyes shifted back to the book as she continued to read. When Shelby looked across the counter at Henry the pleasant look he'd worn upon entering the shop had disappeared.

"Ricky? Is something wrong with Sarah?" Henry asked in a low voice.

Ricky turned his head, face etched with terror. Barely audible, he hissed, "I'm sorry. She knows." He buried his head back into the crook of Shelby's neck.

Shelby watched the lump in Henry's throat bob as he looked back at Sarah. She cast her eyes down at her handsome but sometimes unpredictable boyfriend and noted how he still clung to her. "Ricky? What did you do?"

SARAH TRIED not to fidget. As soon as she saw Henry walk into the store, her agitation had returned full force.

I shouldn't be jealous, she thought as she tried to concentrate on the words she read. Is it because he's standing there lounging against the counter next to Ricky like he owns the place? I'm happy he feels comfortable here or our relationship won't work since I can't ever leave! Ugh, what's wrong with me? And why is he trying to help my nephew be stuck here too? She stumbled over a sentence and forced her thoughts away. Clearing her throat, she looked at the children and forced a pleasant smile.

The door opened and slammed shut as Reggie Nurscher burst inside. Manners and common decency were simply beyond him. She shot him a subdued scowl. At least she'd thought to take the chimes down although it did little good.

Reggie walked in quickly with wild eyes, stopping abruptly when he noticed the group of children. He let out an agitated breath and rested his hands on his hips, one of them holding a lit cigarette. He scanned the room and scowled at the offended mothers. They looked at him in disgust before he turned his attention to the counter. Henry gave him a harsh look, pointed at the cigarette with his index finger, and then jerked his thumb toward the door.

"Good grief," Reggie said, rolling his eyes. He turned and stomped out the door, leaving it half open with his foot. Bending over, his butt clad in tight-blue polyester pants, he rubbed the cigarette out against the outside of the doorframe. A few women gawked at the sight. Reggie slapped his hands together loudly, freeing himself from stray ashes. Oblivious of the attention, he returned inside, rattling the door loudly once again. A few children turned around to locate the distraction with venomous little scowls.

Sarah closed her eyes, praying for strength and then hurried to finish the story. She cringed each time Reggie cleared his throat or sniffed too loudly for the setting. Just what I need—my first fight with Henry and an unexplained visit from Reggie on the same day.

When she finished the story, she bestowed as much of a smile as she could muster on the children and wished them a happy Halloween. She passed out little baggies of candy that she, Shelby, Ricky, and even Henry, had put together the night before. She bid the mothers good-bye and uttered muffled apologies for Reggie's interruption.

Henry held the door open for the women and children as they left the shop. When he came back inside, his eyes found her straight away.

"Hello," she called dejectedly as she walked past him to the counter.

"Sarah, I gotta talk to you," Reggie blurted out as she leaned on the counter and handed her princess hat to Shelby.

"You're doing a good job so far, Reggie," she said in the unenthusiastic tone she reserved whenever she had to speak to the man.

"I think your friend has finally lost her damned mind!" Reggie gestured toward the window like it indicated who he referred to. "I thought it was a joke at first, calling me and whispering weird stuff over the phone, but then…"

"Wait a minute. Who exactly are we talking about?"

"Franci! I'm talking about Franci. Or *Lorna,* if you ask her! She's been calling me the last day and a half, but it's gotten creepier today. She called me Ricardo and Archie, and she keeps telling me to bring her car around or to meet her for a 'lovely stroll through the garden.'" Reggie imitated an elegant feminine voice and waved his hands flamboyantly in the air. "I think she's finally gone over the edge since the old lady died. Maybe the depression's gotten to her. You gotta do something."

"Reggie, it's Halloween. I saw her yesterday morning. She dressed up like Lorna DuClaire this year. That's all there is to it. She's probably just trying to have some fun with it. And can't you be nice? As you so compassionately pointed out, the 'old lady' did just die. Give her a break."

"Yeah, but this goes beyond playing dress up." Reggie flailed his hands in the air and began to pace back and forth. "I think she's trying to *be* Lorna DuClaire."

Sarah eyed Henry who waited patiently and already looked guilty. She glanced at Ricky. As soon as they made eye contact, he diverted his eyes. Great, they'd already conspired. Why do I feel like the bad guy? She let out a sigh and focused back on the rapidly moving Reggie.

"Look, Reggie. She didn't open the shop for a week after her mom passed away. I'm just grateful she's gone back to work to take her mind off things. Maybe this is her way of coping with it. You know, like trying to force herself to be happy. And besides, did you see her in that get-up? I thought she looked great. I almost didn't know it was her."

"She looked gorgeous," Shelby piped in. "She even did her hair in an old-fashioned coiffure. I've never seen her wear it in anything but a bun."

Sarah extended her arms out with her palms up. "There! You see? You're always eyeballing every woman that walks down Blinney Lane. You should be happy one is finally giving you some attention. I can think of worse things than Franci playfully flirting with you when she looks so gorgeous right now."

"Oh, I see how it is!" Reggie threw his hands up and looked around at everyone. "Fine, but don't come crying to me when she starts treating you like her maid or her gardener!" He walked to the door, stopping to peer through the glass as though he were scanning the street for something or someone.

"It's Halloween season, Reggie. You always get nervous around Halloween," Sarah called to him and rubbed the bridge of her nose. "Just go back to your store. I'll talk to Franci tomorrow."

Reggie yanked the door open. "Yeah, if I'm still alive."

The door slammed again, and she sighed as she watched him bound down the steps like an angry troll. She really didn't need any drama right now. She finally looked at Henry, who had been watching her with a look of dread.

"How was *your* day?" he asked with a gentle smile.

She made a flabbergasted sound. Gesturing toward the upstairs she mumbled, "I'm going to go de-princess."

"I'll come up with you."

When Sarah turned away, Ricky mouthed, "Good luck."

SARAH KNEW Henry was there when she heard the floor to her room creak; the room they'd made love in just the night before. His pajama pants still hung draped over a chair in the corner. A pair of his tennis shoes and a few other items rested beside it. As time had passed, she saw more evidence of him in her life. She still wanted to feel good about that but knew the conversation they needed to have might determine that outcome.

She stared out the window as she tried to undo the laces of her dress. He walked up behind her and grazed his fingers over hers. "Can I help you with that?"

Her hands fell away, instinctively accepting the offer. She couldn't find the words to reply, however, and the silence became uncomfortable. She felt Henry's hands move from the back of her dress to her hips. His solid wall of a chest pressed against her back, and his cheek nuzzled hers. She crossed her arms, hugging herself, and rested them over top of his much larger ones. It was now or never. She turned and looked at him. "He told you that I know, didn't he?"

Henry's soft breath touched her hair. "Yeah. You're upset?"

"I'm not exactly thrilled. I don't understand why *you* didn't tell me."

Henry tugged her closer. "I planned to. We just kicked around the idea...in full, yes, but only because there was no slowing that kid down once he got chatting about it. I do think it could be a good idea, and I was trying to take him seriously after what he did for you this summer. I hope you know I wouldn't have agreed to anything for certain without talking to you about it first. Brainstorming, that's all it was."

It was a relief to learn that her opinion hadn't been completely discounted from such a grand scheme but now she had another bone to pick. She turned around in his arms and rested her palms on his chest. "That's good to know," she murmured and fidgeted with one of his shirt buttons. "I wish you hadn't even discussed that much with him, though. Henry, I really don't think it's a good idea if he stays here. At least not until after he turns eighteen. I don't want you encouraging any ideas he might have that would make him more determined to stick around."

"Sarah, he's almost eighteen. He's going to do whatever he wants to do at that age anyway. At least this is something responsible. He hasn't gotten into any trouble since he came here, like he did in New York. It could be a lot worse than him trying to plan a future." Sarah gave him a speaking look. "Okay, he hasn't gotten in any trouble besides taking your book, but if you think about it, he wouldn't have taken it if he'd known what it was capable of."

Crossing her arms, she made a sour face at the logic he presented. "He still took it when he wasn't supposed to and he's not eighteen yet, so I'm still responsible for him."

"Then what's your plan? You're not going to support him in opening a shop?"

"A bar, which I'm not too thrilled about, nor will the other council members be."

"Okay, a bar. But what are your plans? Are you going to force him to leave Blinney Lane?"

"No, but once he gets bored of staying here with me, maybe he'll want to leave on his own...hopefully in time."

Henry sighed and braced her shoulders, forcing her to look at him. "Look, Sarah, he's your family. It's not my place to tell you how to handle him. I just thought he had a good idea. I am proud of him for being responsible. I know it's a bar, but I'd be there to make sure nothing got out of control."

Her hands went to her hips and as soon as they did, she realized it was a stance she'd never used on Henry. She didn't have the right to dictate to him just as he had admitted he didn't have the right to dictate to her about Ricky. But what was his interest in the bar, and how would it affect their relationship? "About that...what would you do? Quit your job?"

"It's a possibility, but I can always do part-time until things got going. You don't think I'm looking for nightlife because of this, do you?"

"No, it's just that... What about us?"

"What do you mean, what about us?"

"If you went into business with him and it didn't work out between us then Ricky would be stuck there trying to juggle things by himself."

"Sarah. I wouldn't start something up with him and then abandon him."

"Then I'd be stuck here with you just down the street as a reminder it didn't work out."

His hands fell away from her shoulders. He looked like she just kicked him instead of asking a simple question. "You really think it might not work out between us?"

"No. I didn't mean that," she said, wringing her hands. "I don't know. Who knows what will happen? You know I'm stuck here forever. What if you get tired of being stuck here too?"

"Sarah, you're here. How could I get tired of that?"

"You don't know that Henry," she offered delicately. "It's a lot for a person. Mary's husband left her when Valerie was only thirteen. Reggie's mother took off as soon as his father died, and Alexander…"

"What about him?"

"After his son disappeared, his wife left." She shook her head and kicked her foot at nothing.

"What happened to them is awful, but Sarah, I won't leave. Can't you see that?"

"And can't you see that there's no way you can know if you'll feel the same way once you've lived here long enough!" She didn't mean to snap, but she had to get him to see reason. She didn't want to think about the possibility that Blinney Lane could become too much for him one day. It would mean she'd lose him. Unfortunately, the look on his face made her worry she had helped him take a step in that direction.

He stared at her for a painfully long time before looking away. She held her breath when he turned and walked to the door. She called out to him, her voice nearly a squeak. "Henry?"

With a hand on the doorknob, he turned back and said, "Sarah...I believe in us enough to know that nothing could ever willingly take me away from you. I just realized though," his voice waivered, "that maybe you don't."

The door closed, leaving her standing there alone—a princess without a deliveryman.

CHAPTER SIX

THE NEXT morning, Sarah sat dejectedly behind the counter of her store. When she'd come out of her room yesterday, Henry was gone. She'd gotten so used to him spending the night, his absence made her worry over the impact of her words. How much had she hurt him? They had never discussed their relationship in a long-term capacity. Now she'd given him the impression she lacked either feelings for him or faith in them as a couple.

Almost noon on Saturday, and half the day wasted. A whole day and a half they could have spent together, but she'd pushed him away with her hasty words. He'd show up some time today, wouldn't he? She'd give him another hour before calling him.

The door burst open and her heart jumped with hope before plummeting at the sight of Reggie. This time he clung to the handle as he walked through, shutting the door behind him with care.

"She's after me!" he cried. He hunkered down and peered through the glass, still clutching the door handle as if to keep someone from entering her shop.

"Shh, keep it down," she warned, looking at her customers. A couple, immersed in their own conversation, browsed the corner of the shop. Fortunately, they hadn't heard Reggie. She hurried over to him. "What the hell are you talking about?"

"Lorna! She just…" His wild eyes roamed around before looking at her and whispering, "Assaulted me."

"*Lorna*? Oh, is Franci playing tricks on you again? I'm sorry. I haven't gotten a chance to talk to her yet. She usually stops by for coffee in the morning, but I haven't seen her in two days…" Why hadn't Franci come by for their usual morning chats?

"Oh, yeah? Aw, that's terrible. I feel *so* sorry for you." His frantic words tumbled out as he scanned the street. "Franci makes coffee. I hate to break this to you but Lorna doesn't. She's probably got a butler who does that for her!"

Sarah stared at him like he was an alien. What on earth had gotten into him?

"And you know what his name is?" Reggie straightened up and pointed at his chest. "Ricardo!"

"Seriously?" she asked in disbelief. Franci's role-playing had clearly gotten out of hand if she expected Reggie to act like someone else too. "Okay, come on. Let's go talk to her together. I'm sure she didn't mean for it to go this far." When she reached for the doorknob, Reggie backed away and pinned himself against the wall. He reminded her of a criminal hiding from the cops.

"No way! I'm not going anywhere near that crazy broad." He darted his eyes across her shop, then leaned closer. He swallowed as if he were traumatized before whispering, "She...came on to me."

"What?"

Reggie nodded rapidly. "I'm telling you, it's not Franci! Franci's gone bye-bye. Lorna struts into my shop like a diva, walks over to my counter, and plops down on it like some purring cat. Then she tells me to 'ravish' her." Reggie made a quotation gesture with his fingers as if she could have missed that remark. "And I laughed and told her to scram. So she attacks me, sticks her tongue down my throat, and starts running her fingers through my hair like I'm some piece of meat!"

She wanted to laugh except his appearance backed up his story. His usually slicked-down hair stuck up everywhere like it had been ruffled by someone's fingers. Around his mouth was a faint hint of red that resembled lipstick. But how did that explain the rosy tint on one of his cheeks?

"Are you serious?" It came out like an accusation, but really—who would willingly kiss Reggie?

"Yes, I'm serious! I tried to tell you yesterday. Do you think I'm saying this for my health? I shoved her off me and she slapped me so hard it felt like my jaw cracked."

That explained his cheek. Jesus. "What the hell has gotten into her?"

"I told you. She thinks she's Lorna DuClaire."

"Oh, boy." No sense wondering how this happened; anything was possible on Blinney Lane. "Just give me a minute. I'll go tell this couple I need to close the shop."

"And then?"

She shook her head at the disheveled sight of him and let out a ragged breath. "Then…I'll go confront your *ravisher*."

VALERIE CARTED a tray of perfume up to the counter where her mother reviewed invoices. It had been three days and Mary still wasn't speaking to her even though Valerie had made an effort to apologize. Instead, she'd received the silent treatment, and Mary wouldn't even look at her.

"I finished the new batch of Helen's Dream. Do you want me to put them out now?"

Mary shrugged then nodded her head toward a display shelf. Valerie pursed her lips, knowing that was as much of a response as she was going to get. She slapped her hands around the box and continued over to the shelf. A simple "yes" would have sufficed. The nod was demeaning. She knew where everything in the shop went just as well as her mother did.

Setting the box down to unload the little bottles, she wondered when Mary would get past their disagreement. Did she forget that she'd insulted her too? She didn't expect an apology, but Mary could try to forgive her.

The door swung open and Franci waltzed in, shoulders slung back, chin high. Valerie stopped and simply stared.

Franci usually dressed dowdy, but she was really pulling off this whole Lorna DuClaire look. Her black hair looked sleeker than usual with rippled waves. The long locks were pulled to the side, twisted into a loose chignon with a jewel-studded lily haircomb inserted into the mass. A sheer, light-green scarf circled her neck and trailed down her back. A form-fitting black gown with a plunging neckline accentuated her tiny waist. Thin straps rested on her bony, bare shoulders and the length came to mid-calf with a short slit up one side. Old-fashioned black heels, which she assumed belonged to Franci's mother, completed the ensemble. They were stylish yet out of date.

She actually smiled for the first time in days when Franci passed by. "Miss DuClaire again, huh Franci?"

Franci stopped, scanning her with a discerning eye. Her gloved hand flowed through the air. "Don't speak to me, shop girl," she said with a snotty tone.

Valerie gaped as she watched Franci saunter over to the counter. Normally she would have found this amusing and laughed. She knew Franci was playing the part of the high-maintenance Lorna DuClaire. Except today it wasn't funny after being dismissed again by her mother. The sooner Franci gave it a rest the better.

Mary, busy ringing up a customer at the counter, glanced at Franci in exasperation.

Franci leaned on the counter with one elbow, her hand still held in its dainty position. She gave a bored perusal of the woman's purchases. "I used to wear that scent. Drove Archie crazy, it did." She spoke the words in a clipped manner reserved for well-bred film characters from long ago. Casting her eyes upward, she sighed. "Remember, Liza?" Franci glanced at Mary who just rolled her eyes.

The customer laughed. "How priceless! You look just like Lorna DuClaire! You even sound like her too," the woman cooed.

"Ah, you've seen my work. How do you do?" Franci offered the fingertips of one of her gloved hands before turning back to Mary.

"Liza, I can't find Archie anywhere. Has he been in today?"

"Franci, I really don't have time for this," Mary scolded, bagging the customer's purchase.

"That's right," the customer marveled. "I read Lorna was friends with Liza Seville, the perfume heiress. Oh, how funny!"

Mary gave the customer a patient smile. She couldn't match the woman's enthusiasm when she was the one caught in this ridiculous game. Handing the woman her bag, she bid her good day.

"Francis," Mary snapped. "Shouldn't you be at your shop? Who's watching it for you?"

"Tsk, I'm bored to death there," Franci complained and traced a finger on the counter. "Ricardo will take care of things while I'm away. He does dote on me so." Franci gazed at the ceiling with a dreamy display of coquettishness.

"It's not funny anymore. Now go home!" Mary walked around the counter, dismissing her. She busied herself at a shelf of facial creams but Franci followed after her.

"Liza, let's go for drinks. I need something to do," Franci whined.

Valerie shook her head as she watched. She didn't need Franci pissing her mother off more than *she* already had. Franci didn't have to live with Mary. "Give it a rest, Franci. It was cute at first, but the party's over now. Okay?

Franci tossed her head back and quipped, "I wasn't speaking to you, tart!"

"Franci!" Mary scolded.

"*Tart*?" Valerie echoed, slamming down a bottle of perfume. She marched over to Franci. "I've had enough. Cut the act, *Lorna*, you're the one who's dressed like a tart."

"Valerie!" Mary scolded again.

Franci gasped, putting her hands on her hips, and thrusting her nose in the air. "How dare you speak to me like that." She turned back to Mary. "Liza, dismiss this...this little tramp immediately! She's probably the one Archie's sneaking off to see."

Valerie threw her hands up. "Oh, that's it! I'm outta here until you come back to your damned senses, Franci. Mom... *Liza*, I'll be over at Sarah's while you rope in your friend."

Valerie stormed out of the shop, ignoring her mother calling after her. Franci didn't even bother to apologize. If she had acted like that, Mary would have had kittens. Why did Mary tolerate Franci's behavior? Her own mother didn't even bother to defend her. And where did the tart and tramp comments come from? Franci never spoke to anyone like that. Maybe Mary had confided in her after their argument the other day.

She reached Allister's just as Sarah was turning the sign on the inside to "closed." Sarah let her in, however, and then locked the door behind her.

"You're closing this early?"

"We're having a little crisis."

"Tell me about it. I had to get out of the shop. Mom's still mad at me and now Franci's lost her damned mind. She's still walking around acting like Lorna DuClaire. It's like she's trying to win a freaking Oscar for best bitch." She noticed Reggie beside the doorframe and gave him a once over. "What the hell happened to you?"

Sarah rubbed her eyes with her fingertips and groaned. "Great, so it's true."

"What's true?"

Reggie pointed toward the street and spoke in a conspiratorial manner. "*She*...molested me and then she assaulted me. She thinks I'm Lorna's husband, Archie Hamlin, or that Ricardo character he used to play."

"What?" she asked in amazement and turned to look out the door with them. "You mean from *The Lady and the Doorman*? I thought she was just screwing around."

"Where is she now, Valerie?" Sarah asked.

She's over at our shop...with her good friend Liza Seville." She grimaced, realizing something definitely was wrong with Franci.

"Oh, boy! I bet your mother's thrilled about that," Sarah muttered.

"Hey, I'd rather be Liza than Archie!" Reggie complained.

"At least you're not some dismissible shop girl who she thinks is a tramp and is sleeping with her husband," Valerie snapped.

"She didn't!" Sarah sighed, rubbing Valerie's back gently.

Reggie looked Sarah up and down. "I wonder who you'll be."

CHAPTER SEVEN

SARAH, VALERIE, and Reggie made their way over to Scents and Suds despite Reggie's protests. On their way across the street, they ran into Ricky and Shelby. Sarah sent Shelby to run the shop while she took care of the "Franci debacle." She also took Ricky up on his offer to help.

When they entered Mary's shop, Sarah locked the door behind them after the last customers in the store departed. Reggie dashed behind a display stand to hide from Franci. Valerie hovered near him to avoid hearing any more of her quips. Ricky spotted Mary and Franci near the register and noticed the agitated look on Mary's face.

"Wow, this is really happening," he said in amazement.

Sarah rolled her eyes and proceeded toward Mary and Franci. "I warned you. You never know what can happen here."

Ricky followed behind her. "Has anything like this ever happened before?"

"Not this bad. When our ancestors first noticed that costumes made on Blinney Lane could possess them they simply got the wearer to take the outfit off and isolated them. It just takes a day or two out of the costume to get the person back to normal, but I don't know how long Franci's been wearing this stuff. I've never heard of anyone wearing a Blinney-made costume for more than a day."

"Do you think it will be the same? Can't you just get her to take the stuff off and then isolate her?"

Sarah sighed as they reached Mary and Franci. "We're certainly going to have to try."

Mary gave a look of relief. "Thank goodness you're here. I was just about to call you. I think something's seriously wrong with Francis."

Sarah grimaced. "We know."

"Who is this, Liza?" Franci looked at Sarah as though it were the first time they were meeting.

Mary's hands turned into fists at her sides. "It's Sarah, Francis. Now stop this nonsense!"

"Miss Francis, a pleasure to meet you." Franci extended a hand to Sarah.

"Just Sarah, please." Sarah smiled and shook Franci's hand. "And you must be the Miss DuClaire who *Liza's* told me so much about."

"Oh, Liza!" Franci swatted a playful hand at Mary, which earned her a scowl. "You really shouldn't brag about me, but I don't mind." She chuckled and turned back to Sarah. "And who is this handsome young man?"

"Ricky," he volunteered. Franci extended her hand, expecting a kiss upon her knuckles. He took it with some hesitation but then complied. "I'm Sarah's nephew."

"Oh, how charming! I wouldn't have guessed you were old enough to have a nephew his age," Franci remarked to Sarah.

Mary crossed her arms, looking like she just ate a lemon. Sarah did her best to battle through the scene. "Um, Miss DuClaire? That's a lovely outfit. Can I ask where you got it?"

"This old thing?" Franci swung her head back and fingered the tail of the scarf around her neck. "It's just something I had in the back of the closet."

Sarah glanced at Mary as she thought. "Have you been to our dressmaker down the street?"

Franci scoffed and inspected one of her gloves. "Yes, but her collection was sorely lacking. I returned that tired looking get-up she sold me the other day. It just didn't suit me."

Mary gasped. "Sarah, you don't think…?"

"I'm afraid so." Sarah sighed. "Would you call Genie and find out how many costumes Franci got from her?"

"Of course." Mary nodded and hurried away.

Sarah motioned to Franci's scarf. "May I? It's so lovely."

Franci fingered the scarf and held the tail out to Sarah. She laughed, enjoying the ruse of flattery. "Be my guest."

Sarah grasped the end of the scarf. She tried to raise it over Franci's shoulder to remove it, but the scarf wouldn't budge. It kept its flimsy form, hanging from her fingers, but acted as if it were bolted into place. Her arm actually began to shake with the strain of lifting it. The force against her hand felt like trying to pull a car by its bumper.

"Oh, my God," she whispered.

Ricky took a step forward. "What?"

"It won't move. I can't get it off her!"

"What?" Ricky grasped the other end of the scarf and tried to lift it. "It's like...it's magnetized to her! Is that supposed to happen?"

"I...I don't think so."

Franci's attention shifted to the doorway, and her eyes narrowed. She marched toward Valerie and Reggie, causing the ends of her scarf to slip from the Allisters' hands. "Archie? What are you doing with that store clerk? I knew you were slinking behind my back with him, you little harlot!"

"Oh, shit," Ricky let out as he and Sarah rushed after her.

Reggie circled around a display stand to shield himself but there was no need. Franci stopped by a table full of soap bars. One by one, she began to throw them at Valerie in quick succession. "Home-wrecker! Temptress! Fortune hunter!" Franci yelled with each toss.

Valerie ducked and swatted at the flying bars. "What the hell? Stop it, Franci! It's me, Valerie!"

Sarah grabbed Franci from behind to stop her, but she continued her attack like an angry T. rex. Ricky shoved the table out of her reach and then stood in front of her. He braced Franci's shoulders to help his aunt.

"Reggie, do something!" Sarah yelled.

Reggie peered over his source of shelter. "Are you nuts?"

"You get your own husband, you little philanderer! I'll have you dismissed!" Franci screamed and struggled against her captors.

"Pretend to be Archie," Ricky suggested as he wrestled with Franci's arms.

"No way! She wants to kill him," Reggie protested.

"Then be Ricardo. Just do something!" Sarah said as she tried to maintain her grip on Franci.

Valerie, crouched behind a table, popped her head up just enough to make eye contact with Franci. She grabbed a bottle of perfume that had fallen over and held it up in the air. "Miss DuClaire! He was just asking me to help him pick out some perfume for you. It was supposed to be a surprise." Valerie cast a warning look to Reggie, still hiding across the aisle. "Right, *Ricardo*?"

Reggie frowned. He was still convinced he didn't want to be either man in this crazy woman's life. However, he'd seen first-hand how Franci, or rather Lorna, became more violent with Archie than Ricardo. He stepped away from the display just enough to make himself visible. "Lorna...it's me... Ricardo," he said awkwardly and eyed the others.

"Oh, Ricardo! Where have you been?" Franci whined and gave up her struggle.

Like an amateur stage actor he let out a monotone decry, "It's true. Archie sent me to buy you a gift."

"Ricardo, you know I don't like surprises. Why didn't you tell me?"

Everyone let out a collective sigh of relief. Mary appeared then, wild eyed at the destruction to her shop. "Lorna! I think it's time for you to go home now," she huffed, nearly tripping over a bottle of shampoo.

"Oh, Liza, I believe you're right. Ricardo, go fetch the car."

Sarah made a motion with her head toward Franci as she looked at Reggie and released her grip on the woman. "Take her home," she mouthed. Reggie shook his head violently.

"Get her out of here," Valerie whispered. "As long as she thinks you're Ricardo, you'll be fine."

"Easy for you to say!" he snapped.

Franci stood primly at the door, fidgeting with her gloves. She tapped the toe of her shoe against the floor. "Ricardo, must you keep me waiting? These people are boring me," she whined and gave Valerie a look.

"I'm coming," Reggie whined. When she went out the door he whispered to Sarah, "What am I supposed to do with her?"

"Get her to take those clothes off!"

"What? No way!" A bar of soap shot through the air and pelted him in the stomach. He found Valerie scowling at him with her hands on her hips.

"You've been trying to get women naked for years. Now you have our encouragement and you're going to complain? I'm not planning on being your abused *harlot* for very much longer so I hope for once you'll finally be successful!"

"Ricardo!" A shrill call came from outside. "I'm waiting!"

"Just take one for the team," Valerie told him. "I'll make something to try and cleanse her of the diva."

Reggie gritted his teeth then went grudgingly out the door. "Well, make it fast!" He poked his head back inside and added, "And strong!"

Once *Ricardo* and Franci were gone, Mary threw her hands up as she looked around at everything on the floor. "Well... this is great for business!"

"I'll clean it up, Mom," Valerie offered.

"Yes, but Reggie's closed. Franci's place is closed. How many people is Lorna going to put out of business with her charades? It's Halloween—one of our busiest times of the year! We can't afford to keep losing customers."

"Mary, what did Genie say?" Sarah asked, trying to focus more on the issue of losing Franci than customers. She'd never read in the Blinney Council journals about anyone becoming this possessed.

"She said she only gave Franci one costume and she returned it the next day. Genie thought Franci was just being cute, in character, when she brought it back." Mary shook her head. "That was three days ago."

"Why is she still acting like Lorna if she doesn't have a costume from Genie's?" Sarah wondered.

"Have you seen what she's been wearing? She's still dressing just like her. Maybe that's enough to make her think she is Lorna. She *is* one of us," Valerie said as she collected soap bars from the floor.

"Maybe." Sarah shook her head and chewed on her thumbnail.

"She watches those ridiculous movies all the time too. I'm sure that hasn't helped," Mary added. "She's been so depressed lately. Maybe she's too weak to fight the urges."

"I hope Reggie can get her out of those clothes." Valerie shuddered at the comment. "Ugh, I never thought I'd ever say that."

"We couldn't get them off her," Ricky interrupted. Valerie and Mary looked at him in disbelief. "We tried to take the scarf off but it was stuck in place. It only moved when she moved it. It's like it wouldn't *let* us take it off her."

Sarah's worry matched the expression on Mary's face. "Valerie, you said you can put something together to help Reggie?"

Valerie was adept at concocting natural remedies. She'd studied holistic medicine, but more importantly, she was knowledgeable of ancient remedies that were only practiced in witchcraft. She was responsible for making most of the miraculous treatments and products in her mother's shop. Mary never appreciated anything that could be associated with the occult. She claimed it was distasteful, but it was more likely that Mary didn't understand it and was simply terrified. Valerie, on the other hand, embraced knowledge—no matter what source it came from. Even when she was a teen, she had her nose in books about herbs and spells.

Valerie studied her mother's reaction to Sarah's request. It was difficult to tell if she was frowning over the suggestion or the growing reality that Franci had lost her mind. "We need to cleanse her of the negative energy."

Mary drew in a sharp breath and crossed her arms. "And just how do we do that?"

"He'll need to dump some salt in her bath and some sage. We'll need sandalwood incense to burn. Franci has some in her shop. He should burn candles too. She needs white light," Valerie continued.

"And burn the place down? I don't think so," Mary said, shaking her head.

"Fine. What do *you* suggest?" Valerie asked.

"Certainly not voodoo dolls and hocus pocus! That's what got her into this mess."

"Hocus pocus?" Valerie extended her arms out. "We're in the land of hocus pocus and you're going to turn your nose up at me when I'm trying to help?"

"Okay, okay," Sarah interrupted. "Everybody calm down. Valerie, you get whatever you need together. Mary, you and I will take it over to Franci's so she doesn't toss Valerie out on her ear. Maybe we can take away all her clothes that look Lorna-ish while we're there."

The Millville women were silent but finally nodded their agreement. Hands on their hips, they avoided each other's eyes like proud, scolded children.

"Ricky, why don't you help Valerie with what she needs," Sarah suggested and began to help Mary clean up the mess.

IN THE back of Mary's shop, Valerie ground dried sage and sea salt with a mortar and pestle while Ricky looked on. She handed him a funnel and a small glass medicine bottle, passing him the bowl when she had refined the mixture to tiny granules.

"This stuff really works?" Ricky asked. He looked around at the shelves above the workbench filled with glass jars containing roots, leaves, and seeds.

"In this case, I'm not sure. But typically it can work for all sorts of things."

"How did you learn about this kind of stuff?"

Valerie shrugged. She'd never discussed her knowledge of the natural powers of herbs and other objects with anyone. Franci, ironically, was the only one on Blinney Lane who had ever taken any interest in it other than herself. Her mother thumbed her nose at it, attributing it to just another indication of Valerie's lack of commitment to anything decent and responsible. Mary seemed to believe that if any of the products they created in her shop had a powerful effect it was either a fluke or caused by the power of Agatha Blinney's curse. She never admitted that Valerie might be onto something by applying her knowledge of things traditionally used by people who practiced "the craft." The products she created certainly helped her mother's business, whether Mary would admit it or not.

"I grew up here, Ricky. None of the stuff around here ever freaked me out, and I just figured I could make the most of it. I knew witchcraft or something like it was the cause of why Blinney Lane is the way it is, so I decided to see if there was a way to use the curse to our benefit. I read every book your aunt ever had in her shop about witchcraft, herbs, potions—anything normal people would consider the occult. Believe me, I've made a lot of mistakes over the years, but I've learned that normal everyday things can be more effective when used in a particular way and what things can be more powerful because of our little curse."

"Hmm, that's pretty smart."

Valerie arched an unbelieving brow. "Thanks, but don't try telling that to my mother. You'll be wasting your breath."

Ricky chuckled. "Are you two always at each other's throats like that?"

Valerie sighed and gathered up an armful of candles. She put a cork stopper in the vial Ricky held out, now filled with the mixture. "Unfortunately, yes."

"I'm sorry you can't leave then. I'd hate to be stuck here if I didn't get along with my aunt as well as I do."

Valerie glanced from Ricky to the wide bracelets on her wrists. "Yeah. Thanks."

REGGIE PACED around Franci's living room. Sarah and Mary had just left, each carrying an armful of clothing they'd removed from Franci's closet. He stopped when he noticed one of the white candles that Sarah had brought was extinguished. Making his way toward the end table next to the couch, he relit it with his lighter.

Glancing at the bathroom door, he took a cigarette out of his shirt pocket and lit it. Closing his eyes, he inhaled and reveled in the feeling of the smoke invading his lungs. He hadn't had a chance to smoke since Franci had burst into his shop early in the day. He coughed, clearing his throat.

"Ricardo, are you smoking again?" Franci shouted from the other side of the bathroom door.

"Uh...no!" Waving his hand through the cloud of smoke, he fumbled with a small potted ivy plant on the table and squashed the cigarette into the soil. Hopefully the bath salts were working and Franci would emerge cleansed of her Lorna-demons. "How's your bath?"

"Heavenly!"

Clearly, she'd at least gotten in the tub. He'd had to insist that it was her usual "bath time," trying to sound like a knowledgeable butler, even though he knew it went well beyond a butler's duties.

"Ricardo, come in here!"

"What?" he squawked. "Why?"

"Do as I say, or I'll box your ears!"

He made his way to the bathroom as if the door led to his inevitable doom. He turned the knob and inched his head around the door. Franci was immersed in a bed of foamy bubbles. She had one foot resting on the edge of the clawed tub, her head leaning back against the other end.

"Close the door! I'll catch a draft," Franci said, her arm sloshing water over the side of the tub.

He turned his eyes away from her as he slinked inside and shut the door behind him, keeping his hand on the knob in case a rapid escape became necessary. "Is...is something the matter?"

"I need you to wash my back."

"No way!"

Franci shot him a dark look. "Don't get cross with me. Grab the sponge; I can't wash my own back."

Reggie gritted his teeth and located the sponge. This is bullshit, he thought. Still, he didn't want her bursting out of the tub in all her naked glory and coming after him. How the hell would he explain that to the others? Was she crazy enough to chase him down the street naked if he got away? He'd been reduced to her personal servant boy. If she ever snapped out of this, she would owe him big time.

Franci leaned forward and clasped her arms around her knees. The bubbles receded to the middle of her. He looked at her glossy bare skin and swallowed. Dropping to one knee behind the tub, he dipped the sponge in the water. Looking away, he slapped it onto her back and moved it around in a rough circular motion.

"Not so hard! You'll leave marks. What will Archie think?"

Reggie rolled his eyes. She was naked, so why was she still acting like Lorna? Maybe it was a good thing she'd demanded a personal sponge bath. Maybe if he lathered her up enough with Valerie's bath mix, it would help to bring her back to normal sooner. "You've got some dirt on you."

"Well, get it off!"

"Hold still then," he muttered. A man could only take so much griping. He swirled the sponge around her back and dipped it into the water again. This time he didn't ring it out, hoping more of the infused water would dribble across her skin. He sloshed the sponge across her shoulders and neck.

Franci leaned her head back and looked up at him, enjoying the pampering. Her smile faded, and she frowned at him. "You know what we're doing next, don't you?"

Dropping the sponge like it was a loaded gun, his hand froze in the air. "What?"

"We're fixing that hair of yours. Really, Ricardo. What have you done to yourself?"

CHAPTER EIGHT

SARAH AND Ricky met up with Walter Freedhof as they made their way to Mary Millville's house in the early morning light. They were all on their way to an emergency meeting of the Blinney Council with the exception of Franci and Reggie.

Sarah had fretted herself to sleep the night before. After she and Mary had whisked through Franci's apartment to commandeer her more risqué clothing and all of her Lorna DuClaire films, she'd returned to her shop and worked until closing time. Distracted, she'd forgotten to call Henry until it was almost ten o'clock. When she called him it went to voicemail. Was he avoiding her? Falling asleep after that hadn't been easy but waking up at this ungodly hour certainly had been.

She woke to loud noises in her room, which almost gave her a heart attack. Grateful it hadn't been a burglar she still wasn't thrilled to find Franci rummaging through her closet, complaining that her own wardrobe was "out at the cleaners." Reggie had been nowhere in sight although seeing him in her bedroom wouldn't have been comforting.

Ricky had come to her rescue when he heard her shouting and helped her escort Franci back to her own apartment. There, they'd found Reggie snoring with his mouth open on Franci's couch. He was wearing an old house robe over his clothes and his hair was combed back instead of its usual slicked-back style.

"What the hell are you doing? I told you to watch her, not play dress up with her!" she yelled at him.

Reggie jumped up off the couch. "She did my hair and made me put this on! What else do I have to do to keep her out of trouble? A guy's gotta sleep sometime!"

"What kind of a butler are you?" she muttered as she and Ricky left him with Franci.

Just as the sleepy trio neared the back of Mary's house, Sarah heard Henry's voice call out her name.

The pressure in her chest died away at the sound of his voice. He'd come to see her. Unfortunately, she couldn't express her full gratitude at the wonderful sight of him just now. She motioned for Ricky and Walter to continue on without her and went to meet Henry in the middle of the courtyard.

Giving him a peck on the cheek, she tightened her robe against the chilly morning air. "Hi. I'm sorry I didn't call until so late last night, but we're having a bit of a crisis."

"What's the problem?"

"I'll try to explain." She filled him in as they walked to Mary's house. He knew enough about Blinney Lane and the curse that there was no harm in him hearing what they would have to discuss at the emergency council meeting. If he was insistent on being a part of her life, he might as well get another good look at what it involved.

Once inside, Sarah led Henry to the kitchen where they found Ricky and Walter seated at the table. Mary was getting coffee cups out of the cabinet and jumped when she saw Henry. "Henry, I didn't realize you were coming."

Sarah let out an exasperated sigh as she took a seat. "Mary, he's already been inside one of the weeping books. Does it really matter if he sits in on a meeting?"

"I can leave if it makes you uncomfortable," Henry offered.

Mary lowered her gaze, releasing some of the tension in her face. "It's all right. You'll have to forgive my manners this morning. Coffee?"

"Coffee would be great." Henry smiled and made his way to the counter. "Let me help you with that."

Valerie strode into the room. Her slippered feet smacked against the tile floor. Her long thin robe hung open, and she stretched her arms over her head as she yawned. The cut-off shirt she wore hiked up, exposing her belly button, just above her mini shorts. "Good morning, fellow campers," she said in a groggy voice.

"Valerie, we have company!" Mary yelled, glaring at her midriff as if it were a dirty magazine.

Valerie ran her fingers through her bedraggled hair. "Yeah, you told me. That's why I came down. Why the hell else would I be up at this ungodly hour?" She avoided Mary's flushed face and looked at their guests. "What's wrong now?"

"Francis is still Lorna," Walter said, dumping a generous portion of sugar into his cup.

"Hmm." Valerie scrunched her face and tied her robe closed when she sensed her mother's disapproving eyes still on her. "Is she less like Lorna than yesterday? It could take a little longer to wear off if she was dressing like Lorna for a few days."

Sarah shook her head. "No. I think she's worse. I woke up to her digging through my closet like it was a department store. I didn't think to take my spare key away from her. Reggie said she sat in that bath for about an hour last night. Then she dressed him like Ricardo and spent the rest of the night talking to him as if he were."

"Are you sure she wasn't just talking to him because she talks to Reggie? I mean, Franci gets along with everyone," Valerie said. Only Franci willingly engaged in conversation with Reggie. Everyone else avoided his whiny dialogue and tasteless jokes like a telemarketer.

"Uh, no. She even blow-dried his hair," Ricky added.

"Ew! Heat damage is no laughing matter," she said jokingly and took a seat at the table.

"This is no time for jokes, young lady! If you're not here to help you can march yourself back upstairs." Mary threw a hand on her hip and pointed to the doorway.

"Oh, lighten up, will you?" Valerie said, biting her tongue.

Mary took a seat as though no one had heard. "What do we do?"

"Are you sure she doesn't have anything else from Genie's shop?" Walter inquired.

"Yes. Sarah and I scoured her apartment yesterday. Genie swears she only gave her the one costume and Francis already returned it."

Sarah looked at Valerie. "Is there anything else we can try besides the candles, sage, and salts?"

"There's other mixtures, but they're supposed to have the same effect. Those are the strongest. It's why I chose them. We can keep applying them and wait to see if the hold of this possession decreases."

"*Decreases*? It's gotten worse," Ricky pointed out. He had never been to a Blinney Council meeting. It certainly wasn't anything official looking, especially with Valerie in her pajamas who was standing in for Reggie and Franci. Mr. Freedhof hadn't even had time to zip up his pants, but he wasn't going to be the one to point that out. Still, he felt oddly important to be included in the mix. He wanted to help.

Walter looked at him. "Well, what do *you* suggest we do?"

Sarah furrowed her brows at the old baker for including Ricky in the conversation. She had been trying to dissuade him from staying on Blinney Lane, not involve him more in their daily lives.

Ricky thought about his only experiences with anything peculiar on Blinney Lane. The only unusual phenomenon he'd witnessed had been when he'd traveled into the book, *The Lands of Farwin Wood,* with Sarah. He actually knew more about Farwin Wood than Blinney Lane. "What about Farwin Wood?"

"What about it?" Sarah asked.

"Remember when I had the duel with Ranthrop?"

"How could I forget that?"

"Well, one of Ranthrop's healers fixed us up after the fight. He even helped Vasimus's healer take care of you."

"What's your point?" Sarah shifted in her chair. She could feel Henry's eyes on her from where he stood at the counter. After their squabble the other night, the last thing she wanted to talk about in front of him was Vasimus.

"My point is that don't you remember how fast we healed? The wound in my leg closed up almost overnight. I still needed a few stitches at the hospital but not near as many as the day prior in Farwin Wood. And most of the pain disappeared when we were still there. That gash you got on your head from diving off the bleachers healed up quicker in Farwin Wood too."

Sarah slumped lower into her chair as her nephew pointed out a source of her embarrassment in front of Henry. She'd been stuck sitting next to Vasimus like some obedient puppy during that duel just before she'd tried to jump from the stands to stop it. "I didn't hurt myself that bad," she mumbled.

"Sarah," Henry cut in, "you fell pretty far. I've seen football players take head blows that weren't that rough and not snap out of it for a few days. You came around the next morning."

Her gaze snapped to Henry. He was agreeing with Ricky? And he was talking about Farwin Wood like it was just any other city. The two of them hadn't even talked about it since they'd come back.

"What are you suggesting, Ricky?" Mary asked. "That we send Franci to Farwin Wood? How will that work and who plans on chasing her around that world, trying to keep up with her?"

"No. I don't think it's a good idea to send her there but what if they have something that could cure her? We could bring it back here." Ricky looked around at the adults. Their silence gave him hope. Hopefully, their lack of swift objections meant he wasn't the only one who thought Farwin Wood might hold a remedy. "Franci's suffering from something because of the curse and the book is...well, *alive* because of the curse. Maybe everything is linked. Maybe it means that something there might help her. You know, like magic treating magic."

Mary patted his hand appreciatively. "We don't know that for certain. Is it even possible to bring anything from this book back to Blinney Lane?"

"Yes! Look at my aunt," Ricky replied. "She's had that bracelet she got there for years."

Sarah cringed as all eyes turned to stare at the cuff bracelet on her wrist with various adornments affixed to it. It was the bracelet her first love, Vasimus, had given her and still had the ring attached to it that he'd proposed with while she'd been in Farwin Wood. She didn't dare look at Henry now. He had never let on what he thought of her still wearing the sentimental, yet necessary, bracelet that hid her scars.

"Okay, so at least that part's possible," Walter commented.

"Even if you can bring something back from Farwin Wood, you don't know what to look for that could help Franci," Sarah piped in.

"No, but a healer might. I could go to Vasimus or Ranthrop and ask to speak to their healers about possessions." Ricky couldn't believe how clever the idea sounded the more he vocalized it. It made perfect sense. Maybe he could finally convince his aunt he was serious about staying on Blinney Lane and help Franci at the same time by finding a cure.

Sarah's spoon clinked against her cup in annoyance as she stirred her coffee. "Ricky, I don't want you stirring up anything else in that book. We left it on a good note. Let's just leave it like that."

"That's right, a good note, which is why it won't be dangerous to go there this time. Vasimus and Ranthrop made peace. The war is over. And what about Franci? If nothing here can help, what will happen to her? Are you just gonna let her be Lorna DuClaire for the rest of her life?"

"Lord, I hope not," Valerie muttered.

"I guess we'll all just have to make some adjustments if that happens." Sarah tried to sound more confident than she felt.

"I certainly don't want to be Liza Seville for the rest of her life!" Mary exclaimed.

Ricky stared at his aunt in disbelief. "How can you say that? She's your friend."

"I don't mean to be the bearer of bad news," Henry cut in, "but if my memory serves me correct, didn't Lorna DuClaire kill herself?"

No one at the table said anything. Henry's words had turned the room into the equivalent of a funeral parlor. Everyone cast their downtrodden eyes to their coffee cups.

Mary broke the silence first. "All right. Who agrees with Ricky's plan?"

Valerie rubbed her hands down her face. "If they have plants that we don't have, it's very possible something there might work."

Walter came out with, "What can it hurt?"

All eyes turned toward Sarah "Fine, but I'm going with Ricky." If it got him off Blinney Lane again before his eighteenth birthday, she would support his ridiculous plan. In the book, the curse of Agatha Blinney couldn't scar him. And she certainly didn't like the idea of him going there alone.

"No, you won't." Everyone turned to look at Henry. Sarah's mouth dropped open at the demand. "I'm not going to risk anything happening to you again. I'll go. I know my way around Farwin Wood enough."

"Absolutely not!" she snapped. "If I'm not going, you're certainly not going." Their eyes remained locked on each other.

Walter gestured to his plump physique and said, "Do we need two people to go? I'm in no shape to be traipsing around the woods."

"I want to help Francis as much as the next person, but I'm not keen on jumping into any kind of book. I've never left Blinney Lane my whole life," Mary said, defending her position. "I doubt I'd be much use fending off animals and brutish men or hiking through nature I've never seen before."

"I'll go," Valerie stated plainly, transfixed on the steam rising from her coffee.

"You? Oh, no! I forbid it!" Mary exclaimed.

"Mom, I'm twenty-six years old. I love you, but you can't forbid me from doing anything. Look, we need at least one person who knows their way around and knows the people. We should be grateful Ricky's willing to go. And I know more about plants and herbs than anyone else here. At least I'll know what to look for and understand what these healers might have to offer. Besides, I think anyone that *Lorna* is intent on harming should remove themselves for the time being while the people she's pleasant to, *Liza*," she gave her mother a knowing look, "should stay here and keep her contained."

"You've never been there. You don't know what you're getting yourself into!"

Valerie got up from the table, ignoring the newest protest from her mother. She looked around at the rest of the make-shift council. "What do *you* think?"

Sarah, tight-lipped, pulled her eyes away from Henry. She nodded. "Fine. But Ricky, you two stay together and look out for each other."

Walter nodded. "You have my vote. Good luck to both of you."

All heads turned toward Mary. She slumped back in her chair, not caring she wasn't sitting proper for once. "Wonderful. Make me the bad guy. Fine, but don't complain to me if something goes wrong." Mary crossed her arms in defiance.

Valerie glared, tapping her foot. She was doing something good for Franci. Why couldn't her mother be supportive? And when had she ever complained about anything other than the way she treated her? She slammed her coffee cup down and looked at Ricky. "Meet me at your aunt's. I'll go wake up Genie to get something to wear."

As Valerie walked out of the room she heard her mother call out, "Make sure it's something tasteful!" She stomped up the stairs to her room. Why hadn't she thought about going to a fantasyland to get a vacation from her mother before?

SARAH LET Valerie into her unlit shop. At least it was Sunday and all the shops on Blinney Lane were closed. It would have been more embarrassing if there were customers to see how she was dressed. Genie didn't have anything medieval left in stock to fit her properly in the bust and everything was picked over with Halloween approaching.

She had nearly fallen to the floor when she saw herself in the mirror at Genie's shop. The vibrant deep-red empire-waist dress she wore was cinched tight underneath her bosom. A soft golden fabric nestled inside the pleated skirt and flashed out each time she took a step, exposing the color. Thin matching golden rickrack zigzagged along the top of the bodice and the puckered short sleeves.

To her dismay, she found her mother and Henry also waiting in Sarah's store. She ignored the wide-eyed look Mary gave her outfit and instead turned to Sarah for approval. "Well, what do you think? Will I meet Farwin Wood standards?"

Sarah eyed the dress up and down. "It's...a little eye catching, but yes. You'll probably pass as a lady there, which will work to your benefit."

"Great. Let's get to it then. Where's the book?"

"I put it downstairs. I'll lock the basement door to make sure no one disturbs you guys while you're inside. That way you won't have to be passed out on my kitchen table. Ricky will be down in a little bit. I set some sleeping tea out for you."

"All right, I'll see you in a few days then." She hugged Sarah.

"Be careful. Do you have any questions?"

"No, I've read enough of the Blinney journals. I think I'll be all right," she replied, referring to the events Sarah and her family had documented about Farwin Wood over the years. "I can always ask Ricky if I have any questions."

"Imagine that, Ricky an authority on Farwin Wood. Be careful and good luck."

Valerie gazed at her mother, but she couldn't think of anything to say that wouldn't be interpreted as sarcasm, so she simply nodded. "Mom."

The nervous sound of her mother's voice drifted after her as she started for the back of the shop. "Wait, I'll come down with you."

Mary's weighty steps followed close on her heels all the way down the basement stairs. Valerie walked over to a workbench where the old leather-bound handwritten book, *The Lands of Farwin Wood,* sat open on the wooden surface. Its yellow-tinted pages were filled with words in mossy-green ink. She ran a finger across the open page and felt a tingle up her arm. She always claimed nothing shocked her but it was quite awe inspiring that a book could transport someone to another world—literally.

She sensed Mary's warm, motherly presence behind her. Mary's fingers grasped her shoulders and nudged her toward a stool at the workbench. "Here, let me fix your hair. You look like a wild woman."

Valerie withheld an exasperated sigh and took a seat. She tried to sit still and drink the tea that Sarah had prepared while her mother tugged her hair out of the unkempt pile on top of her head. Her muscles relaxed as Mary's strong fingers clawed through her hair to straighten it out as she sipped the warm fluid. When she was a child, her mother used to brush her hair before she went to bed. Those days of easy motherly affection were long gone ever since her father left. How she wished they still had that bond now.

Mary twisted two lengths of her long hair along each side of her head. She brought the tails together at the back and braided them into a wide plait. Valerie winced as her mother forced the tail of the braid up into the twist to shorten it. She fingered the results and assumed it was now an intricate-looking bun at the base of her neck.

"You remember not to leave anything of yours there before you come back. I don't want you being pulled back in there like Sarah was last time."

Valerie forced out a labored, "Yes, Mom."

"I don't know why you insisted on doing this! You have no business going in there. Let the Allister's deal with the books. They know more about them than we do."

"Mom, did you see the look on Henry's face? Sarah's finally found someone who loves her. How would it look if she went back where her childhood boyfriend is who tried to kill Henry?"

"More's the point! These book men sound irrational to me. What's to say they'll react any differently to you? You're not exactly as soft spoken as Sarah."

Valerie leaned forward, distancing herself. Mary's comforting warmth now felt suffocating, and the bubble of patience inside her burst. "What else, Mom?" she said angrily. "What else do I lack? What else is wrong with me? I'm too outspoken. I don't dress the way you want or talk the way you want. I certainly don't do my hair the way you want. I don't date the right men. I don't date enough! Then I date too much! Is anything I do ever going to meet your approval?"

"I-I didn't mean that," Mary stammered.

"Not *this* time! But you always have a comment! You're either insulting me or pushing me away. Well, I'm not going anywhere. *I'm* here! I'm not Dad! *I* didn't leave. So why does it feel like I'm always being punished? I'm not as bad or as irresponsible as you think I am even though I second-guess myself since all I hear is you berating me *every* day. I help you out every single day, no matter how you treat me, and I'm trying to help Franci out now, but you're still giving me shit!

"And in spite of what you think of my love life, I'm the one whose heart has been trampled on repeatedly. Did you ever consider that? I don't date these people just to piss you off! Did you ever think I was hoping that it might work out someday? Did you ever stop to think that *I'd* like to meet someone who treats me right and sticks around, maybe even more than you do?" She couldn't hold back the words that poured out of her. Hot tears welled up in her eyes and her throat constricted. She couldn't remember the last time she'd cried in front of her mother.

Mary stood still with a hand over her heart. "I...I don't... know what to say."

"For once just say nothing. Please!" She smeared the back of her hand across her eyes and looked away. The door at the top of the stairwell creaked and she lowered her voice, "Just go, Mom." She felt the warmth still behind her. She couldn't breathe with her judge and jury hovering. "Go!" she insisted.

Ricky passed Mary on his way down the stairwell. Her face looked stricken, and she supported herself on the wall as if she were much older. He heard the muffled sound of sniffling when he reached the bottom of the steps and spotted Valerie. She sat at the workbench with her head in her hands and her back to him. If not for the sniffling, he would have guessed she was already asleep. The bright red dress caught his eye as he walked around the workbench to take the seat opposite her.

On a normal day, he might have lingered on the eye-stopping cleavage that protruded from her dress but not today. The first thing he noticed in the normally unbreakable and sassy woman's eyes was tears. A soft shade of pink colored the lids of her eyes. "Are you all right?"

Valerie snorted in a breath against her fingers and picked up her teacup. "I'm fine."

Clearly, she was upset. It was awkward, but he had to say something. "Are you ready?"

"As I'll ever be." She sniffled once more, set her cup down, and looked at the one on his side of the table. "Shouldn't you get drinking?"

"I chug it. I find that's the best way to get it down." He poured tea into his cup, picked it up, and grimaced. He pinched his nose shut with his other hand and downed the contents in two quick swallows. "Ugh! I hate this stuff!"

Valerie looked smug. "Your taste buds change as you get older."

He shook his head and clacked his tongue against the roof of his mouth as he poured another cup. "I doubt it. I hope I don't have to go back there after this."

"Is it really so bad there?"

He sat down on the stool. His holstered sword clanked against the frame as he shifted to get comfortable. "No. Not really." He looked up in thought. "Not at all actually, now that the war is over. I'm sure it'll be fine. I mean, minus modern plumbing and...wickrits." He shuddered at the memory of the ferocious animals that lurked in the woods.

Valerie grimaced. "Yeah, I remember reading about them. Do you think I should bring a sword too?"

"Nah. Best thing to do if you see a wickrit is outrun it. Aunt Sarah taught me that. Besides, we can get you a sword when we get to Allister Hall," he said, referencing the home his family kept in Farwin Wood. "Better you take as little as possible with you when you go—just whatever you have to wear."

"Right." Valerie looked down at the cuff bracelets on her wrists and remembered what had happened to Sarah, how she'd been pulled back into the book because she'd lost a trinket from her bracelet. Maybe it was a good idea to get rid of them while she had the chance.

She picked up her tea and downed it just as Ricky had, then poured another cup and did the same. Sliding her hands onto her lap, she carefully slid the bracelets off so Ricky wouldn't learn her secret. If he noticed once they got to Farwin Wood, she'd confide in him. He was still a kid, after all. Kids never told adults secrets. If that wasn't enough, she could simply threaten him.

She felt underneath the workbench for the shelf where Sarah kept her tools and set the bracelets there without a sound. Crossing her arms, she carefully rested her elbows on the bench and let her forearms hang down in front of her so Ricky wouldn't see her wrists. She lowered her head onto them once she noticed that Ricky had done the same.

She peered over at him as she rested the side of her face on her elbow. "I hope you fall asleep before I do."

Ricky yawned. "Mm-hmm, no problem. I'm getting tired already." He glanced over at her from where his head lay on the sleeve of his billowy white shirt. "See you in Farwin Wood, Lady Valerie."

CHAPTER NINE

FARWIN WOOD

VALERIE'S MIND and body slowly became aware of sounds and sensations. The chill of a soft breeze prickled the flesh on her arms. The rustle of shifting leaves in the wind stirred, and the coolness of the soft earth against her back seeped through her clothes.

Opening her eyes, she saw treetops above her and beyond their leaves a cloudy, bright blue sky. She breathed in and caught the woodsy smell of dirt and musty bark. Somewhere nearby the sound of water trickled. She sat up and realized the basement had faded away into a forest. Ricky, still in his billowy shirt, gray leather vest, and tight gray legging-like pants, crouched beside her on his knee. His hand clasped the sword's hilt, and his eyes crinkled as he scanned the woods.

"Are we *there*?" she asked in a sleepy voice.

"We're *here*," Ricky whispered and reached out to help her up.

Valerie looked around in awe. She'd read the journals and heard stories from Sarah but couldn't believe her eyes now that she was really in Farwin Wood. She bent down and picked up a deep magenta leaf. It had nine points and twice as many veins as any leaf she'd ever seen. "It's cold here, just like at home." She peered up at the trees. Their branches were full of leaves in warm yellows, oranges, and reds. "And the leaves are different colors...like it's autumn here too." A giddy chuckle of fascination bubbled out of her.

"Shh," Ricky warned, his eyes still fixed on the thick woods around them. "Yeah, I think they have seasons that follow ours at home. Come on. Let's get moving. And keep your voice down, will you?"

"Why? Are we in any danger here?" she asked, her volume still a normal speaking voice as she looked around the woods.

"I'm not waiting around to find out," Ricky whispered over his shoulder and stepped over a fallen branch. "The wickrits live in the woods."

"Do they really look like a unicorn? Or are they more like a rhinoceros? I couldn't get a clear picture from what I read in the Blinney journals."

"You don't want one. Trust me. A wickrit looks like mother nature got drunk, put a horse and a rhino in a cocktail shaker, fed it to a dragon, and then that dragon threw up."

"That leaves a lot to the imagination," she said, picking up the fabric of her dress as she followed him.

"What's so wrong with leaving things to the imagination?"

A shrill *tieeeeeerumpt* sound cut through the woods, and a flash of red swooped past Valerie's head. She crouched down instinctively at the flutter of rapidly beating wings. "What the hell was that!"

"Shh!" Ricky crouched down and waved a hand. "It's just a bird. Now would you *please* be—" A familiar grunt echoed in the trees to his right. "Oh, shit."

"What? What is it?" she asked quietly.

Now she whispers, Ricky thought. He backed up toward the road to Allister Hall, motioning for her to follow.

She complied without a sound, and they made it about twenty feet before Valerie tripped on a downed branch, causing it to crack loudly.

A snort sounded behind them, and they snapped their heads around to locate its source. A sickening snarl followed, and the bushes shook. "Run," Ricky rasped in Valerie's ear.

When she saw his look of terror, she decided to comply rather than inquire why he looked like he was about to soil his pants. She gathered two handfuls of the obnoxious dress and started to run through the woods in the direction they had been going. Ricky followed right behind her.

Another rumbling snort and the thrashing and breaking of tree limbs sounded behind them. A sharp, horrid squeal cut through the air. Valerie felt the thump of something heavy hit the ground behind them. She kept running but spared a quick glance behind her and saw the ugliest creature she'd ever seen in her life.

Its skin was a leathery blackish-brown, and it stood at least eight feet tall on long, meaty horse-like legs with clawed feet. An enormous horn on the end of its snout came to a sharp point. As it snarled, she saw its blood-red eyes look at her. Her mouth went dry at the sight of fangs protruding from its slimy upper lip.

"Oh, my God! *That's* a wickrit?" she screamed, jolting forward as fast as her legs would take her.

"Run!" Ricky yelled. "Come on, keep up!"

The rush of adrenaline coursed through her, and she bounded over a log. "*Keep up*?" she yelled to Ricky as she sped by. "My swordless ass is leaving you behind!"

Ricky watched as the bright red of Valerie's dress flew by him. He tried to keep pace, to increase the distance between them and the charging wickrit. Its massive head thrashed against a branch and the wood splintered. It was nearly upon him. He could smell its foul stench and feel the heat of its breath nearing him. Just ahead, he spotted a tree with a wide trunk. He leaped over a branch on the forest floor and ducked behind the tree as he couldn't outrun the beast.

When the wickrit stepped on the branch, he jumped from his hiding place, thrusting his sword and lodging it into the side of the beast's shoulder. It reared up on its hind legs with an angry snarl. He stumbled back and scurried on all fours around the other side of the tree. The wickrit's front hooves slammed back down, and he watched in shock as it commenced charging toward the road to Oedher Village where Allister Hall called home. "Valerie," he said with a gasp. Scrambling to his feet, he chased after it. The irony of him *pursuing* a wickrit!

Up ahead, Valerie weaved frantically around trees and stumps, crashing through the forest chanting "Oh, my God!" over and over. Through the trees, she saw a road and prayed it would somehow prevent the monster from trampling her into the ground or tearing her to shreds.

Bounding onto the dirt road, she screamed as a grizzly-bear-looking beast with a massive head like a Saint Bernard, complete with floppy ears, reared up and let out a low growl.

Behind her, the bushes rustled and snapped in the forest. The wickrit emerged from the forest, revealing its sharp, yellow teeth, and cornering her between the two beasts. She screamed as it leaped at her. Shuffling backward, her foot tangled in the hem of her dress, and slammed her onto her back, knocking the wind out of her. She pinched her eyes closed and braced herself, fearing the pain.

Something whirred through the air, followed by a gushing *thunk*. An ear-curdling screech pierced her ears, and the ground shook with a massive thud. She peered through her fingers and found no wickrit. She scrambled to her feet and then she saw it. It lay in a heap on the side of the road with an ax in its neck, a sword sticking out of its shoulder, and a creepy red eye staring lifelessly up at her.

"Missy, are you all right?" a man called.

She whipped her head around and found a redheaded man standing next to her. His clothing was similar to Ricky's but drabber in color and style. A wagon was hitched to the dog-like animal that had startled her. She threw her arms around the man's neck when it clicked he had killed the wickrit. "Oh, thank you! Thank you! You…" She looked up at his face as though doing so would help her find the correct way to address him. "…You *ugly*...but very brave man!"

The man laughed and patted her arm. "Deacon Wortwart at your service. My brother's actually the ugly one though."

"Hey, I object to that!" A man appeared behind Deacon. "Baisley's the name. Older by a minute."

Valerie looked from Baisley to Deacon and gawked. They were identical with their frizzy red hair and big noses. They were even dressed the same in dirty long-sleeved shirts and brown loose-fitting trousers that stopped at the knees. "I'm...I'm very grateful to you."

The bushes at the side of the road shook, and Deacon jerked her behind him as he and Baisley faced the woods. Baisley held out a dagger and stood in a wide stance as if he were ready for another beast to come flying out of the woods. All that emerged, however, was Ricky, panting for air.

"Lord Ricky!" Deacon declared. "You gave us a start."

Ricky stopped when he saw the wickrit at the edge of the road. He bent over to rest his hands on his knees and catch his breath. "Wortwarts," he said with equal parts bitterness and gratitude, noting the ax in the wickrit's neck. He hadn't seen them since they'd abandoned him and Henry when they'd been jumped by Ranthrop's men on their trip into the book to save his aunt.

He spotted his sword still sticking out of the wickrit's shoulder. Looking up at the brothers, he narrowed his eyes when he saw Deacon with one hand tightly clasped around Valerie's forearm. Even though he had made his peace with these two bumpkins after they had given Shelby to Ranthrop like some piece of property, he couldn't forget the despicable act entirely. Now Deacon looked like he had taken possession of Valerie. Didn't they learn their lesson the last time? He strode over to the wickrit, yanked his sword from its flesh in one swift movement and thrust the bloody point in Deacon's direction.

"You can take your damned hands off her right now or I can give you what you should have had coming when you took Shelby. And don't think I've forgotten how you left us in the middle of the road at the first sight of Ranthrop's men. Some escort you were!"

Deacon released his grasp from Valerie's arm immediately and held his hands up. "Whoa, Lord Ricky! It's not what you think. We thought you were another wickrit coming to pound her into the ground."

"Likely story. What kind of an idiot do you think I am?"

"A big one!" Valerie replied, stepping between them. "Honestly, they helped me. I'd be dead if they hadn't stopped that...thing."

"Yeah, but you don't know the history I have with these two shifty oafs."

Baisley said, "Lord Ricky, we meant no harm to that little blonde girl. Truly. We were even ashamed we sunk so low to do such a thing, but the war made everyone desperate. We're on the straight and narrow now since they've made peace in the land. I swear to you."

"This coming from a man who I paid a fair amount of troogies to take me and my guard to Daundecort Hall and left us in the middle of nowhere at the first sign of trouble?" Ricky shifted the end of his blade toward Baisley.

Valerie stood by helpless. Clearly, these must have been the two men who'd taken Shelby when she'd accidentally arrived in the book some months ago although they seemed remorseful. She had no idea what Ricky was talking about now since she hadn't read the recent journal entries. She didn't know what to think. As much as she felt the instinct to defuse the situation, she kept her mouth shut. Maybe Ricky actually knew what he was doing.

"Lord Ricky, please!" Baisley urged. "How would it have looked if Ranthrop's men had seen us with you? Then we would have had no friends on either side of the war."

"Let us make it up to you now," Deacon said. "Are you headed to Allister Hall? You seem to be without any stroomphblutels. We would happily take you there."

Ricky grimaced at the large furry beast hitched to their wagon. Now that the threat was gone, it stood with its wide tongue lolling from its mouth. "Still breeding stroomphblutels, are you?"

"Yes," Deacon replied, sounding relieved. He backed up carefully and scratched the side of the beast's neck behind one of its long, floppy brown ears. It let out a satisfied throaty groan and canted its head to the side. "This is one of our strongest sires."

"We were able to purchase a few more with the troogies we earned from you," Baisley said, beaming at Ricky and earning a glare from Deacon.

Ricky smiled and slid his sword back into the holster. "Good. Then you won't mind giving me one when we get to the village in reparation for only taking me *half* the distance that you promised last time."

Deacon's expression darkened before replying, "Of course. That's the least we can do."

"Great. Are you up for a ride?" Ricky looked at Valerie.

She glanced at the dead wickrit and then into the woods. It looked like a bulldozer had plowed through the forest. "Sure, if it keeps us away from those things."

The pair hopped onto the back of the Wortwart's wagon, and Deacon set the stroomphblutel onward with a flick of his wrist to the reins. Valerie watched the wickrit and shuddered as they pulled away. She'd come close to being nothing more than a fairy tale herself—history. Humiliated she had screamed like a wild banshee, she knew how lucky she was to be alive. If she weren't so proud, she'd admit that the day had been traumatizing already and it wasn't even noon. Who knew what time it was here and did it even matter?

She sighed and grasped onto the side of the wobbly wagon as they bounded along. Had her mother been right? She'd nearly died within the first fifteen minutes. At least Mary wasn't there to see it.

"Are you okay?" Ricky's voice broke through her thoughts.

"Yeah. I hoped this would be a vacation from my mother in spite of the obvious reasons we came here. I was thinking about what she said and how she might have been right about me not coming."

"Do *you* think that?" Ricky sounded worried.

"No, of course not. We need to help Franci. I'm fine. I could have done without that creature from hell trying to make me its breakfast, but I'll get over it."

"Okay, good. I was worried you were getting weak on me already." He flashed her a wiry grin.

She clucked her tongue. "Easy, half-pint. I had the appropriate reaction to that freakish thing back there. Besides, *you* were screaming right along with me."

Ricky snorted and crossed his arms. "Ha, hardly! You've got some lungs on you. My ears are still ringing."

Valerie cracked a smile and chuckled. "I didn't know my vocal chords could make those noises." They laughed and rode along in comfortable silence.

"Where do we find this healer?" Valerie asked after a while.

"After we get settled at Allister Hall and see if Dergus and Netta have any news we need to know then we can go see Vasimus Daundecort. He has a healer at his fortress. If his healer isn't there or can't help, we can go to the swamp and see Ranthrop Groslivo. They're the two lords of the land."

Valerie peered over her shoulder where Baisley and Deacon sat, driving the wagon. She leaned closer to Ricky and asked, "Is there anything I need to know before I meet any of these people?"

Ricky looked her over and made a face. "Can't you take that stupid nose ring out? Just put it somewhere safe if you do."

"No way! Then I'll be walking around with a hole in my nose."

"You should have thought about that in the first place," he said under his breath. Valerie gave him a sharp whack to the shoulder, making him flinch.

"I'm older than you, not deaf! How old do you think I am? Fifty? Don't get cute with me, kid. I'm grateful you tried to stop that thing back there, but it doesn't give you a free pass to be a smart ass."

"Who you calling kid? You're the one with a piercing like some hipster. And what the hell is that on your arm?" Ricky's eyes widened as he spied the tattoo poking out from under the sleeve of her gown. "You have a tattoo? And I'm the kid? What are you, a rebellious teenager? Cover that thing up!" Ricky tugged her sleeve over the image. "People don't have tattoos here."

Valerie swatted his hand away and frowned. She pulled the sleeves, causing the gown to slide further down her shoulders. "What's wrong with people here? Are they saints or something? I thought you guys just explained everything away by telling them you're from another land. Why should it be any different in my case? I'm not here to make friends. I'm here to work. I didn't know there was such a high beauty standard," she said and shimmied her shoulders back and forth until her sleeve hid the tattoo.

"Holy...shit!"

"What?" Valerie snapped her eyes to the forest instinctively.

"Can you deal with those developments, please! You'll have babies before we even get to the hall looking like that."

Valerie scowled when she noticed he was looking bug-eyed at her chest. She tried to force her "girls" down into her gown. The effort only made her sleeves slide back up her arms, forcing her to readjust everything again. "Make up your damned mind. Tattoo or tits 'cause I can't really get rid of either."

Ricky's face turned red and he looked away, shaking his head.

"I'm not the one who looks like one of the New Kids On The Block."

"I'm not a new kid, I've been here more times than you have."

She rolled her eyes. Clearly, the nine-year-age difference between them made her older if he didn't catch her reference to the boy-band she listened to when she was younger. "Nice hair," she enunciated sarcastically, determined to get a dig in.

Ricky patted his hair as if it were out of place. He jerked his chin in defiance. "We'll get you a cloak. A *big* one."

Valerie settled her hand back onto the side of the wagon and inspected herself again. Two small bumps now protruded from the front of her bodice. "Good," her voice nonchalant to show his insults hadn't bested her, "because I'm cold."

CHAPTER TEN

ALLISTER HALL

THE WORTWART brothers took Ricky and Valerie to Allister Hall, which sat at the end of Oedher Village. Ricky made arrangements with them to bring by the stroomphblutel they had promised, while Valerie took in the sight of the village. When Ricky noticed Baisley ogling her, he swore under his breath. He latched onto her wrist and tugged her toward the gate where they were met by the faithful Dergus.

Dergus was clad in a familiar light beige shirt, gray trousers, and faded leather vest, and he wore the same dirty boots. He wondered if the man chose to look this downtrodden or if he simply wasn't compensated well by the Allister household's troogie funds.

Ricky exchanged jovial greetings with the man and introduced Valerie as Lady Valerie Millville of Blinney of the North. He quickly urged her through the gate so none of the menfolk lingering in the village could gawk at her.

"Would you quit yanking me around and pushing me," she hissed once Dergus had shut the gate behind them.

"I'm just protecting your reputation, m'lady," he said dryly.

"Yeah, well piss on my reputation," she said and started across the courtyard to the hall.

Dergus scratched at his beard. "You said she's a *lady* of Sarah's court?"

Ricky sighed. "Yes. It was a long journey. She's not in the best of moods."

"Ah, that'll do it." They followed after Valerie toward the hall, Dergus stepping in stride with him. "You won't find Netta up and about today, I'm afraid. She's still down with the drumsy."

"What's the drumsy?"

The towering wooden door to the hall creaked as Dergus pushed it shut. Ricky peered up at the ceiling. The hole in the roof had been repaired since his last trip. There were also new chairs at the lengthy dining table in the center of the main hall. Vasimus had kept his word about maintaining the place even if the Allisters never returned.

"You don't have drumsy in Blinney? Maybe you call it something else. It gets you to coughing up a fit and sweating through the night. It doesn't let you keep much down either. Quite a few people have had it lately. I was lucky myself, but I swear the beetleburry ale helps keep it at bay. But you know Netta. She won't touch the stuff unless she's celebrating something."

"Does she need a healer? Can anything be done to help her?'

Dergus patted his shoulder. "Don't you worry, son. It shouldn't be too serious. It's true it's worse in the very young and old, but she's a tough old bird. She'll pull through. Vasimus sent his healer to Oedher Village straight away when he heard the drumsy had hit."

"Really? That was good of Vasimus. Is his healer still around? I'd like to talk to him."

"He was here a few hours ago, but I can ask around the village and see if he's still about. Netta's in her room." Dergus nodded toward a doorway on the other side of the hall that led to the servant's quarters. He turned to head back outside but stopped and whispered conspiratorially. "I don't suppose the lady can cook, can she?" He held a hand to his stomach as it growled. "I'm not much in the kitchen. Netta always boots me out of there."

"We'll fix up something." Ricky smiled. The poor old codger had likely been left to fend for himself with Netta out of commission. Guilt hit him as he watched the old man go. Dergus and Netta were devoted to his family and they insisted on maintaining the hall even though they knew the Allisters weren't likely to return. That was loyalty if he ever saw it.

"It's beautiful," Valerie called out breathlessly as she glanced around the hall.

Ricky made a face, but Valerie was so transfixed she didn't see it. Allister Hall was cool, but the sound of her praising something's beauty sounded odd. She was like a tomboy with dangerous curves, not someone who appreciated the ambiance of anything. Shelby hadn't been too happy when he'd called to tell her he was going into the book. He'd been met with silence on the other end of the line when he'd told her Valerie would be accompanying him. Had his little darling been jealous? The memory brightened his mood.

He started toward the servant's wing. "Come on, I want to see how Netta's doing. I'll show you to a room later, but if we're lucky we might not need it. Dergus said Vasimus's healer might still be in town."

"Oh?" Valerie said with disappointment as she followed. She'd never seen anything like a castle in her life. Allister Hall was like an old manor with its cut stone walls, arched ceilings, and wooden candelabras. They needed to hurry because of Franci but one night in a place where she felt oddly at home would be nice.

Ricky walked under the arch that led to the servant's rooms. He hated the title servant. He wanted to see if he could do something to improve Dergus's and Netta's lot before going back home. He stopped in front of the second door but paused mid-knock.

"What's the matter?" Valerie looked up and down the hallway. "Wrong room?"

"No. Dergus said she has something called drumsy. I don't know what it is, but they get a cough and fever. That's why the healer's in town."

"So what?"

"*So what*? For someone who knows about medicinal things, you're not very keen on the outcomes of illness are you?"

"What do you mean?"

"We came here to get rid of an illness, not contract a new one. What if we get this drumsy? I survived a wickrit attack. I don't feel like dying from some mythical cold."

"Pfft," Valerie said, pushing him aside. She rapped on the door, her other hand on her hip. "She's an old woman, right? What are you going to do, just let her suffer or die?"

"No!"

"Come in," a cracked, muffled voice called out from the other side of the door.

Before Ricky could stop her, Valerie forced the door open and entered the quaint room. A wooden nightstand with a single candle burning stood next to a small window, which had its shutters closed. Next to it, in a narrow wooden bed, lay Netta French. Her white hair, devoid of its usual bun, was strewn out over a handmade feather pillow. A coarse quilted blanket covered her tiny frame up to her chest, where she lay with one hand grasping the fabric.

"Hello, Netta," Ricky called from the doorway. "It's Ricky."

"Ricky? What in Oedher are you doing here?" Netta's voice sounded strained, and she broke into a coughing fit. She brought one of her wrinkled hands up to cover her mouth.

"We've actually come to seek out a healer for someone from Blinney, but I see that you might need one just as badly."

Valerie made her way over to Netta's bedside. She picked up a stool next to a small wooden table on her way and set it down in front of the nightstand. Smiling tenderly as she looked down, she felt Netta's forehead. "Hello, Miss French. I've heard so much about you. I'm Valerie Millville. I'm a friend of Sarah's."

Netta's coughing died down, and she looked up at Valerie. "Please, dear, just call me Netta. And from the look of you, you're more likely Lady Valerie. You can't fool me."

Valerie smiled at the gentle scolding, but her look turned to worry at her temperature. She found a cup and pitcher on the nightstand and poured a glass of water for the old woman.

"You're even prettier than Sarah, if you ask me, and I didn't think that was possible," Netta said in awe.

Valerie's first reaction was that she was being mocked. She'd never been called pretty except by the cruel girls at school who'd teased her when she was younger. This little old woman, however, didn't look like she would hurt a soul. Just as she reached to help Netta take a drink, Netta pressed a weak hand against hers.

"I can't have you waiting on me. I'll get up and cook you all something to eat."

As Netta tried to sit up, Valerie quickly guided her back to the pillow. "I can't let you do that when you're feeling so poorly. You need to rest, Netta. We'll be fine on our own. I know how to cook."

"Oh, I couldn't," Netta began but broke into another fit of coughing that racked her whole body with the force.

"I insist. Please, just rest."

Ricky fidgeted. As much as he didn't want to see Netta in any discomfort, he wasn't comfortable standing in the confines of her room, which was full of germs he knew nothing about. "Netta, I'll go take care of the kitchen for you."

"Don't you burn the place down," she said. "I don't even want to think about what it looks like in there with Dergus roaming free these last few days."

"I'm sure it's fine. I'll clean up any messes. Don't worry," he offered and hurried away.

Valerie smiled at the woman and handed her the cup again. "I'll venture you haven't had a decent meal since you took ill."

Netta rolled her glazed sky-blue eyes and sighed. "You have no idea, dear."

RICKY SHUDDERED as he walked toward the kitchen, imagining cooties tumbling off him. He hated being around sick people. This had better not be like the plague.

He passed through the kitchen doorway and stopped in his tracks. The long worktable that ran the length of the room was cluttered with dirty pots, pans, bowls, and utensils. Amidst the mess were bottles of beetleburry ale, breadcrumbs, a spilled sack of grain, and little bones of some creature stripped of its meat. An image of Shel Silverstein's *Sarah Cynthia Sylvia Stout,* that his aunt used to read to him when he was little, popped into his head.

"Oh Dergus...you dirty, old pig."

If Netta got over the drumsy, she would die of shock at the sight of filth one old man had created in mere days. Instead of rewarding him with more help, he needed to teach him some serious hygiene lessons instead.

He set to the task of sorting through the filth. Elbow deep in murky dishwater, scouring a bowl somewhere underneath the bubbles, he hated the irony that he was willingly doing dishes and not a single adult was in sight to witness the act. Globs of mushy foreign food floated on the surface and clung to his skin. He shook it off and sent it splashing back into the brine. The work Netta had to go through just to do dishes each day baffled him. He had to get the embers in the fireplace going, cart a pot of water over, and let it boil before he could even start scouring the pots.

Behind him, Valerie cried out, "Holy hovel, Batman!" She lifted her foot and shook off what looked like a potato peel. "Do they all live like this here?"

"No," he said and set a dripping bowl on the counter. He watched Valerie use his sword to spear some renegade food particles off the floor. "Hey, watch it! You'll dull the tip doing that."

"No, I won't. What the hell happened here?"

"*Dergus* happened here. Speak of the devil."

Dergus walked in with a younger man. He wore a loose-fitted black robe tied about the waist and a leather satchel slung across his shoulder rested on his hip. His hair was close cut like a monk's.

"This is Menklow, Lord Vasimus's healer," Dergus said. "Menklow, this is Lord Ricky Allister and Lady Valerie Millville."

Ricky flicked the water from his hands and wiped them on the linen apron he had tied around his waist. He rested his hands on his hips and gave Dergus a disapproving look, but he ignored him. "Menklow, thank you for coming."

"My pleasure, m'lord. Has someone else fallen ill?"

"Dergus will be if he keeps using the kitchen while Netta's sick," Valerie said.

Ricky watched in disbelief as Dergus looked away like a guilty child. How the mighty crumble when a woman criticizes.

"I-I can't find anything in this kitchen when Netta's not here," the old man whimpered.

"Really? Cause it looks like you found *everything*," Valerie added. "Here." She handed him Ricky's sword, which now resembled a giant kabob skewer filled with food scraps. She wiped her hands together and reached to shake hands with Menklow, who grasped the tips of her fingers, bent his head, and bowed. She shot Ricky a look of surprise and found him trying not to laugh. She decided to ignore him and focused her attention on the healer.

Clearing her throat, Valerie tried to match Menklow's proper speech. Her voice sounded foreign as she spoke. "Menklow, we've come to seek your counsel. There's a woman in our homeland that is very ill, but we can't seem to find anything to cure her."

"Does she have the drumsy as well? Oh, forgive me. Master Dergus did inform me that drumsy doesn't ail you in Blinney."

"No, we don't have that there, but I'm certain it's nothing like drumsy. I've just seen Netta, and I'm somewhat of a healer in Blinney," she explained.

"My stars! A lady healer? I've never heard of such a thing. No offense, m'lady." Menklow smiled, his eyes alight with curiosity. "I think that's quite fascinating, you see."

"None taken, and thank you. What's wrong with this woman is what we call possession. She thinks she's someone else and no longer answers to her own name. We were hoping you knew how to treat this. Do you have any experience in something of this nature?"

"I do not, I'm afraid. Fortunately, I should say."

Ricky said, "I don't think I saw you at Daundecort Hall when I was last there. Lord Vasimus had a healer who treated my aunt when she fell at the duel. He was an older man. Has he ever treated anything like that?"

Menklow raised his brows thoughtfully but the expression quickly faded. "He very well might have, but Healer Norston passed away several weeks ago."

Ricky swatted at the dishwater with his fingertips. "Great. I mean…that's terrible."

"He was quite old, you see, and quite stubborn. He got the drumsy just as the cooler weather set in and was out treating villagers when he ought not to have been. A brilliant healer, for sure, although he didn't treat himself or let anyone know about his illness. The sickness took him in his sleep."

Valerie, already taken with Netta in the short time she'd spent with the old woman, asked, "You don't think Netta will die, do you?" She reminded her of her grandmother, long past.

"Oh, no. I have high hopes for Miss French. She is a strong-spirited woman. As long as she stays in bed, rests, and gets plenty of nourishment, I'm sure she will flourish with the tonics I'm giving her."

"Good." Valerie let out a sigh of relief. "Have you ever heard of someone suffering from possession as we've described?" She exchanged a worried look with Ricky. Had they come here for nothing?

"I have heard of what you speak of...instances where a person goes mad and speaks in tongues or acts in ways that make you believe they are being controlled by someone or something," Menklow said as though he were recounting a horror story.

"Can something be done to cure them?" Valerie asked.

Menklow wrung his hands together. "I...you'll have to forgive me. I dare not speak of things I know nothing about. I've only heard tales from the healer who trained me. He knew of a place where this possession had occurred. We've never experienced this in Farwin Wood, you see."

Ricky inclined his head. "What do you mean never in Farwin Wood? Then where?"

Dergus jabbed the tip of Ricky's sword into a floorboard. "Beyond Farwin Wood."

Ricky caught his breath as Valerie shot him a look. It had better not be some myth the locals heard about Blinney Lane from one of his ancestors. He'd look like an idiot if he went back home empty handed. "What do you mean, *beyond Farwin Wood*?"

Menklow and Dergus glanced at each other as silence enveloped the room. Menklow swallowed then replied, "In Terradoon."

"Where the hell is Terradoon?"

"I do not know how to get there, my lord, but I believe it lies to the south. My teacher could tell you."

Ricky couldn't believe his ears. His aunt had never told him about any place in this world other than Farwin Wood. From what he knew, she wasn't aware that anything besides Farwin Wood existed in the book. Farwin Wood was *it*, was supposed to be it! Is this how Christopher Columbus felt when he hit the Americas? How was it possible that there was another land in this land? Had the book taken on a mind of its own? And why did these two men look as afraid to mention it as the people back home did the name Agatha Blinney? It was giving him the willies.

Valerie's impatience took over. "Menklow, where can we find this healer who taught you?"

"His name is Bernryn. He is the Healer of Groslivo Stronghold, home to Lord Ranthrop Groslivo of the Southlands."

"Ricky, you know how to get there, don't you?" she asked.

Grasping the table for support, Ricky stared at it, still in shock. "My aunt told me how to get there, but I've never actually been there myself."

"I'm sure we can find it. We'll go to this stronghold and seek out this healer."

After Menklow left, Valerie looked for something edible to cook for Netta, seemingly oblivious to the severity of the information they'd just learned. Ricky planted his butt in a seat at the table. He pondered on how great the expanse of the world inside the book could possibly be and realized now it might be endless. Why had they never heard of anything else but Farwin Wood before, and why were there other places if his ancestors hadn't written about them? This stupid curse never gave anyone a break.

"What is Terradoon like, Dergus?" he asked the old man.

Dergus glanced at him with an incredulous display. "I have never been there. I've never even liked venturing to the swamplands." He sighed and slid the food particles off Ricky's sword into a bucket, handing him the hilt. "They say it is a dark place of wonders and mysteries that outsiders cannot understand, nor care to. Creatures and beings exist there that have never graced Farwin Wood, and nor have the Terradoonians."

"But why?" Ricky glanced over his shoulder and saw that the topic had finally peaked Valerie's interest. She watched Dergus while she sliced vegetables into a pot.

"Perhaps they have no desire to venture here just as we have no desire to travel there. When people do not understand each other's ways; they stick to their own, I suppose."

"And where exactly is Terradoon?" Ricky pressed.

Dergus pursed his lower lip and steadied his eyes on him. "It's south of the swamplands, a great distance, I believe. No one goes there, so I can't say for sure. And best it stays that way since we've just found peace after this war."

Ricky nodded and watched him stomp out of the room. After he snapped out of his daze, he resumed cleaning while Valerie cooked lunch. She took a serving of stew to Netta and then returned to join him at the kitchen table. The room was much cozier than the great hall with the fire going in its stone pit to help ward off the autumn chill.

The aroma brought Dergus back into the room with a curious twitching nose, and he joined them. He informed them that the Wortwart brothers had delivered the new stroomphblutel and that he'd settled it into the barn at the back of the courtyard.

Ricky and Valerie discussed their game plan and agreed to leave for the swamplands after their meal. Ricky sent Dergus to ready two stroomphblutels and then showed Valerie to Sarah's old room to pack for their trip.

Valerie searched half-heartedly through the clothing she found in a wardrobe cabinet. She still wasn't enthused about playing dress-up. How long would they be in Farwin Wood?

The cabinet contained a mix of sizes that had likely belonged to Sarah and Sarah's mother. The dresses that would have belonged to Mrs. Allister looked like they would fit her better than those made for Sarah's narrower frame. The hairs on her arms stood up as she fingered the soft linen fabric. She remembered Mrs. Allister from her childhood. To think of her living a partial life on the weekends in this strange place put things into a different perspective.

Mrs. Allister had never left Blinney Lane, just like her own mother. She remembered Mrs. Allister as a friendly and happy woman. Was it her trips to this place that had caused that? And if so, had it been worth it to run from wickrits each weekend? She used to think arguing with her mother was one of the most horrible things she had to endure in her life. Wickrits definitely topped that.

When this was over, she had to go back and resolve the void between them. Had Mrs. Allister ever quarreled like that with her children or Mr. Allister? Was that how she escaped from the troubles of life on Blinney Lane? It was a beautiful place, raging creatures aside. Sarah had fallen in love here from what Franci had told her. Who was she kidding? There was no perfect world that could solve life's problems. She shook the thoughts away and folded some dresses into a small trunk at the end of the bed.

She tossed in a nightgown more glamorous than anything she owned. It belonged in an historical romance novel, not her temporary suitcase, but she didn't have any other options. The breeze streaming in through the open window prickled her skin. She spotted a gray cloak that matched one of the dresses she packed and fastened it about her shoulders.

"I weigh an extra fifty pounds with all this crap on," she complained, looking down at herself.

The domed trunk lid creaked as she closed it. She grasped its rope handles and carted it out to the hallway where she found Ricky waiting with a trunk of his own. He hauled both containers outside, surprising her with his clumsy, unexpected chivalry. Dergus helped him fasten the parcels to the backs of the stroomphblutels.

She watched as the pudgy beasts obediently dropped to their bellies for the men. One sat with its tongue lopped out and sniffed at the new stroomphblutel the Wortwarts had brought. She walked over to the new beast, all gray with black paws and a black splotch that covered most of its lower jaw, ears peppered with black speckles. There were two faint dark marks where it appeared to have whiskers sticking out like eyebrows. She smiled and reached to scratch its neck the way she had seen Deacon Wortwart do earlier on the road. It turned its massive head and sniffed her. She froze, waiting for its reaction. It let out a loud snort, flaring its nostrils. A light mist sprayed from its nose, settling on her arm.

She grimaced and wiped the slimy dew from her skin. When she turned, she noticed Ricky was already mounted in his saddle, his beast again on all fours.

Dergus approached from behind and gave her stroomphblutel two slaps on the side, causing it to lumber to a stand. "Here, m'lady, I'll help you up."

Valerie looked at the saddle, a good foot above her head. She'd never ridden an animal. The fact her first time would be on one which shouldn't exist wasn't reassuring. She grasped the saddle horn with one hand and braced Dergus's shoulder with the other. Putting one foot in the stirrup, she sensed Dergus urging her body into a sidesaddle position. She hoisted herself up and sat down but began to slide off the shined leather seat when the stroomphblutel shifted beneath her. Dergus braced her foot, and she was able to shift her bottom back to higher ground. The stroomphblutel rustled from side to side, the jostling causing her to slide again. She clung to the saddle horn, holding herself up with nothing more than her upper body strength.

"Oh, quit that now, you blasted thing," Dergus said. The beast looked back and groaned in protest.

"Damned Wortwarts," Ricky groused.

"This is ridiculous," Valerie said in exasperation. She flipped over on her stomach and threw one leg over the saddle. Straddling the mount, she bent down and straightened her bunched dress to cover her legs, now bare from the knee down. She caught a wide-eyed Dergus looking at her. "What?"

"Do you always ride like that, m'lady?"

"I— " She looked to Ricky, his face buried in his hands. "I don't ride often." She spread her cloak around her to cover as much of her legs as possible. Her cheeks grew hot when she realized both men were still gawking at her. "Let's get moving, shall we?" She flicked the reins so she wouldn't have to remain an object of scrutiny any longer.

Dergus waved to Ricky. "Safe travels, m'lord."

"Thanks, Dergus. We'll be back soon. Take care of Netta." Ricky glanced back at Allister Hall as he followed after Valerie.

His heart was forlorn, knowing they might not actually have to come back. They could go home through any large enough source of water once—*if*—they found a cure for Franci.

He would have to ask Ranthrop if he could help him find some workers to assist Dergus and Netta. That is, if he safely found Ranthrop's place. He'd gotten directions from Dergus. Normally he wouldn't be worried but now that he knew about other places, such as Terradoon, what would happen if he got lost? He didn't want to end up in a "dark place full of wonders and mysteries" as Dergus had described. Hastily volunteering, he noted, was something he needed to work on.

CHAPTER ELEVEN

SEVERAL HOURS PRIOR—BLINNEY LANE

MARY MILLVILLE walked in a daze through Sarah's shop. She'd never seen Valerie so upset. Her daughter hadn't cried since she was a child and when she had it was rarely the result of anything Mary had done. Her feet robotically descended the steps to the main floor of the shop. She was a horrible mother.

"Did everything go okay?" Sarah asked as she leaned against the counter next to Henry.

Mary paused then said, "Yes, they're going in now." She walked over to one of the sofas at the front of the shop and took a seat. Sarah and Henry exchanged curious glances. In a quiet voice Mary said, "If you don't mind, I'm going to wait here for a while. I'd like to check on them."

Sarah knew Mary always worried, but the poor woman looked like she was going to a funeral. She had to know that Valerie was coming back, just as she had each time she had gone into the book. Perhaps it just needed some time to sink in. "Of course, Mary," she replied, motioning to Henry to go upstairs.

In her apartment, Sarah heard Henry shut the door behind him. She grasped the back of a chair in the kitchen and stared out the window. There was no avoiding their argument now that they were alone. She could feel his eyes on her—the tension in the room almost palatable. If she spoke first, at least she'd have a chance to say what was on her mind in case the conversation didn't go as planned. Without turning around she blurted, "I think I should have gone with him."

"Ricky will be fine on his own this time now that there's peace in Farwin Wood," Henry said in a calm voice.

"You don't know that."

"No, but I *believe* that. And if you don't think he'll be fine, what makes you think something wouldn't happen to you if you go down there and go in with him?"

She whipped around, ready to defend her cause. "Because I know the people there better!"

The muscles in his jaw clenched. "I *know* you know them better."

"That's not what I meant!"

"Sarah…*why* do you still wear that bracelet?"

She reached for the leather cuff on her wrist instinctively. The charms affixed to it jingled, adding to her embarrassment. She wrapped her fingers around them to silence the reminder. "I...I have to. You know that," she replied. "I have—"

"Scars. Yes. I know, but *why*...why do you still wear *that* bracelet?"

"That's not fair, Henry," she whispered. She'd walked right into the trap she'd wanted to avoid.

Henry swallowed, looking pained. "I've never said anything until now, but I have to. I don't think it's fair either."

Her lower lip dropped when she absorbed his meaning. She knew why he didn't want her to go to Farwin Wood. He thought she'd run back to Vasimus. Didn't he trust her? She'd never considered that. Would he always be wondering if she would go back into the book? How long would it take for his paranoia and jealousy to get the best of him? This revelation, on top of her fears about him growing tired of life on Blinney Lane, gave her the answer to the thought he had left her with the other day. Maybe she *didn't* have faith in their relationship. They had been doomed from the beginning.

The room suddenly felt far too small for the both of them and the uncomfortable silence. She was going to vomit or cry, perhaps both. Her heart felt lodged in her throat. She started for the door but remembered that Mary was still downstairs. There was nowhere to run from their relationship crumbling right before her eyes. She needed to get out of here. She looked at the narrow door leading to the roof access stairs as if it were her salvation. With a shaky hand, she jerked it open and rushed up the steep stairwell to the roof.

Henry called out, "Sarah, wait!" threatening to suppress her with the ultimatum she didn't want to hear.

"No, I need some air!"

She forced the rooftop door open and burst through it. The rush of autumn air and soft morning light hit her face. She pinched her eyes closed against the fast-forming tears. Henry's footsteps behind her on the stairwell sent chills up her spine. She turned and walked toward the middle of the roof, stopping when her foot caught on something. Opening her eyes, she froze in place as she gazed in wonder.

Her tar and chip sealed rooftop, usually devoid of any objects, lay transformed before her. At her feet she saw what she had kicked: a wooden railroad tie forming the base of a flowerbed. Filled with bright green grass, a small flowering tree sat in the center of it.

More flowerbeds scattered across the entire rooftop in different shapes and sizes, each with flowers, bushes, or small trees. Between the raised spaces of each bed lay green outdoor turf carpet, creating a walkway through the ornate maze of vegetation. A birdbath, small trees, and a wrought iron garden bench with matching table and chairs completed the now transformed surface, which could pass as an elaborate botanical garden.

She turned around and found Henry standing by the access door. "It was supposed to be a surprise."

Marveling at the little eco system, she murmured, "When did you have time to do all of this?"

"Before you got up in the mornings. When you were at the Blinney cookouts on the weekends when I said I couldn't be there." His voice grew closer. "When you'd run over to see Franci or Mary. I had some help too. Ricky, Shelby, even Franci. Whoever could get away when you weren't looking."

"How long have you been doing this?" she whispered.

"About two months. Do you like it?" he asked with a trace of hope, his voice now directly behind her.

Her lower lip trembled, and she hugged her arms tight around her. "Yes," she gasped. "I love it." No longer able to hide her tears, she turned around, still determined to say what she needed to tell him. "Henry, I don't know why I still wear this bracelet. I really am just used to it being there, but I would be lying if I said it didn't remind me of Vasimus. It does. It reminds me of what it felt like to fall in love for the first time. And it reminds me of what it was like to get my heart broken.

"But it's so much more than that. It reminds me of my childhood, of when Richard was still here. It even reminds me of my parents since they were still alive when I got it. I think of Netta and Dergus too when I look at it. I think of when I was there with Ricky and Shelby. And it even reminds me of *you,* and how I wished I could have seen the look on your face when you woke up in Farwin Wood to come rescue me. How I felt the moment I saw you at Daundecort Hall. I didn't want to go to Farwin Wood to run back to Vasimus. I hope you know that."

Henry cupped the side of her cheek, wiping a tear away with his thumb. "Sarah, I wasn't worried about you running back to him. I didn't want you being chased. I know you have memories. We all do. I don't want to take those away from you. They make you who I'm in love with, but I know how much you care about what happens to people. You might think you made amends with Vasimus but what if he saw you again and decided he could try to keep you there? He might not listen to reason and then you'd be stuck there. I just wanted to protect you. I wasn't trying to control you or doubt you. I'm sorry I said anything about your bracelet. I'd just hate to think you feel like you owe him a kindness that he could take advantage of so I got scared when you wanted to go with Ricky. I don't know what I'd do if I lost you."

She reached up and clasped her hand around his. The warmth of his palm against her cheek reminded her of the love she'd doubted just moments ago. "Can't you see that's how I feel? I love you too much. It scares me to think that someday you'll have had enough of Blinney Lane. I know you say you won't, but it could happen. I don't want to see that look in your eyes, knowing you're miserable, and I'm the one keeping you here. I can't ask you to stay if it could make you unhappy. I'd hate to see you go, Henry, but I'd rather you go than one day realize you're stuck here because of me."

Henry stared at her, but she couldn't read his expression. When he dropped his hand, her panic returned. She watched as he reached into his pocket and pulled out a small velour-covered box. Dropping to his knee, he held up the little container in front of her. "If you can't ask me to stay then at least let me ask you if I can stay." His hands trembled as he opened the box, revealing a silver ring with a square-cut diamond in the center. "This is the other part of the surprise," he whispered, smiling at her.

With hot tears still upon her cheeks, she looked from the ring to Henry like a paralyzed mute. His green eyes were filled with hope and worry.

"Don't make me go, Sarah. Everything I want is right in front of me."

Her heart flipped inside her chest, but one question still nagged at her, holding back the excitement that begged to burst. "And Ricky? The bar?"

"Call me clingy, but I figured we'd get to spend more time together if I worked close by and he's almost as stubborn as you. When I saw that he wasn't going to change his mind, I figured somebody had better be around to keep him out of trouble."

"Oh," she managed, the strained sound a mixture of relief and laughter.

"What do you say? Can I go nowhere with you for the rest of my life?"

Even her chin quivered, but it didn't matter if she looked a mess. Only Henry mattered. "Nowhere sounds wonderful."

CHAPTER
TWELVE

FARWIN WOOD

AFTER AN hour on the road from Oedher Village to the swamplands, Valerie untied her cloak and let it fall behind her onto the stroomphblutel. The afternoon sun beat down a cozy warmth as they traversed down the dirt road. The air was more humid than in Oedher Village as the landscape began to change to a swamp with the mossy covered trees that lined the path.

A man approached on foot around the bend in the road. He carried a cloth sack over his shoulder, and she could see bright yellow feathers sticking out where he held it gathered in one of his hands. He nodded as they neared, bowing his head. "M'lord. M'lady."

"Good day," Ricky replied.

When the man raised his head, his eyes snapped to Valerie, his mouth dropping open. Ricky followed his gaze and scowled as the man hurried away. He whispered harshly to

Valerie, "Can't you ride sidesaddle? I don't think that's how women are supposed to ride here."

Valerie looked down at her knees and made a face. "Kid, if you knew where my thong went when I tried to sit like that you wouldn't be so quick to judge."

"You're telling me of the one choice of underwear you could bring *that's* what you decided to wear?"

Valerie shrugged her shoulders. "Give yourself a few years, and I'm sure you'll appreciate them more."

"Whatever," he managed and averted his attention back to the road.

Lumbering along, Valerie peered through the trees around them. The forest floor became more of a marshland the farther they went. Even portions of the road were damp, but she saw no sign of a river or lake.

"So where's the portal we use to go home?" she asked.

"What do you mean portal?"

"I read in the journals you have to go through water to get back to Blinney Lane. Is there a certain lake or river where this portal is that brings you back through?"

Ricky laughed. "Wow, I guess a lot can be lost in context. Did you read the *CliffsNotes* version?"

"What are you talking about?"

"There's no specific place. It doesn't matter where the water is. It just has to be deep enough so you can drown."

"What do you mean drown?"

"You just hold yourself under the water until you drown. When you wake up, you're back on Blinney Lane. Don't worry. I know it sounds scary but it works. I'm still breathing, aren't I?"

"You have got to be shitting me!"

"What? I thought you knew that. What's the big deal?"

Her voice rose."Big deal? I'm not freaking drowning myself!"

"Calm down. I said you don't actually drown. You'll just *feel* like you're drowning, but when you wake up, you'll be back at home. There's no other way to go back."

"But I can't swim." She watched as Ricky chuckled and shook his head. Why didn't he comprehend the severity of this crisis?

"You don't need to know how to swim. Don't you understand what I'm telling you?"

"Yes! I understand what you're telling me, but I'm telling you that I can't freaking swim. I hate the water, and I have no intention of drowning myself!"

Ricky stared at her as his chest puffed out. "You could have said something sooner!"

"I didn't know I had to pretend I was Houdini or I would have said something sooner!"

"Then how in the heck do you plan on getting home?"

She thrust her index finger in his direction. "You're the Farwin Wood expert and the leader of this expedition, that's for *you* to figure out."

"Me? Why the hell should I be in charge of getting you home? Don't you want to go back? I told you how it works so quit freaking out about it."

"Hey, I'm the healer on this trip. That's my contribution. You're gainfully unemployed as far as I'm concerned. I suggest you put that little college brain of yours to work and figure something out. Either that or you can go home and deal with my mother and explain why you left me here." She turned her attention to the road, ending the discussion.

"You can't blackmail me! She isn't even my mother. What do I care?" Ricky waited for a rebuttal or concession, but Valerie ignored him. He used the silence to contemplate her threat. While it would be absurd for anyone to blame him for Valerie not coming home, they would blame him for not *getting her* to come home. What crap! "What if there's no other way to get home? Don't you think somebody would have figured out if there was by now?"

"Why would they need to try if they already found a way home?" she asked.

"Exactly!"

"Don't tell me you enjoy drowning."

"Of course not."

"Then quit acting like I'm being unreasonable. Don't you think it would be beneficial to both of us if you found some other way to get home? What do you do if you ever have to come here in the winter and hypothermia sets in before you drown? Do you still make it home then? Maybe you should stop making me look like a cry baby and give it some thought."

"Sheesh, Red Queen, calm down," Ricky replied. "Fine! I'll think about it."

She whipped her head around and pierced him with her eyes. "You better think about it every second that we're here because I'm *not* going anywhere near water. Got it?"

Ricky held up his hands. "Okay, okay!"

The pair rode in silence through Naublock Village and the next village after that, all the way to the outskirts of Groslivo Stronghold. By the time they reached the gate to Ranthrop's massive complex, the sun was about to set.

They were escorted through a massive courtyard down a dirt path, abutted by moss-covered stones and knobby trees, which led to the main doorway of an ominous stone keep in the middle of the sprawling stronghold. A guard showed them inside to a vestibule.

A wooden bench sat next to the wall. Above it hung a long red banner with an image of a bright golden eagle-like head in the center. A man brought their trunks in and carried them down the hallway and up a flight of stairs.

Valerie heard another set of footsteps approach from a room to her right. A man of equal height emerged through the doorway. His dark brown hair curved under at the ends and stopped just below the collar of his red tunic. His goatee was peppered with gray whiskers. He wore a black undershirt and skintight pants that were tucked into knee-high leather boots. The symbol on the wall banner matched the one on his tunic, which gathered at his waist with a black belt. A gleaming silver sword rested in a scabbard, and his hand clasped its hilt. His other hand hung in a loose fist at his side, giving him a militaristic pose.

"Lord Ricky, greetings. This is a surprise."

Ricky clasped the man's forearm with a smile. "Varmeer, it's good to see you."

"And you, my lord. Fortunately for more pleasant matters than last time, I hope?"

"Not to worry. I didn't even want that duel with Ranthrop last time. I consider him a true friend for what he did, calling it a draw in the end. I only hope I'm still in his favor."

"Aye, m'lord."

"Great. May we speak to him? I've come to seek his counsel on a matter and was hoping he would grant me an audience," Ricky said, trying to sound official.

"Yes. I'll show you to the hall." Varmeer glanced at Valerie. "And...the lady, m'lord?"

"This is Lady Valerie Millville. She has traveled from Blinney with me on official business."

Varmeer took Valerie's hand by the fingertips and bowed. "Lady Valerie, how do you do?"

Ricky watched the awkward curtsey she made as she replied, "How do you do?"

She looked grumpy and pale. One of her hands rested on her stomach. How would her usual bristly behavior and sour mood go over with Ranthrop?

He gave her a beseeching look. "Lady Valerie, would you mind waiting for me while I speak to Lord Ranthrop?"

A gleam of acknowledgement flashed in her eyes, and he was grateful when she nodded. "Of course."

Varmeer indicated a doorway opposite the one he had just come through. "Here, m'lady. You can relax from your journey in the front alcove. There is always a nice view of the sunset over the courtyard there."

Valerie followed Varmeer to the doorway and thanked him before she stepped through it. Ricky was happy to see she'd roused some manners for Varmeer. He hadn't planned on her being baggage. She was older than him. She should be low-maintenance. He barely knew how to calm his aunt down when she was upset, now he had to figure out how to handle a moody twenty-something hydrophobic. What a nightmare this was becoming.

Varmeer patted him on the shoulder. "I must say, my lord, you gave me a start at first, but I am glad you've come. Lord Ranthrop will be pleased. He could use the distraction."

"Oh? What does he need to be distracted from?"

"The responsibilities that come with leadership, I suppose."

"Believe me, I completely understand where he's coming from."

CHAPTER THIRTEEN

GROSLIVO KEEP

VALERIE AMBLED down the alcove through pools of sunlight that spilled in from the windows. Admiring the upholstery work of a bench against the wall, she draped her cloak over its arm. Her hair, still bound in a braided plait against the back of her head, pulled against her scalp, begging for release. Massaging the irritated skin, she smelled the doggish scent of the stroomphblutel on her hands. A hot bath and a soft bed sounded better than winning the lottery. At least their trek through the woods was over for the day.

She walked over to the window and leaned against the sill. The fading sunlight warmed her skin against the cool breeze, bringing in a plethora of foreign scents. She closed her eyes and inhaled, trying to guess what the fragrances were, although she knew that was impossible. At least the queasiness in her stomach, brought on by her fear of drowning, had finally settled down enough so she could appreciate her surroundings. It felt liberating to see and to experience things much different from her small corner of Salem. Leaning her head back, she smiled, grateful to be oblivious of the day's worries for a quiet moment.

RANTHROP TRIED to walk off his restlessness as he left the training arena. It had only succeeded in leaving him sore after he'd bested a handful of his reluctant guards. The nagging boredom of late still coursed through his veins. Distracted and vexed by his agitation, he stopped short under the doorframe of the alcove, taking in the sight before him. He couldn't remember the last time anything had stopped him in his tracks. She was lovely. Her raven-black hair shined in the sunlight, the yellow rays lighting up her red dress like a beacon against her pale skin, as she basked in its glow. He studied her profile from the shadows—high cheekbones, dainty nose, an inviting smile upon lush lips. His eyes trailed down the curve of her neck to the swell at the top of her dress, causing him to swallow hard.

Perhaps Varmeer had sent him a new wench after all. Who was she? Damned if he cared—she was his now! Maybe he hadn't grown as tired of wenches as he had thought.

Stepping forward to capture her attention, he realized he held his breath in anticipation of feeling her eyes on him. When his foot scraped the floor, she turned her gaze upon him, stepping back from the window. Her hand fluttered to her chest, a movement he had grown accustomed to when ladies first laid their eyes upon him. He didn't care if her reaction was genuine or feigned.

"You startled me. I didn't see you standing there," she said. Valerie snapped her mouth shut, realizing she was staring at him. She'd never seen such a masculine display before. He towered over her. Even the way he stood radiated power and strength. "How...how do you do?" she managed to blurt out.

"Madam," his voice like velvet as he inclined his head, "are you here to see about work?" he asked.

She glanced at the doorway of the vestibule where she had last seen Varmeer and Ricky. She was there to work, but who was he to be asking her any questions? His tanned skin held a glaze of sweat and a layer of mud covered his boots. He could be a guard or a knight. His clothes were similar to Varmeer's. He wore a black undershirt but no red overtunic. His partially unlaced shirt exposed a hint of sandy blond hairs on his sculpted chest. She needed to say something. She decided the safest route would be to offer as little information as possible.

"Sort of."

He smiled at her reply and closed the distance between them. "Well, then...let's see how you do."

Ranthrop clasped his fingers around the woman's hip, pressing her against him as he cupped the edge of her jaw. His eager fingertips dove into her hair and he brought his hungry mouth down against her lips. His tongue swirled against hers, pulling him into an instant daze. She tasted like warm nectar in the sunlight. His skin tingled at the thought of devouring her, but then she pulled away. Why would she halt such a sweet exchange? He opened his eyes, hoping for an answer. It came in the form of her fist as it slammed into his eye, followed by his toes being crunched beneath the heel of her boot.

He yelped as he released her and brought a hand up to cover the sharp sting below his eye. Hopping back, he instinctively brought his other hand to the hilt of his sword.

"Who the hell do you think you are?" Valerie yelled once she'd scrambled out of his reach.

At the vestibule doorway, Varmeer marveled at what he'd just witnessed. Never had he seen a woman hit his lord, few men for that matter. Sometimes it felt as if he were guiding a teenager when it came to Ranthrop. Although none of the guards would bother Lady Valerie in the alcove, he didn't consider that she would be in danger of the lord himself.

"Stars collide! You hit like a man!" Ranthrop exclaimed.

"And you smell like a pig and kiss like a horny teenager!"

Ranthrop dropped his hand and squinted through his swelling eye. "What the blazes is a pig?"

Varmeer cleared his throat. "*Lord* Ranthrop," he called. "You have guests."

Valerie thrust a thumb toward Ranthrop. "*He's* Ranthrop?"

"Guests?" Ranthrop asked, rubbing his eye.

Varmeer made a tired noise before continuing his polite announcements. "This is the Lady Valerie Millville—"

"*Lady*?" Ranthrop interrupted.

"Yes, m'lord. Lady Valerie of Blinney. She just arrived with Lord Richard Allister the Second to seek your counsel."

"Ricky's here?" Ranthrop's tone brightened. "Ha! Why didn't you come get me?"

"I'm doing that now, m'lord."

Ranthrop turned to Valerie, who met him with a perfect scowl. In spite of her venomous look and the throbbing in his eye and toes, warm sparks flickered inside of him at the sight of her. It was something oddly exhilarating that she had come to seek his counsel. "Lady Valerie, I…mistook you for someone else," he said.

She crossed her arms against her chest, raising an eyebrow. "Apparently."

"Varmeer says you need my assistance. Just say the word, and I will make it up to you."

"I wouldn't seek a drop of water from you if I was on fire!"

Her reply doused his smile. Did she always speak like that or had he offended her to the brink of combativeness? Tugging at the base of his shirt, he became aware of his unkempt appearance.

"Well...I shouldn't keep Lord Ricky waiting." He waited for a reply but received no response other than the glare from her angry gray eyes. Following Varmeer, he stole a glance back. People from Blinney never stuck around for very long. Because of this, he had a strange urge not to let her out of his sight. Her steely eyes connected with his again so he looked away. A good thing, because he nearly ran into the doorframe.

RICKY THREW his head back with a laugh as Ranthrop whirled a tierumpt bone in the air and regaled another story. They sat at the end of a table that ran the length of the long dining hall. Ranthrop's men filled the table from end to end. An impressive room but less formal than Vasimus's great room with Ranthrop sitting at the head of the table rather than a separate table from his men.

The room was less fashionable than the great room at Daundecort Hall but equal in size. Dimly lit with standing candelabras in the corners, sparse beams of moonlight filtered through the windows. At the end of the room, a large fireplace blazed. The cool night air seeped in through the windows and brought moments of freshness amongst the earthy-smelling men and rich aromas of food.

Ranthrop easily agreed for him to meet with his healer. After that, he and Valerie were escorted to guest rooms on the second floor to freshen up. Ricky had just joined Ranthrop for the evening meal. He had yet to see the healer or Valerie since his arrival. For the moment, he was content to forget his pressing obligations with a pint of beetleburry ale and Ranthrop's good-natured company.

Valerie followed a maid who directed her to the dining hall. She could hear the rumble of men's voices. She wondered if she would be the only woman present. She glanced down at the bright-red gown she wore. It wasn't an outfit she wanted to flaunt in front of a room full of men but the thought of discarding what she needed to wear to go home made her nervous. With a deep breath to bolster her confidence, she strode through the doorway.

Instantly, the roar of voices ceased. She froze and the scent of cooked meat, vegetables, and woodsy, sweaty men wafted around her. Every face in the room looked at her, and every single face belonged to a man. She bit the inside of her cheek and scanned the room for Ricky. Her teeth dug in deeper when she spotted him at the far end of the table next to Ranthrop.

Even from the forty-odd feet away, she could see Ranthrop's potent emerald green eyes on her, spotting a burgundy half-moon under the one she'd pummeled. She managed a tight-lipped smile and began what felt like a walk of shame as the gruff characters studied her.

As she proceeded, the silence turned to whispers. Gradually, the volume increased until she was forgotten. She exhaled in relief but her uneasiness returned when she noticed she was now the object of Ranthrop's attention. What the hell was he looking at?

She ignored him and instead focused on the empty chair next to him, which would place her across from Ricky. She jumped when Ranthrop shot out of his chair, and hurried over to pull her chair out.

No man had ever pulled out a chair for her. She didn't expect this jackass to be the first. She stepped into place and heard the chair creak as he slid her into place. His fingers dusted her shoulders and sent a shiver down her arms.

"Lady Valerie," she heard him murmur before he returned to his seat.

Ricky gave her a quizzical look. She returned his look, and he made a defeated noise, shaking his head. Apparently, he had no idea what had happened nor cared to find out.

She eyed the food on the serving tray in front of her with a mix of curiosity and terror. Her stomach growled, but what should she choose? It smelled like meat and vegetables with a mix of spices she couldn't identify.

Using the three-pronged fork by her plate, she speared what looked to be a bright, lime-green potato. Next, she jabbed what had possibly been a small bird and felt a pang of sympathy as she added it to her plate. It was so tiny it should have been a house pet, not an appetizer. She stared at the morsels in contemplation. The potato held no surprises when she sliced it open so she popped a chunk of it into her mouth.

As she chewed, her eyes rounded. Without thinking, she looked at Ranthrop and declared, "It tastes like almonds!"

"What are almonds?"

Why couldn't she ever meet a man with brains? It wasn't fair to ridicule him for his lack of knowledge about food from a world he'd never been to, even if she only did so in her head, but she didn't care. Why had she addressed him? She noticed he sat with his chin perched in his hand as though engrossed by her every action. Giving him a perturbed look, she sank her teeth into the potato.

"You have never had kierberts?" he asked.

"No." She cast her eyes down. Her cheeks burned under the scrutiny, and she covered her mouth as she chewed. She had an unexplainable urge to hide her lips from him.

"Is this your first time to Farwin Wood?"

"Yes, it is."

"I thought so!" he exclaimed like a trivia champion.

"Aren't you the genius?"

"Valerie," Ricky scolded.

"It's all right," Ranthrop said. "The lady and I had a misunderstanding earlier. I suppose she has the right to be cross with me."

Valerie stabbed her fork into the Tweety-bird carcass. "You *suppose*?"

Ranthrop frowned and shifted in his chair.

"What kind of misunderstanding?" Ricky asked.

Valerie sighed. "The kind where he *accidentally* stuck his tongue down my throat."

"I did no such thing! How could I possibly reach down your throat?" Ranthrop's confusion left him, and he reached for her face. "Madam, you have a gem on your nose."

Valerie swatted his hand with a loud smack. "Yes, I know I do! What's the matter? Didn't you notice it when you were searching for my tonsils earlier?"

Ricky coughed, almost choking on his food.

Ranthrop stared at her a moment and then threw back his head, howling with laughter.

"What's so damned funny?" she asked.

"You, m'lady. You have the most pleasing wit even though you're staring daggers at me."

She rolled her eyes and looked down at her plate. Oh, so he knows what tonsils are. Hilarious. She stabbed the other half of her kierbert. "And you have the most unusual habit of trying to touch people without their permission."

Ranthrop laughed again and shook his head. He turned to Ricky and picked up the pitcher of beetleburry ale. "She is not like your aunt, Ricky."

Ricky held out his goblet and wiped his mouth. "No, she certainly isn't." He watched Ranthrop fill the goblet in front of Valerie and then set the decanter back down. Frowning at his still empty cup, he snatched the pitcher.

Ranthrop continued his vocalized thoughts, "Sarah is more...soft spoken I believe...and patient."

Valerie chewed furiously. "I'm still sitting here, you know. I can hear you."

Ranthrop chuckled, oblivious to Valerie's threatening gaze. An old man in a black robe similar to the one Menklow had worn walked up to the table and caught his attention.

"Ah, Bernryn! Good of you to come. I'd like you to meet Lord Ricky and Lady Valerie of Blinney. This is Bernryn, the healer of Groslivo Keep."

Ricky watched as Bernryn tilted his baldhead. Due to the old man's hunched posture, it gave the semblance of a bow.

His clasped, knobby-knuckled hands rested over the lump of his belly. Skin speckled with age spots, an arched bridge for a nose, and eyes so dark they looked almost black. What had they seen to give them such a vacant look? The man neither frowned nor smiled, and there was something about his face which said he never did.

Valerie set her fork down and stood up. "Bernryn, thank you for coming. Do you have an apothecary where we could talk?"

"Yes, m'lady. It is just down the hall at the back of the keep."

Valerie turned back to the table. "You two enjoy your meal. Since I'm the one with the medical knowledge, I'll go speak to Bernryn about our questions. Good night."

Ranthrop watched her walk away. Some of his men also watched her with interest as she passed, causing him a twinge of hostility. Where on the winds had that come from? He drained his goblet and then refilled it.

"Ricky, I believe she does not like me."

"I *believe* you may be right." Ricky spat out a sliver of bone and picked at his teeth. "Don't take any offense, though. She treats me like that sometimes."

Ranthrop leaned toward him and lowered his voice. "Have you…"

"Have I what?"

"Been…under covers with her?"

"Absolutely not!" Ricky nearly choked on a morsel of food and had to down a gulp of ale to recover. "You just met her, didn't you? She's like a cornered wickrit half the time! Who in the hell would be crazy enough to deal with that?"

Ranthrop arched a brow. "She can't be like that all the time. All women have their feminine sides."

Ricky shrugged and stripped the meat off another bone. "Maybe. She's a hard worker, I know that. And she can be genuinely compassionate when she wants to be. She took care of our housekeeper as soon as she learned she was sick with the drumsy. She volunteered to come here to help our friend from back home, even though she didn't have to."

Ranthrop pictured himself lying sick in bed without his shirt, and Valerie coming over to cool his forehead with a damp cloth. He imagined her touch would be gentle but then reached up and felt the tender, swollen skin under his eye.

Ricky continued, "The rest of the time, you have to be careful you don't rub her the wrong way. I think she's just one of those perpetually angry women, if you know what I mean."

Ranthrop sat back in his chair with his goblet, and said under his breath, "Well, there is a cure for that."

CHAPTER FOURTEEN

VALERIE LISTENED intently as Bernryn spoke about his knowledge of madness. The atmosphere of the room, with only a few candles cradled in the fixtures on the walls, matched his gloomy accounts. They stood before a workbench full of vials, bottles of tonics, powders, and herbs. It resembled her workspace at home, although she had electricity and had no idea of the contents in his bottles.

Bernryn continued speaking, his voice a frail baritone. "The craze took them over, sometimes slowly, sometimes overnight, I was told. Some completely forgot who they were and were left without an identity. Others were left more as you speak of, like this friend of yours. Terradoon is a place of myths and secrets that we know nothing of here. They have spirits and rituals that guide their world. People in Farwin Wood would not understand this as we see no evidence of spirit guidance here, but I tell you...spend one day in Terradoon, and you will feel it. You will feel the presence of something other than the people who walk the land."

A chill shot up her spine. She didn't doubt him. She'd been ostracized her entire life for believing bizarre things were possible, but now she was grateful to have the intuition to take the man seriously. "And this cure you spoke of before. Can it be made in Farwin Wood?"

Bernryn moved to the end of the workbench and reached inside a shelf beneath it. Pulling out a leather-bound book, he blew a layer of dust off the top. Without a word, he set it down and slowly flipped the pages.

She came over to his side and watched. Finally, he stopped and pointed with a crooked finger to a sketch on the stained, brittle page. "Here," he rasped. "The venstra. It grows only in the caves of Terradoon where there is no light. No one can explain it."

Valerie studied the drawing. It was of a flower with lily petals. There were five long tendrils in the center of the bloom, each with a round berry on the end.

"And how do you administer this to the person with the madness?"

"You must burn an object of their possession with white light. The venstra berries must be crushed with the blood of the maddened one. Mix this with a pinch of the ashes from what you burned and make them drink it."

"Ashes and blood? You've seen this work?"

"Only once. It was painful afterward with some sickness but then the madness left," Bernryn replied, closing the book.

Valerie didn't miss his choice of words. "This happened to you?"

"Yes, but I have met others who suffered the same. I ventured to Terradoon when I was young and did not know of the dangers there. The healer who treated me showed me his methods."

A scraping sound came by the door, causing Valerie to jump. Ranthrop stood there holding a plate of food. Whether it was for her or Bernryn, it seemed too thoughtful a gesture for such a mannerless ogre. His dark expression, however, spoke of anything but generosity.

"What is this nonsense about Terradoon you are speaking of?" he asked Bernryn.

Valerie looked to Bernryn. The old man's eyes were on Ranthrop, but if he'd had a reaction she couldn't discern it through his placid mask.

"Are you finished here?" Ranthrop demanded.

"Yes, my lord," Bernryn rasped. He turned to her and added, "The lady has *everything* she needs. I bid you good night." With that, he shuffled around Ranthrop and out of the room.

Ranthrop made an exasperated noise and set the plate of food down on the workbench. "I thought you might be hungry since your dinner was cut short."

Valerie's mind tried to grasp what had just occurred. What reason was there for him to snap at such an old man—one who'd been helping her? "Could you have been more rude to him? I thought you said we could seek his counsel?"

Ranthrop placed his hands on his hips and gave a calm reply. "He said you have everything you need so there is no issue."

"No issue? I need him to take me to Terradoon! Can't you call him back?" There was actually a cure and it might help Franci. She wasn't going to give up without a fight, even if she had to grovel to this idiot.

Ranthrop's fist slammed down on the workbench, rattling the bottles with its force. Valerie flinched. His eyes were wild with anger. "No! No one goes to Terradoon. I forbid it!" he yelled.

She took a step back from the thunderous velocity of his words. He was more intimidating and commanding than a drill sergeant. Her hands trembled at her sides, but she mustered her courage. "I need to help our friend or she will die." With desperation in her voice, she added, "Please."

Ranthrop straightened up and swallowed. Some of the rage drained from his face as he looked at her, but then he turned on his heel and headed to the door. Without glancing back, he said, "Better you take your chances."

He was dismissing her, just like that? She saw red and looked for the nearest object. With loathsome disgust, she plucked a dinner roll off the plate and lobbed it just as he passed through the door. "You worthless, selfish coward! Wait until life takes something from you—you pompous, spoiled ass!"

She waited as anger rippled through her, but he didn't return. She wanted to scream. Should she have thrown herself at his feet? Should she have given him what he seemed to have wanted in the alcove earlier? Had her unpleasantness doomed both her and Franci? God, was her mom right? The look he had given her said he meant it when he declared that no one could go to Terradoon.

Thoughts of Franci killing herself like Lorna DuClaire had swarmed in her mind. She pictured Sarah or her mother walking into Franci's shop, finding her hanging from a noose. The poor woman didn't deserve to be another casualty of Blinney Lane. She didn't want to be the one who'd failed the most harmless and compassionate soul she'd ever met. How could she remain there if that happened? Disgusted with herself, she wanted to weep. Instead, she picked up the plate of food and threw it across the room at the wall.

CHAPTER FIFTEEN

VALERIE STARED into the cloudy, mirror-like object with a blank expression as she sat brushing her hair at the vanity in her room. The hot buckets of water provided for the wooden tub in her room had helped to wash away both the tension and the griminess of traveling. She didn't appreciate relieving herself in a bucket—no matter how ornate the piss pot looked—but she felt more content than when she'd left the apothecary.

Setting down the brush, she eyed her reflection. She wore a thin bone-colored silky nightgown, which she'd packed. The round neckline swooped down to her sternum, and the slit elbow-length sleeves parted whenever she moved her arms. Tiny buttons flowed down the back to the fitted waist, while a slit on each side of the skirt allowed for ease of movement. She looked like an old film star and scoffed at the irony.

She got up to close the shutters and walked to the fireplace. Grabbing the poker, she stirred the logs and then curled up in the wide-slatted chair in front of the hearth.

Bringing her feet up, she hugged her knees to her chest, staring into the orange glow of the dancing flames, contemplating the day's events.

RANTHROP STEPPED with apprehension toward Valerie's room. It had been ages since he'd lost his temper. The last time he came close was when Sarah Allister had shown up after everyone thought she had died twenty years ago. Why did the Blinney women rile him so?

He had mistaken Sarah as a messenger sent by her brother—the one who'd stolen his long-ago betrothed. Sarah had done nothing to rile him, nor had Valerie for that matter, although he doubted she would see it that way. Of all the things to hear her discussing with Bernryn, it had to be Terradoon.

He'd only gone to the apothecary to offer an apology. All he really wanted was a chance to see her again, to hear any remark from the unusual spitfire who dazzled him. And stars and wickrits, had he heard remarks! As if those weren't enough, she had to throw in that bit about letting someone he loved die. She didn't know. How could she? He'd let that happen...more than once.

There were many things he didn't know, but losing someone he loved wasn't one of them. It was the reason he'd become Lord of the Southlands at such a young age. He'd made a mistake that had likely cost him his father. He wouldn't repeat it again, not after he saw the pleading look in Valerie's shale-gray eyes.

She came all the way from Blinney to find a cure; her ailed friend meant a lot to her. Although he detected some apprehension about Terradoon, she had never faltered. He admired her commitment and that she would do whatever was necessary, no matter the cost. It was the other reason why he'd shot her hopes down so swiftly.

How could he let a woman, the first to awaken both his body and soul in twenty years, charge off to a horrid place like Terradoon? His fear that she might be bold enough to go on her own had brought him to her door. He knew it was probably the dumbest thing he would ever do—and he'd done some pretty dumb things in his life—but he decided if she wanted to go to Terradoon, he would be the one to take her.

He knocked and a few moments later, Valerie opened the door. She stared up at him curiously, waiting for him to speak. Except he couldn't.

The glow of the candle on the wall fluttered across the soft skin of her bare arms. The warm flash of the fireplace illuminated the very large bed, which he calculated would be only three impassioned steps behind her. Her long tresses spilled in waves over her shoulders and down her pale gown. He yearned to slide his hand down the doorframe and capture hers where it rested on the opposite side.

"Yes?" she asked in a clipped tone.

He wanted to slap his brain. Instead, he forced his eyes to focus on her face. "I…I owe you an apology, Lady Valerie." She pursed her lips, so he added, "I probably owe you several apologies. We rarely have a lady grace the keep since my mother passed away fifteen years ago."

Valerie's defenses softened. It was difficult to scowl when someone talked about losing a parent, even if that someone was a six-foot-six brute with social etiquette worse than her own.

"Apology accepted." She began to close the door but Ranthrop pressed his palm to the surface, keeping it open.

"I also wanted to let you know I will take you to Terradoon tomorrow if you still wish to go."

"You want to take me to Terradoon?"

"Yes. I offer myself as an escort. Please accept this gesture as my full apology."

"If you've changed your mind, why not allow Bernryn to take me? You don't need to trouble yourself."

Ranthrop snorted. "Bernryn was old when I was a child. He is not fit to travel to the next village. No. I will take you along with a party of my men. This is the only way I will allow a lady to travel to such a place."

It sounded like an ultimatum, but she wasn't in a position to argue. At least he had relented on her going there. The thought of his infuriating and unpredictable masculine company, however, tightened around her like a noose. "But do you know how to get to Terradoon? Bernryn has been where I need to go."

"The trip would kill Bernryn. And yes, I have been to Terradoon."

He had? She studied his unsettled expression. "All right. I accept your offer. May I ask what changed your mind?"

He shook his head. "No." His eyes widened, and he started to reach for her shoulder, stopping his hand mid-air. He pointed, eyes transfixed. "What is that?"

Valerie glanced at her shoulder. The sleeve of her nightgown had wafted open, revealing a dragon tattoo with its tail wrapping all the way around her arm. She quickly covered it with her hand. "It's called a tattoo. I know. Ricky said you don't have them here. We put them on our skin with permanent ink."

"No, we don't have such things. May I ask what is this creature?" Ranthrop's curious eyes danced.

Like an obedient child, she lowered her hand without thinking. His fingertip brushed against her skin as he slid her sleeve to the side. She was never nervous around men—attracted, disgusted, or disinterested, but never nervous. Her heart fluttered as if she were a delicate mouse, and her voice came out shaky. "It's...a dragon."

He looked like a child at Christmas as he studied the artwork. "We have something here which looks similar. We call them skithers."

Real dragons? She couldn't take much more of Farwin Wood if dragons existed! Stroomphblutels, wickrits…giant, golden-haired men like walking sex you only read about in… Where the hell did that just come from? "What did you say?"

"I asked why you chose this *dragon* to put on your skin."

"Oh. I once read a story that if you are dying and a dragon gives you half of its heart, you will live. I admired them for making that sacrifice." Heat burned in her cheeks when she realized the sentiment she had just admitted. Crossing her arms against her chest, she quickly added, "It's not true of course. Just a silly myth."

Ranthrop's hand fell lazily away from her arm. A somber look crossed his face as he whispered, "You are a strange woman, my lady."

"It wouldn't be the first time I've heard that." She reached for the door again. "I'll see you in the morning."

"Sleep well."

She gave him an odd look at his choice of words, but nodded and closed the door. Walking toward the fireplace, she rubbed the gooseflesh on her arms—except she wasn't cold. She decided to go to bed, and hoisted herself onto the high frame, settling her head upon the pillow. The room smelled earthy—a mix of pine, smoke, and leather. She reached up, rubbing her hand across the dragon tattoo. He had called her *my lady*. Why did it sound so much more different than *m'lady*?

CHAPTER SIXTEEN

IN THE morning, Valerie went to Ricky's room to discuss the trip to Terradoon.

"What do you mean it's a four day trip? What if that's too long for Franci to be Lorna?" Ricky asked as they sat by the fireplace.

"That's what Varmeer told me. What other choice is there?"

"I don't know. And are you sure we should go there? What if they found a way to cure her already? I mean that stuff you mixed up back home could have had a delayed effect while we've been gone."

"And what if it didn't and we waste time going back to find out?" she pointed out. They stared at the fireplace in silence. They were short on time, manpower, and solutions. Valerie knew what had to be done. "I'll go to Terradoon in case she isn't better. You go home and check on Franci and let them know how long it will take me to get back. No sense in both of us going to this 'forbidden' place. I don't want your aunt to have a hissy fit that you went off the grid, especially since you guys didn't know about Terradoon."

"So you get all the fun and glory, and I'm demoted to errand boy? What if you don't come back? How will I know if you need help while you're there? How do I find you? I'm not dealing with your mother if I come back without you."

She cast him an incredulous look. "Fun and glory? Is that why we're here? This isn't my idea of fun, and sometimes people need an errand boy. You're only seventeen. I'm twenty-six. My mother knows I'll do what I want whether she likes it or not. Believe me, she'll know if I went on my own that there was no way you could stop me."

"That still doesn't answer everything," Ricky said.

Valerie avoided the subject. Thinking about it might give it merit.

Ricky added, "What if you don't come back? Wouldn't you rather we were both there together so we can watch each other's backs?"

He had to say it, didn't he? "No. I'd rather have you safe here or back on Blinney Lane. I'll be fine with Ranthrop and his party of merry men. They're supposed to be the equivalent of knights or warriors, aren't they?"

Ricky crossed his arms and shook his head, demonstrating his lack of faith in her decision.

"Besides, you need to stay here and figure out how to get me home."

"I told you how to get home!"

"Damn it, Ricky! And I told you that I'm not freaking—"

"Drowning yourself! I know. I don't understand how you can be willing to go off half-cocked to this creepy place that scares the locals shitless, but you're not willing to go home the only way we can. I've assured you it's perfectly safe, in spite of your phobias."

Valerie jolted out of her seat and patted him on the shoulder, giving him a tight-lipped smile. "I decide how and when I risk my life. You're a smart kid. I'm sure you'll figure out something else when you're finished with your errands. Besides, think of the glory you'll get if you manage to pull it off."

Ricky scrambled out of his chair, pointing his index finger at her. "And you just remember what you need to do to get home if you get into any trouble! I'm telling you, just stay under the water even when you can't stand it anymore. Stay under even if you feel like your lungs will burst. If something happens, just make sure you're wearing everything you came here with and head for water. You got me?"

She bit her lip. "Actually, I thought about that this morning. I've decided to leave my red dress here with you...where it'll be safe."

"Why? So you don't have to think about going home? Valerie, you're going to have to do it sooner or later! What if I can't find another way for you to get back?"

"What if I get robbed? They all make this Terradoon place sound dangerous. What if something like a wickrit tears off a shred of my clothes and I never get it back? Did you think about that? Of course you didn't. My things will be safer here. I left them in the trunk I brought. You can hide it here in your wardrobe."

Ricky groaned and tugged at his hair. "Ugh, I don't like this! This is getting way too complicated."

Valerie gave his shoulder a squeeze. "I'll be fine. I need to go before Ranthrop and his men change their minds. Just promise me you'll still try to find a different way to get back home."

Ricky's hands slid down his face. "And promise me that you'll come back."

"I promise."

"Fine! I'll leave a note inside the wardrobe if I won't be at the keep when you get back."

"Thank you." A rap on the door caused them both to jump.

"Lord Ricky?" Varmeer's voice called.

"I'd better go," Valerie whispered. They patted each other on the back in an awkward hug. Valerie opened the door to a surprised Varmeer. "I was just saying good-bye. Ricky won't be joining us after all."

Valerie followed Varmeer through the alcove. She turned back and caught a glimpse of Ricky who stood at the end of the room. He held up his palm in a half-hearted wave.

LIGHT FLOODED the passage as Varmeer pushed open the door to the outside. She walked past him and stepped out onto a stone balcony that ran along the back expanse of the keep. In the far corner, Ranthrop leaned against the railing. He made a loud phlegmy noise and spit on the stone by his feet, and then grasped the fabric at his crotch, adjusting himself.

"Charming," she said to herself as she continued to approach.

Ranthrop looked up at the sound of footsteps, the bright white embroidered trim on Valerie's gray dress catching his eye. She had dressed more modest than the previous day, yet it made her look even more appealing. The long sleeves trailed as she walked, and she wore a matching cloak. Her raven-black hair flowed in the gentle morning breeze, and two plaits of the shiny ebony were twisted and braided along the sides of her head.

He noted a hint of disgust in her mottled expression. He hadn't shaved, and his face was peppered with sandy colored whiskers. It was autumn, and they were about to set off on a journey through the wilderness. What was the point of being well groomed with an exposed face for such an event?

His black leather pants had been one of his more comfortable pairs to travel and battle in...last year. After tugging at the waistline to loosen the laces against his abdomen, he had wondered how much weight he had gained since the war ended. It had been difficult to tuck the excess of his long black linen waist shirt into the restrictive pants. In his defense, however, he did think he looked a bit more regal today, wearing his fine red and gold vest. Lined on the inside with leather, the outside represented his house's colors. It fastened snugly at his sides and came down just below his backside, which also helped to hide the fact that last year's pants were snugger this year. He couldn't remember the last time he'd ever given his appearance a second thought and wasn't sure why he felt compelled to do so now under her scrutiny.

"Good morning."

"Good morning, Lady Valerie. I trust you slept well." Ranthrop fastened a black leather belt and sword scabbard about his waist.

"Fine, thank you." Like he really cares how I slept. Don't tell me people have the same pretentious manners here as they do back home.

"Ready for our journey?"

Was she dressed appropriately? She'd be much more comfortable in pants if they rode stroomphblutels all day long, but she had yet to see a woman in Farwin Wood wearing pants.

"I'm as ready as I can be. Varmeer gave me a sack for my extra clothes and had them sent to the escort party. I didn't bring very much, so it shouldn't overload my stroomphblutel."

Ranthrop raised an eyebrow. "Don't tell me you're going to insist on taking your stroomphblutel with us."

"Why not? Then you won't have to provide one for me. You're already going out of your way to take me to Terradoon. I don't want to be a burden."

"I wouldn't provide you with a stroomphblutel if you asked," he replied with a smirk.

"I'm certainly not planning on walking there. Are you?"

Ranthrop chuckled, shaking his head. "Of course not, which is why the men are saddling the skithers for us." He turned toward the wall of the balcony and extended an arm for her to approach.

She gave him a quizzical look as she made her way to the stonewall that ran along the edge of the terrace. A set of stairs ran off the corner and when she looked down she saw how steep they were.

The stone below the wall steadily dropped off to a level patch of ground covered with rocks and trees. Devoid of grass, it looked muddy, as though it received a lot of foot traffic. She noticed a high wall made from stacked stones running behind the keep at a great distance. It looked like the view one would have at a zoo, peering down into an animal's pit, and she wondered what inhabited this place. A high-pitched screech broke the silence and her eyes shot to a far corner of the pen. She located a large lean-to structure but could not see what had made the strange sound through the trees that blocked her view.

Ranthrop's arm brushed against hers as he pointed. "Look over there. Can you see?"

Her breath caught in her throat. A man led a shiny mustard-colored creature by a set of reins out from behind a tree. Massive scales covered its body all the way up its long erect neck. Lizard-like skin ran over its head, rounding off at the snout where two oblong nostrils ended before curving down into a pointed beak. It screeched again, and Valerie thrilled in both fascination and terror at the sight of it. Tiny sharp teeth in its lower jaw caught her attention as it squawked out the shrill noise. Its black reptilian eyes were flecked with gold as they shifted back and forth in a predatory gaze.

"Do they bite?" she asked in a low murmur.

"Only the untrained ones. Don't worry, there aren't many left in the wild." Ranthrop smiled as though pleased by her fascination. "You have never seen a skither before?"

She shook her head and studied the rest of the animal's body as the guard led it closer toward them. Its head towered more than fifteen feet high with its body just as long, and its back lay fairly flat in the middle. There was a leather-covered seat affixed to it with a strap that circled under its belly. It had four long, solid legs, which looked like the paws of a lion covered in reptilian scales. It walked with the same steady gait of a feline and it looked capable of fast speeds. Two tiny ears shaped like Aspen leaves sat at the back of its skull with a small splay of reptilian spikes behind each one. The length of its body tapered into a wide tail similar to that of an alligator. Once it had fully emerged from the trees, she saw two more guards appear, leading another pair of the animals.

"Is this the animal on your family's crest?" she asked.

"Yes. Skithers are only found in the swampland. They can travel almost anywhere, but they prefer to nest here."

Ranthrop motioned for her to follow him down the stairwell that led to the pit. She complied, still in a daze over the sight of the creatures.

At the base of the stairwell, they passed through a heavy iron gate into the pit, which contained ten skithers. Each had a saddle chair affixed to its back. Large woven baskets were strapped to the end of each seat that rested on the backs of the animals for storage. She felt silly about her stroomphblutel comment. Each skither looked like it could carry a sedan, let alone her meager belongings.

Varmeer walked over to one of the skithers, patting its shoulder. Swinging its head to look at him, the skither's long, narrow tongue stuck out, emitting a soft, vibrating hiss. Climbing up a rope ladder connected to the base of the seat, he reached for the chair's armrest and stepped onto the skither's back. It didn't move as he gathered up the reins and turned around, settling into the seat. As he pulled a wooden ball on the armrest, Valerie figured out it was attached to a rope hidden inside the wicker chair. The rope ladder collapsed as he pulled the cord and wrapped it around a wooden disc on the side in one fluid movement.

A guard gestured to Valerie's skither, holding its reins in his hand. "M'lady."

She closed her mouth, realizing it had been open ever since she'd set eyes on the peculiar creatures. No longer afraid, she gathered two handfuls of her dress and walked over to the skither, amazed she would be riding it.

The guard extended his hand, but she decided to demonstrate that she wouldn't be a handicap on this journey. She reached for the ladder with both hands, mimicking Varmeer's movements. She felt Ranthrop's eyes on her as he passed by to mount his own beast. The ladder shifted under her feet, causing her to pause until it swung back underneath her frame, and then she continued her ascent. She hesitated for a moment, then stepped onto the giant lizard's back, finding it firm and solid.

Stepping up on the ladder, the guard handed her the reins as she settled into the seat. When he stepped down, she reached for the ladder retrieval, recoiling the device with ease and securing its end in place. Looking up, she found Ranthrop mounted on a skither beside her, staring at her with a peculiar look on his face. Before she could ask if she'd done something wrong, he looked away and set his skither in motion.

Three guards mounted on their own skithers led their party out of the pit through a passage with a wide iron gate into the surrounding wilderness. Valerie looked back and noticed Varmeer directly behind them and four more guards riding behind him. Each armed man carried a long sword at the waist with a shield affixed to the chair's side.

As her skither lumbered along, the thud of its feet reverberated through her with every step. She didn't have to guide; it knew to follow those ahead of it.

Clinging to the reins for security, she saw Ranthrop leaning against the rounded back of his seat. One hand held the reins gingerly, the other lay relaxed over the armrest. Two beams jutted out from the base of the saddle with a rocker arm across the skither's neck where he rested one foot. Was it as easy as it looked?

Settling farther back into the chair, she rested her forearms on the armrests, realizing she could enjoy riding this beast with little threat.

The thick swamp had strange trees with many sporting pitch-black bark and furry moss. Plants sprang up from the ground with clusters of giant leaves bigger than her head. Unlike the changing foliage farther north by Oedher Village, everything here was still green.

"Do you have winter here in the Southlands?" she called to Ranthrop who trotted beside her.

"Yes, of course."

"Do the leaves fall off the vegetation or change color?" she clarified.

"Some of them wilt and fall, but many do not change color as you probably see in the north. Only a few things thrive well in the winter. The crasen flowers, for one, are quite plentiful in the colder months and easy to see once the other foliage is gone."

She looked around, trying to locate the flowers.

"You will not find any of them now. They are about waist high with red spiky leaves and a prickly yellow flower blooms in the center. The zoozles and other creatures feed off them in the winter to sustain them through the season."

She wanted to ask what zoozles were but returned to her visual exploration of the wilderness.

"You have an interest in nature?" he asked with curiosity.

"Yes, don't you?"

"I know everything there is to know about the land already. I have lived here my entire life," he simply stated.

How could someone surrounded by this scenery care so little for it? She would love to be engulfed by this habitat day in and day out. The secrets and capabilities each species might possess could be endless, and the sheer beauty took her breath away. It provided an easy distraction, one that kept her eyes turned away from Ranthrop—one that also helped to avoid engaging in conversation with him.

CHAPTER
SEVENTEEN

BLINNEY LANE

THERE REALLY should be an easier way to do this Ricky thought, holding his breath as he submerged his head in the water barrel at Allister Hall's kitchen.

He sat up at the workbench in his aunt's basement and gasped for air, recalling the feel of panic as his lungs had burned. He was home. Once again, the torturous mode of passage from Farwin Wood to reality had worked. He let out a ragged breath and looked at the open book in front of him. Valerie still slept, her head resting on the table. She certainly wouldn't like what he had just gone through.

Netta was in no condition to help him hold her down. He couldn't imagine Dergus going for it—if he even knew about the book.

"I know, I know," he said, looking at the silent woman. "Figure out how to find a way."

He trudged up the basement stairs and peered down at his clothing when he reached the landing to the store. He saw his aunt standing behind the counter, dressed in a Robin Hood costume.

"I guess I'll fit right in."

The Halloween season made coming back easy. He didn't feel like changing his clothes just to inform her about the delay in Farwin Wood.

He took his time walking to the front of the store. Sarah could be reactionary and his news, although not bad, wasn't good either.

Vibrant neon green caught his eye as he descended the steps to the main floor, and he smiled when he saw Shelby. Wearing a mesh tutu with iridescent wings, she was immersed in conversation with a customer.

He walked up to her and the woman. Shelby gasped in surprise. "Mind if I borrow your fairy for a few moments?" he asked the customer.

The woman chuckled. "Sure, go ahead. I found what I needed."

Once they moved away from the customer, Shelby's arms squeezed around his waist and she whispered, "Are you finished already?"

"No. I just came back to see how things are going here and to give my aunt some news. How's Franci?"

"The same from what we can tell. Still bossing Reggie around and trying to sneak off to see Liza whenever she can."

"I knew hoping she'd just snap out of it wouldn't work," he said.

Sarah inched to the edge of the counter. "You're back soon. Did you find something already?"

"Not exactly."

"Where's Valerie?" Sarah looked past him toward the back of the store.

"Still in the book." He swallowed and reared his shoulders back. This wasn't going to be fun. "They said it could take about four days."

Sarah's eyes snapped back to him. "Four days? I didn't expect a miracle, but why did you leave her in there by herself?"

"She made me come back to let you guys know how long it would take them." He couldn't get defensive. It would just piss her off.

Sarah jutted her hip out, placing a hand over the tan belt on her green tunic. "When do you ever do what you're told?"

"Since you sent me in there with that she-cat!"

"This was your idea, Einstein. I didn't want you to go at all." The feather in her hat bobbed along with her head.

Ricky felt Shelby tug at his sleeve, and he relented. "Fine. Fair enough."

His aunt abandoned her teapot stance and straightened a stack of papers on the edge of the counter. "Wait...why did you say *them*? Who exactly is them?"

He bit his lip. Shelby gave him the same intrigued expression as his aunt. "Valerie...and Ranthrop."

"Ranthrop!" Shelby shouted. "You left her in there with Ranthrop? He's the one who kept me hostage at his grungy castle!"

Great. Now he had two of them to deal with!

"It's fine, really. The war's over. Everything's peaceful. Ranthrop said he and Vasimus get along now. And he's really sorry about the whole hostage thing, by the way. He told me so himself."

"Why did you even get hooked up with Ranthrop in the first place?" Sarah asked.

"We talked to Vasimus's healer, but he couldn't tell us much, so we had to go to Groslivo Stronghold to find Ranthrop's healer. I couldn't just barge in without saying hello. I asked for his permission. It seemed like the right thing to do, and he was fine with it...sort of."

"What does sort of mean?" Sarah asked, watching him closely.

"You might want to sit down for this."

"I don't feel like sitting down."

Ricky regaled what they had learned about Terradoon, which didn't take long, since they had learned very little. He spared telling them about Ranthrop's reaction to going there. No need to rile his aunt up more. The shock of learning that Farwin Wood wasn't the only world in the book appeared to be enough.

Sarah slumped into the stool behind the counter. "How is that possible? No one ever said anything about places other than Farwin Wood in all the time I spent there." Her voice sounded distant and hollow.

"I got the impression the locals didn't always know about Terradoon either. Maybe the world grew with the book as the story inside of it grew." He reached over and squeezed Shelby's hand. She looked flabbergasted too. "Well, I don't mean to shock and run, but I'd better get back. I just wanted to let you know it's going to take longer than we hoped."

Sarah jerked out of her daze. "Now? Why don't you just stay here? You said it'll take Valerie four days to get back to Groslivo Stronghold, right? You don't need to be in there if you don't have to."

"There's some things I need to take care of." He shrugged, accentuating their lack of importance.

"What things?"

"Valerie wants me to find a different way to get home other than drowning. I guess she can't swim."

"She doesn't need to swim!" Sarah said, popping out of her seat.

"Don't you think I told her that?" All right, now he could get defensive! He didn't come back to be interrogated.

"Well, tell her again! You can just stay here for the next four days while she's off gallivanting with the barbarian. Go back and dunk her the day she's supposed to get back. End of story." Sarah waved her hands out like someone was safe at home plate.

"No, it's not the end of story! Netta's sick with something called the drumsy. The hall is a disaster because Dergus is like a feral cat wandering around looking for table scraps without her, and have you ever seen Valerie when she's got her mind set on something? You could have warned me about that!" He waved his arms. "And Ranthrop is not a barbarian. He's… he's just a man's man."

Sarah put a hand to her heart. "Netta's sick? Will she be all right?"

"I think so," he said, his tone softening. "Vasimus's healer said she's tough, and Valerie helped take care of her before she left."

"Oh, thank God." Sarah sighed, bringing her hand to her forehead. A sparkle on her finger caught his eye, and he grabbed her hand.

"He asked you already?"

"I… Yes." Sarah tugged her hand away and looked at the ring on her finger. "I said yes."

Sighing in exasperation, he staggered back. "Oh, that's great. I can't make plans for my future, but you're out here having a party while I'm in there getting my ass kicked by wickrits trying to help your friends."

"You saw a wickrit?" Shelby said, gasping.

He squeezed his arm around her. "Just one, but we got the best of it."

Sarah took a step toward him. "Ricky, it's not like that. I saw the garden upstairs by accident, so he asked me. I'm sure he wouldn't have with everything that's going on if I hadn't.

Look, why don't you just change into something normal and sleep in your own bed tonight. I'm sure Henry would like to share the news with you in-person, and it'll give us a chance to all sit down and talk about your silly pub idea."

Change his clothes, and sleep in his own bed? When did he become twelve?

"It's not a silly idea. It's a plan! What do you think I'm going to college for? Keggers?"

"No, but there's dozens of other things you'd probably rather do than be stuck working here for the rest of your life. Maybe Henry and I can help point you in the right direction."

"Yeah, like the door! That's where you want to point me. I don't mind work. I told you that already. I'm going to have to work no matter where I end up. And speaking of work, I have plenty to do. Let me get out of your hair since you seem to be trying so hard to keep me from sticking around."

He spun on his heel, Shelby's hand still clasped in his, and headed to the back of the shop. Sarah's footsteps sounded after him, and he stopped when he heard her subdued voice.

"That's not what I meant, Ricky. Don't rush off just because you're not getting your way."

"Getting my way? Is that what you think this is about? How old do you think I am, Aunt Sarah? I'm not a little kid anymore. Valerie needs me. Netta needs me. Franci needs our help! As far as the bar, if the council turns me down, fine. I can accept that, but you won't even ask them! Can't you see this has nothing to do with me getting my way? This is me being forced to do things *your way*."

Sarah stared at him, speechless. He waved a hand and murmured, "I'll see you Saturday."

As he walked back to the basement with Shelby in tow, he glanced down at her. "I'm sorry. I didn't mean to get all reality TV back there."

"I know. I actually get where both of you are coming from."

"Oh? So you're not on team Ricky?"

Shelby adjusted his tunic and smiled. "I'm on team Ricky, but I also sit in the visitor's section for team Sarah. She just worries about you. I worry about you too." The look in her eyes said she meant it. "Do you really think there's a different way to come home?"

"I don't know. I have to try. I just want to be responsible and not let anyone down. Otherwise, I'd stay here and curl up on the couch with you for the next few days." He leaned down and placed a soft kiss on her lips.

She rested her forehead against his and whispered, "You're responsible. You'll figure something out. Just be careful."

"Thanks, I will. I'll see you in a few days." He walked to the cellar door and stopped. "Speaking of responsible…you wouldn't mind doing my accounting homework for me, would you?" He bared his teeth impishly.

Shelby furrowed her blonde brows, but she gave a nod, waving a dismissive hand.

ACROSS THE street, above Spices and Stems, Reggie Nurscher eyed Franci as she sauntered out of her kitchen with a Bloody Mary in hand. He stirred his own drink, still not keen on boozing it up with the sassy film star. He had only relented at her insistence when he decided it might help him relax through the babysitting stint from hell. He'd learned two things about Lorna in the last few days: she liked to drink, and she was much easier to deal with when you agreed with her.

What a perfect habit to go along with a chemical imbalance. It was too damned early to drink. He couldn't believe he was freaking missing his workout for the third day in a row, let alone all the business lost with his shop closed.

He stepped carefully into the living room, donning a checkered robe over his shirt and pants, which Franci insisted he wear. Reaching up, he patted his head, feeling ridiculous with the fluffy hairstyle she preferred. He located Franci on the couch, clicking the remote.

She wore an old-fashioned full-length silk slip with thin straps. It could have belonged to her; however, it wasn't her typical attire. Her hair looked beautiful, and she had arranged it in an artful style at the base of her head. He wondered why she'd never worn it like that before she'd become possessed. Leaning back, she rested one elbow on the back of the sofa as she changed channels. Her other hand clutched the drink he had mixed for her with a light splash of alcohol.

He'd mashed up a sleeping pill and added it to the liquid when she wasn't looking. He didn't care what the other Blinney residents might say if they knew he needed to drug her into a few hours of silence so he could get some sleep. She was like the freaking Energizer bunny and nobody was helping him out.

"Archie, there's nothing on television," Franci complained.

Great. Now he was Archie again. Why couldn't he be Ricardo?

He came over and sat as far away from her on the couch as possible. "Here, let me find something." He gestured for the remote, doing his best to appear helpful. She tossed it, hitting him in the thigh.

Franci took another long sip of her drink, bobbing her foot up and down over her crossed legs. She picked up a picture frame off the end table and stared at it. "My word, she's a drab looking thing."

Reggie looked at the photo of Franci in the frame, remembering the day it had been taken. Every Sunday they held a cookout in the courtyard. He'd drank far too much and, at her insistence, wore the "dancing boots"—a pair inherited from his ancestors which came to life, forcing the wearer to frolic about to music whenever worn. He'd fallen, nearly splitting his head open, but she'd patched him up. He remembered how kind and apologetic she had been since she had requested the entertainment. In the photo, Franci smiled, waving at the camera, standing over a picnic table about to cut her strawberry rhubarb pie. He let out a sigh. God, he loved that pie. Lorna certainly wouldn't make him one.

"Who is she, Archie? Should I know her?"

He stared at her, still amazed she had no recollection, even though he knew he shouldn't expect anything different. She really had gone bye-bye. "That's our friend, Franci. Don't you remember her?" he asked hopefully.

"Pfft. I can't say that I do. She's quite pitiful looking, and I don't care to know or remember anyone pitiful." Franci dropped the frame onto the end table, causing the glass to crack.

"Hey! Be careful with that."

"Oh, heavens! What do you care? I'm sure we don't know her. It probably just came with the frame."

He crossed his free arm over his chest, scowling. "Franci's a good woman, even if she is a little silly," he said more to himself than her. He couldn't believe he really missed Franci.

The hint of her silence took a moment to register since Lorna never stopped chattering. The cushion shifted as Franci scooted closer to him. Wearing a pleasant smile, she set her drink on the end table. "I can be silly, Archie. Don't you remember the fun we used to have?"

Her bare arm reached out, and she rested a hand on his shoulder. He noticed just how provocative the dainty slip looked on her frame—*Franci's frame*. She still was Franci. He considered her body for the first time; he'd never seen it so bared before.

Franci's words clicked in his head. Franci *was* silly. She was the only one on Blinney Lane who could really make him laugh. They both shared the same sense of humor that everyone else thought was odd. She was the only one who ever laughed at his jokes. He'd never stopped to appreciate that before.

Franci grazed the side of his neck with her fingertips. Re-crossing her legs, she aimed her knees in his direction, forcing her torso toward him. He looked from her red lipstick smile down past the faint scars around the svelte-looking skin on her neck. The swoop of her neckline clung to her body, showcasing her full and firm thirty-eight-year-old breasts against the silky fabric. They were both the same age. He needed to work out today, especially if women their age still had bodies that looked like this. Tearing his eyes away, he caught sight of her bare legs, exposed from the knee down.

The skin looked soft and perfect; calves plump in just the right place, narrowing down to dainty ankles. Franci had nice gams. An electrifying shiver ran down his spine as he felt her hand rest just above his knee, her fingertip grazing up his neck to his earlobe. Sucking in a breath, he looked at her. The soft glow of morning light crept in through the windows, chasing away the shadows, increasing the intimate moment.

"Didn't you think I was fun?" Franci whispered in a seductive pout as she leaned in closer.

"Yeah," he stammered. "You were fun."

She smiled, moving her hand farther up his thigh. He casually brought his hand down to rest on his leg in an effort to block her passage.

The pout returned to her face. Delving her fingers into the base of his hairline, she swirled her fingertips against his scalp. "What's wrong? Am I not attractive?"

He swallowed so loudly he swore she could hear it. He shifted his head, but her fingers followed, continuing their torturous onslaught. Taking a sip from his drink, he fixed his eyes on a random spot on the wall. Maybe if he sat perfectly still and avoided eye contact, she'd grow bored of her game. He felt her hand move from his leg to the top of his hand. She picked it up, pressing it to the center of her chest. The soft flesh touched the base of his palm, causing his mouth to water.

"Aren't you going to tell me? Don't you find me attractive?" Franci whispered, her warm breath on his ear.

His abdominal muscles quivered; his breath caught in his throat. Too afraid to move, he shifted his eyes, noticing a slight bulge in his polyester pants. Oh, man! It was too late for morning wood!

He felt paralyzed as her words floated through his mind, shivers racing over his body. "I...I think you're very attractive," he managed.

He felt her heartbeat beneath his sweaty palm. She moved, causing his hand to fall around the soft curve of her breast before landing on her slender waist like a dead limb. Dead—that's exactly what he was, especially when her hand glided sensuously up the inside of his thigh.

The cushion of the sofa shifted, and he watched her bring a knee up to support herself, leaning into his chest. His knuckles brushed against her thigh where they sat lifeless by his side. He felt the full weight of her breasts press against his thin shirt. Her hand trailed across his groin, up the side of his ribs to his chest, and stopped on his cheek. "Good," she purred, her lips just in front of his, "because I still find you... *incredibly* handsome."

He couldn't take it anymore. Nearly whimpering, he parted his lips in hunger. Franci closed the distance between their mouths, joining their lips and letting her body collapse against his. The anticipation and tension in him evaporated as their tongues melded, and he inhaled the intoxicating scent of her perfume. His drink slipped from his hand, crashing to the floor.

Franci grazed her other leg against his knee, tugging his shirt out of his pants, her warm hand slipping underneath, sliding across his chest. He flinched when she touched the scars marring his chest. Every woman he'd been intimate with had cringed at the sight of them. Leaning his head back, he waited for her reaction to his deformity.

She kissed his neck and then his collarbone. Her hand moved out of his shirt, and she tore open its top button, fully exposing the edge of one of the marks.

Reggie watched as her lips came down with heavy breaths, planting a kiss on the skin, oblivious to the marks he despised. When she stopped, his stomach clenched, knowing this was the moment. His entire body tensed, waiting.

She looked up at him, her hand still pressed to his skin. A genuine pout formed on her face, and she asked with hurt in her voice, "What's the matter? Don't you want me?"

He stared at her in disbelief for two seconds. That's all it took for him to realize she still wanted him, scars and all. He groaned, reaching for her. "Yes!"

He shot off the couch, one hand supporting her back. The other found a happy home around her hip and laid her down across the cushions. He yanked the ridiculous robe off, chucked it into the air, and then quickly settled down on top of her. His lips came down to meet hers, and it was exhilarating to find them so eager. He slid his hand up the soft skin of her arm, to where hers still delved in his hair, entwining their fingers. Her one hand was gentle while the other was eager and wild, just like his, and he marveled at the duality of her passion.

Franci ripped open the front of his shirt and gave a satisfied sigh. She moved her hand across the expanse of his skin, scars and all. He equaled her exploration and slid a hand down the shiny fabric of her slip, up the back of her knee, helping her to guide it around his hips. She moved her hips up to meet his, and he could feel the agonizing pressure within his tight pants as their pelvises connected.

Somewhere in the back of his mind, two voices began to battle. They each screamed, and he vaguely wondered if *he* was becoming possessed. Over and over, the words "this is wrong" followed by "it's not wrong" warred in his head.

"Oh, Archie, I want you!"

He snapped his head up. "What?"

"Archie," Franci moaned, tugging at the flaps of his shirt.

He felt his face sag instantly along with the tension in his pants. Sitting up on one knee, he stared at Franci, panting against the hammering of his heart. He felt crushed and ashamed all at once as he saw the pleading expression on her face. What had he done?

"I can't do this," he whispered.

"Archie, whatever's the matter?"

He grimaced upon hearing that name again and pushed off the couch. "I can't do this," he said more clearly, turning away from her.

Franci came up behind him. "What's wrong?"

"Nothing." He shrugged her hand away from his shoulder, her touch making him cringe now. He felt as if he had just violated his oldest friend or a mental patient. Isn't that what you just did? he screamed inside his head. Franci wasn't some tourist he could forget about who would leave in the morning. He shook his head in disgust.

"What do you mean *nothing*? Don't you still want me?" Franci cried.

"No! Just leave me alone!" He spun around just in time to see the shock and hurt on her face. Her lips were still plump from his kisses. Distracted, he didn't see her hand come up to slap him, but he sure felt it. Her palm cracked across his cheekbone, forcing his head in the opposite direction.

"You bastard!" she screamed, running away in tears to her bedroom.

Reggie stretched his jaw and brought a hand to his stinging cheek. The door to Franci's room slammed shut, and he heard the lock click into place. He walked over to it, but stopped when he heard the heart-wrenching sound of her crying from the other side. "Great," he said, stomping back over to the couch.

Maybe she'd cry herself to sleep. That would keep her busy for a while. Even if it were a possibility, he didn't feel good about it.

Looking down at his ripped, open shirt, he realized the remaining source of his agitation. Franci didn't want him. Lorna just wanted Archie. What baffled him was why it he couldn't understand was why that bothered him.

CHAPTER EIGHTEEN

FARWIN WOOD

THE PROCESSION of skithers eventually emerged from the wilderness to a wide dirt road. The passage appeared to see little travel. Small patches of grass sprouted in various places. They traveled in silence for over four hours before stopping. Valerie watched the men dismount and found Ranthrop standing below, motioning for her to get down. Releasing the stepladder, she descended.

At the bottom rung, she felt one of his hands at the small of her back and another cradle her elbow, catching her off guard. Turning quickly to look at him, she nearly lost her footing as the folds of her dress wrapped around her legs. Ranthrop's hands tightened on her as she righted herself.

"Careful. The ground is very soft here."

"I'm fine." She took a step, releasing herself from his grasp. "Why have we stopped? Where did your men go?"

He hooked a thumb through his belt, watching her and smirked. "They are likely in the trees, away from the eyes of a lady."

"Oh," she replied, catching his meaning.

Ranthrop removed an animal-skin canteen from his shoulder and took a drink, handing it to her when he finished. She resisted the impulse to wipe the brim as he stared at her with his obnoxious eyes. Looking away, she took a few swallows, then handed it back. The awkward silence between them grew as they exchanged glances.

Finally, Ranthrop spoke. "Do you need to...do what nature intended, as well?"

Valerie's cheeks flushed. Of course she did. Why was he asking? "Yes. I was just waiting for some privacy." She started for the opposite side of the road away from the other men. Hearing footsteps behind her, she turned around and saw Ranthrop following her. "Do you plan on watching me?"

He stopped as if he ran into a wall, snorting. "I don't make a habit of it."

"Then why don't you stay right there. I can manage just fine on my own," she replied, continuing into the brush.

"I'm not letting you get mauled by something when you're under my care."

Valerie whipped around but found him on the other side of the bushes. "You're in charge of making sure no one gets mauled? Ha! That's a laugh." She moved to put more distance between them.

Ranthrop rolled his eyes. He turned his back to the tree line so she wouldn't be tempted to tread deeper into the wilderness. "I can't see you now," he called over his shoulder. "Don't walk all the way back to the stronghold, will you?"

"I can still hear you!" her muffled voice called out.

Valerie frowned as she hiked up the bulky skirt of her dress. She could handle relieving herself outdoors, but she hated sounding like a pampered diva who cried when a nail broke. Why was that man so damned argumentative and stubborn? She'd give up arguing with her mother for at least a week to get away from him as soon as possible. Finally, her discomfort with the situation and her relief streamed out of her. She tore a piece of the inside of her dress lining and used it as paper, wishing she'd thought to bring some form of tissue from the keep.

Pushing her way back through the foliage, she stopped when she saw Ranthrop's back. His head was down, and she heard the splattering sound of water.

"Oh, brother." She folded her arms, waiting for him to finish his own business.

Something whirred past her head. Glancing around, she couldn't locate anything flying. Her skin began to crawl as she stood in plants up to her waist, the ground not visible below.

"Ahem," she said, clearing her throat. "Are you about finished there, Lord Waterfall? I'm so grateful you're ready with a weapon in hand to protect me, but I'd like to leave the woods now." She watched his back shift as he shook. Gross!

She disliked acting prissy, but he just made it too easy to find new reasons to loathe him. He turned around to face her as if to say something, and then closed the distance between them in long strides through the bushes.

"What?" she asked. Eyes locked on her, he looked positively livid. Couldn't he take a little sarcasm for all the digs he threw out? "I was only teasing you. What's the matter?"

Ranthrop stood before her, scowling. Reaching up, he grasped her shoulder. She stepped back, putting her hands up, wondering if she needed to defend herself. Her retreat ended when she backed into a tree.

"Hold…still," he whispered.

She heard the sound of sliding metal, and from the corner of her eye she saw his other arm come up from behind him, holding a shiny foot-long dagger. Grasping the fabric of his shirt, she pushed at him until she saw the blade go over her head. Peering up, she noticed his eyes focused above her head. Something tugged at her hair as she stood rigid and confused. She watched as he pulled the blade away and out to his side.

A fat teal worm, half the length of the blade, sat perched on it with eight thin spindly legs. Its large black eyes were glazed over. Antennas poked out of its round head, and two little fangs jutted out from the front of its mouth.

She held her breath, shifting her eyes from it to Ranthrop's face. He extended his arm as far away from them as possible, lowered the blade and flicked his wrist, flinging the creature into the woods.

"What the hell was that?"

Ranthrop resheathed his blade. "A zoozle. They sting, and it itches like a fury."

She relinquished her hold on his tunic and stood very still. "Are there any more on me?"

Ranthrop studied her face, his hand still clasping her shoulder. He'd never seen a woman react so calmly to nature or ride a skither. He'd never seen a lady relieve herself in the woods. And while she had a scathing tongue that easily found fault in everything he did, she managed to do it in such a graceful manner that he couldn't really find fault in her. He would have laughed at the Lord Waterfall pun, but assumed it would only infuriate her more.

"What? Is there one on my face?" She brushed her fingertips over her cheeks.

Ranthrop frowned, jerking her away from the tree. Spinning her around, he inspected her back. When he jerked her back around, he found her scowling at him. Grabbing her about the waist, he hefted her into his arms as if she weighed no more than a feather. "Best not let anything crawl up those skirts," he said, starting for the road.

"Hey! What do you think you're doing?"

Ranthrop glared at her as he had during their argument in the apothecary. She decided to remain quiet.

"Damn it, woman! Do you never let anyone help you?" he asked in annoyance.

Valerie blushed and looked away. Pressing her lips together, she avoided the eyes of the men who had reassembled on the road. Let anyone help her? No one had ever tried before.

CHAPTER NINETEEN

ALLISTER HALL

RICKY MADE it through the glade entryway to Farwin Wood without being chased by a wickrit. It was the first time, and he was grateful for the anomaly. He walked to Oedher Village with a heavy heart, his argument with Aunt Sarah still fresh on his mind.

Finding an alternate way home for Valerie seemed even more pressing now that his abilities were doubted once again. The more he wanted to succeed, the farther away success appeared. He had no idea where to begin.

He'd spoken to Bernryn before he left Groslivo Keep that morning about the properties of water. The peculiar old man couldn't offer insight on any special powers the substance might have. He'd listened patiently as the old man launched into a lengthy description about the different medicines that could be made by adding water to other substances before he'd grown frustrated and left for Allister Hall to get back to Blinney Lane through the kitchen's rain barrel.

Stopping by an old smithy shop at the edge of town, Ricky watched a young man, a few years older than himself, struggle to reset a beam on the roof of a ramshackle workshop. Ricky entered the yard, which was cluttered with broken wagon wheels, buckets, and battered armor.

"Looks like you've got your hands full there," he called up to the man.

"Mine and three more pair's worth," the man said without looking down at him as he forced the beam into place.

Ricky perused the cottage that sat at the edge of the work yard. The shutters hung precariously from their hinges. A haphazard patch job covered a charred section of roof. Several fluffy kouklas (plump, furry chicken-like creatures) scampered free range near some potted flowers by the doorway. He noted a small pen with coops, but its fence was in as poor shape as everything else.

"Have you thought about starting new somewhere else? Seems you might be working the rest of your life to get this place back in order."

The young man began climbing down from the roof. His blond hair shined like a beacon against his tanned skin. Sinewy arms clung to the bracer posts as he slung his legs over the side of the roof, hopping down with a youthful, but tired ease. His dirty hands were calloused and cracked, and he grumbled as he dusted them off on the leather apron covering his mud-stained shirt. "Somewhere else? Where have you been the last twenty years? I'd like to see a smithy shop in Farwin Wood that's fared any better than mine."

When the man lifted his head and made eye contact with Ricky, his eyes rounded as he stammered, "Lord Ricky."

Ricky stepped forward and offered his hand. The man smeared his hand on his apron again before accepting the handshake. "I'm sorry. I didn't realize it was you. I've only seen you from afar several times."

"No worries. I'm not here often. Master…"

"Tyson. Tyson Ryker."

"Pleasure to meet you, Master Ryker. So this is your smithy?"

"It belonged to my father." Tyson grimaced as he looked around at his workspace. "He was killed early in the war. I've done my best to build on what he taught me but between the skirmishes and guarding the village, I haven't had much time until late to repair the neglect. I know it must be a sore sight."

"I'm sorry for your loss, but no need to apologize for the state of things. I can't imagine trying to maintain this all by yourself. Even Allister Hall needs its repairs, and my family has been negligent at that."

"Why I'd give my right arm to have a smithy shop like the one at Allister Hall. Mine is certainly no comparison to it right now."

The flapping of wings and squawking of the kouklas drew their attention to the cottage door. A comely blonde woman steadied herself, nearly tumbling over the scattered birds.

"Tyson! You really need to repair that pen. I'm going to break my neck one of these days on…" She balked as her eyes met Ricky's.

Ricky noticed a faint red scar running across the right side of her jaw. It disappeared in a curve behind her ear. His cheeks warmed as he watched her hand cover it in haste as she lowered her eyes.

"I'm sorry. I didn't know we had company," she called, the feistiness gone from her voice.

"This is Lord Ricky Allister of Allister Hall," Tyson announced. He turned to Ricky with a smile and gestured. "My sister, Ophelia."

"Lord Ricky. My apologies," she murmured, bowing her head.

"Lady Ophelia, the pleasure is mine." Ricky bowed. As he stood upright, he noticed brother and sister exchanging awkward looks.

"I'm no lady," Ophelia said. He didn't miss the forlorn tremble in her voice. She combed her long blonde hair to hide the scar, smoothing out the ragged apron covering her worn mauve-colored dress.

"Ophelia is a wonderful cook, Lord Ricky. Could we offer you a meal?" Tyson asked.

Ricky took another glance around the yard and then again at the brother and sister. His mouth turned into a broad smile. "I have a better idea."

TWO HOURS later, Ricky returned to Allister Hall with Tyson and Ophelia in tow. It was still unclear to him how Ophelia felt about his proposed arrangement of coming to live and work at Allister Hall, but Tyson had practically kissed him at the idea. However, when he'd mentioned he needed someone to help the currently bedridden Netta, Ophelia's skittish weariness had decayed, and she offered to tend the kitchen until Netta was well.

Dergus took Tyson under his wing, straight away, likely starved for male companionship from all his years at Allister Hall with only Netta to pass the time. Ricky knew Dergus would also get Tyson to do some of his own work, but he didn't mind. In fact, it was why he had procured the arrangement.

Silence filled the hall as he sat in front of the crackling fire with an array of books open before him on the table. Allister Hall never had a healer in residence, but he'd found some books in a library upstairs. Among them a journal, penned by several of his ancestors, containing notes and descriptions about the plant and animal life in Farwin Wood. Interesting and nostalgic, it held no information to spark any ideas to help Franci if Valerie and Ranthrop didn't succeed, or any hope of finding a different means of returning to Blinney Lane.

The door to the hall creaked behind him, and he turned to see if it was Dergus and Tyson returning. A dusty blue cloak wafted in with the breeze, and he followed the giant frame it silhouetted to see the face of Vasimus Daundecort.

"Lord Ricky! I heard you were here," Vasimus called.

Ricky heaved the book onto the end table and hopped out of the chair. "Lord Vasimus! I'm sorry Dergus isn't at the gate. He's out back showing around a new smithy I took on."

"Ah, why didn't you tell me you were seeking a smithy? I could have found one for you."

Ricky met Vasimus in the center of the room, clasping arms with him. It was such an odd change from the man he'd seen on his last trip to Farwin Wood. There was joy in his eyes, a contentment that had not been there before.

"How are you, my young friend?" Vasimus asked.

Ranthrop had been right. One look at the man smiling at him and Ricky could tell he had mellowed from his bitterness. He had wondered how Vasimus had gotten on after his Aunt Sarah had gone back to Blinney Lane with him and Henry. Perhaps he didn't hold any grudges.

"I'm well, thank you. And I hear the peace is going well in Farwin Wood. My aunt will be happy to hear this."

"She did not come with you?"

"No. Henry was not eager to let her go," he replied, studying the man's face.

Vasimus gave him a genuine smile, patting him on the shoulder as they walked to the chairs by the hearth. "Master Henry is a wise man. You must tell them they are both welcome at Daundecort Hall any time. I would add that the better man won, but you understand I must keep some of my pride," he said in a conspiratorial tone near Ricky's ear.

Ricky let out a breath and fist bumped Vasimus's arm. "You're a better man than me."

"It takes stupidity and mistakes to become a better man," Vasimus added with a pained expression. "Don't be too jealous."

"Ha, okay, I won't."

They settled into the chairs by the fire. After a while, Ricky excused himself to rouse Ophelia in the kitchen, informing her of their guest and requesting ale. Although it had only been a few hours, the kitchen looked greatly improved, and he noticed a masked look of pride when he complimented her on her work.

Returning to the fireplace, he delved back into easy conversation with Vasimus. "Speaking of mistakes…I realize now that we should have found some help for Netta and Dergus before we left. They're not exactly getting any younger, and we don't come here very often."

"You didn't come all the way from Blinney to remedy that did you? I'm sorry I didn't think of it. I would have seen to it for you. I'm sure I can find someone who can help them."

"I believe I've remedied it already. Tyson Ryker has agreed to take up as the hall's smithy and his sister Ophelia has come temporarily to take care of Netta. As long as she agrees to stay, I won't need to look for anyone else to help Netta with the housework."

"Ryker? I believe I remember their father. He was an adept smithy and just as skilled a warrior. I remember the day he fell, poor fellow."

Ricky felt a chill go up his spine. It was difficult to imagine that people in this beautiful land had actually killed each other. He saw regret on Vasimus's face, and the guilt of stirring such a memory gnawed at Ricky's insides. He decided to change the subject before altering the man's good mood.

"I have to thank you for the repairs you've done to the hall since we left. You really didn't have to see to all of that. I'm sure you've had plenty of other things to do."

Vasimus waved a dismissive hand. "No more of that, Ricky. It was the least I could do."

Ricky could see his gratitude made the man uncomfortable. He really had changed for the better. He wasn't horrible before but love could make anyone go off the deep end.

Vasimus's expression changed from embarrassment to surprise, and Ricky turned his head as feet shuffled behind him. Following the man's gaze, he located Ophelia approaching with goblets and a bottle of beetleburry ale in her hands.

Vasimus jumped to his feet so quickly the chair rocked backward, and the legs returned to the floor with a loud thump, stopping Ophelia in her tracks.

Ricky motioned her forward. "Ophelia, this is Lord Vasimus. Lord Vasimus, Ophelia Ryker."

"Mistress," Vasimus said, putting an arm across his stomach as he bowed, "may I assist you?" He reached for the goblets, and Ricky noticed the flustered blush painting Ophelia's cheeks. She inclined her head away from Vasimus as she handed over the goblets. The poor woman seemed ashamed of her face. She had no need to be. She was quite attractive in spite of her modest clothing.

"Thank you, m'lord," she barely whispered.

Ricky steadied his goblet as she poured with a shaky hand. Either she was a terrible server or Vasimus unsettled her with his staring.

"I hope you will be very happy here, Mistress," Vasimus said in a gentle hush.

"Will that be all, Lord Ricky?"

"Hmm? Yes. Thank you, Ophelia." He took the bottle from her grasp, and she turned abruptly, whisking herself back to the kitchen. He noticed Vasimus still standing, watching Ophelia's departure.

"Did you need something else?"

"No, I'm fine." Vasimus took his seat again, glancing back toward the kitchen. "You've hired some caretakers. Is that all you need settled while you are here?"

"I came looking for a cure for my friend, Franci who is back in Blinney. She seems to think she's someone else. It's as if she's forgotten who she is, and she's been taken over by someone else's identity."

Vasimus frowned. Resting his elbow on the chair, he rubbed the whiskers on his chin. "Ricky, we have nothing like that here in Farwin Wood…" His mouth hung open as if he meant to say more.

"But...maybe in Terradoon?"

"I did not know if you knew of such things. Yes, I have heard that strange things happen in Terradoon. Ranthrop could tell you more."

"I came here with a lady from Blinney who is a healer where we are from. She met with Bernryn, Ranthrop's healer, and he told us about a cure that could be found in Terradoon."

Vasimus glanced around the room before returning his gaze back to Ricky. "A lady healer? Is she here now?"

"Ranthrop is taking her to Terradoon to obtain the cure. They left from Groslivo Stronghold this morning."

"*Ranthrop* has gone to Terradoon?"

Ricky nodded. Why was everyone so afraid of Terradoon? "I know, everyone told us it's a dangerous place, but he offered to escort her there himself."

"Really?" Vasimus stared into the fire, shaking his head. "He spoke of craving adventure," he said to himself. "What a damned fool."

Great. Even he thinks it's foolish for them to have gone. "They said they should be back in about four days. Do you really think it's dangerous in Terradoon?"

"Hmm?" Vasimus looked up. "I wouldn't recommend it, not after all of the stories I have heard. I must say, I'm glad you stayed behind. Why did you, might I ask?"

Ricky sighed, glancing around to be sure Dergus hadn't returned. He remembered his aunt had told Vasimus about the book. Since he seemed so pleasant and generous now, it couldn't hurt to seek his advice. "Lady Valerie, the woman who came with me, would like me to find a different way to…to get back to Blinney. Do you remember how we get home?"

Vasimus scoffed. "How could I forget it? I nearly fell asleep in my washtub one night and jolted up thinking I might be transported to some other place far worse than Terradoon."

Ricky chuckled. Leaning forward, he rested his elbows on his knees. "I hate to ask you for any more help, but how do you feel about drowning a woman who is afraid of the water if that's the only way she can get home?"

Vasimus gawked at him. "Ricky, I've done some despicable things the last twenty years during the war, but I refuse to drown a woman."

Ricky gestured with his goblet. "You said you understood how we get home. It's to help Lady Valerie, the woman who came with me. She's terrified of water, and she's insisting that I find some other way for her to get back to Blinney."

Vasimus swirled the ale around in his goblet. "Well, I have to agree with the lady. You should find a more civilized way to go back and forth. I hated seeing your aunt in the river when she left here the last time. It took everything in me not to dive in to make sure she wasn't lifeless with her body simply waiting to float to the surface." He shifted uncomfortably in his chair.

Ricky sat back, chewing on his lip. "If I could think of something more civilized, I would do it, believe me. I'm worried I won't find a way. It's impossible to get Lady Valerie into the water to come home. I can't leave her here, but at the same time I don't think I'll be able to hold her under the water by myself." He folded his arms across his chest. "She's uncooperative."

"You want me to volunteer to help you commit murder?" Ricky gave him a speaking look and Vasimus sighed. "Well, it would feel like murder. It's a shame you don't have a door to your world that just opens up here and sends you back."

"Tell me about it! A door? Can you imagine that? Who would guard the door here to make sure people from Farwin Wood didn't wander through it and get the shock of their life when they ended up where I live?"

"I would see to that."

Ricky cast him a quizzical look. "You wouldn't...want to go through the door yourself?"

"To see your aunt, you mean?"

"Maybe..."

Vasimus chuckled. "And see if Master Henry were waiting to treat me as hospitable as I treated him while he was here?"

Ricky shook his head. "Henry would never harm anyone without provocation. He loves—"

"He loves your aunt?" Vasimus added calmly and nodded.

"Yeah."

Vasimus smiled, staring at the glowing flames. "Then there would be no need for me to go through the door. My lands and people need me here. This is where I belong, just as your aunt belongs there. We both understood that...finally." He cast Ricky a thoughtful smile. "People like to believe in fairy tales, but I believe time and space exist for a reason. There is only one reason I would challenge that phenomenon. For love," he held up a finger, indicating he wasn't finished, "but not for the kind of love you suspect. I do love your aunt. I imagine I always will. But she has the kind of love that makes the woman she is today happy. We are but strangers now. It would be an awkward dance for the both of us."

Ricky felt dumbstruck by the wisdom the man had just spewed. His head hit the back of his chair with a thump as he took it in. Wow. He wondered how much stupidity and how many mistakes it would take him to get like this? Durley, his ancestor who'd written *The Lands of Farwin Wood,* had certainly broken the mold with this guy.

He wanted to tell him he had a man-crush on him, but doubted he'd understand the meaning. "If there was such a door, I'd pass through it more often to come and help you out if you ever needed anything."

Vasimus extended his hand, and he and Ricky clasped forearms. "You are a good friend, Ricky. You have the same promise from me. It's a shame there is no such door. I fear I'm with this Lady Valerie, for I have seen too many people from Farwin Wood drown. Their bodies reappear here at the surface, so I know they do not go to Blinney with you."

"If only there was a book in Farwin Wood like we have in Blinney," Ricky said. He stared at the fire. Suddenly, his breath caught in his throat. Wide-eyed, he looked at Vasimus.

"Have you tried to write this book that you have, I mean a copy of it, while you are here?" Vasimus asked, leaning on his armrest.

Ricky felt as if he would burst from his excitement. "No! But our book is about your world. I'd have to write a book about *The Lands of…*"

"*Blinney Lane,*" they said together in amazement.

CHAPTER TWENTY

THE SOUTHLANDS, FARWIN WOOD

AFTER THE fiasco with Valerie, Ranthrop ordered the skithers to a trot. He didn't feel like talking, but she wouldn't be able to either if the motion bounced her around in her saddle. He felt guilty, which was new to him, and he glanced to check on her. Her usual scowl appeared on her face. He wondered if it was because of him or if she was miserable from the ride? She didn't appear to be bouncing around a lot. In fact, she sat leaning back against her chair with a foot pressed against the brace as if she were a natural. Damn it, she continued to baffle him.

How long would she stay mad at him? Maybe Ricky was right, and she's just an angry woman. But what made her so angry all the time?

Flicking his reins, he urged his skither to a faster pace until it was alongside Varmeer, who acted as if he didn't see the giant beast by his side. It screeched loudly, nuzzling its head against Varmeer's skither.

"Any new instructions, m'lord?" the man finally called out. "Or have you simply stopped by to complain about your saddle sores?"

Ranthrop scowled. "New instructions? Are you ready to turn around and head home already, old man?"

Varmeer was only five years older than Ranthrop but if he had a stone for each time Ranthrop had called him "old," he would have enough to build his own hall. "I go where I'm bid, m'lord. 'Twas you I thought might come to your senses by now."

"My senses!" Ranthrop yelled.

Varmeer turned his head, realizing how his comment had been interpreted. "Ranthrop, you know what I meant. 'Tis this journey to Terradoon that is senseless. I meant nothing more."

Ranthrop flicked his reins, bolting his skither forward. The beast raced ahead, not breaking stride, until Ranthrop cleared the group. He lead at a pace far away from the others, letting Varmeer know he did not care to speak to anyone nor was he calling off the trip.

For over three hours, they traveled at the quickened pace. Varmeer caught Ranthrop glancing back several times, with his eyes always looking past him to Valerie.

Varmeer began to suspect the man's foul mood had to do with more than the comments he'd made. Perhaps Ranthrop had said or done something inappropriate to the lady again, and she was ignoring him. He'd never seen a woman so willfully dismiss any kind of attention from the brawny man who was much too handsome for his own good. The shock alone must be eating at him. It was no laughing matter if Ranthrop dedicated himself to this foolish quest in order to win the lady's affections for a night. He'd never broken his unspoken code of secrecy to his lord, but he might have to drop a word in the lady's ear if he got the chance.

RANTHROP FINALLY slowed, and the party lumbered along at a steady pace for another hour. Valerie could see a mountain range beyond the trees ahead—the rocks were a creamy white hue as far as the eye could see. She would protest if Ranthrop gave any indication that they would be scaling up the mountain this evening. Her back and legs were sore from holding herself in the saddle all day, and she was in dire need of using the bushes again, preferably without any zoozles.

The party veered off the road to a clearing in the forest as they neared the base of the mountain. The landscape had turned from swampy to more deciduous looking vegetation some time ago, and Valerie wondered if it meant they had officially left Ranthrop's lands. How could one man rule and care for such a vast expanse of territory? How could a spitting, pissing, thickheaded, womanizer be responsible for anything? she wondered.

Ranthrop stopped the party in the clearing and ordered the men to dismount. Valerie happily stood up on the skither and stretched. She noticed the men unpacking the baskets behind their saddles and she inspected her own.

Finding her clothing sack, she tossed it down to the ground. There were also large folded leather skins and fur hides. Ranthrop's men took similar materials from their baskets and tossed them to the ground as well. Some of the men had posts affixed to the sides of their baskets, which they also dropped to the ground. Unless they were dull spears, they were likely materials to make tents for the night.

She tugged the pelts from her basket, flipping her loose hair over her shoulder and pulling up the bothersome sleeves of her dress. Freeing the material from the confines of its container, she tossed the heavy load away from the skither to the ground. When she looked up, she noticed everyone staring at her.

"Don't we need these things to make camp for the night?" she called to Varmeer.

"Yes, m'lady, but the men will do this for you. No need to trouble yourself."

"Oh."

The men continued unpacking. As she sidestepped around the basket and saddle chair, she noticed Ranthrop watching her. He looked agitated with his hands on his hips. She arched a steely brow at him, but received no change in his expression, so she turned her back on him and unfurled her stepladder.

When she descended, he was nowhere in sight. Varmeer walked toward her, picking up her clothing sack. As she went to take it from him, he moved it away from her reach, as though he meant to gesture with that hand and not slight her.

"Would you like to sit with me while I make a fire?"

She tried to smile, understanding his kindness to keep her from manual labor. She wasn't used to sitting on her laurels. She nodded for him to continue without her. "I'll be right there."

Varmeer walked away as if he were hesitant to leave her. Walking up to her skither, she patted its shoulder. Careening its head back, it let out a quiet screech. She trailed her fingers over its vinyl-like skin, caressing its scales. "Thank you for the safe journey," she whispered.

The skither nudged her shoulder with the edge of its snout. It snorted a soft hissing breath, swinging its head back around then headed past where Varmeer sat crouched by a pile of broken branches. She followed and watched it trot over to join its companions who drank from a stream up ahead.

Valerie found a smooth rock near Varmeer that came up to her knees and sat down on it as she watched him start a fire. He used a dried twig and some dead grass to kindle a flame. She'd seen this on television before but never in person. She wanted to try, however, she suspected it wasn't something a lady did. In spite of the chivalry she'd seen in Farwin Wood and her lack of elegance, she had to admit that everyone so far seemed accepting of her. Well, everyone except for Ranthrop. Maybe it was her feigned status of being a lady, which meant she wasn't to be questioned. Regardless, it felt nice not to be a total outcast for once.

"Lady Valerie," Varmeer called as he stood up and dusted off his hands once the fire began to take, "might I have a word while the men are out hunting for dinner?"

"Of course." How wonderful would it be if people like Reggie asked for permission to speak?

"Might I ask...that is, do you know the reason why Lord Ranthrop agreed to take you to Terradoon?"

Valerie pulled her cloak around her, feeling goose bumps on her arms. "I told him about my friend who may die if I cannot find a cure for her."

Varmeer stared at her for a moment. "And may I inquire what the lady suffers from?"

Valerie hesitated, looking around. She saw a single man twenty feet away setting up a tent, but there was no sign of the others. She didn't know if she should speak openly about possession to Ranthrop's men, but she got the impression that Varmeer was his most trusted confidant. He seemed like a pleasant and kind enough fellow. "Has Ranthrop not told you?"

"He knows I counsel him against anything...too foolish, so he did not give me a reason for taking you to Terradoon other than he would act as your escort."

"You objected to him going to Terradoon?"

"Yes. Most adamantly."

She frowned. Tit for tat had always been a decent policy. If these men were being forced to take her to a place they feared for her benefit, they at least deserved to know her motives. "My friend is possessed by someone else. She does not remember her true self. It's a form of madness, which you might call it, that we have found no way to cure."

"I see." Varmeer scratched at his goatee and ambled over, crouching down on a knee. "Madness? You're sure?"

"Yes. There's no other way to put it. I can't really explain." She couldn't describe magic and curses to him when she'd seen none of that in Farwin Wood. "Why did you not want Ranthrop to go to Terradoon?"

Varmeer let out a quiet breath and returned his gaze to the fire. "M'lady, I think this may be something you should hear from the lord. If he found out I told you, he might do me in."

"Do you in? You think Ranthrop will tell me if I ask him? I don't know if you've noticed, but our conversations don't last very long or accomplish very much."

Varmeer cracked a half smile. "You would have to pry the information from his dying breath, m'lady. He does not speak of this. Not even to me."

Valerie waited, but he said nothing more, leaving her with a giant cliffhanger.

"Varmeer, I told you why I need to go to Terradoon even though Ranthrop would not. I think it is only honorable that you tell me why you didn't want him to go."

"It may be unpleasant to hear."

"I can handle unpleasant." She scooted to the edge of the rock, showing she was prepared.

Varmeer glanced around, speaking in a hushed tone. "It happened many years ago when Ranthrop was a young man, and his father Lord Gharen Groslivo was Lord of the Southlands. He was even a wilder man than Ranthrop is—perpetually restless. Lord Gharen was the first person bold enough to cross the Farwin Mountains. The first from Farwin Wood to sail the Greunie Sea. He was eager to take Ranthrop exploring with him when Ranthrop came of age. I was but a young guard then myself, chosen to serve Ranthrop by his father. I was honored I'd been selected to go with the party."

Varmeer tugged at his glove, staring into the fire. Valerie waited in anticipation to hear what he had to say. "We crossed the sea and discovered Terradoon. I will not tell you what caused the madness, as I am sure I still do not understand it, but something occurred there to change Lord Gharen. He was not himself. He merely sat in a daze, not knowing who he was one minute and then the next he was screaming and bashing everyone about like a wild animal. We met a man on the way back from Terradoon, something like a healer in their land. He claimed he could cure this madness, but Ranthrop did not trust the area after all that we had already seen. Ranthrop swiftly ordered the exploration over, and we returned to Farwin Wood. Lord Gharen's condition worsened each passing day. The old lord's guard, at one point, suggested chaining Gharen in his room to keep him from harming himself and others, but Ranthrop would not hear of doing such a thing to his father."

Valerie was as still as the stone she sat upon. She could not picture Ranthrop as a young man nor devoted to someone in any way. She could not imagine him having to face such a thing as a parent losing their mind. Varmeer continued as she dug her nails into her knees, afraid to learn what he would add to the story.

"One morning, they found Lord Gharen missing. Ranthrop ordered every able body to search the Southlands. We found him that afternoon, west of the swamp, his feet bare and his clothing tattered. He had been set upon by wickrits, scarcely alive. The lord sat there and held him as his father babbled on, before dying in his arms." Varmeer shook his head, eyes in a daze from the memory.

"How horrible." She sat up and stared into the fire with him. The visions she mustered were enough to make her cringe. She hated to think of a helpless man, out of his wits, lost in the woods and defenseless to the very animal that had nearly killed her on her first day in this land. And Ranthrop. That explained why he had been so adamant about not going to Terradoon. *Adamant.* That was the word Varmeer had used when he described his attempts to dissuade Ranthrop from going. Ranthrop had been adamant until he had come to her room that night and changed his mind. The words she screamed at him in the apothecary came back to her, dousing her senses with guilt.

"Yes. 'Twas quite horrible. From that day, Ranthrop forbade anyone to go to Terradoon and it has been so until now."

"And you think he has changed his mind because of me?"

"No, m'lady. I know he has changed his mind because of you."

She couldn't look at him any longer. She knew it was true. Still, her words came out defensive. "He is even more stubborn than I am. I doubt I could make him do anything he truly isn't willing to do."

"Varmeer!" Ranthrop's voice bellowed from the tree line, giving her a start. He stood holding several dead, furry creatures by their tails, each the size of a raccoon. "You can see to my tent now."

Varmeer nodded, turning back to her as he stood. "Lady Valerie," he murmured, "I think you possess the power to make him do a great many things, if you so choose."

What the hell did that mean? She watched him walk away as Ranthrop instructed one of his men about the pile of dead rodents, oblivious to the mysterious conversation. Deciding to forgo another scene, she walked over to him.

"I need to use the bushes."

"It is safe here. I will keep an eye out from afar."

Lovely, she thought, refraining from saying it out loud. She gave him a nod and walked into the tree line, inspecting the area for critters.

Later, she learned their dinner consisted of fire-roasted gorble, or rather, over-sized forest rat. Chewing in silence, she listened as the men sat around the fire and chatted over their food. Varmeer gave her a flask of beetleburry ale. The watermelon and lime flavor tasted refreshing after the long day's ride and helped to wash down the pungent meat. When she had finished her meal, Ranthrop gestured for her to follow him. She bid her goodnights and glanced at Varmeer, who had the annoying habit of ignoring her the same way he did to Ranthrop when he chose.

Through the fluttering firelight, she followed Ranthrop to the front of one of the tents. He pulled its flap back for her to enter.

"Goodnight," she called in a humble voice and stepped inside.

She surveyed the arrangement of the ten-by-ten foot area, more than enough room for her to sleep. A fur pelt covered the ground and another sat rolled up in the corner. Five wooden stakes held up the leather covering. The center post was tallest, giving the abode a circus tent ambiance. Her saddle chair sat in a corner—quite clever for its dual use as furniture now. Someone had lit a candle on a stump of wood in the center of the room.

"I hope this will suffice for the evening," Ranthrop's voice said behind her.

She spun around, finding his towering presence blocking the doorway. "It will be fine. Thank you."

He looked around the tent. "Do you require anything else?"

A toilet and a toothbrush would be nice. A rush of heat washed over her. Was it from the ale she drank or from having him in her tent? She brought a hand to her forehead and found it to be warm in spite of the chill outside. Sitting down in the saddle chair helped provide some distance from her intruder. "No. The only thing I require now is sleep."

Ranthrop stepped closer, kneeling near her chair. He gave her an appreciative smile. "You rode well today. It was a long journey."

Fidgeting with the edge of her cloak didn't help alleviate the discomfort of being near him. "You all suffered the same... and because of me. I am very grateful that you are taking me to Terradoon. I hope you know that."

Ranthrop's expression grew serious, his voice lowering. "I should not have spoken so harshly to you in the apothecary. You will have to forgive my manners." He plucked a dried blade of grass off the rug and tossed it through the air. "Varmeer has tried to make me a proper lord over the years, but I fear I will never be the kind of man who says what's appropriate." Valerie chuckled in spite of herself. "Ah, I see that you agree with him?"

"No. It's just that...my mother feels the same way about me."

"Is she a strict woman?"

"Very. I never seem to say the right thing where she's concerned."

He laughed as she took off her cloak. "I don't remember my mother well, but she was like that in some ways. What about your father?"

Valerie curled her toes inside her boots, letting the cloak fall over the back of the chair. She inspected her fingernails, avoiding his curious gaze. "My father left us...when I was thirteen. He did not care for life in Blinney. We have not seen him since. It's just my mother and I."

"He abandoned you?" Ranthrop asked in a loud voice. She looked away when she saw his shock over the information. Didn't couples ever separate in Farwin Wood? "How could a man do such a thing?"

"I don't know," she murmured and shook her head. With more confidence she added, "I don't care."

"This must be why you are such a strong woman."

She couldn't detect any malice in the comment. Her instincts told her he was mocking her, but the tenderness in his face seemed genuine. It was humbling. "I don't think that I'm strong. I'm stubborn. I know that, as much as I can't change it. Strength and doing what you have to do are two different things."

"And you have to go to Terradoon to help this woman?"

His damned scrutinizing gaze made her squirm in the chair. "No. I want to help this woman."

"There. You see? That is what lets me know you have strength. You cannot teach compassion, and you cannot have strength without it. There are a lucky few who have the capacity for strength. Those that do rarely know it is not a choice they can control. I have never met such a woman...until now."

His words permeated as she stared at him. It may have been the greatest compliment she'd ever received, although she didn't feel worthy of it. The day's events seemed to transform him before her eyes. He'd gone from a bumbling moron with poor social skills to a considerate philosopher. Her stomach turned again. Gorble meat or her nerves? Placing a hand there to quell the discomfort, she turned her thoughts to what Varmeer had told her.

"Ranthrop, why did you agree to take me to Terradoon when I know you have no desire to go there?"

"How can I allow this woman to die if you feel there is a cure for her in Terradoon?"

She had no right, but she had to ask. "Is it because you feel you failed your father?"

Ranthrop went rigid, inhaling so much air it caused his nostrils to flare. He shot to his feet. "You've been listening to Varmeer's tales of woe, have you? M'lady, I keep my promises, regardless of the ones I failed to make in the past. We will head up the mountain tomorrow. No need to worry why I go. I am capable of making sound judgments in spite of what my squeamish counselor thinks." He turned on his heel and started for the tent door.

She shot out of her chair, rushing after him. "Ranthrop, wait!" She managed to catch his arm before he went through the door. He turned around to face her, fists clenched at his sides, jaw set tight. "I can't let you go if it will cause you pain or endanger you and your men. You should have told me your reasons! I didn't mean to cause you guilt. I know what it's like to disappoint a parent. It doesn't mean you have to do anything foolish to try and prove something to yourself. It isn't your fault that your father died, and it won't be your fault if my friend dies. It's called life— it's dirty and messy and we're supposed to be born not knowing the rules. Just tell me where to go, and I can go by myself. You've brought me this far. Don't ask me to torment you by taking you any farther," she pleaded.

The tension in Ranthrop's face dissipated as he looked into her eyes. He took in the force of emotions, her pleading look, the way she desperately clung to his arm. So much courage and selflessness, and now a level of empathy he had never known. A feeling of warmth and an unexplainable pull to be as near to her as possible came over him.

He would go to Terradoon, just as he had decided. However, gazing now into her intoxicating eyes, he knew it would not be for the original reasons he intended. It would be for something much more foolish as she had just described. It would be for the purpose of being near her every second of the journey and making sure she returned each step by his side. He committed himself to the decision and made his first endeavor at that foolishness. Reaching out, he clasped her waist, cupping her jaw. He closed the distance between them and whispered near her lips. "My darling lady, you already torment me."

Valerie stood paralyzed the moment she felt his sinewy hands on her. Like a spell, the breath of his husky words sent a tingle from her heart to her toes. Her eyes were mesmerized by the intensity of his gaze as he spoke. Pulling her to his chest, he captured her parted lips, brushing slowly against one and then the other. She tasted the sweetness of his mouth, and it awed her that such a gruff looking man could be so tender.

Just as her judgment was about to falter and give in to the tempting urge to explore his kiss, he pulled away. She though she heard a muffled growl as his grasp on her waist tightened. His mouth moved to her forehead, placing a soft kiss on it. She breathed in the exhilarating scent of bark and sugar that lingered on his skin and clothes. A waft of cool air hit her face, and she opened her dazed eyes to see him exiting the tent.

"Sleep well, my lady," he called as he left.

CHAPTER TWENTY-ONE

THE SOUTHLANDS, FARWIN WOOD

VALERIE DROPPED to her knees outside of her tent, coughing as the contents of her stomach lurched out of her. She held her hair to the side with a shaky hand. The frigid night breeze whipped through the thin fabric of her nightgown, and she basked in the relief it brought to her hot flesh. She had awoken, covered in sweat. She coughed, spitting out the vile phlegm that lingered at the back of her throat. Leaning against the tree where she crouched, she closed her eyes and moaned.

"Lady Valerie?" A deep voice sounded from behind her.

She let out a whimper, turning her head to identify the speaker. Ranthrop crouched down beside her, his bare chest gleaming in the moonlight, the wind tickling his hair. Seeing him so close, she held up a hand instinctively, motioning him back after just having vomited.

"You are ill?"

She groaned and straightened up on her knees, preparing to stand. "I'll be fine. I think it was the rat."

"The rat?"

Another sound of discomfort escaped her as she said breathlessly, "The gorbley thingy we ate." She felt the rigid backs of Ranthrop's fingers against her forehead and closed her eyes.

"You are very warm. Food doesn't do that to people." He frowned, scooping her up into his arms.

"It doesn't?"

"No," he said, looking at her as she dropped her head onto his shoulder.

"Netta had the drumsy when I was at Allister Hall. Maybe I got it from her." She felt a tent flap brush against her arm as he carried her. He lowered her to the fur pelt, and she collapsed onto it without protest.

"I will take you back to the Southlands tomorrow."

"No!" she yelled, sitting up to protest. Her lungs clenched from the minor strain, sending her into a harsh coughing fit. She turned her head away from him, covering her mouth. Didn't he worry about catching it? "I'm not going...back!" she wheezed between fits. "I'll be fine. Just...let me sleep."

"Lie down, woman!" he said, pushing her shoulder back gently.

She dropped back onto the pelt and noticed red and black clothing slumped in a pile in the corner. There was a chunk of wood with a candle on it, but it didn't look like the one in her tent, nor was it in the same place as she remembered. "This isn't my tent."

"I won't have you stumbling outside in your night things by yourself, should you feel the need to do so again," he warned.

"I—" She tried to protest, but another bout of coughing racked through her.

"Don't try to speak. It makes the coughing worse." He remained kneeling by her side with his hands on his hips, appearing enormous above her. She was grateful that the battle with her congestion forced her eyes wide open—maybe he wouldn't notice her gazing at his bare, bronze chest. "'Tis the perfect illness for you, I think," he teased.

"Ugh," she said with a groan as the coughing died down. "What can I do for it?"

Ranthrop leaned to the side and came back with a flask. "Here. Drink this. I'll be right back. Don't go anywhere."

Valerie watched him leave and uncapped the flask. Beetleburry ale. She doubted alcohol would cure her ailment, but she drank it anyway.

A little while later, Ranthrop returned and dropped down by her side again. He held a dried black twig in his hand and began to break it. Taking the pieces, he rubbed his palms together quickly. Cupping the crumbled fragments in one hand, he placed them in her palm.

"Eat this. It will help with the fever."

Valerie looked at him from where she lay on her side. Taking one of the pieces, she popped it into her mouth. A sour sensation infiltrated her saliva. "Ugh, that's horrible!"

Ranthrop got up, grabbing a discarded pelt. "You won't notice after you've eaten all of it."

She made a face at the amount of root shards in her hand while his back was turned. The coughing returned and she winced, holding a hand to her chest. As the fit subsided, she sighed and closed her eyes. Bringing her cupped hand up to her mouth, she inserted another piece of the bark. Something moved behind her, and she felt the soft fur of blanket being pulled over her body. She turned her head, moving up on her elbow when she saw him settling down behind her.

"What are you doing?" she cried.

"Keeping you warm." His voice was incredulous as he pushed her shoulder back to the ground, giving her a speaking look. "You wanted to know what makes it better," he added.

She stared at him for a moment before looking away. "Won't you get sick if you stay too close to me?" Her body went rigid as she felt his legs brush against hers, and his chest press against her back.

"I drink enough beetleburry that I rarely get it," he murmured at the back of her neck. The feel of his breath gave her gooseflesh. His arm brushed against hers as the blanket shifted over them. "But if you're so worried I will die," he continued and hooked his fingers into her cupped palm for a piece of the bark, "I'll take a piece of your poison."

Valerie swallowed. His entire body now pressed against her as his lips moved just above her ear. "Will I die?" she asked. Worry mixed with the haziness in her head and the rapid beating of her heart.

Chuckling, he rested his face against the back of her head. "No. I won't let you."

His arm circled around her once more, and she turned her cupped hand with the bark so he could access it. Instead, he slung his arm over her ribs, tugging her against him. His forearm dropped over the thin fabric covering her belly. It remained there; an indication that he wouldn't be moving it.

She lay very still. Finally, she shoved the remainder of the bark in her mouth all at once. Closing her eyes and tucking her arms to her chest, she chewed and swallowed the foul pieces down as quickly as possible. Her body shook with another cough as the juices oozed down her throat, and she clenched her fists to her mouth. Ranthrop's arm tightened around her as his fingers rubbed her arm in a soothing manner. Breathing heavily, she inhaled the intoxicating smell she had detected earlier on his skin. She opened her palm and realized it was the same smell as the bark. The scent made her feel completely encompassed by him as though he were the blanket swaddled around them.

Her body relaxed and exhaustion overtook her. This is kind of nice, she thought dreamily. Her mind drifted into the blackness with the soothing, strong heartbeat at her back. Very nice.

IN THE morning, Ranthrop awoke to an unfamiliar feeling—a fully clothed woman pressed against him. Surprisingly, it was more enjoyable than any memory he had of the naked ones. He smiled and nuzzled his face into the blanket of silky black hair strewn out on the pelt beneath them. A soft moan came from Valerie, and he leaned up on an elbow. She rolled into him, and he took the opportunity to rest his other hand on the ground beside her. "Good morning," he called in a husky voice.

Valerie rubbed her eyes. "Good morning."

"How are you feeling?"

"A little better. I think I'll be fine."

"Good. Then I'll have the men ready the skithers." He started to get up but felt her hand grab his forearm.

"I...I don't want you to go."

He studied her face, thinking what a powerful effect the words had on him. "Tell me that some other time."

Dropping a kiss on her forehead, he got up and donned his clothing. When he turned around, he noticed her slipping out the back of the tent.

As he emerged through the front, Varmeer strode past him. "I was wondering if you'd ever rouse from your tent. Should I assume there is no cause for alarm that Lady Valerie has not done the same?" he asked.

Ranthrop walked up to him, falling in step with his stride. Tossing an arm around the man's neck, he caught him gruffly by the tunic, pulling him closer into his grip. "Varmeer, my dear old friend. You would do well not to assume as often as you do. And why are you watching Lady Valerie's tent so closely?"

"M'lord, you instructed me to see that she comes to no harm."

"Really? Or is it perhaps that you hoped to catch her ear and plant more misgivings as to why we should not travel to Terradoon?"

Varmeer stopped, hanging them both up, and careened his head in Ranthrop's grip with an impish look. "I was looking out for your best interests, m'lord. I thought the lady should know what may await us in Terradoon."

"And you feel it's in my best interest to allow a lady to travel there alone?"

Varmeer pressed his lips together. "I think it's in your best interest not to feel the need to prove something to yourself or this lady. 'Tis a fool's errand."

Ranthrop released him as the muscles in his face hardened. "I feel no desire to prove anything to anyone, Varmeer. Do not cast me the fool so quickly. 'Tis simply a matter of doing what is right, so rest easy."

"M'lord, it is your need to do what is right that troubles me."

Ranthrop's nostrils flared as he stared at him. They both turned their heads as they heard Valerie emerge from her tent in the distance. Ranthrop squeezed Varmeer's shoulder, leaning in and speaking with controlled heat. "Trouble yourself with this old friend. When you are old and in your dotage, they may say a great many things about me. But never will you hear there goes Varmeer, the man who served Ranthrop the Coward."

CHAPTER TWENTY-TWO

BLINNEY LANE

REGGIE SAT on the chair next to Franci's bed with his elbows on his knees, cradling his chin in his hand. His head bobbed as he woke from another intermittent bout of sleep. A quick look at Franci showed her still curled under the covers in her bed. He leaned over and heard the sound of steady breathing. Thank God, she was still alive. It had been a horrible day.

He'd taken a very cold shower that morning after it became clear Franci wouldn't leave her room. She hadn't come out the night before after their tussle on the couch when he'd had a lapse in sanity and libido. He'd listened to her sobbing for as long as he could, but when he tried to talk to her, she'd only yelled at him through the door to leave her alone. Pulling guard duty on the dreaded couch all night, he hadn't slept a wink, too worried she would sneak out to get away from him.

Silence had greeted the apartment when he came out of the shower. He had decided not to disturb Franci, hoping she had finally fallen asleep.

He had gone into the kitchen for something to clean up the shattered Bloody Mary glass still littering the living room floor. That's when he noticed the bottle of sleeping pills he'd set on the counter the previous day. It was tipped over with the lid off…empty.

He had bolted through the apartment to Franci's bedroom, finding the door locked.

"Damn it!" Swearing under his breath, he began beating on the door. "Franci? Franci, open the door!" he yelled, pounding over and over, but no sound came from the other side. How long had he'd been in the shower? Thirty minutes? Forty-five? Jesus!

Stepping back, he hefted his knee into the air, thrusting it against the door. It only made a loud thud. He hopped, thrust again, and then hobbled as sharp pains jolted through his knee and leg. "Fuck! Fuck the fucking movies!" he yelled, running back to the kitchen. Jerking the drawers open, he searched frantically until he found an ice pick.

With urgent, hobbling steps, he raced back to the door and forced the pick into the locking mechanism. He rattled it around and jiggled the door handle until it finally clicked, and the knob turned. Franci lay in bed on her stomach, snoring faintly.

Dashing to the bed, he turned her over in his arms, shaking her as he yelled her name, pleading with her to wake up. She only snored in response. He shook her again, slapping her face once, twice. She answered with a sluggish groan.

"God damn it! Don't do this to me!"

He slung his legs over the side of the bed, pulling her across his lap so her head faced the floor. One hand clasped around her jaw, he stuck his finger into her throat to bring the pills back up. She coughed, her body jolting, as the contents of her stomach spilled out onto the floor. As it subsided, she moaned insensible words. "Damn it, Franci," he said, rocking her in his arms. "What the hell were you thinking?"

"Archie, go away," she whispered.

Now, hours later, the relief that Franci was still alive had worn off. A new misery nagged at him as he watched over her. He knew how this had happened—he couldn't be bothered with her problems. The other shopkeepers had constantly pointed out to him that he was selfish and uncaring. Until today, it had never backfired on him.

Being selfish was the only way he knew how to survive on Blinney Lane. Keeping to himself and looking out for himself was much easier than getting involved in everyone else's lives or their problems. He only talked to customers who came into his store, and he spent his free time by himself, alone with his hobbies. He only went to the Blinney cookouts because he couldn't resist food. More selfishness. He didn't like being reminded that they were a group of trapped souls. He had assumed everyone else felt the same way: sick of seeing the same people every day.

But right now, he would give anything to see Franci's eyes light up as *Franci* once again. She was the only one who gave a damn about him. There had been someone so close to home who actually saw him for who he really was—saw past his bitter exterior—and he'd missed it. He had always written her off as another unwanted reminder of being stuck on Blinney Lane. For the first time in his life he truly had a friend, and now that friend might never come back. Worse yet, his stupidity was partly to blame.

He looked at Franci's face and silently urged her to re-emerge. He prayed for Valerie and Ricky to find a cure.

And somewhere, in the back of his mind, the selfish part of him wished that if all of that occurred, Franci would snap out of it without forgetting that for a brief moment she'd wanted him just as he was.

CHAPTER TWENTY-THREE

FARWIN WOOD

VALERIE GRIPPED the arms of the saddle as her skither made its way up the mountainside. The path was so narrow now that the party rode in a single column. She had made the mistake of peering down moments ago. The trees where they had camped looked like miniature replicas, making her dizzy. She pressed her back against the chair, forcing her gaze to remain fixed ahead. The sight of Ranthrop's skither in front of her did little to pacify her nerves. Its body was nearly upright on its hind legs due to the steep incline. She fought back another cough, worried he'd turn around to check on her. What if it caused his skither to sway and fall, sending them all down like dominoes? Closing her eyes, she listened to the creaking of the saddle as her weight shifted with each jarring step the animal took toward the summit.

Three hours into the treacherous climb, the wind picked up, and her skither leveled out. She heard the slap of its feet on the ground and opened her eyes, marveling at the sight before her.

Smooth bone-white stone spread out as far as the eye could see, the apex—a flat plateau. So polished, it could be a ballroom dance floor. She looked over the side of her saddle at the slick sheen of stone. Tiny cracks laced across the surface in an irregular wavy pattern like veins in olive wood.

Ranthrop slowed until he was riding alongside her, asking how she was and giving her another piece of the brittle root she had the night before. He scanned the horizon in silence, curiously gazing at her every few minutes. She noticed their opinions of each other had begun to change. She knew hers certainly had.

When he wasn't looking at her, Valerie stole glances at him. The bulge at his shoulder rounded out the top of his sleeve. As his skither moved, the girth of his bicep pressed against the loose black shirt. She recalled his strength when he'd swept her up effortlessly into his arms the night before. She didn't focus on the physical elements of his muscles. Those arms now represented compassion in him she didn't think had existed. They had encircled her to keep her warm during the night. There were no prowling hands, no lewd or veiled comments, no lingering expectation that something more would happen. It wasn't the outcome she would have expected in a situation like that with a man. She sensed he had felt as content as she had with just being held.

Her eyes moved to the hand clasped around his armrest. In spite of the power that hand possessed, it had gently cupped her face right after she'd angered him by mentioning his father. He had control if he could go from rage to tenderness in mere seconds. She still didn't understand fully why he'd kissed her or what he meant about her tormenting him. She had her own torment. Her heart fluttered each time she looked at him now. Waking up that morning in his arms had been different than any memory she had of the ritual. It gave her an odd sense of safety, though she had never felt a lack of it before.

Something about Ranthrop made her feel cared for and protected just by being in his presence. And her femininity could be at the forefront. That self-awareness rarely surfaced because she had to be tough all the time in her world. His mere proximity spoke deep within her, telling her to relax and just be beautiful. It was baffling and more than she deserved.

He certainly didn't owe her anything. She hadn't been very civil to him since they'd met. Yet he'd sparred along, chipping away her defenses until she understood he would give her the help she was so determined not to accept. She came to the conclusion that she was caught between no longer despising him and trying hard not to be attracted to him. She had sworn off men. Shouldn't that include those inside books?

When Ranthrop caught her eye, he struck up a conversation as they continued across the marbled plain. He inquired about her life, how she came to be knowledgeable of healing, and what Blinney was like. Valerie explained as vaguely as possible that everyone in Blinney had a trade or profession. He listened intently as she discussed her studies and the business she ran with her mother.

She spotted a building in the distance. Ranthrop told her it was a guard shack, and that he kept a post of guards stationed on the mountain in case anyone ever crossed over from Terradoon. The hairs on her arms stood up upon hearing that no one had ever witnessed that.

As they traveled on, the sun disappeared behind the amassing clouds above and the velocity of the frigid wind increased. They stopped at the guard shack to rest and eat lunch. Rain drizzled down, spattering against the ivory mountaintop. The men propped small canopies out from the backs of everyone's saddle chairs. The covers were made of leather, and she hoped they were the skins of wickrits.

As they continued on, the makeshift roof did little to keep the lower half of her gown from getting soaked. The rain picked up, pelting them sideways. Her skither huffed, shaking its head and sending droplets into the air. A hazy fog rolled in, limiting her sight.

The skithers clipped along the slick surface, their claws tapping against the stone. The rhythmic noise lulled her like gentle drumming, and she fought to keep her eyes open. Weak from the drumsy, she pulled the hood of her cloak tighter around her face, leaned her head back against the chair, and finally gave into her exhaustion.

She awoke to the sensation of falling. Her eyes fanned open, spying a sharp descent beyond the neck of her skither. Half off her seat, she shrieked as the skither's weight jarred her just as she clasped onto the armrests. The saddle shook under her grip, the force nearly tossing her over the side of the animal's back.

A hand grabbed under her arm, jerking her back up. Whipping her head around, she found Ranthrop clinging precariously to the side of her saddle, standing on her skither's back. Through the inundating fog, she saw his skither next to hers, staggering to keep its hold on the narrow shelf of the mountainside.

"Grab a hold of me! I've got you," Ranthrop yelled, his features wild with concern as the rain pelted his face.

Valerie pushed her feet against the skither's neck, flipping over so her chest rested on the edge of the saddle chair. Taking hold of Ranthrop's arm, she pulled herself closer to the saddle.

"I fell asleep! Did we fall off the edge of the mountain?"

"No. We're descending. I couldn't see you in this fog, or I would have woken you." Ranthrop sidestepped and came around to the front of her chair. He dropped down into the seat, yanking her arm toward him.

She shrieked and slid a knee beside him onto the chair. "We're going to fall! It can't hold both of us!" She wrapped her fingers around the back of the chair, pulling her face against it, next to Ranthrop's shoulder.

"I won't let you fall," he called through the wind.

His arm snaked around her waist. The skither lobbed down another jagged step, and they slid forward. She whimpered and clutched Ranthrop's shirtfront. He tugged them back firmly into the seat and wrapped his other arm under the armrest, holding them in place. She took a starved breath, knowing they had just escaped the danger of plummeting, but she refused to relinquish her hold on the chair.

"A skither can carry four men for an entire day's ride. You have no need to worry," he said in a soothing voice.

She swallowed the lump in her throat as she looked at his rain-soaked face, wanting to believe him. The chair tipped back and the pressure in her tired muscles waned. She looked out through the fog, seeing an expanse of flat stone as they leveled out. She sighed in relief.

"Sit back and relax while you can," Ranthrop said, his voice humming in her ear.

"While I can?"

"Yes. The descent will take a while."

"You mean we haven't reached the bottom yet? I can't see anything. Do they even know where they're going?"

Ranthrop's eyes crinkled as he chuckled. "Yes. Down."

She let out a weary moan as she saw the flat slab ending a few feet ahead. The side of the mountain seemed to be shaped like giant stairs.

Her stomach stirred at the thought of plummeting so soon. Shifting onto her hip in the narrow space next to Ranthrop, she pulled her legs up, kicking through the fabric of her skirt, and hooked her feet behind the armrest on the other side.

"What are you doing?"

"Anything I can to not be a splat mark at the bottom of this mountain," she whined.

His fingers grasped her ankles under the hem of her dress and dragged them up across his lap, helping her reposition her feet. Gathering the folds of her dress, he secured the fabric through the chair handle around the delicate flesh of her skin. He concentrated as he worked to protect her legs from rubbing against the chair as if he were completing a science project. His soaked curls, darker from the rain, clung to the sides of his temples. He smiled as he inspected his work, patting the fabric over her calves.

"There," he declared proudly, "all secure."

"Thank you," she murmured. Practically sitting in his lap, she felt uncomfortable as he fawned over her. It had been easier to deal with him when she viewed him as a thoughtless, bumbling oaf. His delicate tendencies and moments of compassion forced kind feelings and apologetic thoughts to stir inside of her. She had the suspicion she would lose something dear if they continued for too long. She wasn't certain what it was, and she didn't want to find out.

Her queasy stomach growled, battling her lunch. She let her tired arm fall to her lap while the ride was peaceful, finally relinquishing her hold on his shirt. She closed her eyes with a sigh, blocking out the undulating, misty view.

"You really should not have continued."

Valerie cracked her eyes open as his finger brushed damp hair away from her cheek. She studied the fretful face looking back at her, noting a scar curving under his chin, and another at the edge of one eyebrow. His sandy skin was peppered with faint freckles, likely from years of being outdoors.

How rough had his life been? Sarah and Ricky had said the war in Farwin Wood had lasted nearly twenty years—a lifetime to live in such trying conditions. Her petulant squabbles with her mother seemed petty in contrast to what he must have endured. Understanding dawned; she couldn't blame him for being a little brash and unpolished. How else could a person have emerged from two decades of death and despair? He had to be skilled and tough to have come out of the ordeal alive while so many had not. He'd flung himself onto her skither like a mad man to save her. The damned fool could have crashed to his death and been trampled underfoot or skewered by one of the skither's claws. She felt pathetic in front of such valor.

"I can't remember feeling this weak before, but I can assure you I won't quit or complain. You don't have to keep looking at me like I'm going to wilt," she assured him.

"I could never imagine you wilted, m'lady. There's a fire within you that I doubt could ever be extinguished."

Heat ran up her cheeks. He wasn't teasing her, and she didn't know how to handle it. His fingers cupped the underside of her chin, urging her to look at him.

"I could never endure twenty years of war."

"I don't believe you would be foolish enough to engage in a war that long." Remorse was evident in his strained expression. The man had his regrets.

Valerie thought of her mother and a pang of guilt washed through her. Wasn't their relationship like a foolish war? Home seemed so far away now. Would she see her mother again? The thought had not occurred to her before rocketing down the side of the mountain. She might not have the chance to make amends with her. Her lip trembled, but she refused to cry. "I think you give me too much credit. You don't even know me."

The chair rocked violently, and she gasped as her weight shifted on Ranthrop's lap. His arm tightened securely around her waist, and he tucked her head into his neck.

"Hold on. We're dropping again."

"Oh! Don't say drop!" she moaned into the crook of his neck.

"What would you prefer I say?"

"Nothing! Say nothing!"

He rested his head against hers and did just that all the way to the base of the mountain.

CHAPTER TWENTY-FOUR

GREUNIE BEACH, FARWIN WOOD

THE FLAT ground was a welcome sight to Valerie's eyes. She relinquished her hold on Ranthrop, directing her attention ahead as if he were invisible and not something she had clung dearly to for life support. A flat plain of barren gray dirt lay before them.

The wind and rain had died down, but the sky remained a gloomy swirl of smoky clouds. Breathing in the cool air, she smelled a salty dampness.

"How much farther to Terradoon?"

"We are almost there. It lies just beyond the Greunie Sea." Ranthrop pointed to the abyss.

"The sea?" She looked through the parting vapor and saw water lapping, realizing she had been hearing the lull of waves. The dull sparkles of light reflecting off the packed granite-colored earth revealed sand. Her queasiness returned, slamming hard.

"Yes. The Greunie Sea separates Terradoon and Farwin Wood."

"And we have to cross it to get to Terradoon?"

Ranthrop's chuckle tickled her ears. "Well, I can't bring it to you, my dear, or I would."

"How will we get across?"

"I keep a boathouse just yonder." He pointed farther down to the dreary beach where she could see the outline of a building in the distance.

"Boats," she whispered. That little shit, Ricky never said anything about boats! All right, Ricky had never been this deep into Farwin Wood, but she needed to direct her anger at something before panic overtook her. "Are your boats sturdy?"

Ranthrop focused his eyes on the terrain ahead. "Let's hope so. They haven't been used since well before the war."

"*Before* the war? That's like twenty years!" Valerie began imagining several scenarios, and they all ended in a crisis.

"I keep a contingent of men stationed at the docks. They help maintain the lookout over the divide between Farwin Wood and Terradoon. They provide a healthy supply of saltwater fish to be taken back up the mountain for the Southlands people. Part of their duties is to ensure the boats stay maintained. Do not fret. They would not slack in this plight even though they know the boats were not likely ever to be used. My men are dutiful."

Varmeer strolled up next to them, and Valerie's cheeks grew hot under his masked gaze. She unhinged her legs as Ranthrop waved a dismissive hand for him to continue ahead.

"I don't think he likes me," she said, smoothing her dress.

"Varmeer?" Ranthrop snorted. "I doubt that. He's probably not looking forward to seeing the fonskas again."

"Who are the fonskas?"

Ranthrop tapped his fingers on the armrest, watching the men who came out of the boathouse to greet them. His other arm lay draped around her as though it belonged there. He chuckled. "You mean what. The fonskas live in the Greunie Sea."

"Live in the…" She pieced together his vague description and steadied her fearful question. "What exactly are fonskas?"

He glanced at her, quickly returning his focus to the men as they captured the reins of the lead skithers. "They are sea monsters."

She caught the lower half of his jaw between her thumb and fingers and forced his attention back to her. "You never said anything about sea monsters!"

Ranthrop's lips puckered together under the pressure of her grasp. He arched his brows and muttered through his fish lips, "Yer nevuh ashked."

"I'm asking now, damn it!" She jerked her hand for emphasis. "What are we talking here exactly? Friendly, fiery, freaky?"

"Fuh-rocious," he managed.

A delirious noise tumbled out of her throat as she released his face. He lolled his tongue, rubbing his face.

"Big or small?"

Ranthrop clasped his jaw as though he were either contemplating his answer or protecting his face. "Big."

"How big?"

"A little bigger than the boats."

"Bigger than the boats? You can't make boats smaller than a sea monster! Everybody knows that! They'll flip them over!"

Varmeer appeared, interrupting as he stood next to their skither. "Rest easy, m'lady. That's why we have paddles. Just a swift bash, and they scuttle on their way."

Valerie located the guard, narrowing her eyes. He smiled reassuringly as he unslung their ladder.

"That is not what paddles are for! Who do you people think you are? Ishmael? This isn't *Moby Dick*!" She bolted off Ranthrop's lap, steadying herself against the chair as he crawled out of the seat.

"Ishmael? Wasn't that the old fellow who used to run the roomple farm in Tyson?" Varmeer asked Ranthrop.

"No. That was Honnelly. Ishmael was the man who used to bring me skithers before the war," Ranthrop said.

"No, it wasn't," Varmeer replied. "That was Skipsie LeCreedal. Or was it Dernesten?"

"Unbelievable," Valerie said, looking down at the two morons. She sighed, hoping their lack of concern meant it wasn't as high of a risk as she thought. She gathered up her skirts and made her way down. Ranthrop grasped her waist, setting her on the ground.

He continued his debate with Varmeer as though she were just a piece of luggage he'd absently unloaded. "Dernesten wasn't a LeCreedal. He was that villager in Knoblauch who used to climb the roofs when he drank too much."

Varmeer laughed while Valerie surveyed the foggy pier. "I remember now. Poor soul. He fell at the Wibbly skirmish five or…was it six summers ago now?"

The potent smell of fish and salty sea air permeated the area like any seaside port, although it appeared to be more archaic than South River harbor in Salem. Not that anyone on Blinney Lane knew she had sneaked away that far. If they did, she could tell them how much greener the water was here, how the narrow docks that thrust into the sea appeared to be made from trees that were hand-cleaved.

The jagged tops of the pylons had the appearance of dead wood, which were likely once a pale pulp color, but were now encrusted with the salty residue of splashing sea foam. Thick rope and crude metal rivets secured the walkway planks to their supports. A two-story cabin structure sat forty feet away from the water's edge, lifted by stilts. It had a balcony on the second floor. An armed man in Southland colors walked the length, scanning the horizon.

Something odd struck her as she realized she didn't see any boats. Opposite the pier were four very large rafts made of thick timbers. As they bobbed in the water, she saw each had a base two logs deep. An upright post was fastened to the center of each, about twelve feet high, with a shorter, perpendicular beam closer to the base. A pale yellow cloth wrapped around each post, secured in place by ropes.

Four men bounded off the pier and onto the first raft. They unfastened the ropes and unfurled the cloth, securing the end of the triangular piece of fabric to the perpendicular beam. Her breath caught, seeing the shape of a sail evolve before her eyes.

"Where are the boats?" she whispered, gaping at the antiquated transport. Her hand flailed in the air, hoping to connect with either Ranthrop or Varmeer. "These can't be what we're taking."

"Ritchie!" Varmeer said excitedly, snapping his fingers. "Leonard Ritchie. He was the skither drover you're thinking of."

Valerie couldn't believe they were still reminiscing over names like two old-timers on a Sunday afternoon.

"Ahem," she said, clearing her throat.

Ranthrop peered at the sky in thought. "No, it was Luther Ritchie, I think. Definitely a Ritchie though."

"Hey!" she said, slapping each man's chest. "I don't care if it was Lionel Ritchie or Luther Vandross! Where are the boats?"

Varmeer fingered the crest on his tunic, his expression crumpled. "M'lady? The boats are just on yonder side of the pier. The men are readying them now. We know you mean to make haste."

Valerie looked around, making sure she hadn't missed a real vessel. All she found were the rustic concoctions of floating logs, two of them now with sails unfurled. Men continued loading the bundles of tents onto them.

"Those are *not* boats!" She jerked her thumb in the direction of the pier as she turned to face her guides.

Ranthrop stared at her like he was trying to solve algebra problems. Finally he queried, "Lady Valerie, I can assure you those are boats. Do your seafaring vessels in Blinney look so different?"

"Different?" she asked in a shrill voice. "Those are what homeless trappers take up river in a western movie, not something you take out into open waters full of sea monsters!"

Varmeer and Ranthrop exchanged befuddled looks. Wringing her hands, she paced back and forth. She had to think of Franci and not sea monsters. Franci and not timbers cracking beneath her feet or water sloshing around her ankles. Franci and not drowning.

Ranthrop gave his friend a telling look. "Varmeer, would you leave us please?"

Varmeer nodded, casting a curious glance at Valerie. When he was out of earshot, Ranthrop took her by the shoulders, halting her.

"The crossing troubles you, m'lady?"

"Troubles me? I'm terrified!"

Ranthrop noticed the uneasiness in her pretty gray eyes. It was different than what he'd witnessed on their way down the mountain.

"I can't swim."

His anxiety at her state burst like a bubble. He chucked as he tapped the underside of her chin with his index finger. "Is that what has you twisted? Have no fear. You won't need to swim."

"Why does everyone think that's supposed to make me feel better? It's still water. I can't walk on it. Anything could happen."

"You really don't want to do this, do you?"

"No." She swallowed hard, leering at the sea. "But I have to, and I told you I wouldn't complain. I'm sorry I'm being such a coward, but I really hate the water."

He took her face in his hands wanting to remove the horrid sea from her vision. "You don't have to cross. You can stay here. No one will think you a coward."

"Bernryn said the venstras only grow in the Terradoon caves. I have to get them, or Franci could die."

"I will get them for you. You can rest here in the boathouse. My men will take good care of you."

The delicacy in his voice surprised him, but he needed to bring her comfort. He spoke with more sincerity than he ever had with a woman before. He usually saved his whispery tones for drunken evening pillow talks after a feast or a hunt. She'd more than earned her battle stripes, traversing up and down the mountain, racked with the drumsy fever. He realized he didn't feel the least bit ashamed or foolish by his tenderness. He felt proudly taller offering her this useful service he'd never fathomed he possessed.

"I can't let you do that. You didn't even want to make this trip. What kind of person would I be if I left you to travel by yourself?"

The thought of leaving her behind disturbed him. He remembered his last trip to Terradoon, so many years ago with his father. Leaving her behind was a better notion in light of that journey. He had the feeling if he insisted, however, that she would absolutely refuse to stay behind.

"I am not sure of what we will find in Terradoon. It's a land of strange customs and peculiar people. The winds scream like they are calling the names of the lost, and the terrain is much more unpleasant than in Farwin Wood. I'd rather not see you have to endure any of that. It might help me to focus more if I knew you were somewhere safe."

She stared at him, and he held his breath for her answer. Finally, it came in wistful words. "How can you possibly be the same man I met three days ago?"

Had he changed? He didn't know how to respond.

Her lips pursed into a stubborn line. "I can't let you go alone. Just tell me I can do this."

He grazed his thumb over her cheekbone. Her proud, forced bravery and determination were admirable. "You *can* do this. You could do anything you set your mind to, my lady. I will not leave your side." She nodded, and he bent to place a kiss on her salty forehead. "Come. We should depart before the sun sets."

Ranthrop guided Valerie down the pier. Her gait wobbled as she walked on unsure legs. The sight of her terror tore a hole in him. He had the mind to whisk her back to the boathouse and tie her down. When she hesitated to jump down onto the raft, he quickly bounded up the pier, swept her into his arms and leaped back onto the vessel. She moaned, her face pressed firmly into his chest, her arms clenched around his neck like a vice.

"Do you want me to set you down?" he whispered.

She drew her face away from his chest and glared at the sea, then gave a wary look to the timbered deck. She nodded, and loosened her hold on him. He deposited her next to the sail support, which she quickly grasped once her feet touched down.

"I think it would be better if I sat down," she murmured. He held her hand as she slumped down onto her backside, scooting up against the post between two packs of tent leathers that were tied to it. Her head was safe from the pivot bearing, and he was content she had chosen a safe place.

He signaled to his men on the neighboring raft to shove off and then turned to Varmeer. Varmeer stood in front of him, ready to man the rudder of their vessel. He gave

Ranthrop an understanding nod and signaled the other men aboard to start rowing. The men unsheathed the long wooden paddles from their holders on the railing of the raft. The paddles, like giant wood boring drill bits with two-foot spikes jutting out from the end of each thick wooden flap, were hefted into the emerald water as the men shoved them away from the coastline.

Ranthrop settled onto one of the tent bundles and held onto the sail post, his feet akimbo just in front of Valerie's. He took a last look at the men on the pier who watched with forlorn stares. They raised their fists over the crests on their tunics. He returned the gesture with a somber nod. His men did not want him to go to Terradoon. They looked upon him as if he would not return, or worse, would return as his father had.

He caught Varmeer's gaze, the knowing, silent dark eyes, and felt his lip twitch. Ranthrop gave him an *I don't want to hear it again* look and turned his attention to the sea.

The raft oscillated over the growing waves as the craft floated farther out to sea. Stillies swooped down and cawed, then zipped back up into the air. He had not seen one in years, rarely making the trek down the mountain to the boathouse. The black tips of their narrow white wings fluttered in the air, and he watched the pointy yellow beak as it called out its cry. His father had introduced him to the sea birds. His father had introduced him to many things. How much simpler that time had been before having to discover the workings of the world on his own.

Gharen loved the wilderness, loved adventure. It had been his undoing in the end. The sight of the sandy horizon beyond the fog remained a cruel reminder of that ending. Ranthrop knew what lurked through that mist and didn't want to see it, but he could not tear his eyes away. Soon the Kraheny Mountains would appear, the first landmark they'd seen on that exploration to Terradoon so many years ago. A vision of his father standing proud at the railing as he sucked in a deep gust of sea air flooded his memory.

"Ranthrop, my son. No one will ever call you boy again. This is a man's journey," his father had said with a proud smile. "Boys sit at home and wonder where smoke comes from. Men seek out the fire and dive through the flames."

Ranthrop knew his father had, in part, made that journey because of him. It had been a gift, a rite of passage, something that would earn him respect as future leader of the Southlands. It was yet another memory of his father's death that he didn't need to blame himself for. They had no idea what they would find, where the sea would end. They had no idea that Terra-doon existed until they discovered it, nor had they known what would happen the deeper they traveled into the eerie land. It was supposed to be a fun adventure the two of them could share, not a descent into his father's madness. How quickly the boy had become a man that day. Looking out at the looming presence of the approaching mountains, he wondered what would happen this time. What misfortunes might await them on this journey? The boy became a man in the face of the last. What would a man become facing his next?

CHAPTER TWENTY-FIVE

THE GREUNIE SEA

VALERIE OPENED her eyes since keeping them closed did nothing to alleviate her nausea. She twisted her hand tighter around the ropes on the tent bundle when she saw how far they had traveled from the coast. The towering cabin looked vulnerable and small against the backdrop of the mountain they had descended. She had kept her eyes closed for most of that journey with her face buried in Ranthrop's neck, and didn't realize how steep the mountainside had been. The fading sun poked through the hazy clouds on the banks of Farwin Wood, and the mountain stretched as far as the eye could see in either direction.

She wet her lips, tasting the pungent salt, and followed the array of rock steps they had descended. It resembled a ziggurat down to the last dark brown stone ledge, a vast contrast to the ivory rock above. The wet stone glistened in the faint light, and Valerie's breath caught in her throat as she viewed the peculiar topography.

"My God, it's a book," she said with a gasp.

"Did you say something?" Ranthrop called down to her.

She pointed with a trembling hand at the fading mountainside. "The mountain. It looks like an open book...like the edge of the pages."

"Hmm. I never noticed before. Yes, I suppose it does."

Everything made sense now. Well, nearly made sense. No one knew Terradoon existed because Farwin Wood ended with the book, literally ending at a book-like mountain. Anything beyond had a life of its own. The sea they floated in, the land they headed toward which everyone dreaded, all were blank, unwritten pages back home.

How could a book write itself? How could a world grow on its own? She wanted to laugh deliriously. How could it not? This was, after all, a product of Agatha Blinney's magic—her curse. It always did whatever the hell it wanted. There were no rules. Nothing about the curse on Blinney Lane had ever terrified her before, but now she felt stunned and out of her element.

Craning her neck, she looked up at Ranthrop. The rugged stupidity she'd seen in his face had disappeared. She could read the lines in his brow, at the sides of his mouth, as his caring expression met her gaze. She saw concern for her, worry for what was to come, and an aged wisdom in the glint of his eyes, no longer just those of a playful womanizer. She really didn't listen to anyone, did she? Her mother had warned her that she might not know what she would find inside the book. Ranthrop had said it was forbidden to travel to Terradoon. He didn't seem like the kind of man who made any rules. The fact that he had one very insistent one hit home with her now.

"Ranthrop?"

"Yes?"

"Thank you for taking me to Terradoon."

A baffled look crossed his face. "You are very welcome, m'lady."

A gust of laughter fanned through her nostrils, and she smiled. She knew she wouldn't be able to perceive his moronic expressions the same anymore. They were becoming endearing. The warmth of the moment ironed out her frazzled nerves.

Like an earthquake, it erupted violently beneath her, shifting the deck as her head slammed into the tent bundle. The force jolted Ranthrop backward, tossing him toward her. Stopping his fall with an outstretched arm, he grasped the bundle on the other side of her for support. His face hovered next to hers, his eyes crinkling like a man ready for battle, as he uttered with hatred, "Fonskas."

She gripped the ropes on either side of her and rooted her feet firmly to the deck. Ranthrop sat up, stretching one leg in front of her, his boot heel squishing into the mound of leathers. His stance would block her should she tumble forward.

Her eyes searched the cresting waves, but she could see no sign of sea life. Varmeer stood in a wide stance at the rudder, sword drawn and arm at the ready as his eyes scanned the water just below the edge of the craft. The raft rocked violently again, sending the back corner four feet up into the air. Valerie let out an anguished cry as she watched Varmeer stagger back.

A jagged silver strip crested the water at the edge of the raft. The slimy curved body disappeared, and she saw a wide fanned tail of the same color. It splashed out of the water, sending spray over the side. She glanced back to check on Varmeer, and saw him hooking his arm through a loop of rope attached to the rudder. He gave an unsettled look to

Ranthrop and nodded, then quickly returned to his perusal of the sea. She heard yelling in the distance and knew the men in the other raft were now being treated to their turn by the creatures.

Water gushed thirty feet behind the vessel. She stared slack jawed as a massive, plump body shot out of the sea. A long, tubular creature arched into the air, so large that all of its body could not be airborne at once. It had a six-foot long snout like a snorkel that trumpeted at the end. A deafening honk resounded, and its snout inflated like a balloon, peeling back like a blossoming flower all the way to the animal's wide head. Strips of razor teeth flashed as its jaw cracked open with its bellowing cry. The snout rustled and then retracted over the jaws, resuming its snorkel shape, just as its head dove back into the water. Its spindly back fin arched through the dive, bringing its mermaid tail into the air as it descended.

"Here it comes!" Varmeer yelled over his shoulder.

A guard appeared at the side of the raft. He stood akimbo, holding the paddle over the railing, its spike at an angle. Ranthrop bounded off the pelts, lumbering toward the space between the man and the corner of the raft. He planted a foot next to one of the support beams on the railing and wound a length of rope around his wrist. Valerie held her breath as he drew his sword, holding back her cry for him to retreat.

Ranthrop and the guard both geared up at the same time. Valerie braced herself, knowing they had spotted the approaching fonska. Ranthrop brought his blade down with a violent thrust, growling as he punctured the water.

Valerie's head smashed into the sail post, the searing pain forcing her eyes closed. The craft slammed back into the water, spraying it everywhere as it seeped through the cracks of the deck, soaking her backside. Prying her eyes open, she saw the raft had righted itself again, but she couldn't locate Ranthrop. Struggling to free his arm from the rope, Varmeer rushed to the other side. A hand reached up, clasping the railing as a wet black sleeve emerged over the side.

"Ranthrop!" Her heart slammed into her chest. She tried to scoot forward, but the pelt ropes held her in place.

His eyes found hers as if needing assurance she was still aboard. Slinging his bloodied sword around the railing support post, he hugged it with his arms. A guard rushed forward, standing at the ready with paddle in hand, as Varmeer pulled Ranthrop from the water.

Valerie untwisted her hands from the ropes, standing on shaky legs, and started toward the men. Ranthrop yelled, "No, stay back! Varmeer!"

"Go back, m'lady!" Varmeer urged as he tugged Ranthrop's legs over the side of the raft. "We don't want to lose you too!"

Valerie clamped her mouth shut like a scolded child, waddling back to her position between the packs. As she settled back in, she watched the men again. A soaked Ranthrop lay on his back as he and Varmeer clasped each other's forearm. Ranthrop patted his friend's hand, laughing. Varmeer let out a deflated breath and then cracked a smile.

She stared at them as if they were insane. How could they laugh?

Ranthrop got to his feet, approaching her with a smile. "That'll teach him," he said, thrusting his sword into a nearby crevice.

"You ass! You could have been killed!"

Ranthrop frowned, dropping down beside her. Droplets of water flew into the air as his backside hit the beams. He smelled of seaweed and fish. His sandy hair, now springy wet curls, dripped onto her cloak as he leaned toward her, gripping her chin with his cold fingers.

"As you could have been," he said pointedly. "What were you thinking, walking out there when you can't swim?"

Valerie scooted away but didn't get very far with Ranthrop's weight on her dress. "I couldn't let my guide drown before we even get there."

"I am feeling a little breathless…now that you mention it," he murmured before her lips.

She turned her head, leaning back against the sail post. "Then you should stop talking and save your breath."

They were halfway there. In a few more days, they would be back at Groslivo Stronghold, and Ricky would be waiting with a new solution to get home other than what had almost happened to Ranthrop. The damned fool almost got killed. A disgusting fonska could have swallowed him or severed him right before her eyes. Then where would she be? Would his men turn on her? She wouldn't blame them. She was the reason they were all on this road trip from hell. They didn't deserve this. Ranthrop didn't deserve to die because Franci became possessed.

Why was one person's life more important than another's? A part of her felt Ranthrop was only a storybook character and not real. The other part felt his dripping clothes and the lingering scent of him in her memory. She knew he was more than the mere manifestation of words on paper. He existed, and the horrid feeling of watching him go overboard would stay with her well beyond her time in this storybook.

What the hell was wrong with her? If they lived through this, she had to go home. Okay, so he was real—but only in here. No such man truly existed. That made him kind of a Prince Charming—a grade-B Prince Charming, but perhaps he was just written that way. He probably didn't mean half the things he said or did.

There was no man who would willingly be so chivalrous and thoughtful, who was attracted to her, or that made her heart flutter like a schoolgirl. Ranthrop Groslivo was just a story, and she had a job to do. This was like a hero's journey, and she nothing more than a distraction meant to tempt the hero, one that would bring no benefit. The sooner he realized what she just figured out the better off they both would be. Cold shoulder time, and she planned not to give in.

His wistful sigh stirred heat in her veins. He wanted her. She knew that now. It sent delicious thoughts through her frazzled mind, but the rocking of the vessel kept her firmly planted in reality.

The raft jolted again, slamming Ranthrop's weight into her tent bundle. She crossed her arm over her mid-section, quelling the butterflies and holding tight to the ropes.

"Ugh, when will they give up?"

"Probably just getting one last dig in for good measure," Ranthrop said.

She pinched her eyes closed, leaning her head against her arm. She felt Ranthrop's hand as he wound it into the rope next to hers. His skin, cold and clammy.

"You're freezing," she said as water sloshed across the deck and permeated her skirts. She flipped an end of her cloak toward him, knowing it would settle on his lap. The raft rocked violently again, and she didn't dare look. The sour bile in her stomach had made its way up to the back of her throat.

This had to be the price of being in the company of such a beautiful man. Well, it wasn't worth it!

AN HOUR and five more fonska attacks later, the rocking of the raft subsided. The vessel slowed as the men guided it into the shallows of the beach at the base of the Kraheny Mountains before jerking to a stop. They'd made it to Terradoon.

Valerie stirred as Ranthrop stood and helped her to her feet. "We've arrived."

She swayed on her feet. The world seemed to spin out of control.

"Congratulations, Lady Valerie. You're the first woman to ever sail the Greunie Sea," he declared.

The pores on her face began to sweat as she stared at Ranthrop and Varmeer. Lifting her soggy skirts, she raced to the edge of the raft and fell to her knees. Every terrified thought she'd endured poured out of her throat and into the green waters with a lurching sound.

"Yes, congratulations!" Varmeer quipped.

CHAPTER TWENTY-SIX

BLINNEY LANE

ALMOST THREE whole days had passed since Ricky and Valerie left. Although too early to close her shop, Mary wanted to check on her daughter before Sarah locked up for the night. Flipping the store sign to closed, she headed across the street.

"She'll still be sound asleep, Mary. There's nothing to worry about," Sarah told Mary as she headed to the cellar.

"It's a mother's job to worry, dear. I won't feel better until I see for myself."

Mary braced her aching back as she walked down the basement stairs. Running the shop by herself for the first time had exhausted her. With the upcoming Halloween weekend, the swarm of shoppers kept her hopping and a prisoner at the cash register all day with no time to restock shelves. With the work she still had to finish, she wouldn't be getting to bed at a decent hour.

She almost called her niece, Clarissa to help except she had only worked in the shop a few times. She wasn't adept like Valerie, and the time to explain things would slow Mary down instead of alleviating her workload. Valerie truly was the backbone of their business. Mary wished she were there so she could admit it to her.

Valerie's tears still haunted her. She hadn't meant to make her feel rejected. How could she have caused that much pain when she only wanted the best for her? She had been wrong about so many things.

Seeing Valerie's body slumped over the workbench made her heart skip a beat. Ricky looked just as lifeless as he lay in a similar position. She reminded herself they were only asleep as she fought against her rising anxiety.

She walked over, hesitating to touch Valerie's shoulder, afraid it would somehow harm her daughter while she was inside the book. With a shaky hand, she finally grasped Valerie's arm. She let out a breath as she watched her back rise and fall.

Satisfied that she was breathing, Mary pulled out the stool next to her and sat down. Valerie's face looked peaceful, reminding her of when she checked on her as a child at night. Reaching for her hand, she clasped it in her own. Her skin felt cold and clammy, and she had the urge to wrap her in a blanket, although she didn't dare, fearing it might disturb her chances of coming home. Instead, she squeezed the icy hand and rubbed her thumb over her wrist.

Leaning close to Valerie's ear she whispered, "You come home safe to me. You hear?"

She noticed the smooth feel of the skin on Valerie's wrist and froze. Where were her scars? She realized it was the first time she'd ever even seen her without wearing wristbands or bracelets. In the eerie silence of the dank basement, it hit her. If a heart ever broke, it broke then.

Her lower lip trembled as tears pooled in her eyes, the welling emotions growing as she stared at Valerie. The veil that had concealed years of pain, worries, and regrets slipped away like ashes in the wind. Mary dropped her head in her hands and wept.

As Mary sat in the darkness, holding a hand she realized she had not held in years, she heard a faint noise. Sniffling as she wiped her blurry eyes, something moved. She blinked as Ricky sat up. Eyes closed, his moans sounded like a mummy come to life. Flying off the stool, she screamed, tumbling backward and she landed with a painful thud onto her back.

RICKY TRIED to focus through his grogginess, yelling in unison as the shrill cry jolted him awake. He toppled off his stool, slumping against the wall for support. As he became aware, he saw the bookstore basement.

"Is that you, Mary?"

Mary struggled to her feet, curls loose and wild. She held a hand to her backside and another over her heart. "My word, you scared the daylights out of me!"

Ricky beamed upon hearing her familiar, harsh tone. "I'm home!" he declared with wonder. "It worked! Mary, it worked!" He ran over, throwing his arms around her.

"What worked?" Mary asked as he clamped her into a bear hug. "Where's Valerie? I mean...when will she be back?"

"She's still with Ranthrop looking for a cure for Franci."

"Why did you come back? Sarah said you were waiting there for her?"

"I am, but Valerie made me promise to try and find a different way to get home. She's terrified of having to drown to get back to Blinney Lane."

"Oh, my poor girl! I didn't even think about that. She's always been afraid of water ever since she was little. One day she was playing by the rain barrel behind our shop and fell in. I found her and pulled her out just in time."

"No need to do that now!" He couldn't hold back his proud excitement.

"What are you talking about?"

"Mary, I figured it out! I found a different way to get home from Farwin Wood."

"I thought there was only one way?"

Ricky laughed, picking up the stool Mary had knocked over and patting the top of it as he leaned on the workbench. When Mary was settled, he explained how he'd spent almost two days at Allister Hall writing a new book—a book about Blinney Lane.

"And you're sure that's how you got home?"

"I'm here, aren't I?"

"I don't think your aunt will be happy about this. She doesn't like you playing around with things in that book, and I can't say I blame her. What if someone from Farwin Wood can come through this new book? What will we do then?"

Ricky rolled his eyes. "That won't happen. I'll keep the book at Allister Hall, locked in the cellar space where we hide our troogies. Netta's the only one who knows about that crawl space." Mary looked at him with a blank expression. "She's our housekeeper there. I told her before I left, and she knows not to mention it to anyone. We can trust her."

"Still...I think you should have consulted your aunt first before you did this." She sighed. "But I am happy to know that Valerie won't have to go through any pain getting home."

Ricky placed his hand on her shoulder. "Exactly. That's why I did it. It's crazy having to drown every time you want to come home. Let's not mention any of this to Aunt Sarah until Valerie gets back, okay?"

"You mean keep it a secret? We always document changes in the council ledgers once we learn of them," Mary said, protesting.

"I know, but Valerie insisted she isn't going anywhere near water to get back home. I was really worried she'd stay and not come back. It was either that or find someone to help me drown her."

Mary grabbed a handful of his vest, wrenching him toward her. "Don't you dare touch a hair on my daughter's head!"

He tried to unpry her fingers. "Now I know where she gets it from!" he exclaimed.

"I'm sorry," Mary said, releasing him. "I guess you have no other choice." She stood up and rubbed her hands together, casting her worried eyes to Valerie. "Oh, I hate this book business."

"There is another choice now, Mary. A painless, less terrifying choice that worked. I'm going to go back now and head to Groslivo Stronghold to wait for them. I'll bring her back as soon as they return."

Mary looked at him, worry lines still creasing her face. "You really are a clever boy, Ricky. Thank you for doing this for Valerie and for Franci."

He walked over to his stool in front of the book and nodded. "I can't say I'm not happy about it either. I wasn't looking forward to taking another dunk. How's Franci doing?"

"I'm worried something happened. Reggie was acting like a caged animal when I stopped by earlier. She locked herself in her room the other day and wouldn't come out. Now she's taken to bed, moping about and barely speaks to anyone. At least she's staying put for a change, but Henry said that Lorna was a manic-depressive and ended up killing herself. I have to wonder if that part of her has taken hold of Francis now."

Ricky bit the inside of his lip. It was easy to forget the chaos on Blinney Lane while he was busy inside Farwin Wood. The threat to Franci remained real. He'd held up his end of the bargain for Valerie. Would she be as successful as he had been?

The door creaked at the top of the steps, and he heard his aunt's voice call down. "Mary, are you doing all right down there?"

He pressed his hands together as if he were praying and looked at Mary. She covered her mouth as she held her breath. He waved a frantic hand toward the stairwell.

"Yes, Sarah dear! I'm fine. I'll be up in a moment," she called out.

"Take your time." Sarah's voice wafted down with the sound of the door closing.

"Thanks," he whispered once the coast was clear.

Mary tore her eyes away and nodded. Her guilt probably didn't sit well with her.

"We'll see you in a few days. Don't worry." He laid his head back down on the workbench and closed his eyes, knowing there was still much to worry about.

CHAPTER
TWENTY-SEVEN

TERRADOON BAY, TERRADOON

RANTHROP'S MEN took to setting up three tents near a spur of the mountains. Valerie sat on a rock, ridding the sour taste from her mouth with a flask of water as she watched Ranthrop and Varmeer speak to some local fishermen who milled farther down the beach. They had their own semblance of a camp, and she wondered what they thought of the strangers who'd just appeared out of the sea.

From her distant view, they appeared to look human. They wore robes with ponchos on top in shades of pastels, and their skin appeared darker than anyone she'd seen in Farwin Wood. Some held spears, and others had bows strapped to their backs. She saw no swords, no metal of any kind. If they proved to be adversaries, at least Ranthrop and his men would be more advanced in the way of weaponry.

A pen sat next to a row of small huts with strange animals inside. Convinced the local fishermen posed no threat to

Ranthrop and Varmeer, she studied the four-legged animals. The pelts were furry like blow-dried Sherpa with necks sticking four feet into the air. The back legs were jointed, red and rubbery, resembling massive chicken legs, which folded underneath when sitting. The front legs, covered in the same white woolly fur, had hooves on the end of them. One stared at her with round, attentive gray eyes, shifting its head as each eyeball studied her. The snout had a curved beak covered in suede skin with hairy whiskers adorning each lip. The creatures were an odd mix of camel, ostrich, and an oversized chicken.

Finally, Ranthrop and Varmeer made their way back to the forming camp. Several of the foreign men lingered in the distance, staring after them, although they lost interest far sooner than she did.

After the tents were constructed, the guards gathered stones from the beach to make a fire pit. Ranthrop caught her attention, signaling for her to follow him. He led her to the center tent of the three-tent camp, holding the flap open for her to step inside. It had the same setup as the previous tent except it contained two sets of sleeping pelts instead of one. Turning around, she saw Ranthrop didn't follow her inside. Peeking out the tent flap, she watched him return and sit with his men by the fire.

"He better not think he's sleeping in here with me," she said to herself, closing the flap.

Later, a guard brought her a loaf of bread, a haunch of some type of meat, and a bucket of warm water. She set the food aside and quickly disrobed down to her shift, keeping an eye trained on the tent flap as she sponged away the stench of the last two days.

Managing to eat some of the dry food, she settled into the furs farthest from the door and finally felt the rocking motion of the raft die away.

A gust of cool sea air wafted in through the door, bringing Ranthrop in with it. She sat up, hugging the pelt to her chest, gaping at him as he began to unfasten his sword belt. He'd changed into dry clothes, his red overtunic missing. "What are you doing?" she asked.

"It's been a long day. We'd best get some sleep before heading into Terradoon tomorrow morning."

"I agree, but where are you going to sleep?"

His forehead crinkled as he dropped to his knees on the pelts next to her. "Here of course. We've only brought the three tents. I did not think it wise to give everyone their own tent. We don't want to look like a small army come to invade our wary neighbors."

"I can understand that," she said, quieting her hostility. "But why don't you go bunk with Varmeer?"

Ranthrop glanced around the tent as if he were searching for something. "I…someone needs to stay with you to make sure you're safe."

"I'm perfectly safe. I have the nine of you on either side of me, just mere feet away. You post a guard at night, don't you?"

"Yes, but…"

"But what?" she said, snapping at him.

His frown softened as one of his tawny brows arched into a questioning look. Dropping on all fours, he crept forward. "I thought maybe…you might need someone to keep you warm?"

"Well, you thought wrong!" Pressing her hand against his shoulder, he stared at it as if she'd just burned him. "It wouldn't be appropriate for you to stay in the same tent with me, Lord Ranthrop. After all, I am a lady. Surely that custom is the same in Farwin Wood as it is in Blinney?"

Ranthrop sat back on his haunches, frowning. She watched the hamster wheel in his mind turning rapidly as he struggled to find a worthy protest. She sighed in relief as he stood up.

"Yes. Of course it is," he said, running his hand through his golden mane. He picked up his sword and the extra pelt and headed for the door. "You know," he turned around, "I gather you are of enough years…of a heightened age that no one would bat an eye if you were to…to…"

"To what?"

"You're old enough that no one would think anything amiss if you invited a man into your tent and…"

She was old enough that everyone expected her to be a whore? I don't think so, buddy!

"Out!" she yelled, pointing to the door. "Get out!"

Ranthrop jumped back so fast he stumbled through the doorway, landing hard on the sand, and tugged his feet free from the flap. He watched as Valerie quickly secured it behind him with the affixed strings, barring any entry.

VARMEER SIGHED in contentment at the feel of Trina's hands in his hair as they massaged his temples in the oversized tub in the back room of her little cottage. The scent of dried flowers, a bottle of beetleburry ale uncorked on the stool next to them, and a candle emitting soft light permeated the cozy room. It almost seemed real.

Lost in his dream, he saw Trina's face, felt her skin, and touched the firm mound of her belly. How big would that belly be when he returned home? Not much bigger than when he left, surely, but he didn't like leaving her for this trip. He would marry that woman now that the war was over, now that he would have a family. He puckered his lips, accepting her soft kiss, the warmth of his pelts becoming the feel of her caress.

A gust of cold air caused him to shudder, and he stretched his lips to the image of her in his mind. He saw her fingers reach for his mouth as she whispered his name.

"Varmeer?"

"Mmm, Trina," he said in a sleepy voice.

"Varmeer!" a deep masculine voice took over as the sound of Trina faded away.

He cracked an eye open and inhaled at the sight of Ranthrop leering over him, his big fingers fumbling blindly at his face in the darkness.

"Bah!" Varmeer exclaimed as he felt foreign, rough fingertips poke his face. "Ranthrop!" he shrieked, turning his head.

"Are you awake?" Ranthrop asked in a loud whisper.

He turned his head, pinching his eyes closed. "No."

"Yes, you are." Ranthrop grumbled, dropping down next to him on the ground. The man's elbow landed in his shoulder joint, and he winced as pain shot down his arm.

He inched to the side to avoid being crushed, taking his pelt cover with him. "I'm busy," he complained in a sleep-laden voice.

Ranthrop's elbow thrust into his bicep as the big man folded his arms over his chest, taking up more space in the crowded tent. Retreat proved impossible as he was already shoved up against the side.

The sound of rumbling snores ripped though the little abode as Winslow and Shimsley slept only a few feet away. They'd found the peaceful slumber he'd been searching for—the rotted lot.

"Are they asleep?" Ranthrop's pathetic excuse for a whisper rasped in his ear.

He took a patient breath as another eruption of nasally snores cut through the tent. "Winslow and Shimsley are in a coma."

A few moments of silence from his noble lord followed, but it proved too much to hope for.

"Why aren't *you* sleeping?"

"I was, just."

Ranthrop grunted. "No doubt dreaming about your Trina, old man."

"Trina?" Varmeer asked, turning his head in the dark. "Who's Trina?"

Ranthrop snorted and wiggled in place, and he knew the man planned to settle in. "Keep your secrets, my friend. I don't mind."

Scoffing, he rolled over, determined to ignore the disruption. Ranthrop fidgeted again and let out a lengthy sigh. Great. He knew this wayward charade. Something was eating at his friend, and he wouldn't get any sleep until he figured it out. "Weren't you going to share a tent with the lady?"

"No! That wouldn't be appropriate. She's a lady, after all. I wouldn't jeopardize her reputation like that."

"Of course not."

"Exactly," Ranthrop agreed. "Besides…I do not think she likes me."

"This bothers you?"

"Everyone wants to be liked."

"In my experience, you have never cared whether people like you, m'lord."

"Well, the war is over, Varmeer. Things change. Besides, she is from Blinney. Maybe I am simply trying to show diplomacy before she goes back to her people. No need to scatter tarnish on my name wherever it travels."

"Wisely played, m'lord." He let out a yawn.

"Am I boring you?"

"No, sire. I am hanging on every word."

"Cheeky devil," Ranthrop said, slamming an elbow into Varmeer's back. "What do you propose I should I do?"

"Do about what?" he asked in annoyance.

"To get Lady Valerie to be more amiable toward me."

"Have you tried being thoughtful and compassionate to her and her needs?"

"Yes, I believe I have."

His body rocked as Ranthrop shifted beside him. The man's arm thumped into his back several times and the sound of rustling leather filled the air. Varmeer knew Ranthrop was scratching himself in places he didn't want to think about. A nasally rip followed, and he listened as Ranthrop made a spitting noise, releasing a wad of phlegm somewhere onto the tent floor. He pinched his eyes closed again, gathering his pelt tighter.

"Perhaps you could try being more eloquent. The ladies do seem to admire that."

"I can be eloquent," Ranthrop protested.

He breathed into the fur pulled up to his face, realizing he was fully awake. Damn it! "I never doubted it for a moment, m'lord."

"And if I lack eloquence then it is damned well your fault!"

"*My* fault?"

"Yes. You were supposed to be the one to teach me these things over the years. How was I supposed to know I would ever need to woo some baffling, headstrong, stubborn, dizzying lady."

"Woo?"

"You know what I mean."

"My lord, I am truly sorry if I have failed you in any way," he said with sincerity. "Perhaps she just needs more time—time to get to know you."

Ranthrop let out a haggard breath. "You haven't failed me, Varmeer. You've been a good friend."

Had he just heard him correctly? It was probably the nicest thing the man had ever said. Fortunately, his ego didn't expect to hear nice things from Ranthrop, which made the comment that much more momentous.

"It has been an honor to serve you, my lord." He added with bated breath. "You have been a good friend to me, as well."

Several moments passed. He heard no rebuttal, no further query. The only sounds were the faltering breaths of snoring men. Rolling over to see what had gotten Ranthrop's tongue, he learned that two snoring men had now become three. He grumbled and slammed his body back to the ground, all thoughts of Trina and a good night's rest far from his grasp.

CHAPTER TWENTY-EIGHT

TERRADOON

MORNING BROUGHT a different perspective to the banks of Terradoon. The winds were as gusty as they had been on the mountainside, but the noises they carried with them were something new. The constant whistling resembled a howl as the party mounted the strange creatures Valerie saw the night before. She'd learned they were called hockenstotts, and unlike skithers, they could only hold the weight of one rider.

Ranthrop and Varmeer had bartered daggers with the local fishermen for four of the creatures. The rest of their party stayed behind to guard the rafts. She didn't like the diminished numbers but trusted Ranthrop knew best.

Once she had wrangled her way onto the back of a hockenstott with some lifting assistance from Ranthrop, it hopped around in unruly circles before calming down. She noticed Ranthrop, Varmeer, and the two guards joining them didn't have better luck either. A foreboding feeling fell over her. Would anything in Terradoon be as simple as it had been in Farwin Wood?

The hockenstotts skipped up the sandy path where the mountain range split in a wide pass. The terrain was barren and dry. Sand stung Valerie's eyes as the wind whipped it cruelly through the air every moment of the journey. She held her cloak hood across her face as she peeked out.

Craggy hills swept up on either side of them as the road from the beach ascended in the distance. In the haze of the morning air, she detected more hills and mountains on either side of them through the yellow blur on the horizon. As they approached the crest of the road, a looming structure appeared, and she couldn't tear her eyes away from it.

It beckoned like a water tower in the desert. Its base and neck were smooth and as they neared, she saw it was made from paved sand. Gaping upward, she noted three bulbous sections, one atop the other. The eerie monument finally came to a point at the very top nearly fifty feet above and appeared to be floating in the haze of the sky.

Looking around, she realized the party had stopped. A teaming city farther down the road where the hill sloped to a plain took her breath away. Smooth, adobe-style structures filled the horizon as far as the eye could see. In the center stood a much larger building of the same material. Three stories in height, its roof had a similar fixture attached to its pinnacle like the monument next to them.

"Why have we stopped?" she called to Ranthrop and the men, who had all dismounted.

Varmeer and two of the guards each laid something down next to the base of the monument. Strange things littered its circumference. She saw what appeared to be a doll, a pitcher, beaded necklaces, a strange hat covered in sand, and even several wagon wheels propped against it.

One of the guards discarded his dagger into the mix, the other his water flask. Varmeer set his gloves down next to the doll. Ranthrop approached her with his dagger out.

"We must pay tribute," he called up to her. "That is the custom here. It doesn't look as though it's changed since I last journeyed here."

"What are we paying tribute to?"

"To the wind. To the voices it carries." Ranthrop shrugged. "Whatever it is that speaks to this place. I do not know exactly." He patted the side of her hockenstott, and she swallowed at the vague explanation. "What would you like to leave?"

She had nothing. No possessions. All she had were the clothes on her back. Would that count to appease a wayward wind?

"A lock of hair, perhaps?" Ranthrop suggested.

"No!" she cried.

"That would be a shame, wouldn't it?"

"Here." She stuck her foot out, away from the beast. "Can you cut a piece of my dress?" She was thankful she hadn't worn her Blinney clothes.

Ranthrop complied, cutting a small strip of the gown's beautiful border. She watched him work with delicate fingers, trying not to mar the dress. He had no idea she planned to never wear it again. His gentleness touched her as he gave her an apologetic look once he'd freed a strip of the cloth. He walked over to the pile of forgotten items and tucked the cloth underneath the dagger he'd used to cut it, returning to his mount.

They descended the hill and after an hour came to the edge of the city. As they passed through the winding streets, villagers emerged from their huts, staring at the small traveling party. The onlookers grew in numbers. Women and children crept closer. Some reached out to touch Varmeer's leather boots, others the hem of Valerie's dress.

A sea of curious eyes in shades of brown, green, and gray looked up at her. An array of pastel-colored robes soon flooded around her hockenstott. Cocoa skinned arms reached up, their fingers running across her gown, her leather boots.

"Valerie, are you well?" Ranthrop called to her. She noticed a pool of pedestrians also encircled his ride. Children poked at his boots. A woman rubbed the edge of his bright-red tunic between her fingers. She watched Ranthrop's grasp as it tightened on the hilt of his sword.

"No," Varmeer called out, shaking his head.

"I'm fine," she added as she saw his concerned expression. She looked back down at the crowd as they milled about her, reaching her hand down slowly.

"Valerie!" Ranthrop warned.

She spared him a glance but then let her hand brush against a woman's open grasp. The woman smiled at her and she returned a smile of her own. Their fingers parted and the next in line reached up to do the same. It moved the prying hands away from her gown as the people smiled at her as she passed by. Craning her head, she looked over at Ranthrop and gave him a reassuring smile. He sighed, relinquishing the hold on his hilt.

The crowd eventually lost interest, and they approached the center of the city where the lofty mud fortress sat like a symbol of power. Ranthrop guided the party under an archway in the center of a wall that surrounded the adobe palace.

A few robed men gave them wary glances as they entered a sandy courtyard and Valerie lingered back, watching as Ranthrop dismounted to speak with them. When he had finished, he helped her down. The Terradoon guards led their hockenstotts away and another appeared, signaling for them to follow.

Valerie was grateful for the protective arm that Ranthrop held around her as they entered the palace. They passed through a simple vestibule with bird-shaped decorations and reeds adorning the walls. A jagged floor consisting of irregular-cut stones ran its length down a wide hallway, aligned with precarious stone pillars. They were told to wait in a large open room lined with several rugs on either side. At the end sat a mezzanine with an ornate wicker trellis behind an array of pillows and a very large rug.

Varmeer stood like a statue, his hands clasped behind his back, as they waited. She could tell he was a pro at this waiting thing. Ranthrop, on the other hand, paced back and forth before what she guessed was the throne rug on the mezzanine. She fidgeted with her hands and looked about the room.

Torches were mounted to several pillars, and trellis-style grates covered the window openings at the tops of the walls, allowing the sunlight to pool onto the floor. The room smelled of sandalwood and dust, reminding her of the smell of the vacuum cleaner bag when her mother changed it.

A loud whoosh startled her, and she spun around to see a burst of fire disperse behind the trellis at the center of the mezzanine. Sparks floated up with wafts of smoke. The guard who had led them inside stepped around a pillar next to the trellis. "The Donka Arlyle," he announced in a monotone voice.

"Donka?" she whispered to Varmeer.

"That is the title for a clan leader here."

"Oh."

An old man emerged behind the guard, walking tall and straight without the slightest bit of rigidity. His steps, however, were slow and gave the illusion of floating. He stopped in the center of the rug after a long pause, turning to face them. Bending his head, he raised his palms upward. Ranthrop and Varmeer sat down on the rug beneath their feet. Valerie quickly gathered the skirt of her dress as she and the two guards with them followed suit.

After she'd settled herself next to Ranthrop, she looked up in surprise. The Donka looked directly back at her, although his eyes were completely white. The center where his corneas should be was only a shade darker than the rest of the eye.

"Lord Ranthrop Groslivo…from beyond the sea. It has been many years," the man called down to them, his voice like raspy smoke.

"More than twenty, Donka Arlyle," Ranthrop said, his hands resting on his knees.

"Yes, I remember." Arlyle smiled and stared off into a corner of the ceiling. "You are…Lord Ranthrop now. The only lord of the house of Groslivo."

"Yes," Ranthrop said after a pause. Valerie noticed the tension in his jaw. "My father died shortly after our return home."

"I know. I hear his spirit on the wind from time to time. He speaks of you."

A chill ran down her spine, and she looked at Ranthrop for his reaction. His nostrils flared, but his posture remained as rigid as when he'd sat down. Varmeer did little to answer her unspoken curiosity. His eyes told her he found the meeting as uncomfortable as she did.

"I have not come here to talk to the wind, Donka. I have come…"

"On a quest. Yes, I know. You are searching for something and it has brought you here, Ranthrop from beyond the sea." Arlyle's head careened back and forth as he spoke, his snake-like eyes never settling on anything in particular.

"We have come in search of venstras. I have come to ask for your assistance in directing me to a cave. I am told that is where they grow." Ranthrop's voice was more diplomatic and controlled than Valerie had ever heard. He seemed like a completely different person than the free spirit she'd been treated to on their trip.

"Venstras? Ah, so you have come to fight a madness? But no…I don't think it is yours. No, not the son's. He has not yet become like the father." Arlyle's head tilted to the side, and his features pinched as though he were straining to hear a secret being whispered into his ear.

"Where can I find the caves of the venstras?" Ranthrop asked in a firm yet patient tone.

"They are to the south. That is where the caves are you seek. My men will take you." Arlyle's voice faded as if the weight of the words strained him to speak.

Ranthrop let out a soft breath and glanced at Valerie and Varmeer. He gave them a nod and stood up. "I am grateful to you, Donka. We appreciate your hospitality and will be on our way."

As Ranthrop helped Valerie to her feet, she froze when the old man's voice raised a pitch. "It is four days to the southern caves, son beyond the sea. You don't have that kind of time, do you?"

Ranthrop paled as he looked at her. He stepped closer to the old man. "Four days? Is there nothing closer?"

"You have to help her. I see this foreign woman. You have to help her before her light is snuffed out forever." Arlyle stared at one of the windows.

Valerie didn't know why she kept following his gaze. The man was clearly blind as a bat. And how did he know about Franci. She might not have four more days.

"Arlyle, tell me what I must do!" Ranthrop stated loudly.

"The tunnel. Your destiny lies in the tunnel." The old man's voice had grown tired again.

The party exchanged confused looks, none of which solved the old man's riddle. "What tunnel? Is it far?"

"The Tunnel of Whispers."

Ranthrop clenched his fists and shifted impatiently. "How far away is this tunnel?"

"Crupa will take you," Arlyle said, nodding in the direction of his sentry.

Ranthrop looked to the stocky man who stood at the side of the throne. He held out his hands to the man, pleading for an answer.

"It is just outside the village in the valley of the mountains," Crupa said like a trained robot.

"When can we leave?" Ranthrop asked.

Crupa looked to the old man. Valerie watched in awe as Arlyle nodded to the sentry, as though he knew the man looked at him for permission.

"Very well. Thank you," Ranthrop said, nodding to Crupa. "Donka, your guidance is appreciated." He bowed and Valerie watched in awe as Arlyle's head nodded in return.

Ranthrop pulled her by the arm, turning her around as he started for the door. Varmeer and the men wasted no time in joining him to the exit. Her skin still crawled as she glanced back at the old man on the throne. He raised his head up and stared at her with his unseeing eyes.

"Ranthrop!" he called.

Ranthrop stopped and looked down at her, a wary expression on his face. He turned back to face Arlyle, gazing at him in silence.

"Listen for the voice in your heart…son from beyond the sea."

Ranthrop's face contorted. He pursed his lips and nudged Valerie toward the door, not sparing another glance at the old man who let out a boisterous laugh that echoed all the way down the hall as they raced from the building.

CHAPTER TWENTY-NINE

THE TUNNEL OF WHISPERS

VALERIE SAT on a stone ledge at the base of the mountainside that Crupa had led them to, wringing her hands. She'd given up pacing back and forth in the wind and instead hugged her cloak around her for security and warmth. The hockenstotts sat huddled together in a row, bellowing low moos of protest for reasons she did not know.

Ranthrop's guards, Winslow and Shimsley, stood with their hands resting on the hilts of their swords. One looked at Crupa, while the other looked at the path Varmeer and Ranthrop took toward the tunnel. Crupa leaned with a foot propped against the rocks, his hands folded over his stomach, eyes closed. He was either sleeping, meditating, or doing a spectacular job of ignoring them all.

Valerie chewed on the inside of her cheek as Varmeer and Ranthrop disappeared from her view around the craggy curve of the mountainside. Crupa gave no more instruction other than telling them they could only enter the Tunnel of Whispers one at a time.

Ranthrop had refused to let her go with them, ignoring her protests when she insisted that she should be the one to venture inside since the venstras were for her.

"This is non-negotiable, my lady," was all he'd said.

She couldn't take it anymore. That old man had given her the willies. And everyone thought Blinney Lane was weird. Ha! She wanted answers—something more than a cryptic riddle spouted off by a blind nutcase.

"Crupa?" She waited, and the man finally lifted his head, making eye contact with her. "Why do they call it the Tunnel of Whispers?"

His gaze trailed up the crooked, narrow path leading toward the cave. "It is home to the voices of the lost."

"Who are the lost?"

"The dead. The unborn. The living who float between both worlds—souls with hearts that beat but have been split in two."

Valerie glanced at Winslow and Shimsley. Their color paled as they stared at the somber sentry.

"What...will happen to him?"

"What happens to all men. He will meet his destiny."

THE WIND howled, and the sound reverberated into and back out the opening of the tunnel. A strange bird with lengthy wings cut a cry through the wind, causing Ranthrop and Varmeer to jump as it flapped violently past them. Ranthrop steadied himself and peered at the looming darkness in the tunnel. The entryway curved up ahead, hiding further view of its contents. He rubbed at his face, feeling a vibration tickle the skin.

He tightened the rope around his waist that Varmeer had threaded for him and gave it a tug to inspect the knot. Avoiding Varmeer's eyes, he took a bag off the man's shoulder and slung it across his own. The vibrations trembled through him again and pressure built inside his head. He rubbed at his ears trying to stop the sound from tickling his eardrums.

"You feel that too?" Varmeer asked. "I thought it was just me. It's like the sea and a thousand low drums all sounding out of time."

Ranthrop grimaced at his friend's wary expression. "Secure the rope, will you?"

Varmeer clasped a tight grip onto his shoulder. "Ranthrop, you don't have to do this."

"We are here. I will not waste this journey now."

"Let me go. I will get the venstras for the lady."

Ranthrop planted his own hand on Varmeer's shoulder, steadying him with a look. "With a babe on the way?" He shook his head. "No. I will not subject a father-to-be to whatever awaits in that abyss."

Varmeer snapped his mouth shut, squirming under the knowing look. "Your informants…"

"Were correct, I can see." Ranthrop smiled and shook the man's shoulder. "Congratulations, old man."

"I don't care. I'll still go. I'm your personal guard. It should be me anyway."

Ranthrop shook his head. "And I'm still the lord. This is the way it's *going* to be."

"And what if… What if you come out of there like…"

"Like my father?"

Varmeer swallowed hard. "Yes, m'lord. What then?"

Gripping Varmeer's tunic, he tugged him closer and stared into his eyes. "If that happens, you must promise me something."

"What?"

"Promise me first!"

"With your pension for hasty decisions? Tell me what I am to promise," Varmeer demanded, grasping Ranthrop's shirt in return.

"If a madness takes me, do not give me any of that flower concoction the lady seeks. I don't want to spend my days like Bernryn—a shell of what I used to be."

"But sire, what is the alternative?"

Ranthrop clutched the hilt of Varmeer's dagger until the man looked down at it. "If I am truly gone, make it quick for me, old friend."

"No, I won't do that!"

"You would rather see me like my father? Promise me, Varmeer. Promise you won't leave me like that!" he exclaimed, shaking the man by his shirtfront.

Varmeer closed his eyes as he held onto Ranthrop's wrist. "It is not an easy thing you ask of me."

"I have never asked you for easy things."

Varmeer let out a weak chuckle. "No. No, you haven't."

"Will you do it?"

Finally, he uttered, "Don't make me say it."

Ranthrop released his friend, content with his unspoken promise. They stared at each other for a moment. He turned to walk into the tunnel and added, "See that the lady makes it home safely."

Just before the tunnel curved, Ranthrop glanced back. Varmeer stood, unleashing the skein of rope slowly through his hands and gave him a nod. Ranthrop turned back and took a deep breath as he stepped with careful footing around the bend.

He stayed near the walls and walked with measured steps. The vibrations increased, and he braced his hand against the wall when he began to feel dizzy. Under his palm, he felt the pulsations that emitted from the rock coursing through him, and he winced at the sharp pain in his ears. He gritted his teeth and hurried forward, following the tunnel downward into the mountain.

His eyes searched for signs of flowers, but the growing darkness revealed nothing but sand-colored stone. He stopped before another veer and bent down to light the torch Crupa had given him. As he reared up to clank the flints together, he heard the sound of a man's deep scream and jumped.

"Varmeer?" He called the man's name but suspected the scream had not come from the direction of the entrance.

"You're a man now, my boy," came the distinct voice of his father. It wafted around him in an eerie whisper.

His hands froze midair, and he looked around the tunnel. The whirring buzz of the vibration rumbled again inside his skull and he shook his head, intent on focusing on the torch. He slapped the flints together, grinding his teeth as a flutter of whispers tickled his eardrums. Finally a spark caught the dried, oil-soaked moss wrapped on the end of the torch as it came ablaze.

Swaying as he stood, he braced himself against the cavern wall with his outstretched hand. Streaks of color flashed before him in tiny lines, and he pinched his eyes shut behind the glow of the flame, but the unworldly streams remained when he opened his eyes once more.

Letting out a low growl, he moved toward the next passage. His legs grew heavy as though an invisible force were weighing him down. Leaning forward, he pushed his limbs onward with each step.

The voice of his old friend, Grandly, pierced his ears with the words the man had spoken to him just before they'd gone into battle—the battle where Grandly had fallen. "Just over that hill. Do you see them?"

"Grandly's dead," Ranthrop replied, squinting under the glow of the torch as he searched the tunnel. He spotted bright white up ahead, as if it were a beacon, and he pushed himself toward the precious plant he'd come to capture.

His father's whisper floated inside his head. "Why did you leave me to die like that in the swamp?"

He shook his head, forcing it away as he blinked rapidly. When he finally reached the venstras, the dragging force allowed him to drop easily to his knees. The screams and pleading last words of men he'd killed during the war flooded into his ears. He reached with his dagger to cut the flowers, watching his hand shake uncontrollably.

Gasping for breath against the suffocating pressure in his chest, he managed to free a blossom and then another. He slumped into the rock as he struggled to tuck them into the bag. How many did she need? He couldn't come back in here.

Once the flowers were secure in the sack, he wiped his hand across his face, revealing a layer of sweat. The incessant whispers didn't relent, and he felt nauseated. His heart hammered, and he could hear its rapid pulsing along with all the other noises. Pushing himself to his feet, he felt along the wall as he inched toward another set of plants just ahead.

"Sire, I meant to hit Lord Richard," Ferguson's voice ricocheted through his mind. He saw the archer's face just before he slit his throat for accidentally killing his betrothed so many years ago. "Sire, I beg you. I never meant to hit the Lady Deronda."

Ranthrop crumpled to his knees just short of the venstras. Against his will, he lurched out a dry gag, *tasting* Ferguson's fear—and the fears of everyone else he had in some way caused.

Pulling himself forward over the gritty rock, he focused on the flowers, trying to blot out the memories the voices brought. His hand appeared blurry as he reached out for the blossoms. The gasping sounds his father had made when he'd found him dying in the woods, seeped through the deafening cries rumbling in his ears.

A painful cry erupted from him as he blinked back the forming tears. "No! You're not real!"

His hand connected with the waxy petals, and he tore them away from the plant. Shoving them into his pack, he reached out, eyes closed, and felt frantically for more. He could no longer tell if the ground reverberated beneath him or if his body shook so much it merely felt that way. One. Two more flowers. He couldn't be sure. Perhaps he grasped at nothing, and his mind played tricks on him.

He forced his back against the wall, his breaths heavy as he panted. Scraping at his face, he sputtered as sweat dripped down his lips.

"Boys sit at home and wonder where the smoke comes from. Men seek out the fire and dive through the flames," his father's voice felt like it taunted him.

He groaned, bracing his head in his hands. "No! You are just my memories."

The back of his throat contracted again, and he coughed. Sputum dripped out of his mouth, and he spat on the ground as he forced his legs underneath him. He waved the torch violently in front of him, hoping to still the crazed murmurs—now all around him—but it only compounded them, their pitch increasing.

The pressure against his body intensified as he began to double back out of the tunnel. Was he even going the right way? He moaned as if he were mad, his whimpers unintelligible as the whispers swarmed inside his ears.

"Richard," Deronda called painfully with her dying breath. He felt the same hurt she had experienced at that moment, calling out to her lover. He hadn't even been there when she died. Why did he have to hear her too?

The cries of dying men, screaming out for their mothers, their wives, their children, made his head whirl, and he dropped the torch, cradling his head in his hands. He let out a curdling cry and plunged forward into the darkness with as much strength as he could muster.

"No!" He didn't know how deep he had traveled, how much farther he had to go. It seemed infinite, his mind a jumbled mess as all sense of direction ceased to exist. All he felt were the screams in his head, the pain pulsing through his body. Before the gagging overtook him once more, he collapsed onto his hands and knees, crying out with all his might, "Forgive me!"

CHAPTER THIRTY

VALERIE BOLTED off her perch on the ledge as soon as she saw Varmeer racing down the mountain path toward them. He didn't even spare her a glance, stopping only half-way down the ridge to gesture at Winslow and Shimsley.

"Make haste! The lord needs our help," he cried.

The men raced up the ridge after him. Valerie followed, but her dress kept tripping her the faster she ran, slowing her pace. She looked back when she neared the crest and saw Crupa on his hockenstott heading back down the road. Why was he leaving them?

When she turned back around, she saw the men carrying Ranthrop. Varmeer stood behind him, his hands underneath Ranthrop's lifeless arms. Winslow and Shimsley each cradled a leg as they scrambled down the path.

A loop of rope around Ranthrop's waist had been cut, leaving a tail dragging in the dirt. His hair and face were soaked, and he appeared unconscious except for the look of anguish on his face.

"What happened?"

"Make way, m'lady. Let us get him off this mountain," Varmeer answered.

Valerie nodded, hurrying as quickly as possible to the hockenstotts. The men followed behind her, setting Ranthrop gently on the ground. She dropped to her knees beside him, placing a hand to his forehead. It felt cold despite the sweat covering his skin. He moaned a strange sound, his head and facial features twitching.

"What happened up there?"

"I heard him cry out," Varmeer said, panting as he doubled-over. "I ran and found him lying face down just inside the tunnel, but he did not speak again."

"Can we put him on a hockenstott?"

Varmeer looked at the other two men. "We might have to tie him to it so he doesn't fall."

"That's fine. Let's get the hell out of here."

"M'lady," Varmeer called as she stood up, handing her a sack. She opened it and found over two dozen bright-white flowers. "The venstras. He got them."

Her heart plummeted as she looked from the bag to Ranthrop's pale, lifeless face. She wanted to die right then and there.

CHAPTER
THIRTY-ONE

TERRADOON BAY

THE MEN pulled Ranthrop's limp body off the hockenstott with care once they reached the tents on the beach. His limbs spasmed, and they set him on the ground to avoid dropping him. The hockenstott, spooked by the quick movement, took off running toward the fisherman's camp.

Ranthrop let out a yowl, his body contorting from its fetal position to a splayed stance as he writhed on the ground. Valerie rushed over as soon as she dismounted. She reached to calm him, but his legs bashed into hers, sending her onto her backside.

"M'lady, don't get too close," Winslow said as he helped her up off the ground.

"Too close? We have to help him!"

She watched as Ranthrop's lips moved but nothing sensible came from them. He was reduced to making noises a fleeing child made running away from the boogeyman. She looked up at the men. The rest of his guards had emerged from the camp and were staring down at their lord in pity.

Her fingers knotted into fists, and she stamped her foot. "Well, don't just stand there! Take him into the tent," she ordered, pointing to the one she had slept in their first night at the beach.

Four of the men wrestled with the flailing man and managed to get him off the ground. They walked with jerky motions as Ranthrop's body fought them each step of the way. Varmeer remained by her side, looking on as the men carted his lord into the tent.

"Varmeer, what can we do for him?"

He looked at her, his mouth in a tight line. "I'm afraid there's nothing that can be done, m'lady."

That wasn't good enough. There had to be something to do to ease his pain, his distress. "The flowers! What about the flowers?" She raced to the saddle on her hockenstott and returned with the bag. "I remember what Bernryn told me. I can try to make it and see if it helps."

She startled when Varmeer clamped a tight grip around her wrist as she tugged the bag open. "No! No, m'lady. He would not wish it."

"What do you mean he would not wish it? How can you possibly know what he wishes right now?"

"He told me…before he went into the tunnel."

She couldn't believe it. How could he be so stupid as to refuse a treatment if they had one? She'd be damned if she was going to take orders from his servant. "But what if it can help him? You don't want to see him like this, do you?"

"Of course not, but I keep my word." He pulled the bag from her hand with a fierce tug. "M'lady, he does not want to end up like Bernryn. Ranthrop feels the cure Bernyn took for madness ages ago left him severely altered."

Valerie felt her lip pout. She looked at the tent, watching the men come out with haggard expressions. Severely altered? Bernryn was creepy and strange. She couldn't imagine Ranthrop ever being like that. She didn't want to imagine Ranthrop like that. He was younger and stronger. He could never be half the man he was before he went into that god-forsaken tunnel.

"I hope you understand, m'lady. 'Tis what he wanted."

She schooled her features and replied in a tone that wouldn't even convince herself. "I understand. I'll sit with him and do whatever I can to keep him comfortable. Can we take him across the sea in the morning? I think we should at least get him back to Bernryn as soon as we can. Maybe there's something he can do to help him."

"Of course, m'lady. I'll inform the men."

She walked toward the tent, eager to see Ranthrop yet dreading it all the same. How long would he be like this? He had gotten soaked on the sea passage. Perhaps they were being too hasty and he had only come down with a fever. She hadn't felt herself the first day she had come down with the drumsy. She didn't think she had appeared as unresponsive as Ranthrop, but it gave her hope. She was nearly herself again without a spot of nausea today. Maybe all Ranthrop needed was time.

When she entered the tent, her eyes located him by the sound of his moans. The pelts he lay on were undisturbed, and she scowled realizing the men hadn't even bothered to cover him. He turned violently from one side and then back to the other, his arms following as if they were no longer under his control. She untied her cloak and tossed it into the corner.

Kneeling down by the bucket, she wet a cloth from the bag of clothing she'd brought from the keep. She scooted over to him on her knees and began to draw it across his brow. The task proved difficult. Ranthrop's head jerked from side to side as he mumbled like she was coming at him with a hot poker.

"Father? Father!"

"Shh," she soothed and did her best to wash his face.

His legs twisted and thrashed. A bursting pain shot up her shin and she scrambled back, grasping her leg where his boot had connected. Careful to avoid his appendages, she hobbled on her knees behind his head once the pain had subsided and found the cloth again.

"Grandly…behind you!" he roared, clenching his fists. His arm swung up so quickly, she couldn't move out of its path.

Her head jerked to the side as his fist connected with her cheekbone, causing her teeth to click together. She tumbled backward and blinked at the spots in her vision as she brought a hand to her face. Her skin felt warm as it throbbed beneath her hand. Needles shot through her cornea as she tried to steady her gaze back on Ranthrop. She was as useless as a football player on a golf course.

She couldn't bear the cries he made, apparent utterances of regrets. Yet she didn't want to give up and leave him alone in the tent. What if he hurt himself? What if she came back in the morning and found him dead? Her skin crawled at the thought and she scooted back over to him, her face contorting from the pain in her cheek and eye.

Pressing his shoulders forward, she lowered herself down onto the pelts behind him. At least she would be out of his grasp behind his back. She pulled one of the covers over them and cradled his head in her arms while he continued to writhe. His arm swung at nothing again. She clamped her arms over his shoulders, pinning his arms and hugged his chest. The less space between them, the less he would be able to slam into her body. When his feet kicked backward, she quickly bent her knees, tucking her feet under her backside.

Ranthrop whimpered, and she pressed her face into his neck so her lips were close to his ear. "Shh. It's all right. You're going to be all right."

"Ferguson!"

"Shh. Ranthrop, I'm here. I won't leave you."

"Ferguson! What have you done? Now there'll be a war!"

Valerie's face scrunched in wonder at his cries. Who were all these people he spoke to—or did they speak to him? She hugged him tighter when she realized that they were all likely dead. After twenty years of war, she imagined his ghosts were plenty.

"Ranthrop. Listen to my voice. They're not real. None of them are real. They're just your memories. Stay here with me," she whispered into his ear and held on tight when he rocked them back and forth.

She felt his muscles relent beneath her grasp each time she offered a comforting whisper. If it worked long term, she had yet to find out, but it appeared to ease his present torment.

After a while, Varmeer announced himself. She didn't move from her cradling when he entered, not wanting to get caught in a deathblow again. Varmeer set a pail of warm water down in the corner and placed a candle on the wood block, careful to move it out of Ranthrop's reach.

"How is he?"

She shook her head from where she lay, clutching Ranthrop's back to her breast. She braced herself as he arched back, squeezing her eyes closed when he groaned a painful noise. She opened them to find Varmeer shaking his head, looking down at them as though he were at a funeral.

"Thank you, Varmeer."

"M'lady! Your face!"

Valerie tucked her head back into Ranthrop's neck to hide her cheek from his view. "I'm fine. You can leave us now."

He hesitated but finally turned, ducking under the tent flap into the night. Valerie resumed her tender support once he left. She released Ranthrop briefly to wash her face and the grimy places on her skin. When she had finished, she washed him as much as possible without sustaining further injury. She tried giving him water, but it only dribbled down his chin, causing him to gurgle in a choking manner.

Taking up her previous hold, she tucked herself tightly to his back and drew the hair away from his forehead. Tender words came from a place she didn't know existed inside of her—sweet consolations, gentle reassurances, words of loving encouragement.

Franci was possibly doomed to be someone else for the rest of her life and now Ranthrop didn't even know who or where he was, trapped in a hell of nightmares. How could life be so cruel? He had been trying to help someone. Shouldn't helping someone be easier than this? Ranthrop didn't even know Franci and whatever his reasons, he'd still insisted on being the one to go into the tunnel. She'd sworn to avoid his flirtations, to just thank him and be on her way. Now he might never be sane enough again for her to even give her gratitude.

"Ranthrop," she murmured at his shoulder, settling her head onto the ground, "come back. I was wrong about you."

A CHILL seeped under the covers, tugging Valerie back toward consciousness. Her mind fought to wake up, remembering the crisis at hand, while her body yearned for the silent blackness of her slumber. Ranthrop stirred under her arm, and a shiver ran across her skin as if she were being watched. A silly premonition—she wasn't alone, not with Ranthrop tucked in next to her.

A sputter noise above her, too high to have come from Ranthrop, drew her eyes open wide. Varmeer loomed above them, kneeling on the ground in front of Ranthrop. In his hands, he gripped his dagger, the blade glinting in the dying glow of the candlelight. She wasn't dreaming! She gasped and tried to scramble away while trying to pull Ranthrop's dead weight along with her.

"Varmeer! What are you doing?"

Ranthrop mumbled as his arms shadowboxed at the air. She panted, coming up on her knees to cover his body with her own. She watched Varmeer, noticing he had yet to look at her. She saw tears in his eyes just before he dropped his head. His arms sagged, and the dagger slumped to the ground with them.

"I can't…I can't do it," he managed.

"Do what? Murder us in our sleep?" she asked in a seething voice.

He lifted his head as his lip trembled. "I promised him. I promised I wouldn't let him live like this, but…I can't do it." He broke down, sobbing as he covered his eyes.

"It's not over yet, Varmeer. Give him time. He's strong, isn't he? Isn't he?" she asked, prodding him when she got no answer.

Varmeer smeared a hand underneath his nose, nodding.

"Good. Then he has a chance. Let him fight this. I can't imagine someone as colorful as Ranthrop being wiped away by a mere walk through a tunnel. I'll do everything I can to bring him back but give us time."

Varmeer nodded again, composing himself. "Yes, m'lady."

When he stood, he walked out as if he were the one in a daze. Valerie felt her breath rush out of her. She dropped back to the pelt and squeezed Ranthrop's arm, sidling up to him now more for her own comfort than his. She wasn't going to sleep a wink.

CHAPTER THIRTY-TWO

IN THE morning, the men came and loaded Ranthrop onto one of the rafts. He groaned and snarled in delusional protest as they tied him to the sail post. Varmeer seemed to avoid eye contact with Valerie. There were no words exchanged among the entire party. The mood for idle chitchat was a far-reaching dream.

Boarding the raft and even setting out to sea, strangely enough, did not concern her as much as it had on her first passage across the water. She nestled down next to Ranthrop, immersed in watching his facial expressions and talking him out of his madness. The fonskas did not spare them, even though the group had enough troubles without the buffeting attacks. Valerie remembered what Ranthrop had told her when they'd first crossed the sea: *I will not leave your side.*

She clung to him and that promise through the bashing of the vessel. She steadied his head in her hands to keep it from pounding into the sail post. The last thing he needed was a concussion. Before she knew it, the crafts had made it to the beach of Farwin Wood. She looked back over the misty waters, flummoxed that she had made the journey with such little distress and without any moral support.

Varmeer roused the men who had been left behind at the boathouse. He barked commands and walked with an urgency she had not seen him display until now. Her heart went out to him. She'd known Ranthrop just shy of a week. Varmeer had known him his entire life. To see the mighty lord fallen showed its toll on the loyal guard. He approached her as the men readied the skithers for the mountain ascent.

"M'lady, will you ride with the lord again or do you require your own skither?"

"I'd prefer to ride with Ranthrop to make sure he doesn't get hurt."

His features softened. "Very good, m'lady." He led her to the skither where Ranthrop was tied into the saddle chair, holding the ladder in place for her.

"I…I'm very sorry, Varmeer. I know this is all my fault."

Varmeer cast his eyes to the ground. "M'lady, I would not dare to blame you for the workings of foreign winds and spirits."

"No, but it was me who… He would not have come on this journey if I had not asked to go to Terradoon. He would never have gone into that tunnel." Saying the words aloud whittled away any remaining pride she had. Her guilt gnawed at her like a hungry animal.

Varmeer looked up at her and said, "I was wrong to plant any of my misgivings about your request. You sought to aid someone else just as Ranthrop sought to aid you by going into the tunnel. You both showed great bravery. I fear I may not have been so selfless if our roles were reversed. Even now," he gestured up to Ranthrop who writhed against his bindings in the saddle, "you bear the brunt of it. 'Tis I who owe the apologies."

She wanted to offer him words of comfort like she had all night to Ranthrop. Words that would erase the guilt he felt for not carrying out his request to kill Ranthrop and words to take away the guilt he felt for actually contemplating the request. Before she could think of what to say, he turned away and walked to his skither.

Valerie did her best to stay in the saddle, seated in the same position as she had been on the way down the mountain just days ago. Her weight on Ranthrop's lap kept his legs from thrashing around, but he jostled her whenever he flinched. He moaned in agony all the way up the mountain and halfway across the apex, arguing and pleading with faceless names. She did her best to distract him, and his rants gradually died down.

Shortly after they passed the guard shack on the shiny surface of the mountaintop, she heard the soft whistle of snoring. It was the first time since leaving the tunnel that he'd truly fallen asleep. What would be left of him when he awoke?

They reached the base on the other side of the mountain late in the afternoon. Varmeer led the party back to where they had camped the first night. Although they had made good time and there was still enough daylight that they could continue farther, she was grateful he decided to stop. Her eyes begged for rest, and she silently hoped that Ranthrop would continue sleeping if it brought him some semblance of peace. She didn't think she could stay awake through another night of guard duty if Varmeer mustered the courage to carry out Ranthrop's request. Something told her that the request had been long forgotten, but she wouldn't forgive herself if she found out the hard way.

She waited for her skither to stop so she could dismount with the others. She crawled gingerly off Ranthrop's lap, careful not to wake him, and climbed down the ladder. Varmeer and Winslow stood waiting when she touched the ground. The three of them jumped in unison at the sound of a groggy command from above.

"Varmeer?"

Varmeer's eyes traveled to the man in the saddle. "Yes, my lord?"

"Why do I feel…like I am tied to this saddle?"

"Ha!" Varmeer clamped Valerie's shoulder with a look of glee in his eyes, beaming from ear to ear.

"I'll have the men get the tents ready," she said with equal enthusiasm and hurried to rouse the other guards.

AFTER VALERIE finished brushing the knots out of her hair, the urgency to see Ranthrop returned. The sleep deprivation that had clung to her throughout the day was overruled by the curiosity pulsing through her veins. She set the brush in the cradle of her nightgown and picked at the bristles as she looked around her tent.

Her stomach was full of gorble meat, and she was happy it agreed with her much better than the first time she'd tried it. The mood of the men around the campfire during dinner had improved greatly from two days prior. Ranthrop had not joined them, but she saw Varmeer take a haunch of meat into his tent. The men had braced him between their shoulders as he'd staggered into it earlier, but at least he had walked on his own two feet.

Varmeer had told her over dinner that Ranthrop was much improved, but she would not sleep until she saw it for herself. She'd even snuck out the back of her tent to dump her bath bucket in the hopes of running into him. No longer able to suppress the anticipation, she slung her cloak over her shoulders and peered out the front of her tent.

The fire was waning, and the stones and stumps around it where the men had sat were empty. She pushed out the flap and ran on tiptoe over the cold dirt to the front of Ranthrop's tent. Her hand waivered in front of the leather flap. She patted it several times, bringing her mouth near the opening and called out, "Lord Ranthrop?"

It didn't seem odd to say that title now. He was a lord, after all—and this was his world. He'd certainly earned the title in her eyes.

"Enter," a familiar voice called from within.

Valerie pushed through the doorway and glanced across the tent. The sleeping pelts where they had slept were in the same location but Ranthrop wasn't.

"Lady Valerie. You are still awake?"

She followed the sound of his voice, staggering back when she located him. He sat bare-chested in his saddle chair in the corner of the tent. His skin glistened all the way down to his bare legs from the glowing candle on the woodblock. Wrapped around his waist was a thin cloth that stopped just above his knees.

"I didn't realize you were…I should go," she stammered, hiding her eyes as her back hit the wall of the tent.

"No. No, stay. Please. I wanted to see you, but I thought you would have already turned in for the night."

She drew her hand away from her cloak, showing only her profile. She focused on the ground, looking for a spot to settle. "You…are feeling better?"

"Here. Take my chair." The wicker creaked, and she looked up to find him standing in front of her.

"No. You can take…"

"Your face! What happened? Who did that to you?" His words came in a panic.

An instinctive hand went up to her cheek, feeling the side of her eye. She hadn't looked in a mirror for four days. Her fingers felt the puffiness, and she winced at the soreness. It was disconcerting to look at him when she had no idea how she appeared.

"I… You did."

She would have lied if she'd known the reaction it brought him. His hand reached for her face but halfway there his fingers closed, and he turned away.

"Varmeer said you tended to me throughout the night." His voice floated over his shoulder. "I dare say I deserved such diligent treatment."

"Deserved?" She watched the cords of muscles on his back shift as he reached up and rested his hand on the center post of the tent. "What was I supposed to do? Just leave you there alone to suffer?"

"You would have been better off. Look what it got you."

"I'm fine. It probably looks worse than it is. I'm just glad you're feeling better. I…was worried about you." She watched him drop his head, but he did not speak. "Ranthrop? What happened in that tunnel?"

His back rose with the sound of his breath, and he ran a hand through his damp hair. "I learned that I am a monster."

He was a lot of things but certainly not a monster. "Why would you say that?"

"I saw every horror I ever unleashed on anyone. I heard the cries and felt the pain of every man I killed in battle."

Her skin prickled with gooseflesh. How could he not think himself a monster after that? "But…it was a war. Death comes with war."

"Yes. And it stays. It stays long after the dead have gone."

"I don't doubt that you already knew that before today. Don't let this reminder destroy you. Someone could have killed you in the war too."

"Yes, but I lived. And when you are alive it is a conscious eternity to revisit your past. War makes you re-evaluate every moment of your life. It wasn't just them… I saw my father die all over again. I saw a woman I… A woman who…"

"Vasimus's sister?"

Between Ricky's and Sarah's stories, and what she'd skimmed through in the Blinney journals, she remembered the story of love rebuked. How the betrothed of Vasimus's sister, Deronda, had sent men after her lover—Ricky's father. She hadn't stopped before to piece together that the betrothed had been Ranthrop. As destructive as his actions sounded, she knew what it was like to feel duped, to be rejected.

She imagined a much younger, less controlled Ranthrop—it seemed an appropriate history for the man she had come to know. She couldn't believe, however, that anyone who'd floundered because of a hasty, impassioned decision hadn't paid for it with a wealth of remorse for the rest of their life. Or what it must have felt like to learn he'd unintentionally been the cause of Deronda's death. A weaker man would have been driven to madness years ago. His treatment of her, the way he insisted on protecting her—it all made sense now.

"So you know of Deronda," he said with a sigh. "I've often wondered what her life would have been like had she not met me, not been promised to me like property. She could have had children with Richard. They would have been Ricky's age by now."

"I can't imagine you haven't already spent years beating yourself up over her death…or your father's, for that matter," she added as she moved to his side. "You didn't kill them."

"My decisions killed them," he replied with bitterness and turned away from her. "It is the same thing."

Valerie pursued him with careful steps. "Do you think that's what Arlyle meant about your destiny? That you were supposed to be doused with a new flood of remorse? All that will do is leave you angry and bitter like this for the rest of your life. How do you think that will impact any decision you ever make again?" Ranthrop finally stopped pivoting away from her, and she halted once she faced him. "We all have to make decisions. It's the toss of a coin. I had no idea what my decision to come to Terradoon would bring. I never imagined any harm coming to you because of something I decided. Remorse is not your destiny, Ranthrop. I'm sure of it."

He finally looked at her, the expression on his face strained. "I have lived with remorse my entire life. It was not remorse that I learned from that tunnel," he murmured in a hushed tone. "It was gratitude."

"Gratitude? What do you have to be grateful for?"

"You, m'lady."

"Me?"

He continued as though he were fascinated, "Through the storm inside my head, I finally felt a sense of peace begin to pull me free. I heard your voice begging me to come back, assuring me that I was not lost. It gave me the strength to believe it was so."

A tingle ran down her arms as she listened. He had heard her. It had worked or at least helped. She felt less foolish for all the utterances she had doled out while he was unconscious, but now somewhat vulnerable, even though he didn't seem to realize they had actually occurred.

"Arlyle said to listen to the voice in my heart. It was you. It was your voice that I found there." He looked away, clearly embarrassed to admit such a remark. "I know you likely do not wish me to imagine you in such a way, but doing so saved me. That is why I am grateful. I am grateful to you." He let out a sour laugh. "It is a selfish thing to use your vision so ill, even in madness. I know. I apologize to you for that. Perhaps, I am still mad, for the memories sustain me even now as I see you standing here—a presence likely attributed only to dutiful pity and the kindness you so like to try and hide." He gave her a shy smile.

Her lungs expanded as the shock from his confession released her starvation. His skin called out to her, begging to be caressed, begging her to discover by touch that the man was back in his mortal shell. She stepped forward and cupped his face in her hands.

"You are not mad," she whispered, staring into his stormy green eyes. "I didn't think you would hear me, but it was the only thing I could think to do. I prayed, and I begged." She didn't understand why, but her words began to sound weepy. She grazed her thumb across his cheek as he stared at her in disbelief. "I have a lot to be grateful for too since my demands were answered."

Ranthrop reached for her face, cupping a gentle hand to her cheek. He stared at the tender skin below her eye. Her lashes fluttered as he leaned forward, placing a soft kiss there. The scent of his soapy skin, returned to its bark and sugary aroma, was like a warm breeze encompassing her. She opened her eyes to find his lips just before hers.

He murmured, "Someday I must find a way to thank this woman whose illness sent you here."

Her incredulous laugh was cut short as his lips captured hers. Gone was the fiery insistence and careless prying that he'd exhibited in the alcove of Groslivo Keep. His mouth was dutiful now, capturing one of her lips, lingering, and then the other. His hand found her waist while the other fingered a lock of her long black mane. His lips circled her face, placing kisses on her forehead, her cheek, her chin, and then finally returned to where she wanted them most as she wrapped her arms around his neck.

The Ranthrop she knew, the barely domesticated animal, purred as their bodies drew each other together with eager hands. The tongue that had wagged every husky, confounding, tempting, and delicate word met hers for a welcomed dance, and she reveled in tasting their maker as if it were a well-earned reward. The seasoned fingers that had wielded his sword against the fonskas, that had held her tight to him down the mountain, that had brushed her cheek, now drew away the tie of her cloak, sending it to the floor in a whoosh. Gooseflesh rippled across her arms, and she knew it was from the giddiness of excitement and not the chill of the night air.

Her fingers ventured across his shoulders and down his chest. She had to do something to increase his exploration. She needed his hands on her, needed to feel the warmth of his palms make contact with her flesh. He had more in him than this timid display of gentle pawing about her waist or the tender hand that trailed up and down her back.

He thought her a delicate flower, and she was flattered by it, but now she wanted the old Ranthrop—the less humbled one—and to discover all the unbridled passion she imagined him to possess. Her hand found the place where his waistcloth was secured. With a tug of her fingers she sent it sailing to the floor, hoping it would send the signal she wanted. Appropriate be damned. She'd earned a night of heaven.

Ranthrop's animal instincts kicked in. He moaned and wrapped his arms around her, erasing every inch of space that remained between them. A zip of electricity shot through her as his hand caressed her bottom, and he arched her backward to delve further into their kiss.

His head pulled slowly away, and she panted when she could no longer reach his lips. She opened her eyes and found him staring at her, his mouth open in wonder.

"What?" she asked in a panicked breath.

"Just…tell me I'm not still dreaming."

Her arms went slack against his chest, and she fought the urge to laugh. She pushed away enough to grasp the sides of her nightgown. With one swift movement, she brought the fabric up over her head and flung it across the tent. She watched his eyes as they trailed down her body. Her cheeks warmed at his awestruck perusal. She stepped forward, slid her hands up his massive arms, and whispered, "I don't care if you are dreaming as long as I can stay."

His intake of breath warmed her belly as he tugged her back to him, smiling as he brought his lips down to her mouth. A delicious dizziness swept through her head, and she ran her fingers into his wavy hair. The strong hand sliding down her thigh froze at the same time her heart stopped. Her eyes shot to the rustling tent flap as Ranthrop clenched her in his grasp.

Varmeer's muffled call came from the other side. "My lord, are you speaking to someone? Are you unwell again?"

Further proof they had nearly been one, they yelled in unison, "Go away!"

The flap fluttered, and she heard the sound of shuffling boots against the dirt outside. A thud from the other side of the precarious doorway followed along with a grumble. She turned her head to look at Ranthrop just in time to see a smirk creep across his face.

He swept her up into his arms, making her feel weightless, and shot over his shoulder, "I am more than well, Varmeer! Go to bed!"

Valerie tucked her head into his neck in her embarrassment, but she couldn't wipe the smile from her face. Lips nuzzled her earlobe, making her quiver.

"If you've gone shy on me now, I will break his neck," Ranthrop murmured as he set her down on the pelts.

Valerie took in the sight of the bared and brawny giant kneeling beside her. Resting on her elbows, her eyes trailed all the way to his face. "I think it would be impossible to be shy around you."

Her words betrayed her emotions as she blushed. Who wouldn't in front of all that masculinity waiting to devour them? His features softened, and he slid down next to her.

He drew a strand of hair away from her forehead. "I don't care. I love every shade of you, even your anger…because you are still there in the middle of it."

Valerie moved her lips but couldn't find any words. She remembered thinking she didn't need a man to feel like a woman. It was still true but there was something about feeling like a woman, especially because of him, that she didn't mind. She didn't mind it at all. She didn't feel owned or beholden. She knew exactly who she was and now there was a man who had seen exactly who she was and liked what he saw.

"Now…" Ranthrop purred, propping himself up on an elbow. He walked his index and middle finger in a path, starting at her neck and continuing down between her breasts. "What could I do for a lady in the same tent that would be deemed *appropriate*?"

Valerie smiled at his mischievous grin and slung her arms around his neck. "Stop talking, and kiss me."

"We should agree more often."

Ranthrop assured his silence when his lips captured hers. His hand slid up and down her ribcage, her arms—he couldn't seem to touch her enough. His curls tickled her collarbone when he bent to treat her breasts to his eager lips. Her nails dug into the muscles on his shoulders until her sanity reminded her she would never want to harm this man in the slightest.

She found a scar on his hand when it cupped her breast, his mouth distracted with peppering her belly. She tugged it to her, kissing the jagged line. When she discovered another across his forearm, she pampered it the same way. As he drew himself back up to her, she fingered another mar of his flesh just above his nipple. Tilting her head, she let her lips graze across the long line in several places. Sensing the stillness above her, she found him smiling down at her.

"It won't heal them," he whispered.

She cupped his face and rubbed her thumb across the pale line that curved under his chin. "I don't mind trying."

He stared at her, and she wondered what was going through his mind. What had she said or done to give him pause? His features seemed too serious compared to the playfulness she'd seen only moments ago. He lowered his body and his lips onto hers, and her curiosity drifted away. Again, his mouth was gentle, but soon the insistency overtook them.

Valerie reveled in how real every inch of his skin felt beneath her hands. A swirling giddiness built inside of her as he shifted to join them. Her breath caught in her throat as reality and storybook united with their bodies. She wrapped her legs around him as he rocked with steady, calculating movements, driving her to a fever.

"Where have you been all these years?" he said, moaning in her ear.

She felt her mouth curve at his words, more sensual than anything she'd ever heard from a lover. It couldn't be real, but somehow it was. He couldn't be real, but he was. His arms went around her waist and swept her up in a rush. She found herself on top of his lap, wrapped around him as the passionate dance continued.

The fur of the pelts tickled her toes. The soles of her feet nudged his backside. The skin there was warm, far from fictional. He cradled her in his arms and swam his fingers through the hair trailing down her back. Not shy at all, she thought as he let out sounds of satisfaction and took in the sight of her body.

It felt wondrous clinging to his powerful shoulders, feeling so delicate, and yet knowing she was the source of his passion. She was the pen, and he was the paper. The pressure inside her built and built like some unnatural thing. Lord, what would happen? Would she disappear? Would she wake up naked on the floor of the Allister's basement? Would he burst from the pages into oblivion?

The answer to what existed after the pinnacle came in the form of Ranthrop's husky gasps dusting the skin of her neck. He lowered her back to the ground with him. His heart pounded underneath her sweaty palm. Her awestruck eyes scanned the ceiling of the tent. She was still under the canopy made from the skins of fantastical animals. Still in the middle of mystical woods. Still in the arms of a fabricated man.

He nuzzled his lips against her cheek. "Why do you look as though you are searching for something?"

"I'm searching for myself," she said, panting as she chuckled. "I thought I would disappear."

"Tsk," he said, clucking his tongue and pulling the covers over them. "Don't do that. I wouldn't know how to search the thin air to find you."

The pangs of delicious excitement crumbled inside of her. Tomorrow. Tomorrow she would be no more than thin air in his world.

CHAPTER THIRTY-THREE

THROUGH MORNING and early afternoon, Valerie smiled at the rapt attention Ranthrop paid her on the ride back to Groslivo Stronghold the next day. He didn't seem to mind if any of his guards or Varmeer noticed. If the men had any opinions, they kept them to themselves. The guards laughed and joked with each other as they rode, clearly grateful to be alive and returning home unscathed after their quest.

They reached the stronghold a little after noon and returned the skithers to their lairs. Valerie gave a silent thanks to hers, wondering if she would ever see one again. The animal snuffed a powerful breath into her shoulder then turned with a screech to the comfort of its dwelling.

A pair of powerful arms swept around her waist, and she laughed as Ranthrop lifted and spun her around. He treated her to a hungry kiss as he lowered her back to the ground. She watched with astonishment as he snapped up her hand in his and began to walk in stride with her to the keep.

"When are you leaving?"

"I…I should go as soon as possible." Why did it pain her to say the words? She was eager to get back to see if she could help Franci. She should have no regret.

"We will have a feast to celebrate our successful journey. Can you delay your departure until then?"

"I would love to, but I really shouldn't." The disappointment in his eyes was touching. She looked away, suspecting he could easily change her mind if he prodded further. Her eyes locked with Ricky's who stood on the patio at the edge of the keep. His head was tilted, and she noticed the arch of his brow as he stared at her and Ranthrop. She tugged her hand out of his grasp, smoothing it over the billows of her dress as they approached him.

"Had a good time, did you?" Ricky asked.

Valerie shot him a don't-go-there look. "No. It was horrible actually." She sighed and wrapped her arms around him for a hug. "You're lucky you didn't go, believe me," she murmured into his ear.

She felt Ricky's hand pat her awkwardly, and she drew back, realizing just how out of character the embrace was for her. She released him, combing her fingers casually through her hair as though she hadn't lost her wits and gone sentimental.

"Lord Ricky! What an adventure you missed, my boy!" Ranthrop threw an arm around Ricky's shoulder as they continued into the keep. "And what a brave lady you brought from Blinney with you. I owe her my life."

"Your life?"

Valerie waved her hand through the air. "He's exaggerating."

"'Tis no exaggeration at all! Why, I was just saying this occasion deserves a feast. I know you must make haste to return to your ill friend, but can you not convince Lady Valerie to delay your departure for several hours?"

Valerie cast a dark look at Ricky. "A feast? Of course!" he exclaimed.

"Wonderful!" Ranthrop slapped Ricky on the back. "I'll go alert the kitchen staff. It will be ready in no time. Make yourselves comfortable until then."

After Ranthrop disappeared into the keep, she snapped, "Ricky! Did you forget why we came here? The clock is ticking, and we don't know what could have happened to Franci by now!"

"Oh, come on. It's not like they'll be waiting to throw us a parade when we get back. And what could a few more hours hurt?"

"Hopefully nothing," she said, grumbling. "Fine, but not a word of this to anyone. Agreed?"

"You don't have to tell me twice. As soon as we're done eating, we'll head back to Allister Hall and go home."

"Good."

"Good? What? No protests?"

"Protests? Why would I protest? I know we have to go home." Didn't she sound convincing enough? Her mind was busy contemplating the feasibility of slipping into the book periodically to visit Ranthrop. What good could come of it? Yet, what harm?

She stopped when she noticed Ricky was no longer beside her. She turned around and found him two steps behind. He met her with an emphatic query. "What's with you? You haven't even asked me what I did while you were gone."

"What?" She rubbed her forehead. "I'm sorry. What happened while I was gone?"

Ricky gawked at her. "Um...do the words *I can't swim* ring a bell?"

"Oh. Yeah, speaking of that, you didn't tell me I'd have to cross a sea to get to Terradoon."

"There's a sea here?"

She threw a hand on her hip, finding her haughtiness returning. "Yeah. Complete with sea monsters, thank you very much."

"Wow." Ricky stared in wonder, his imagination taking hold of him. "Then you'll probably be even more happy to know that I found a solution to your phobia."

She waited for the answer to his riddle. Clearly, she was missing something. His shoulders dropped, and he splayed his fingers out, palms up. She shook her head as if to signal she still couldn't read his mind.

"I found a new way home! We don't have to drown ourselves."

"Oh. What do we have to do?"

Ricky schooled his features, animating his head as he began having a conversation with an invisible version of her. "*Congratulations, Ricky!* Why, thank you. *How did you do it, Ricky?* Well, it's an interesting story. What? What was that? *I can't believe you went to all that trouble just for me. Thank you, Ricky!*"

A swift crack to his bicep jolted him from his charades. "How do we get home now, *Ricky?*"

He rubbed his arm, scowling. "I wrote a book about Blinney Lane at Allister Hall and it worked. I fell asleep next to it and woke up back at home by the book in my aunt's shop."

"Really?" She gaped at him as they entered the keep and walked down the alcove. "That's so brilliantly simple I wouldn't have thought of it."

"You're welcome."

He still looked annoyed so she raised her hand to pat his shoulder. He flinched, but she completed the affectionate congratulations. "Thank you. I'm impressed."

"So…you and Ranthrop got along on your adventure?"

She shrugged as they strolled along. "Yes. Well, enough."

"Really? And here I thought you would have spent the whole time arguing."

"Arguing? No. Well, he was a little difficult at first, but we straightened everything out. He's a good guide, actually. Better than I would have expected." The feel of skin on her hand pulled her gaze, and she flinched when she saw Ricky holding her hand. She yanked it away, her lip curling. "What the hell are you doing?"

"Oh, I'm sorry," Ricky crooned, placing his hand over his heart. "I thought holding hands was your new thing. Or was Ranthrop just being a *good guide* on your way up the stairs?"

She rolled her eyes. "What? Should I have refused? You're the one who seemed to be worried about offending people here."

"Ah, maybe you're right. I mean, this is certainly a step up from the last time I saw you two together. He doesn't look like he got any more black eyes since you left. Or is it because he gave you one?"

"I fell," she said, gritting her teeth as she touched her cheek.

"Well done on not getting pummeled. We'll have to elect you the new ambassador of peace between our two nations."

She swung at him again, missing on purpose. "Oh, piss off!" Against her nature, however, her mouth curved up at the corner.

"Just do me a favor and don't start any wars like my father did," he whispered conspiratorially to her as they rounded the corner into the vestibule by the main door.

Valerie stopped in her tracks at the sound of laughter coming from farther down the spacious hallway that ran the width of the keep. Some forty feet away, near the kitchen doorway, she located the source of feminine sounds coming from two curvaceous women. They were difficult to miss given the provocative cut of their dresses and how they clung to Ranthrop. One, in particular, clung to him with her lips...on his!

As the woman's lips left Ranthrop's, she saw a smile spread across his face. Her heart slammed into her throat. The women whispered to him, tugging at his arms, and beckoning him to follow them to the stairwell leading to the sleeping quarters. Ears at attention, she listened intently.

"Maybe later," he responded, patting one woman on the bottom and sending them on their way.

Ricky chuckled at her side. "Man, that guy has to shake them off with a stick."

A rush of rage-filled blood coursed through her as she watched a laughing Ranthrop saunter into the kitchen. The silly visions she had entertained of riding stroomphblutels back to Groslivo Stronghold to see him in the near future mutated into something less pleasant. Images of laughing women, perched on his lap, as he waved for her to join the masses that stood in line to please him, clouded her head like a doomsday storm. Through the thunderous humiliation, she felt something tug at her sleeve.

Ricky's voice penetrated her thoughts. "Earth to Valerie."

"We need to leave," she said, grinding her teeth together.

"But…the feast."

"Ricky!" Her heart hammered erratically like it had lost a vital screw. Tears threatened her eyes. Her fingernails dug into the palms of her hands. "Get me the hell out of here! Right now!"

CHAPTER THIRTY-FOUR

BLINNEY LANE

FRANCI'S HAND felt like ice in Valerie's grasp as she sat next to the woman's bed. Her frail friend had fallen asleep after she'd administered the venstra concoction. The sight was more reassuring than the thousand-mile stare she'd found on the woman's face upon returning from Farwin Wood. Franci had refused to focus on anyone who came to visit her. It was as if she had given up. Perhaps Valerie was projecting her own heartache, but she sensed something had broken either Franci's or Lorna's heart as well. The sympathy she had for the women was apt.

Sarah had closed her shop to watch Valerie mix and administer the venstra potion. Ricky, Shelby, Reggie, and Mary had also been present for the event. Valerie had been so lost staring down at their old friend that the large audience didn't bother her. The room gradually cleared out when everyone realized the results wouldn't be instantaneous. Mary, however, had lingered, and she eventually noticed her mother's worried gaze was for more than Franci's condition.

"Are you all right?" Mary had asked at one point.

"I'm fine."

Mary sat in silence for several hours, her chair occasionally creaking under her impatient weight. Valerie mustered only short answers to her inquiries but oddly, her mother didn't have many. Around ten o'clock, Mary finally got up, the silence likely more than she could tolerate.

She walked over and squeezed Valerie's shoulder. "Don't worry about working tomorrow. You look exhausted. Try to get some rest."

The tenderness in Mary's voice caught her off-guard. She nodded and watched her walk out of the room. Looking down at herself, she realized she still wore the ridiculous red dress she'd had on when she left Farwin Wood. At least her diligence to Franci hadn't been sidelined by the selfish feelings of betrayal that swam inside her. She'd come straight to Franci's after she emerged in Sarah's basement.

The recent memories of riding away from Groslivo Stronghold, urging her stroomphblutel to a speed it did not appreciate, embarrassed her now. She should be thinking of Franci and only Franci, but the bitter thoughts crept in against her will.

Ranthrop was a womanizer. The ink on the pages that created him must have given him that DNA. There was nothing she could do to change that. He was a storybook character with flaws like any real-life person. *The Lands of Farwin Wood* wasn't meant to be a fairy tale for women to find their Prince Charmings. She hadn't even been looking for a Prince Charming, so why did it hurt so much? How had she been swept away by his charm so quickly? She had been a fool. They say God protects the foolish, but she had seen no evidence of this.

A storybook character. What had she been thinking? Her error left a pungent vulnerability that seemed to rob her of valuable wisdom points in the game of life. How long would it take to get them back?

IN THE wee hours of the night, Reggie made his way into the room. Valerie knew this because the sound of his constant pacing in the living room had stopped. Why had he been out there all evening?

He grasped the foot of the bed railing and asked, "How much longer?"

"I don't know."

"Will she...be the same? I mean, will she be her old self again when it's over?"

Valerie turned her tired eyes to Reggie's. His hair was a mess and there was a five o'clock shadow peppering the lower half of his jaw. When had he last slept? The respect that welled up inside her for him was surreal. Respect for Reggie Nurscher, imagine that. It had been a day of surprises. Would Ranthrop look the same way if she were the one lying in the bed right now? Probably not. She let out a selfish puff of air and looked back at Franci's sleeping face.

"I don't know, Reggie. I hope so. I'm sorry I can't give you a more positive answer."

"She doesn't deserve this," he muttered, pacing at the foot of the bed.

She watched his agitated movements. It was so unlike him to be concerned about anyone but himself. From what she'd gathered, he had done the bulk of looking after Franci while she'd been away.

Around four in the morning, Franci began to toss and turn. Her moaning brought Reggie back into the room. He rushed to the other side of the bed, his face white with worry.

"What's happening? Why's she making that noise?"

"I don't know. Maybe it's finally taking effect." Valerie struggled to take hold of Franci's hand again. She patted it and called out, "Franci? Franci, it's Valerie. Are you all right?"

"Is it making her sick? It's making her sick. Can't you stop it?"

Reggie sat on the bed and cradled Franci in his arms. Valerie's heartbeat quickened, waiting to see what would happen. Her breath caught in her throat at the sight of Reggie working himself into a tizzy. He was genuinely concerned for the woman. Didn't that beat all?

Franci coughed, and her body jerked. She sputtered, making a horrid gagging sound. A brown, slimy substance spewed out of her mouth and projected onto the front of Reggie's shirt, the same color of the mixture that Valerie had given her. To her surprise, Reggie didn't balk at being soiled. He clasped onto Franci's jaw and turned her in his arms so she could expel anything else onto the floor.

Valerie grabbed the wastebasket and a box of tissues from the nightstand. She rushed to Reggie's side of the bed and placed the bucket in Franci's line of view as the woman continued to cough.

"Come on, Franci! Wake up! You're okay. You're going to be okay!" Reggie pleaded.

Franci's eyes fluttered open, and she moaned. Her glazed stare focused down at the wastebasket as she heaved for breath. Valerie reached for the corner of the woman's mouth with a tissue.

"Franci? Are you all right?"

"Ugh. What did I eat?" Franci said, groaning.

"Nothing sweetie, you've been out of it for a few days." She wiped Franci's chin and swept her hair away from her face. "Do you know where you are?"

Franci's brow wrinkled as she looked at Valerie, but then she glanced over her shoulder at the room. "I'm in my bedroom. Why?"

"Do you know…*who* you are?"

"What?" Franci coughed again, bringing a hand to her mouth. "I'm *me*. Why are you asking me that?"

Reggie turned Franci in his arms, using a gentle voice that Valerie had never heard him use before. "You haven't been yourself, old girl. Do you know who I am?" He gazed down at her with a hopeful look on his face.

"You're Reggie."

Reggie let out a breath and laughed. He squeezed Franci against him, nearly pulling her into the pool of vomit on his shirt.

"Careful there, Reggie," Valerie warned, bracing her hand on Franci's shoulder to keep her clear of the stain. "You're going to run her through the Lorna juice."

"Lorna juice?" Franci scrunched her face and then looked back at Reggie. "Why are you holding me, and why are you sitting on my bed?"

Valerie watched Reggie's face sag. His hold on Franci went limp as the woman sat up. "You…don't remember anything?" he asked, sounding disappointed.

"What are you two talking about?"

"Franci, what's the last thing you remember?" Valerie asked and helped Franci sit up on the bed.

"I was…having tea and making my Halloween costume."

Reggie slid off the bed and stared at Franci. "That's the last thing you remember?"

Franci looked down at the baggie T-shirt she wore over her underwear. She tucked her bare legs under the covers, pulling the sheet up over her chest. "Well, yes." Valerie watched as Franci ran her hand through her long, loose hair, clearly feeling self-conscious. "I'm sorry I threw up on you. Why are you here?"

Reggie glanced down at his shirt. "I…don't worry about it. I just came by to check on you. I'm glad you're feeling better." He got up as if he were in a daze and walked out of the room.

"Are you feeling okay now, Franci?" Valerie inquired. She heard the main door of the apartment close. Reggie had wasted no time in leaving.

"I have a bit of a headache, but my stomach is starting to feel better. What day is it? How long have I been in bed?"

Valerie got Franci a glass of water and began to break the news to the woman once she returned. "It's Friday morning, Franci."

"I made that costume last night, Thursday."

"No, Franci. You must have made it *last* Thursday. You haven't been yourself for over a week. You dressed up like Lorna DuClaire, and we think it took a hold on you. You were acting just like her and treating everyone like people she knew or like characters from her films."

"What? A week! How could I lose a whole week and not remember it?"

Valerie grimaced. "You might be glad that you don't remember it."

"Why? What did I do?"

She chuckled and patted Franci's hand. "You gave the performance of a lifetime."

"Oh." Franci's voice sounded wary as she stared down at the bed. "Did I offend anyone or do anything embarrassing?"

"Nothing too awful. Don't worry."

Franci surveyed Valerie's outfit. "Who are you supposed to be?"

A walking disaster, she wanted to reply. "I'm just me. We had a council meeting and decided that someone would go to Farwin Wood to try and find a cure for you. Ricky and I went and found something we thought might help and brought it back. I gave it to you late yesterday afternoon."

"Oh."

She could tell Franci's mind was in overdrive. The poor thing.

"Is that what made me sick just now?"

"Yes. I'm sorry, but we didn't know what else to try."

"*You're* sorry? Why should you be sorry? I'm sorry you had to go to so much trouble for me. I can't believe Sarah let Ricky go back into the book. And Mary. I bet Mary put up a fuss over you going."

"Well, they were overruled," she murmured, picking at a thread on her gown.

The lingering silence broke as Franci spoke with forlorn words. "I just wanted to be someone else, you know? Someone a little more glamorous than me. I still wanted to be me, just a better version of me. Now that mother's gone I…realized how alone I'm going to be. I don't imagine that anyone would want…this," Franci said, touching the scars on her neck with one hand while gesturing at herself with another. Valerie made a pained expression, and before she could disagree, Franci held up a hand. "No. Really. I've convinced myself I'm no looker. I'm not denying I did it, hoping to catch some man's eye, but it's more than that. I looked in the mirror and didn't like what I saw anymore. I thought if I…updated my packaging, I would love myself more. I guess I got a little carried away though." Franci smiled and looked away. "That probably sounds silly, doesn't it?"

"I don't think it's silly at all. You know…you were quite the eye-catcher in your Lorna get-ups." She cracked a smile when her comment caught Franci's interest. She reached for a strand of Franci's hair and ran it through her fingers. "I'd recommend a braid. You still have gorgeous, shiny black hair, and I think something simple like that wouldn't look as if you were trying too hard. And, it would still be a change from those buns you always pile on top of your head. I didn't realize your hair was so long."

"What did I wear? Did anyone see my scars?"

"You looked like you were going to a cocktail party in the thirties, but I only saw you twice before I went into the book."

"Oh, that's right. I'm sorry. I'm worrying about what I looked like and here you must have had the adventure of a lifetime at my expense."

"No, it's okay. You looked gorgeous, but I have a few turtlenecks you can have if you like. Maybe wear a nice skirt to go with them. I don't think it's a good idea to wear anything that looks like something Lorna might have worn for a while. I didn't mind getting that cure for you, but I have no desire to ever go back there."

"That sounds nice. Thank you," Franci said in a humble voice. "Why wouldn't you go back? I've always wondered what it was like in that book. Did you meet Sarah's Vasimus?" Franci brought a hand to her mouth. "Don't tell Henry I asked, or Sarah for that matter."

"No, I didn't meet him." She ignored Franci's other question, hoping the woman would forget and not press for a response.

"Did you meet any other men?"

Valerie got up off the bed. The curious and lucid questions were proof enough that Franci was in the clear. "Yes. A few. Why don't you try and get some real rest now. I'll bring the clothes by for you later."

"I will." Franci slipped back under the covers, and Valerie brought the comforter up over her. "Were they handsome?"

"Who?"

"The men in Farwin Wood? I imagine them all as tall, handsome, and charming."

"Some of them were."

"I knew it! Real knights in shining armor. How did you resist it, Val?"

Valerie stopped at the doorway, squeezing her hand on the knob. "They *aren't* real, Franci. And charm can be overrated."

CHAPTER
THIRTY-FIVE

FARWIN WOOD

MY LORD! I have been searching every village from here to Naublock for you. Why didn't you wait for me?" Varmeer asked, calling out from on top his stroomphblutel as he met Ranthrop on the road.

"Because you've proved to be utterly useless in looking out for my best interests!" Ranthrop exclaimed as his beast neared Varmeer's.

"Useless? I thought I nearly saved your life a few days ago? Does that not count for something?"

Ranthrop's face hurt from the sour expression he'd been wearing since yesterday afternoon when he'd discovered Ricky and Valerie were gone. Ricky, he could do without a good-bye from, but Valerie… He had things to do with Valerie, sentiments to convey, things to learn about her, and now…words to speak. How could she leave without letting him know?

"It counts for nothing if you let my guests slip through my fingers without so much as a smidgeon of effort to keep track of them!" He directed his stroomphblutel to continue its ragged trot right past Varmeer.

"My lord, I thought all was well and a feast was to be had. I commenced my bath and then informed the wenches the men would be gathering for the evening's festivities. It wasn't until then that I discovered Lord Ricky and the lady had gone. I came to you straight away when I heard the news of their quick departure from the stable master."

"Wenches?" He whipped his head around and saw Varmeer struggling to turn his stroomphblutel around to pursue him. "You were busying yourself with wenches when you were calling out for your Trina just the other night? Ha! Your loyalty falters at me, I see."

"The wenches were not for me!"

"Oh? And do you always bathe before you simply converse with wenches?"

"I thought after the long journey that I would be allowed the luxury of a bath, m'lord. I do apologize if you prefer me to stink."

"Ha! So you don't deny it?"

"That I am clean?" Varmeer asked as he caught up to him.

"No! That you wasted no time in dallying with the wenches instead of tending to my guests!" He waited for Varmeer's innocent expression to fade now that he had cornered him in the verbal spar.

"I told you. I informed the ladies that their presence would be welcomed by the men at the feast last evening and then I came straight away to you once the stable master sought me out."

"Ladies? They are not ladies. They are wenches. There's no need for them to laze about my keep when they can certainly meet men outside of my walls."

When Ranthrop heard no reply, he glanced over. Varmeer gave him an incredulous look, as they trotted along.

"What?" Ranthrop snapped.

In a suspicious voice, Varmeer asked, "Where have you been?"

"I have been to Allister Hall only to learn from Miss French that Lord Ricky and Lady Valerie headed back to Blinney. I've spent all last night searching every village from the stronghold to the base of the northern mountains for any word of which way they have gone."

"Oh," Varmeer replied. After they had traversed down the road for several more minutes back to the south, he asked curiously, "And where are we going now?"

"We are not going anywhere. I am headed back to speak to Miss French for directions on how the blazes to get to Blinney! You are going back to the stronghold."

How did he get stuck with such an obnoxious confidant? The silent pauses between queries annoyed him to no end. He knew each would be followed by a placating riddle meant to sway him from whatever he was trying to do. His temper often guided his decisions, he realized, but not this time. Now his task was clear to him, all feelings aside.

People from Blinney rarely came to Farwin Wood. If he didn't stop Valerie before she returned home, he might never see her again. Something was wrong. After what had passed between them, she wouldn't leave without telling him goodbye unless she had a change of heart. What worried him was that he had misread her heart. What perplexed him was that he desperately cared what was in her heart. It had hit him the moment he realized she was gone.

"And what am I to do at the keep when I get there?" Varmeer's voice interrupted his thoughts.

"Rouse the drunken men to clean up the hall, see to the stable repairs, dismiss the wenches! Why are you asking me this? You know what needs to be done!"

They approached a fork in the road, and Ranthrop continued on course for the one leading to Oedher Village. "Very well, my lord," Varmeer said.

"VASIMUS! THANK the stars you are here. How in the blazes do you get to Blinney?" Ranthrop exclaimed as he strode through the courtyard outside of Allister Hall.

"Blinney? Why in the world would you need to know that?"

"Lady Valerie, the woman Lord Ricky brought here with him…I need to find her."

"Ranthrop, you cannot go to Blinney," Vasimus warned and clasped a hand on the man's shoulder.

Ranthrop shrugged his arm away. "What do you mean I *cannot* go? You'll do well to remember I rule half the territory here. We are equals, old boy! You cannot command when and where I may travel."

"Ranthrop, calm down. It's not like that. I'm sure there's no pressing need for you to go is all."

"That means you're not going to help me. Some ally you are. You were a better enemy." He stormed away as he continued speaking, his voice carrying from the hall. "Fine! I don't need you. Perhaps I can persuade the workers of Allister Hall to come to their senses."

"Oh, fire and wind," Vasimus muttered and hurried after him. "What the blazes has gotten into him?" He waved for Dergus to return to his duties. There was no need to put the old man into the crossfire.

Inside the hall, he found Ranthrop prowling as he took giant steps back and forth, shouting, "Miss French? Netta! Show yourself!"

From the corner of his eye, he noticed Ophelia poking her head out of the kitchen. He glanced back and saw Ranthrop pacing away from her. He looked back to her and shook his head. She retreated back into the kitchen.

"Ranthrop! Stop this now, and tell me what is troubling you," he called as he walked over to meet him.

"Troubling me?" Ranthrop whirled around, flailing his arms. "For one, I'm learning that everyone treats me either like a child who deserves no worthy answers or a contagious invalid that should be avoided. Tell me, which is your perspective?"

"That is not the case. Just calm down and explain to me why you need to get to Blinney so badly?"

"I already told you! I need to speak to Lady Valerie. There's been…a misunderstanding of sorts."

"What kind of misunderstanding?"

"The kind I don't care to share with you! Now, are you going to tell me how to get there or not?"

Vasimus frowned, setting his hands on his hips. "Not if you plan on going there with that temper. I feel a sense of obligation to protect them from such a visitor."

"Protect them?" Ranthrop stepped forward. "From me? I have no intention of doing harm to anyone ever again. I only wish to speak on terms of friendship to one person." He held up his finger to accentuate his demand. "One person and as soon as I have done that I will return. Now are you going to help me or are you just going to stand there and waste air?"

"Pfft, what a convincing show of diplomacy." He shook his head, gesturing toward Ranthrop. "Tell me, is that the amiable face you plan on wearing when you deliver these terms of friendship to this lady?"

Ranthrop let out a growl. He lunged forward and grabbed Vasimus's tunic in his fists, yanking the man forward. Vasimus planted his feet, countering Ranthrop's hold with his own grip on the man's clothing.

"Don't be a wickrit's ass, tell me which way to go!"

"Not…if my life…depended on it, you thickheaded knuckle dragger!" Vasimus said, gritting his teeth as Ranthrop backed him into one of the chairs by the hearth. "Are you trying to start another war? What's gotten into you?"

"Don't come at me with threats of war! This has nothing to do with our people, only their selfish leader and I," Ranthrop yelled as Vasimus spun them round, getting the upper hand, and backing him over the chair.

"Selfish? How am I being selfish?"

"You know how to get there! You've been blessed with love from Blinney. I've paid for my sins long enough. You know I regret all that happened with your sister and the war, so why won't you tell me? Why should I be denied my chance at happiness?"

Vasimus felt his footing slip as the shock of Ranthrop's words hit him. His lapse of judgment allowed Ranthrop enough leeway to force him backward and into the table. He winced as the pain shot up his spine, ignoring it as he gazed in astonishment at the angry man over top of him. "You've fallen in love with her," he said, gasping.

A stinging sensation pierced his cheek, and he squeezed his eyes shut as the prickly object jabbed his skin. Ranthrop's hold loosened, and he heard the bristle of reeds. Sitting up, he deflected whatever was attacking him.

Netta's voice shrieked beside them. "Stop it! Stop it this instant. Both of you!"

Vasimus peered over the crook of his elbow as Netta's broom came at him again. He rolled off the side of the table and used it as a barricade between the livid housekeeper who now jabbed at Ranthrop.

"Me?" Ranthrop said, holding his forearms up to block her onslaught. He jerked a thumb toward Vasimus. "He started it!"

"I started it?" Instinctively, he grabbed ahold of Ranthrop's shoulder. Ranthrop smacked his hand away. Vasimus flinched when he saw the broom come at his face again and deflected the fanned reeds with his arm. He heard Ranthrop chuckle until Netta bashed the man in the face with the flat side of the broom's reeds.

"All right! All right," Ranthrop complained and wiped at his face.

"What a pair of lords you two are!" Netta yelled. "I've known you both since you were shorter than my knee! Knew both your parents too! They never raised you to squabble like hungry kouklas."

Vasimus offered his guilty condolences. "I'm sorry, Miss French. We should not be fighting in your hall."

Netta nodded at him, turning her gaze to Ranthrop. "Shouldn't be fighting at all! Not after the last twenty years!"

"No. Of course not, Miss French," Ranthrop muttered and straightened out his tunic.

Netta adjusted her apron and the handkerchief round her head. She rested the end of her broom on the ground and took a deep breath. "Now, what is all this fuss about?"

Ranthrop began to pace again, his hands on his hips. Vasimus gave Netta a speaking look and said, "Ranthrop has a pressing desire to travel to Blinney."

Netta's eyes rounded. "To Blinney? Well…that's not possible."

"I know. I've told him as much."

"Not possible?" Ranthrop flailed his arms. "What do you mean *not possible*? First Sarah and Richard, then Shelby and Ricky, now Valerie. It seems quite possible that there is a way from here to there. Why will the only two people who seem to know how to get there not give me some simple directions so I can be on my way?"

"It's not that simple," Vasimus replied.

"Look, yes it is! I'll show you," Ranthrop said, his voice growing high. He stuck out his index finger and spun around in a circle. "Just point, damn it!"

"It's not possible," Netta repeated. "We don't travel to Blinney. End of story."

"We? Well, what about me?"

"We *is* you!" Netta added.

Ranthrop growled and pulled at his hair. He laughed hysterically, dropping his face in his hands. "Have I lost my mind—"

"I made a promise to Ricky that I would never tell anyone how to get to Blinney," Vasimus replied.

"Ricky? He and I are on good terms. I've just helped them find a cure for a friend of theirs in Blinney. I'm sure he would not mean to exclude me. I could send him a message and request his permission first if they have such strict guidelines on visitors."

Vasimus rubbed the bridge of his nose and shook his head. "No…you can't."

"You won't even send a simple message on my behalf? This is getting preposterous! Even for you, Vasimus."

"It's not that I will not. I cannot! It's not possible!"

"Argh!" Ranthrop yelled. The man picked a weighty chair up and heaved it into the air. It tumbled several feet away, sending a clatter echoing up to the rafters. Dropping to his knees, Ranthrop gripped onto the hair at his temples. "Will no one have mercy on me? I have to find her!"

Netta gawked at the giant man sprawled on the floor by her feet. With a slack jaw, she turned her questioning expression to Vasimus.

His haggard breath cut through the silence, and he waved his fingers in the air. "Oh, let him go, Netta. I don't care to deal with all the complaints I'll get should we let him stay here like this. You know how long he broods. After all, it's not every day Ranthrop Groslivo falls in love."

"Hmm," Netta said, snorting. "That's not what I've heard."

CHAPTER
THIRTY-SIX

BLINNEY LANE

HEY, MARY," Ricky called as he approached her store counter. Mary straightened her stack of receipts and noticed the book bag slung over his shoulder.

"On your way to class or coming home?"

"Nah, I'm done for the day, but I've got enough homework here from last week to keep me busy the rest of the day."

"Oh, I bet. You really shouldn't have gone, especially when you had other obligations."

Ricky dropped his bag on the floor. "It had to be done. How's Franci doing? My aunt said she came around early this morning."

Mary pursed her lips. She didn't mean to sound disparaging all the time. Thanks to Ricky, Franci had recovered and he'd brought her daughter home safe. It was plenty to be grateful for; she just never managed to convey what she really felt. Anyone she'd known as a child were always children in her mind. She'd learned the hard way this week not to think like that.

"Francis is doing well," she added in a more gentle voice. "She called me a little while ago to say she's up on her feet. She doesn't remember anything, thank goodness, but at least she knows she's Francis again."

"Good." Ricky nodded, letting out a breath.

"Did you happen to notice if Regis opened his shop today?"

"No, I haven't been down that way. I just stopped here to see if you'd heard anything about Franci."

"Oh. All right." Mary frowned and fussed with the receipts again.

"Why?"

"It's nothing really. It's just that..."

"What is it, Mary?"

Mary huffed. She was going to have a difficult time getting used to treating Ricky and Valerie like adults. She was the adult. She wasn't supposed to confide her worries to them. "The night before you and Valerie came back I...I smelled something burning and heard a noise in the courtyard. I looked out from my porch and found Regis burning something behind Franci's place." Mary wrung her hands together. She didn't know why the sight had made her uncomfortable other than it seemed so unlike the man.

"What was he burning?"

"He... Well, I walked over to find out. He seemed rather upset, beside himself almost." Reggie actually had tears in his eyes, but she wasn't going to divulge that. It didn't seem appropriate to talk about someone else's misery. And she still didn't quite understand how the whiny, grump of a man had been moved to such an act of compassion. "He...was burning all of Francis's clothes."

Ricky was thoughtful in his silence before he responded. "That was smart, actually. If the clothes made her act like

Lorna, the best thing to do would be to get rid of anything that looked like something Lorna might have worn."

"Yes, I suppose you're right," she murmured. He hadn't seen Reggie stuffing the clothes violently into the burn barrel, nor had he heard Reggie scream, "She has to come back, Mary! We can't lose her!" It was more than she knew how to handle. She'd finally calmed him down enough and got him to go back inside.

Ricky interrupted her thoughts. "Is Valerie in the back?"

"No, she's…resting at the house."

"Oh. Well, tell her I… Tell her I stopped by." He picked up his bag, weaving his arms through the straps.

"Ricky, what happened in Farwin Wood?"

"We went to Ranthrop Groslivo's keep to talk to a healer about a cure, and Valerie went with them to find it."

"Yes, I know that, but did anything else happen?"

"What do you mean?"

Mary glanced at some customers in her shop and ran her fingers through the side of her swept-up hair. "Did something happen to my daughter? She…doesn't seem the same."

Valerie had been awake when she went up to her room to check on her that morning. She knew this because she'd come around the side of the bed. She wanted to look at her face, assuring herself that she really was back home. Valerie's slack hand was petting her loyal cat, Jackal. When she looked down, Valerie closed her eyes the moment Mary appeared, but she knew Valerie's eyes had been red from crying.

Valerie didn't cry. Even as a child, she had been tough and happy-go-lucky. She had to be tough growing up on Blinney Lane. And now, tears. Twice in just a little over a week. The first time she knew she'd been to blame, but now? If Ricky didn't know what had broken her fiery girl's spirit, she might never find out. They had never shared their heartaches or weaknesses with each other. She was trapped being the only kind of mother she knew how to be to a daughter that likely needed more than she possessed.

"If something happened, she'd have to tell you about it. Sorry, I can't help."

She wanted to believe he was hiding something, but he looked too sympathetic for her to cast judgment. "You have helped, Ricky. You kept her from having to go through the water. I'm sure I couldn't have endured that."

Ricky let out a nervous chuckle. "Let's just keep that on the down…let's just keep that quiet, okay?"

She nodded. "I haven't forgotten. Your secret's safe with me. No one will ever find out."

"Yeah. Sure. I can imagine what my aunt would say if she ever found out." His lack of confidence betrayed him as he started to turn away.

"Ricky? You might think about giving her a little more credit than you do." She pulled open a drawer behind the counter and produced a set of keys, holding them out to him. "The council voted while you were away. If you're still determined…the public house is yours."

"What? Really?" Ricky turned to look through the window toward his aunt's shop and then back at the keys. He reached for them as if he were afraid to touch them. "Are you serious?"

"When am I not serious?"

Ricky ran his hand through his hair, letting out a breath. "I…I can't believe it. She was so dead set against the idea."

"People can change. Not often, but they can. Are you going to take them or not?"

"Oh, I'm taking them!" He snatched the keys from her. Before she knew what was happening, he leaned over the counter and threw his arms around her. He planted a kiss on her cheek and said, "Mary, you're the best!"

She adjusted her dress when he released her and fussed with her hair. Heat crept across her cheeks, but she couldn't tamp down a smile. Ricky almost sprinted out of the shop. Her heart leaped, watching his giddiness as he went. With the clang of the bells once the door had closed, she looked around and realized she was still alone, still without Valerie. The best, she thought. She'd made one young person's dreams come true today. One down. One to go. The other one wasn't going to be so easy.

CHAPTER THIRTY-SEVEN

ALLISTER'S BOOKS

THE RUSH of Ricky's excited announcement had finally passed, allowing Shelby to focus on doing something productive. She and Sarah decided the register was the best place to station him for the afternoon. Once Sarah gave him the blueprints for the old public house, he hadn't been able to take his eyes off them. He would be useless on the floor today with the bustle of Halloween shoppers and their children.

When she'd arrived at the shop after school, he'd only tore his eyes away from the floor plans long enough to tell her the news. He had squeezed her so hard her ribs nearly cracked. Spontaneous, he certainly was that. She didn't mind it and actually welcomed it. He added flare to her studious and dedicated personality. Life would never be boring with Ricky Allister. She looked back and smiled at the sight of seeing him so happy. He looked up as though he'd sensed her eyes through his impermeable distraction and gave her a wink. She wasn't forgotten and that satisfied her enough to get back to work.

Sarah was waist deep in a circle of children who had come in and found the shelf of toys near the young readers' section. Candy wrappers littered the floor near the kiddie table set up for holidays. Shelby smiled at the taxed Sarah and mouthed, "I'll go get the broom," as she pointed to the mess.

She walked to the upper level toward the back of the store. As she neared the back shelf, just before the cellar door, she paused. She never used to pay much attention to the weeping books, but that was before she'd found out what they did—before she'd been inside one of them. Now each time she passed, she stopped and eyed them for just a moment with appreciation and wariness. The audible drip caught her attention, and she walked over to stand in front of the glass case where the five eerie dated books sat, each on its own pedestal.

Just as she'd never stopped to notice them before, the dripping sound had never caught her attention. It was always a slow phenomenon, not one that sounded like a leaky faucet. Today, however, the plopping noise seemed constant as the tears of the weeping books dripped into the metal base, trickling toward the drain in their case. Scanning the books, she identified the source of the rapid flow. All of the books had their usual damp appearance, but *The Lands of Farwin Wood* was seeping.

Leaning her face closer to the case, she whispered and timed the drops coming out of the book. "One Scooby Doo. Two Scooby Doo…" *Plop.* "One Scooby Doo. Two Scooby Doo…" *Plop,* another. "Wow." Was it because Ricky and Valerie had just been inside of it?

Maybe the dripping would die down after a few days. She'd stayed far away from the back shelf when she had returned from Farwin Wood, so she had no basis for comparison. She'd mention it to Sarah later. There was no need to raise any alarm if it wasn't necessary. The woman already had her hands full with Halloween tomorrow.

She headed down to the cellar steps to fetch the broom, and retrieved it where it sat propped against the wall on the third step. Just as she grabbed the handle, she heard a thump on the other side of the wall where the weeping bookshelf sat.

No one was allowed on the upper level this week. Sarah had instructed them it was off limits. The shop would be too busy to keep an eye on the collection of rare and out-of-print books housed there. Great. She hurried up the steps and shut the door to play security guard. She rounded the corner, prepared to confront either a lost or disobedient customer.

She didn't expect to come face to face with the man she'd been given to in Farwin Wood like a peace offering—Ranthrop Groslivo. She sucked in a breath, staggering back and slammed into the wall, dropping the broom in the process. She blinked but found that he still stood before her in the flesh. It really was him!

Black leather pants, and a billowy black linen shirt covered by the red overtunic, which she remembered. The golden creature crest on the front grew larger as he stepped forward, towering over her. She splayed her fingers out against the wall, unable to retreat any farther. She squeezed her eyes shut and braced herself as she listened to his footsteps approach.

"Lady Shelby. It is so good to see you. I was not sure if it would work. I thought Vasimus and Netta were playing a farce on me. Oh…forgive me. I have frightened you."

She peeled an eye open and looked up at his face, which was surrounded by a wild mane of sandy hair. He was really there. The flesh on his face was as vivid as anyone else alive. She glanced at the bookcase and through the glass, and saw *The Lands of Farwin Wood* sitting open on its pedestal. It dangled precariously on the little platform, threatening to fall off. Had it been forced open with the man's arrival? How was that possible?

Shelby flinched as Ranthrop kneeled in front of her, bringing him even closer. He spoke in a delicate tone that she did not remember hearing when they last met. "Lady Shelby, please accept my apology for your unnecessary detainment at my keep. I did not know who you were and hope I can make it up to you. Can you forgive me?"

She watched as his eyes looked at her as if they were pleading. Wanting to do anything to redirect the stormy green lenses, she nodded with vigor. "Sure. I forgive you."

"Oh, good." He sighed and grasped one of her hands. He placed his other over top of it and added, "I am your humble servant then, m'lady. Whenever you require anything of me, simply ask."

She tugged her hand away. "Anything?"

"Anything in my power, my dear."

With a shaky finger, she pointed to the case and croaked, "Get back in that book."

Ranthrop frowned and stood up. "Sadly, I cannot do that just yet. I have come to speak with Lady Valerie Millville. Do you know where I may find her?"

"Valerie? She's…across the street." She wasn't sure why she pointed, especially since it resulted in Ranthrop thanking her. He patted her on the head and turned on his heel to the front of the store.

RICKY COULDN'T believe Aunt Sarah had caved in and asked the council to rent him the public house. The future was big, bright, and endless with possibilities. It was really happening. He had a future all of his own, one that he was in control of as an adult. It felt sweeter knowing he had worked hard for it and would continue to do so through school and the hours he planned to invest in the place. He was on top of the world. Nothing could knock him off, not even the occasional tricks of Agatha Blinney's curse.

Vaguely he noted the creak of the floor on the other side of the counter as he jotted down notes for changes to the public house. He glanced up as someone called his name.

"Lord Ricky." Ranthrop gave him a nod on his way to the door.

"Hey, Ranthrop," he said with a lazy wave, going back to his plans. It wasn't until the chime of the doorbells that it hit him. He slapped his pencil down hard on the counter, his eyes drawn to the door. There was no mistaking the broad back clad in red or the tall stature and unruly mop of hair of the man who bounded down the front steps of the shop.

Ricky turned so fast to search for his aunt that his neck cracked. He found her across the room, standing paralyzed among a sea of excited children, looking like she was having a stroke. The chair nearly toppled over as he scrambled to his feet and raced around the counter to the shop door. His hands planted on the glass like Spiderman. His nose bent as he pressed his face to the glass, trying to get closer to what he hoped was an illusion. Ranthrop strode in long, purposeful steps right across the street to Scents and Suds.

"Ricky!" Sarah's thick whisper came at his side. "That was Ranthrop! Wasn't it?"

"No. No, it can't be," he mumbled to convince himself.

"I know it can't be, but it was! What the hell is Ranthrop doing here!"

His knees shook. He was going to pass out or pee his pants. Maybe he would melt into a puddle on the floor. His sweaty palms made a squeaking sound against the glass as he turned to look at his aunt.

"I… I…Ranthrop!" He pointed like a babbling idiot.

"Ricky…"

"What did you do?" Shelby's accusing tone from behind him completed his aunt's sentence as he turned around to face his judge and jury.

"I… Ranthrop," he said, laughing hysterically and pointed over his shoulder.

"How did he get here?" Shelby huffed.

"I may have…written another book."

"Another book?" Sarah spun him around by the shoulder. "What do you mean another book?"

"Uh… Didn't I tell you that? I wrote a book when I was in Farwin Wood. I thought I mentioned it."

"Oh, Ricky," Shelby added.

"What kind of book?" Sarah asked, gritting her teeth.

"Oh…just a book about the land of…Blinney Lane."

CHAPTER
THIRTY-EIGHT

SCENTS AND SUDS

YOU DON'T need to do that," Mary's voice scolded as Valerie stood restocking shelves. "Why don't you take the day off?"

"Mom, you've been slammed since I got here. Why didn't you call and wake me up?"

"I…I can manage. I can call your cousin Clarissa if I need to. You look like you need more rest. You were up until all hours with Franci."

"I'm fine. And Clarissa hasn't helped out in over a year. She wouldn't have a clue what to do."

Valerie wanted to welcome her mother's concern, but her pride and bitterness over the past few days refused to let her. It distracted her so much that she couldn't focus on her mother's peculiar change of heart toward her, which was probably for the best.

"Fine, but if you feel unwell, just duck out and don't worry about any of this." Mary turned to a customer who was trying to get her attention. "I'll be with you in a moment," she nearly snapped. Turning back to Valerie, she continued, "I don't care what we sell today. You had a long trip. If you…"

"If I what?" She arched a brow. What was the deal with her today?

"If you want to go see that Dexter and let him know you're back, I won't mind."

"Dexter? Are you serious? Mom…" She collected the boxes she'd just emptied and shook her head. "Dexter's ancient history."

"Yes, but are you still upset about what happened between the two of you? Something's bothering you. I can tell."

"Pfft, I could care less about Dexter. I'm way over it, really."

"Then what's bothering you? Did something happen? You've been out of sorts ever since you came back from that book," Mary whispered.

The boxes slipped out of her hands. She stared at her mother's sympathetic eyes and wanted to cry. "Nothing is bothering me. It was just…unpleasant, that's all."

"Unpleasant? How?"

"I don't want to talk about it!" She scooped up the boxes and rushed to the back room. If she started crying again, she wouldn't stop. It had taken her all morning to halt the water works enough to clean up her face and come to the shop. For once, Mary looked like she would be on her side no matter what she told her. She wanted to throw her arms around her and let the tears flow. She wanted to tell her what a fool she'd been, how she'd met the most infuriating yet caring man in the world, and how he'd broken her heart in a matter of days.

"TWENTY-SEVEN NINETY-FIVE," Mary said with a grumble as she made change for the customer. She forced a pleasant look on her face. "Happy Halloween. Come back and see us, won't you?"

Glancing back at the doorway to the storeroom, she saw no sign of Valerie. What was wrong with that girl? She hadn't seen her mope so much since Jackal nearly died from a raccoon bite.

The sound of whispers and cooing drew her gaze to the front of the shop, and she spotted several women gawking at a towering man. He looked like he got lost on his way to Medieval Times, decked out from head to toe in red and black, complete with a sword strapped at his hip. His weighty steps rattled jars on the shelves as he marched up to the counter. She didn't have time to take a man by the hand and explain the beauty products in her store. He seemed fairly well-kempt, but there was a ruggedness about him that cried out for cosmetic and hygienic help.

"Can I help you?"

"I hope that you can, mistress. I seek the Lady Millville. Do you know where I may find her?"

Mary put her hands on her hips. "You are speaking to Mary Millville."

"Ah! Lady Millville!" The man stepped up to the counter and bowed. "You are the mother of Lady Valerie Millville, I presume?"

Mistress? Lady Valerie? She would be glad when Halloween was over. She'd had enough of role-playing after the Franci debacle.

"Valerie is my daughter, but you can drop the whole mistress and lady business. Just get to the point. I don't have time for shenanigans today if this is some kind of joke."

"I can assure you, La...madam, I have come here neither for antics nor to waste your time. I seek an audience with your daughter with your permission."

"With my permission?" Mary's posture went slack. Boy, this guy poured on the manners. He must be a professional, one of those theatre actors from across town. "Just a moment, please. Valerie! There's someone here to... Can you come out here?"

The man nodded at Mary, a pleasant smile on his chiseled face. She peered around him and noticed the women in the shop gathering in a huddle to stare at him. He smelled of oak and sweet blossoms. She needed to bottle his scent and slap his face on the label if he had this kind of effect on women.

"I'm sorry, I didn't catch your name."

"Pardon my manners. It has been an interesting journey from Farwin Wood. I am..."

"Farwin Wood?"

"Yes. I am Lord Ranthrop Groslivo, Lord of the Southlands of Farwin Wood."

VALERIE DROPPED the carton of lip balms she carried and gasped. "Ranthrop?"

"Ranthrop?" Mary looked dumbstruck as she glanced from Valerie to Ranthrop. "Ranthrop Groz...Grozzlevow?"

"Groslivo," Ranthrop corrected.

He drew his sword from his belt in one swift movement and dropped to a knee. Mary jumped when the tip of his blade stuck in the floorboard beside him.

"Lady Valerie, I do not know why you parted so abruptly, and I apologize for coming here without warning of my arrival, but there is something I wish to discuss with you."

Valerie was too shocked to speak. How had he gotten through? She wanted to run to him and punch him in the nose at the same time. She heard her mother whimpering a strange sound but could not tear her eyes away from the man kneeling before her.

"Valerie, my tender flame, my sweet flower. I wished for an adventure before you arrived. You have given me the greatest adventure of my life. I have torn through the woods searching for you and now across pages to this strange place—a journey I do not understand how is possible, but am grateful for from the depths of my soul. I was lost and did not know it, but you brought me back to life in more ways than one. I will repay you with my lifelong devotion and offer you my hands, my sword, and my heart. Lady Mary," Ranthrop continued and turned to the older woman, "I pledge to cherish and protect your daughter as long as there is breath in my body. I humbly ask for your permission to take her hand in marriage."

Valerie couldn't breathe. The women behind Ranthrop whispered excitedly to each other. Mary moaned and crashed to the floor with a massive thud.

"Mom!" She rushed to Mary's side where her mother lay crumpled on the floor, passed out. She searched for signs of broken bones and felt a strong hand clasp her shoulder.

Ranthrop bellowed, "Mother? Can you hear me?"

She swatted his hand from her shoulder. "Mother? She's not *your* mother! Get the hell out of here!"

"What?" Ranthrop drew back. "But I..."

"Oh, my God! What happened?" Sarah appeared, pushing around Ranthrop with Ricky close on her heels.

Valerie fanned her hand above Mary's face. "She fainted!"

"Mary, can you hear me?" Sarah patted Mary's cheek.

"Does this happen often? Is she ill?" Ranthrop suggested.

Valerie couldn't take it anymore. She shot to her feet and pushed at his chest. "Out! Out! Right now! Get out of here! I hate you, you lying man-whore!"

"Hate me?" Ranthrop yelped as he staggered back with each forceful shove.

Valerie felt her face wither as the threatening tears caused her face to scrunch up. She turned and dashed to the back of the store.

Ricky tugged at Ranthrop's elbow. "Come on, man. Let's get out of here."

CHAPTER THIRTY-NINE

RICKY IGNORED Ranthrop's ramblings about his run-in with Valerie as they walked around Blinney Lane. The man didn't seem to require responses to the questions he asked anyway.

"She says she hates me. How can that be possible? We had become so amiable, more than amiable, in fact, on the last leg of our journey. I cannot believe her heart would change so quickly. Why did you depart without telling me?"

"We...had to get back to give Franci the cure," he said in a rush. "How did you get here?"

"Through your book, of course. I had no idea. Why didn't you tell me?"

"Our world isn't exactly similar to yours. I don't think Far-win Wooders would mix well here. We have a lot of rules."

"We call ourselves Woodlanders. Yes, Blinney is quite different."

Ricky gave Ranthrop a penny tour of Blinney Lane. Near the end of the street, they found Alexander Rainsford in the work yard in front of his smithy shop. The stone-piled building had a wooden post fence that cordoned off the yard from the street. The stakes looked like they had been painted about a hundred times over the years.

Ricky moseyed through the yard and introduced the men. Alexander's comparable size and old-fashioned leather smithy apron made Ranthrop appear less out of place among the shoppers that passed by. Alexander's sun-and-heat-baked face went slack when he realized where Ranthrop came from. The brawny blacksmith did well to school his features after Ricky's weighted explanation.

The man's shock was forgotten as Ranthrop walked freely around the yard and through the shop, barraging him with all sorts of inquiries about the tools and old-fashioned weapons he made. Ranthrop admired the craftsmanship and unsheathed his sword like a proud parent.

Ricky still didn't know Alexander all that well. He was polite and sometimes quipped a joke but more often than not kept to himself with a brooding expression. He seemed to prefer forging—hammering out wrought iron and steel as if the tireless job killed pent up demons—over conversing with people. Today with Ranthrop, his mood was light, and his eyes glistened with appreciation for the man's knowledge of his work. They could be fast friends if Ricky didn't have to try and shove Ranthrop back into the book like a genie in the bottle.

The distraction proved too good to be true. Ranthrop's eyes soon began to wander to Scents and Suds. There was no way he would be willing to go back right now. Ricky needed to find something else to occupy him before he broached the subject.

He announced his recent acquisition of the public house and asked Ranthrop to take a look with him. Alexander seemed pleased with the news and held them up long enough to provide a bucket of ice.

"You can't christen a pub without a drink. It's bad luck," he said.

Ricky nearly forgot the misery of his foreign friend upon entering the pub. The smell of dry dust clinging in his nostrils was the scent of joyous possibilities. Cobwebs hung from two brass chandeliers. The interior was wood from floor to ceiling. A bar with elaborate molding curved on the end by the entrance. It had a chalice shape, bulging out in front of the bar stools and tapering off with raised panel work near the footrests. Four wide arches with pillar bases and rope crown molding made up the bar back. Through the grimy mirrors, inlaid between the arches, he could see a hint of his reflection.

"It is fancier than any tavern I have seen, but it needs a lot of work, Ricky." Ranthrop tilted a three-legged chair, causing it to wobble. "Do all lords operate establishments here?"

"Uh, yeah. Only the lords, actually, or masters of trade like Henry and Alex. Come on, let's clean it up a bit and see what's left behind the bar."

A few hours later, the bar and tables were free of their thick dust. The ploy had worked in Ricky's favor, giving him an extra pair of hands for the first round of many needed cleanings. He had interjected the task with busy chatter and questions to keep Ranthrop's thoughts from returning to Valerie.

Marry her? He'd been just in time to hear the tail end of Ranthrop's proposal before Mary dropped like a ton of bricks. What the hell had happened on their trip to Terradoon? He was dying to know but didn't dare ask. If he knew his aunt, she'd want Ranthrop gone yesterday. Baiting the man for details certainly wouldn't get him out the door and back to the swamp.

He'd temporarily distracted Ranthrop with the task of finding a name for his new establishment. Ranthrop looked out of his element trying to wield a broom as he spouted off suggestions. "Lord Ricky's Blinney Brothel and Ale House."

"No. We don't have brothels. And that's a bit long, don't you think?"

"No brothels? Really? What is allowed in a public house here?"

"Drinking, eating, dancing, games… I guess that's it."

"Do you have knick knack here?"

Ricky pointed at Ranthrop and beamed, remembering the drinking game the townsfolk in Farwin Wood played. "That's it! I'll call it The Knick Knack!"

The door opened and Alexander walked in, wiping his brow, a six-pack of soda in each of his massive hands like tiny dumbbells. Ricky could see the dim blue sky as he looked out the window. The sun had nearly set.

"Ah, Master Alex. Good. I've had enough of this woman's work. Ricky, give over the ale now, will you?" Ranthrop asked and discarded his broom to take a seat at one of the tables.

"Looks like you need some light, little friend," Alexander said and set the soda on the bar. He walked to the back of the pub and opened what Ricky had thought was a cabinet, revealing a fuse box. "Let's see if we can get the juice back on."

Ricky watched as Alexander flipped the main breaker. He flinched as sparks burst out of the box, but Alexander acted as if they were no more than raindrops. The lights flickered above, and he smiled as he stared at the glow under the blossom bulb covers.

"All right. What've you got?" Alexander's voice brought him back to reality. The man stood in front of him on the other side of the bar. Ranthrop too stared eagerly from his place at the table. He had his first customers.

He scanned a row of foggy bottles behind the bar and found one that was unopened. "Uh… Whiskey?"

"That'll do," Alexander drawled and took a seat next to Ranthrop.

Ricky came around the bar with three glasses of whiskey and cola chilling his hands. He set them down on the table and took a seat to join them. It appeared neither were going to object that he wasn't legally old enough to drink in this land.

"To The Knick Knack!" He raised his glass with a grin.

"The Knick Knack?" Alexander arched a brow. "That's certainly different. To new neighbors."

"To the good people of Blinney," Ranthrop added in a rather gloomy voice.

The door opened before Ricky could take a sip. He grimaced as he followed the polyester pants up to the tight pocket-protector style shirt and stared at the face of Reggie Nurscher. "Damn it," he muttered.

"I thought I saw a light on over here."

"WHAT DO women want?" Ranthrop asked. It had taken less than half an hour for the conversation to turn away from things pub-related.

"They want you and then they don't," Reggie complained, pouring himself and Alexander another drink.

"They blame you for things that are beyond your control," Alexander chimed in. He downed his second shot, having forgone the cola.

Him too? What was his beef? Great. Now Ricky had three of them to deal with.

"I was thinking about a dartboard, maybe a pool table. What do you think?" he asked.

Ranthrop leaned on the table and took turns addressing Alexander and Reggie. "I know. Are women here all this mystifying?"

"Where are you from?" Reggie asked.

"The south!" Ricky blurted. "He's from the south."

Reggie nodded, then continued. "Women are mystifying everywhere. It don't matter where they're from. One day they're tearing your clothes off, the next they act like they don't know you."

Ricky washed the vomit taste in his throat, brought on by Reggie's comment, down with the rest of his drink. Maybe he could get Ranthrop drunk enough to pass out and haul his big carcass over to the book. He decided to switch to shots and retrieved another bottle. He poured a round for everyone, making sure to slide Ranthrop's close to the man's hand. Ranthrop took the bait, and he continued to refill the little glass vessels. However, a problem soon ensued. Each time he did, the men raised their shots, forcing him to do the same.

Alexander's eyes started to droop, and his head began to bob. Reggie stood up abruptly, causing his chair to squeak.

"This place sucks. If I wanted to be depressed I could have stayed at home," Reggie muttered and staggered out the door. Ricky tried to focus on the man but felt himself sway in the chair.

"Huh?" Alexander snorted and popped his eyes open. "Uh, I must have nodded off. Long day today."

Alexander got up, but Ranthrop stopped him. "Master Alex. One for the moon, as we say." He held up a shot, and the man smiled and accepted it.

"For the moon, aye?" Alex chuckled. "Why not."

Ricky toasted, feeling his throat constrict as the liquid burned on its way down. He wiped his tongue across his lips as he watched Alexander leave. He could smell the potent vapors on his breath and knew he'd had enough.

"Good fellows, Ricky," Ranthrop said and poured another round. "Good fellows."

He stared at Ranthrop and noticed the man's eyes were glassy. It wasn't the first time he'd repeated a phrase in the last hour. Both of their hands swayed as they tried to clink the other's shot glass. Ricky sneered, coughing once the amber liquid had gone down.

"What happened, Ricky? Why did she leave so quickly?"

"We…had to get back to give Franci the cure," he slurred.

"I know, but what happened? Why is she so upset with me? Did she say something to you since you got back?"

"Since we got back? No." He let out a hiccup and clamped a hand over his mouth.

"What about before you left Farwin Wood? Do you have any idea why she would be cross with me? Did I do something to offend her?"

He tried to hide behind his hiccups, but each time his head bobbed from the pressure, he found Ranthrop's inquisitive eyes on him. "I can't…*hiccup*…really think of anything."

"Ricky, she called me a lying…man-whore! Why would she say that? We were so agreeable with each other. There must be something I missed. Something I said or did that I am sure I can explain to her. You have to help me."

His stomach gurgled. Was it from pity or one too many shots? "Okay, so…*hiccup*…she may have seen you locking lips in the hall with…*hiccup*…some women at your keep when you guys got back…*hiccup*… Ugh."

"Locking…" Ranthrop stared at the bottle of whiskey on the table. "Oh, piss." The words tumbled out of his mouth like a fat drop from a faucet. "What did she say?"

Ricky shook his head. "Nothing. She just wanted to leave."

"What else? She didn't say anything about it? I thought you wanted to stay for the feast. Didn't you object?"

"I… I may have accidentally said something… *hiccup*… about how you had to keep women away with a stick."

"What?" Ranthrop said, growling. The chair toppled over as the man jumped to his feet.

Ranthrop lunged across the table, and Ricky felt himself jerked out of his chair by his shirtfront. His toes scraped the floor, and he clamped his hands over Ranthrop's wrists as the room seemed to spin.

"I didn't know you guys were a thing!"

"You told her I must fight women off with a stick? Why would you say that?"

"Cause it's true!"

"Yes! But *why* would you say that?"

"Ranthrop! I'm on your side! I didn't know she was going to freak out. Let me try to help you!" he pleaded from behind the collar of his shirt. He dropped back into his chair as Ranthrop released him.

"I don't need anymore of your kind of help!"

Smoothing out the stretched portions of his shirt, he followed the scrape and thud of chairs. Ranthrop bounded out the door, leaving it swung open behind him.

"Ah, crap!" *...hiccup...*

CHAPTER
FORTY

SARAH RACED across the street with Henry at her side. They ran through the passageway between Mary's and Franci's shops. It wasn't difficult to locate the thunderous bellowing of Ranthrop's voice. Poor Mary. The woman didn't need to call. Sarah would have soon heard the man all the way from her apartment.

"Valerie! Lady Valerie!" Ranthrop's voice echoed across the courtyard.

"Ouch!" she yowled, twisting her ankle when one of her slippers gave way.

"Are you all right?" Henry whispered.

"I will be when I kill him and my nephew," she complained and hobbled a few steps until she found her footing again.

She located the source of a screech, followed by a rattling sound. Valerie stuck her head out of one of the upstairs windows to her house.

"What do you want? Haven't you ever heard of knocking?" Valerie's harsh whisper came as she glowered down at Ranthrop who stood in the yard below.

"Valerie!" Ranthrop staggered as he focused on the woman. "You cast me out! I did not think you would welcome me at your door!"

"I wouldn't! I won't! Now go back to your swamp before you wake up the whole freaking town!"

"Ranthrop! Come back, buddy…*hiccup…* We can work this out." Ricky's slurred words came from Sarah's left. She located him just in time to see him fall like a felled tree, flat on his face. His legs kicked up with the force, and he stayed plastered where he landed.

"Oh, perfect," she said and looked at Henry. He winced as though he felt the pain of Ricky's fall.

"But I must speak with you!" Ranthrop continued.

"No, you mustn't! Because I don't wish to speak to you! Now go home and don't come back! You already scared the hell out of my mother!"

Ranthrop dropped to his knees. "But I will die without you!"

"Good! Then drop dead!" The window rattled closed, and Valerie disappeared from view. The lights upstairs went out a second later.

Ranthrop let out a pathetic moan and dropped his head in his hands. Fortunately, he said no more. Sarah didn't want to see Henry try and grapple with the guy. He'd had enough tangles with Farwin Wood men.

Henry let out a sigh and turned to her. "All right. You get Dumb and I'll get Dumber."

"You might have to be more specific."

They hauled the drunken pair back across the street. Sarah shoved Ricky up the steps and dumped him onto his bed. Henry tried to deposit Ranthrop on the floor by the bookcase at Sarah's insistence, but Ranthrop was still lucid enough to protest.

"I don't want him in my apartment," she whispered.

"Where are we supposed to put him? You don't want him wandering back across the street. Can we lock him downstairs?"

"This is a man who pees in a bucket. I'm not letting him down there around all of my book binding equipment. There's too many valuables down there for him to destroy." She peeked around Henry's shoulder and cringed as Ranthrop leaned on an island rack. It swayed under his weight, and he fumbled to keep the books from falling on the floor. "Can't we shackle him or something?"

Henry raised a brow. "You have shackles?"

"No."

"Sarah, he's a human being who's done nothing wrong other than fall for a woman who doesn't want him. We can't treat him like an animal."

A belch cut through the air, and they both turned to look at its maker. Ranthrop dug in his ear and snorted in an audible breath.

"Really? Cause he belongs outside." Sarah put her hands on her hips. She felt her tension drain away as her eyes looked up at the ceiling. "And he needs to be contained."

"Your garden? I thought you didn't want him to destroy anything. You haven't even got to enjoy it yet."

"I know, but the door to the rooftop locks. I don't think he'll do as much damage up there as down here. Besides, I can help you replant anything he ruins. I wouldn't mind getting my hands dirty with you." She smiled and pressed her hands to his chest.

Henry bent down and kissed her. "Fine, but if he jumps off the roof and breaks his neck, I had nothing to do with this."

CHAPTER FORTY-ONE

SARAH SCANNED the shop out of habit. These perfunctory glances were second nature after working there for so many years. She could spot dissatisfaction, curiosity, intrigue, and shoplifters in a split second. They stood out like Valentine decorations at Easter. The smallest fraction of a split second was how long it took her to identify the most glaring round peg in a square hole this morning—Ranthrop.

He was seated in one of the child-sized chairs that abutted a table of equal height. How it hadn't broken under the weight of him, she couldn't fathom. He sat next to a young boy with dark brown hair, round black-rimmed glasses, and a black cloak—clearly a Halloween impersonation of a fictional idol.

Ranthrop rested one hand on his knee and leaned on the table with his other arm, immersed in conversation with the boy. What struck her as odd was how he didn't appear to be humoring the boy. His expression was one of rapt intrigue and intensity that could not be feigned. He probably wasn't capable of showboating a grand facade to humor a child. No. Ranthrop, in some ways, was like a child himself—a very, very large child. Anything he felt was clearly written across his face. He had but two perpetual expressions—intensity and confusion. He could appear quite scary wearing either due to his size. To have that hostile display of brutishness now staring into the eyes of a young child in her shop made her nervous.

She crept up to a bookrack closer to them and eavesdropped. The boy was explaining the story plot of *Harry Potter*. As she listened, she noticed the little fellow spoke in terms well beyond his years. No wonder Ranthrop looked confused.

"You mean to tell me that there are all of these adults with years of experience in magical powers, and they left poor Harry to do battle on his own? And brooms that fly? That has to be the most uncomfortable mode of transport I have ever heard. Really, someone should speak to this…" Ranthrop picked up the book from the table and read the back. "…Lord J.K. Rowling about this fip fop."

Sarah squeezed her eyes shut and grimaced. The little boy let out an exasperated sigh and slapped a hand to his forehead. She watched as the boy snatched the book back from Ranthrop. "It's *Lady* Rowling. She's a girl!"

Ranthrop sat back and snorted. "A lady? Writing stories? Ha! Who ever heard of such a thing!"

"Idiot," the boy mumbled under his breath and shoved away from the table.

"Ranthrop?" She tapped him on the shoulder. "Shouldn't you be getting back to Farwin Wood? I'm sure your men need you or something."

"No, thanks to you and Ricky we've been at peace for some months. The days are as carefree as when I was a boy."

"Yes, but...you don't belong here." She spoke with her hands like people foolishly do when a foreigner doesn't understand their language. "You can't stay in my shop all day."

"Oh. Forgive me. I don't want to be a burden on your establishment. May I assist you with anything? I can earn my keep, or perhaps you know of some other lodging available in trade for work. Maybe with Master Alexander? I am adept with a sword." He stepped closer and whispered near her ear. "I have to ask though, Lady Sarah. Do you not have piss pots here? I had to relieve myself into one of those potted trees on your rooftop forest this morning."

She rubbed her temples and groaned. When he mentioned Alexander her heart leaped, but she couldn't do that to Alex.

"Look, Ranthrop. How long did you plan on staying here? Did you even have a plan?"

"My plan was only to speak to Lady Valerie, but I have yet to resolve my dilemma with her."

"I got the impression yesterday that she doesn't exactly want to talk to you."

"I know, but if I could just explain to her that my eye has not wandered since I met her, nor will it ever again, then I am sure she would like to hear what I have to say. You and Vasimus quarreled and made amends. Have you not ever quarreled with Master Henry? Please tell me you understand that some things cannot be left unresolved."

Damn it, now she was actually starting to feel sorry for him. "Yes, I understand. All right. You need a plan. Do something nice for her. How bad did you screw up?"

"I didn't screw up anything."

"Let me rephrase that. How bad does *she* think you screwed up?"

Ranthrop drew his palm down his face. "I suppose she thinks my actions were unforgivable."

"Great. How about flowers? Women here like getting flowers from men. I'll call Franci across the street to make you a nice bouquet. I'm sure she'd be happy to oblige since you played your part in bringing her back to her senses."

"Flowers? That's all I need to do?" Ranthrop's dismal face brightened.

"No. That'll just make it easier for you to get in the door." She eyed him up and down. "I think you could do with a wardrobe change too. Maybe it would help for her to see you as a normal…I mean *different* than how you looked when she got mad at you. Come on."

She led him over to the counter. Ricky sat with his head slumped onto his arms at the register. His eyes were concealed with a pair of black sunglasses. The whistle of his rhythmic breathing made her blood boil. She raised her hand and slammed it down on the metal customer bell. He rocketed up in time with the ding.

"Hey! Roy Orbison!"

"Huh? I'm awake! I'm awake."

"I need you to take your friend upstairs and give him some of Henry's clothes. They're on the right side of my closet."

Ricky let out a yawn, and she wrinkled her nose when the stale smell of last night's binging hit her. "What's that now?"

"Ranthrop! Henry's clothes! Upstairs closet! Right side!"

"Closet. Right side. Got it." Ricky saluted and walked like a blind robot toward the steps.

She shook her head as she watched the pair go upstairs. Halfway up, Ricky staggered back into Ranthrop, and she cringed. Ranthrop's sword got temporarily lodged between two balusters, and she heard the wood creak when he freed it. She closed her eyes, not wanting to witness more and muttered, "More like Dumb and Dumbass."

CHAPTER FORTY-TWO

SCENTS AND SUDS

MARY'S CURIOSITY was eating a hole in her from the looks of it. Valerie didn't want to glower at her after what the woman had endured yesterday, but she took on an expression close to it each time she caught her mother's eyes studying her. Mary apparently understood it was an I-don't-want-to-talk-about-it face because she hadn't mentioned either ordeal all day. She did, however, grab her by the shoulders at one point and ask, "Just tell me…are you all right?"

"No, but I will be." It was all she had been able to offer at the time.

Marriage? Was he serious? She slammed jars of face cream onto the shelf. What happened after the honeymoon? Oh, see you later darling, I'm off to frolic with one of my wenches. Ha! Some kind of paradise that would be.

She stepped off the ladder and slid it to the end of the wall. She kicked the box with her foot harder than she needed to scoot it to the back of the store.

They barely knew each other. *Marriage*? He didn't seem like the kind of man who would want to get married. Why her? She had nursed him back to health. Maybe he wanted someone to lean on and take care of him waiting at home.

She rested her hands on her hips and scanned the shelves, realizing she had nothing left to stock. She had been so energized by her agitation that she'd worked on overdrive.

My tender flame, my sweet flower. I have torn through the woods searching for you.

Her cheeks grew flush as she remembered his words. She remembered everything else too—the tender moments in the tent, his lips on hers, the way he held her, the way she thought his eyes had looked at her adoringly. All of that only to come back to the keep and hear him tell some strumpet "maybe later." Did any more men need to make her feel like she was expendable?

She turned as she heard a familiar deep voice behind her and found Ranthrop addressing her mother. At least she thought it was Ranthrop. He wore work boots, khaki slacks, and a green polo shirt tucked into his pants. She listened with bated breath as he apologized to her mother for last night's raucous and inquired about her well-being. Mary smiled, actually smiled, and put her hand to her heart like swooning women did!

Sure, win over the mother to get to the daughter. Was that his new tactic?

He turned, and she noticed a large bouquet of flowers in his hand. His hair looked swept back. Good grief. There was no way he'd done this all on his own. She bit the inside of her lip knowing someone on Blinney Lane was a traitor.

"Lady Valerie." He bowed. "It is good to see you. How are you this afternoon?"

She folded her arms and shifted her weight onto one leg. "Exhausted. There was a drunk outside my house last night, but I told him to leave town, so I'm sure I'll get some rest tonight. No worries."

A line formed in his forehead, then faded when he captured her meaning. She wanted to roll her eyes and apologize for being rude at the same time.

"Please accept my apologies for the intrusion. I should not have woken you. Here." He handed her the bouquet. "A token of my regret."

The hairs on her arm stood up when his fingers brushed against hers. She looked down at the flowers. Pink and white daffodils and Star of Bethlehem. They were beautiful and thoughtfully arranged, not some cheap bouquet from a grocery store cooler.

"Where did you get these?"

"Lady Francis, next door, assisted me. She's a pleasant woman. She asked me to assure you that she is feeling much better."

Franci. There was traitor number one. Figures. One look at Ranthrop, and Franci would have given him anything in her store.

"Do you like them?"

"The flowers?" She knew it was petulant, but she shrugged. "They're nice."

"These daftdils, Lady Francis said…"

"Daffodils," she murmured.

"Yes, I'm sorry, daffodils. She said they represent affection." He gave her a warm smile.

She chewed on the inside of her lip and remained mute. She wasn't going to give him any points for being clever. Behind him, she noticed her mother was arched back where she stood at the counter, craning her neck to view the exchange.

"Do you want to smell them?"

"Smell them?"

"Yes, they have a unique scent," he added.

She began to lift the bouquet but stopped. She knew what the flowers smelled like. Why did she need to smell them? *Affection*.

Her nostrils flared as she eyed the flowers now. One thing she and Franci had in common was their knowledge of plants. She'd had many a conversation with the woman over the meanings of herbs and flowers. She knew daffodils represented affection or…unrequited love. She hadn't given it any thought when he'd handed them to her, but that was before she remembered Franci's method of arranging.

She remembered what Franci had told her: I use one flower to represent the stance or mood of the giver. The others represent the desired effect on the recipient.

Daffodils—regard and unrequited love—Ranthrop. That left the Star of Bethlehem. She didn't have to think too hard because she knew Franci used them often in bouquets for people seeking forgiveness. They signified atonement. *She* was the recipient. She was supposed to forgive him. Her heart was already conflicted, one whiff of those and she might falter.

Damn it, Franci! Just give him my soul and the keys to my house while you're at it!

"Here!" She thrust the flowers back at Ranthrop. "I can't accept these."

"Why not? You haven't even smelled them."

"I don't want your *stinking* flowers! What did you think? I'd take one whiff and forgive you for treating me like just another one of your wenches?"

"No, it's not like that! You are different!"

"Ugh!" She tossed the flowers to the floor. Ranthrop's pleading hands were in no position to accept them. "You know what? You're not a monster like you thought. But you're an animal with an appetite that I don't care to help fill anymore. I just wish you hadn't wasted my time with your charm. It's deadlier than your sword. And I resent the fact that you'd stoop to tricking me with magic instead of trying to earn my forgiveness."

Ranthrop dropped to a knee and placed his fist over his heart. The gesture made his new outfit even more absurd.

"Tell me what it is that I must do to earn your forgiveness and the task will be toppled."

"Oh, for God's sake, get up!"

Mary and some customers looked on the scene as Ranthrop scrambled to his feet. She ignored their eyes, one hand back on her hip. Ranthrop was akimbo again, staring at her. She jarred her head and threw a hand up—but he didn't understand the universal sign for "what?"

"Are you kidding me?" She threw both hands in the air when she realized he thought he'd just completed his task for forgiveness. This crisis he was stuck in left him a puppet and her pulling the strings. It would be easier to deal with him if he had his gumption back. She pointed to the door. "I will forgive you if you leave and never come back."

"You cannot possibly mean that," his voice but a whisper.

It hurt to mean it, but it was for the best. "Yes. I do."

Ranthrop took a step back as though a wind had hit him. His entire posture withered and for a moment, she thought he might drop to the floor. He looked at her but seemed to be looking through her instead.

"Yes, m'lady," he murmured and turned away.

She watched him walk to the door. His steps were awkward, and he grasped onto one of the displays halfway there. His hand slid off it like dead weight dropping to his side. His other hand lifted to rest where the hilt of his sword usually was, the way he did when he was thinking. No one else probably knew that. His palm came down, and his fist clenched when it found no iron to rest on at the waist of his dress slacks. She felt herself breathe again when he finally made it out the door.

Beside her, she heard a rustle and found her mother rescuing the discarded bouquet. Mary looked up and said, "You know, you didn't have to be so harsh, Valerie. I think he's heartbroken."

"He's heartbroken? I'm heartbroken."

Mary's hand froze with a loose daffodil in it. "You are?"

"Never mind what I am. Here, I'll get those." Valerie grasped Mary's elbow and helped her up. She took the flowers from her and walked behind the counter to throw them away but stopped to see if she could spot Ranthrop. Only halfway across the street, he walked as if he'd been hit by a car.

Mary rested a hand on her shoulder. "You care for him, don't you?"

"I did. I don't anymore." She picked at the flowers to avoid her scrutiny. "The garbage can's full. I'll go throw these out back." As she stepped away, her mother took hold of her wrist.

"Oh, no you don't!"

"What? I don't want them, Mom. They'll just remind me of…"

"Of how much it hurts?"

"Yes," the word fell from her lips. Why did her mother look like she understood for once?

Mary ran a finger across Valerie's temple, drawing her hair away. She smiled and said proudly, "I know. I have you. I see a little bit of your father in you every day and sometimes it still breaks my heart."

Valerie dropped her eyes and dug her thumbnail into one of the stems. Nothing like being kicked when you're already down. "Well, I'm sorry. You know I can't leave."

Mary's fingers nudged her chin back up, giving her a scolding look. "I wasn't finished. That breaks my heart some of the time, but when I see you every day I'm reminded that the man I married didn't just abandon me. He abandoned our wonderful, talented, intelligent, compassionate daughter. And that…that breaks my heart every second of the day." Mary's voice quivered, the older woman's curls shaking with emphasis. "You have your father's hair, his eyes, his height…" She chuckled, glancing down at herself. "And luckily, his waistline, but you're my daughter too. You're stubborn just like me. Too stubborn." Mary gently grabbed her wrist and held it up in the air. "And you *can* leave."

"I…" Valerie squeaked.

"I know you can, but you never have—even after all the grief I gave you. And you never planned to leave, did you?"

She was afraid to speak. It felt as if any response would be the wrong answer. "No."

"Because you don't want to abandon me like your father?"

"Because I love you." She didn't know the last time she had said those words, but they relieved a pressure inside of her.

Mary cupped her face. "And I love you, but you don't have to stay to make up for what he did. You're cheating yourself out of a whole world out there."

"I stayed because I wanted to, Mom."

"Let's do each other a favor. You don't wear these bracelets anymore, and I won't mention that you should leave for greener pastures again. Okay?"

Valerie closed her eyes and nodded. She smiled, enjoying the feel of her mother's affectionate touch on her face. Mary let go as she opened her eyes, and they both looked out the shop window—Ranthrop was no longer in view.

"What did he do that was so unforgivable?"

She took in a deep breath, contemplating what to say. Why break a winning streak of openness? "I saw him kissing another woman."

"I'm sorry. Do you know who she was to him?"

Could her mother handle the truth? "Um…one of the hall wenches apparently."

Mary's upper lip curled. "Oh. Is that…common there? Wenches?"

"I don't know, but there were two of them pawing all over him the second we got back as if it were their common greeting ritual."

"Two of them?" Mary's eyes rounded, and she glanced back out the window.

Valerie picked up the bouquet again. "Can I get rid of these now?"

Mary pondered, then replied, "He seems so well-mannered and sincere, Valerie. It's not right to throw away a gift given with sincerity, even if you don't agree with the person. He said he wants to marry you."

"He lives in a storybook, Mom," she said, walking around her mother. "How am I supposed to live in a storybook?"

"Well, quite easily, now that I think about it. After Ricky wrote that book in Farwin Wood, he disappeared right in front of me when he went back to sleep. Your body wouldn't be left behind, looking cold and dead for me to fuss over." Mary looked deep, in thought, contemplating the possibilities. "I'd certainly never have to worry about knowing where you were."

"Wow! I never thought I'd live to see the day Mary Millville promoted the weeping books."

"Shh!" Mary warned, glancing at the customers.

"Look. Can we be done with this now? It…" She looked at the flowers as her voice faltered. "It makes me sick thinking about it."

"That's what bothers me, Valerie. I've been on the sidelines for all your breakups, and I've never seen you like this."

"I'm just tired." Her lip began to tremble. She couldn't hold back the tears. "I'm sick and tired of being treated like I don't matter. I'm tired of being used. And I'm humiliated because I keep doing it to myself. It's not them! It's me! They're a brick wall that I keep running right into. I don't want to feel that hope, that excitement anymore and think," she rubbed her forehead, turning her tear-filled eyes to the ceiling, "…maybe this one is different. Because they're not different! They never are, that's the thing. I really thought he *was* different." She detested her high-pitched voice as she spoke. She smeared her hand underneath her nose.

Mary crushed Valerie against her, holding her tight.

"I don't want to hurt anymore," Valerie whispered, letting her head collapse on her mother's shoulder.

"Shh," Mary said, stroking Valerie's hair. "It gets better. Don't worry."

"When?" she demanded as she drew her head back.

Mary laughed, wiping Valerie's tears. "You never were patient with anything."

ALLISTER'S BOOKS

IT TOOK Sarah several minutes to break away from her customers to get to Ranthrop. He still stood by the door where he'd stopped when he came in, his chin nearly touching his chest.

Someone could use him as a model for a sketch of a hangman's victim. Ricky was useless as he snored at the register.

"Ranthrop, is something wrong? How did it go?"

"She does not want me," he mumbled.

"I'm so sorry." The phone rang, and she tried snapping her fingers in front of Ricky so she didn't have to abandon Ranthrop in his misery. "Did you try the flowers?"

"She does not...want me," he repeated as if it were an epiphany.

The phone chirped and chirped. "Would you excuse me a moment?" She hoisted herself up, leaning across the counter to grab the cordless phone. "Allister's Books."

"Sarah? It's Mary."

"Mary," she whispered, covering the speaker with one hand. "What happened over there? I've got a dead man walking on my hands."

"And I've got his twin over here. She went in the back, but I don't know when she'll come out again. Can I talk to Ranthrop?"

"Talk to him?"

"Yes. Hurry, please. I don't want Valerie to catch me."

"All right." Sarah turned around and handed the phone to Ranthrop. "Here, it's for you."

He broke from his daze, giving the phone a contemplative look. "Thank you, Lady Sarah." His voice sounded unenthused as he took the handset, stuffing it into his pocket. "I do not see though why I deserve a gift."

"Hello?" Mary's muffled voice came from inside the fabric.

Sarah scrambled to tug the phone out of his pocket. "No, it's a phone. It... Here. You put it up to your ear like this, and you can talk to other people. It's Mary. Mary Millville from across the street. She wants to talk to you." Sarah forced the phone up to Ranthrop's ear.

"Lady Mary?" Ranthrop yelled. "Where are you?"

Sarah spun around, trying to hold the phone to his ear as he turned and looked out the window toward Scent and Suds. She grabbed his hand, placing it on the receiver.

"And I am at the Allister's shop!" Ranthrop continued.

"Shh! You don't have to yell," Sarah warned.

"What about Valerie?" His posture straightened as his eyes squinted, trying to see Mary in the shop across the street. "But she said she wants me to leave!"

"Shh!"

"A cookout? What is that?"

"A feast," Sarah whispered. "It's like a feast."

"Yes, I'd be happy to attend. Will Valerie be there?" He nodded, his expression serious. "Yes, I see. I thank you for the invitation. Nine o'clock this eve? I'll see you then. Thank you, Lady Mary."

Ranthrop dropped his hand and waved out the window. Sarah snagged the handset from him, drawing his attention back to her.

"What a marvelous invention."

"Yeah, it's pretty remarkable." She wasn't daft. Never would she have expected Mary to invite Ranthrop to the annual Halloween cookout. With Halloween on Saturday this year, they had moved the regular Sunday cookout up a day so everyone could recover on Sunday from the chaotic week.

"Well!" Ranthrop inhaled, drawing himself up to his full height as he rubbed his hands together. "I require a washtub."

"Excuse me?"

"A washtub. I require a bath, perhaps a shave as well. I will also need to clean my colors. No offense, Sarah, but your suggestions did not work. I have been given another interview with Valerie, and I'd prefer to go in my own attire. Maybe it will remind her of the man she met. Can you provide me with a washtub?"

Sarah gawked at him, feeling reduced to a maid. "Why don't you try waking up Sleeping Beauty?"

"I beg your pardon?"

"Ricky." She nodded toward her snoring nephew. "The washtub is his department."

CHAPTER
FORTY-THREE

THE COURTYARD

REGGIE INCHED his way over to the spread on the picnic table. Pumpkin pie, honey ham, and even Walter Freedhof's barbecue ribs didn't interest him. He'd been watching Franci from afar while he nursed his drink. She wasn't Lorna anymore, but she wasn't quite the old Franci either.

She looked incredible. He knew she looked incredible because his mind kept repeating this every time he stole a glance at her. She had woven her long black hair into a wide-plaited braid that trailed over her shoulder and down her breast. The black turtleneck, true to her usual colors, made her look fresher. He loved the knee-length tan suede skirt with the black panty hose and calf-high boots. It was a modern twist on the classic Franci he knew. She still looked like a lady as she sat with her legs crossed and hands folded in her lap.

She looks incredible. But a new thought popped into his head, one that made him start meandering toward the table. She looks uncomfortable.

Franci loved the cookouts more than anyone. She was usually bubbly and chatted with everyone about their day. She made sure each person had a heaping pile of food and often walked around to offer second helpings. The first to insist on music, she always played something lively and got everyone to dance. Not tonight, however. Tonight, Franci sat alone on the edge of the picnic table. She nodded and greeted people with a smile as they milled by but returned to fidgeting with her hands once they were gone. Occasionally, she'd adjust her glasses, setting them right back in the place they had been.

"Happy Halloween, Franci," he called as he approached.

"Oh, hello, Reggie. Happy Halloween to you too."

Nothing. There it was again. Her gaze constantly shifted from one person to another to the flames in the fire pit. They both began speaking at the same time.

"What were you going to say?" he asked.

"No, you go ahead."

"How are you feeling?"

"Fine. Much better. Thank you. I... Well, technically I don't know if I'm better because I don't remember anything being wrong with me."

He braved his nerves and straddled the bench opposite her. "You're better, trust me."

"Sarah said you stayed with me most of the time. Thank you for doing that."

"Ah, you'd do the same for me."

"Yes, I suppose you're right, but still…" She lowered her voice and looked at him with her deep brown eyes. "Did I embarrass myself?"

You look…incredible. Snap out of it, Reggie! Focus! "No, Franci. I wouldn't let you embarrass yourself."

Her smile was genuine this time. It warmed his heart until she said, "You're a good friend, Reggie."

He didn't just want to be friends anymore. It was selfish. Having Franci back to normal was more than anyone had hoped for, but he'd had a glimpse of what the two of them had missed out on all these years. He wanted to show her, wanted to see if she reciprocated the spark.

"You know what I do remember?"

"What?" His heart skipped a beat.

"That you're never without a cigarette for more than twenty minutes, and I haven't seen you smoke since you got here."

"Oh. I'm trying to quit."

"Really? Good for you. I never understood why you exercise and smoke. It seems to defeat the purpose."

He worked out to compensate for his maimed chest. The one-night stands he was able to manage certainly wouldn't have been very eager if he'd been scarred and flabby. None of that mattered now. This was Franci, and she wouldn't judge him for his scars. "If you expect me to stay this size, I'm going to have to double my workouts because I've been eating garbage all week."

Franci giggled. "I don't care what size you are, Reggie."

Lord, she said his name again. *His* name. It sounded so good each time she did. It let him know he was the current center of her attention, a place he wanted to stay.

She leaned forward and whispered, "Does that mean you don't want any of my pie?"

"What kind of pie?"

"Your favorite—strawberry rhubarb."

"You made it?"

"Of course." She stood up and brought him a serving. "I know what a picky eater you are. That's why I always make this one so I know you'll at least find a dish you like at these things."

"You do?"

"Mm-hmm, sure."

She got better and better every minute. He'd missed it, all these little things that made her great. What an ass he'd been. He stared at the pie like it was a trophy.

"Aren't you going to try it?"

"Sure." He ruptured her work of art, putting a bite in his mouth. The tangy rhubarb mingled with the sweet berries and melted in his mouth. It tasted like home. He wanted to cry.

"How is it?"

He shielded his eyes with his hand, resting his forehead against it to hide his misty eyes. Through a weepy bite, he managed, "It's good. Really good."

"Reggie, are you all right?" Franci's hand reached out and covered his.

He dropped his fork and clasped onto her. "Geez, you're freezing. Here. Take my jacket."

"No. I'm fine. I was going to go inside soon anyway."

He had already rounded the table and taken off his brown leather jacket. He held it out for her to put on. "You can't go in yet. You just got here. You haven't even danced."

"Oh, I'm not in the mood after what happened. It doesn't seem right to be frolicking about when I was running around town out of my mind."

"Looks good on you." He nodded to his jacket on her slender frame.

"Thanks." She sniffed at the coat. "Did you get new cologne?"

"No. It's the same I always use. Why?"

"Hmm. I like it. I never noticed before."

He pointed a warning finger at her in jest. "Hey, don't start actin' like me now. You only get the jacket for an hour, tops!"

Franci giggled. "I won't." She sighed and hugged the lapels across her front. "I let Mary pick out the music tonight and you know she doesn't like anything lively like we do."

He followed Franci's gaze to the couples on the concrete slab in the center of the common area. Walter's petite wife had her arms stretched to the limit to reach his neck, while his belly held her at bay. One of Walter's boys was dancing with Genie Mathers's girl. Ricky looked like he was sucking up to his girlfriend as he held her close. Henry and Sarah were whispering and smiling as they swayed in time to the music.

"We've never slow danced, have we?"

Franci laughed again. "I've certainly never slow danced. With anyone."

No one? How many times had he felt sorry for himself for his lack of success with women and Franci's track record was even worse than his. She made the best damned pie in the world. She made pie just for him. She deserved more than that.

"That ain't right, Franci."

"Maybe, but it's all right."

"No it ain't. Come on." He grabbed her hand and led her onto the patio.

"How am I doing?" she asked, resting her hands on his shoulders.

He took one of her hands in his. "Here, like this."

"You don't have to feel sorry for me, you know? I'm used to being on my own."

"I don't. I wanted to dance." He moved them to the music in silence. She didn't look uncomfortable, but he had hoped she'd appear to enjoy it more than she was. "Franci, what else haven't you done?"

"What do you mean?"

"I mean in the way of romance. Stuff men and women do together."

"What?" She pulled her head back and looked at him wide-eyed. "Reggie, I may be on the brink of spinsterhood, but I've at least found out what it's like between the sheets."

"No, that's not what I meant!" Jesus. He didn't want to imagine that.

"Oh." Her cheeks reddened, and she looked away.

"Why don't you make me a list? A list of all the things you've wanted to do but haven't had the chance."

"What are you now, Reggie? My fairy godmother?" She chuckled. "My, you're acting strange tonight."

"You really don't remember…anything?"

"No. I told you already. Maybe someday I will. If I do, you'll be the first to know."

He swallowed the lump in his throat and stopped dancing. "Franci, I gotta tell you something."

"What is it?"

"When you were…bonkers. You…thought I was Archie Hamlin or that Ricardo guy he played. You…acted like you were in love with me and kept coming onto me."

"I what?" Franci slapped her hands over her mouth. "Oh, my word! Did we… Did we…"

"No! No! Of course not! I couldn't!"

Her hands fell away from her mouth, and her voice became dejected. "Oh. No, of course not. Sorry, I didn't mean to assume that you would…want to do something like that… with me."

"What? Are you crazy again? Of course, I wanted to! I…" Ah, shit! He said that out loud.

He realized that he had grabbed her by the shoulders. She turned her downcast eyes up at him. "You did?" she asked.

Please don't slap me in front of everybody, he thought. "Yeah. I'm sorry. I couldn't help it. You kept kissing me and… then I remembered it wasn't really you, it was just that psycho Lorna. Who really has an attitude problem, by the way. You don't want to be her, trust me! I didn't mean to take advantage of you, though Franci. I'm sorry I gave in, but I stopped in time. You're my oldest friend, I wouldn't do that to you. Please don't be mad at me." He squeezed her shoulders and waited for her reaction.

She stared at him, her arms folded across her stomach. Lorna would know what to say in a heartbeat. Why wasn't she saying anything? "We…kissed?" she finally managed.

"Yes, but that's it. I swear." Okay, that wasn't totally it, but he wasn't going for sainthood. He was already the leper of Blinney Lane, he didn't need any more black marks against him.

"What…" She shrugged her shoulders, and her gaze moved to his lips. "What was it like?"

That was a green light, if he ever saw one. "It…it was like this…"

THE HALLOWEEN cookout was the last place Valerie wanted to be tonight. Just another reminder of how life had come to a screeching halt on a dead-end road. She used to love this place and the quirky people in it. Looking around at her little community, the future looked like the prison that so many of them found Blinney Lane to be. At least she had made amends with her mother. It was comforting to be in her proximity at the drinks table while everyone else milled about the courtyard. The rest of her comfort came in liquid form.

The spread of liquor bottles and mixers they had setup on the banquet table either tasted sour or bitter to her. She'd been put in charge of the punch, which she later realized was watermelon flavored. The extra kick she added had been to warm the dull ache inside of her against the crisp chill of the night air. Now the sweet aftertaste only reminded her of beetleburry ale.

"Hey, why don't you take it easy on that?" Her mother said.

"Yeah, it's lost its appeal." She set the cup down, folding her arms.

"You look very nice, by the way."

Valerie glanced down at the long-sleeved black chenille dress she'd worn at her mother's suggestion. It had bell sleeves and an A-line cut that fell just below her knees. She'd braided two strands of her hair and connected them at the back of her head. On her ears were two large golden hoops. Mary had said that looking good might make her feel better except she didn't. She felt more feminine and vulnerable. With the slow, old music playing, she imagined she resembled a go-go girl, which just made her feel stupid.

"Thanks, but it didn't work. I don't feel any better. And what's with the music, Mom? I don't think you could have picked anything more depressing."

"It's a nice change. Everyone else seems to be enjoying it."

She looked at the couples dancing, and her jaw dropped. Amidst the partners on the patio, she saw Franci and Reggie—lip locked. She looked at her mother who appeared dumbstruck. "Yeah. They seem to be enjoying a little more than that!"

Mary adjusted the stacks of cups. "Yes, well…that's none of our business."

Valerie gawked at her. It was going to take time to get used to her new, nonchalant attitude. A flash of red approaching out of the darkness caught her eye.

"Valerie, what is it?" Mary turned to see what had caught her attention.

"Lady Mary." Ranthrop bowed in front of her mother.

"Ranthrop! Uh, welcome," Mary said in a nervous voice. She turned to Valerie and added, "I think I'll grab a plate before the food gets cold."

Mary scrambled away, and she was left on shaky knees, standing in front of him. He had on his Farwin Wood garb again, which looked pressed from head to toe and smelled of soap.

"Lady Valerie," he greeted. His husky voice gave her tingles.

"What are you doing here? I thought you would have left by now."

"I've had the fortune of meeting some of your townsfolk. I've only come to say good-bye to everyone properly and to give my thanks to the Allister's for boarding me during my stay. Don't fret, m'lady. I plan to respect your wishes. I will return to Farwin Wood within the hour."

"Within the hour?"

"Yes. I'm sure Varmeer will be beside himself if I do not return soon since he has no idea where I've gone." He glanced out at the rest of the Blinney residents. The glow of the firelight and Halloween candles ruffled shadows on his face. "You have your own version of feasts here, as well. It is a peculiar place, but I am glad to find similarities."

She was speechless. He acted resigned, but she could see the melancholy in his eyes, hear it in the tone of his voice.

"Again, I thank you for what you have done for me, and I am deeply sorry that I caused you pain. It was not my intention. I had hoped things would have turned out differently for us."

Her throat constricted, listening to his sincerity. She couldn't let herself cry in front of him. He was really leaving. She was hardly capable of braving his world on her own but neither was he. Not knowing what would become of him there bothered her. She thought of his protector, Varmeer.

"Give my best to Varmeer," she blurted.

"Yes. Of course." He put a hand on the hilt of his sword, his forearm across his chest, and bowed. "Lady Valerie, it has been an honor. I wish you every happiness."

He turned and walked away before she knew what had happened. Bracing her hands on the table, she watched as he made his way over to Sarah and Henry. She couldn't make out his words, but he moved on from them to Alexander, then to Reggie and Franci. It was surreal to witness him with people in her world. She watched his easy charm effect them. He managed to say something to each person, causing a laugh or smile. They shook his hand or patted him on the shoulder. Possessiveness washed over her, knowing that he wasn't always a joker. He could be tender and vulnerable—a side he'd shown only to her. He moved on to Ricky and Shelby, as Mary sat a plate of food down at the end of the drink table.

"What did Ranthrop want?"

"He came to say good-bye. He's…leaving."

"You asked him to. Why do you sound so bothered?"

"I'm not bothered," she said and fussed with some bottles. "I…" Her voice trailed off as she spotted Ranthrop approaching again.

"Lady Mary."

"Ranthrop, I hear you're leaving."

"Yes, m'lady. I would like to offer my apologies for the upset I gave you whilst I was here."

Mary waved a dismissive hand. "Oh, this place could use a little livening up from time to time. I'm sure I've seen and heard worse." Mary arched a brow and spared Valerie a fleeting glance.

"All the same, I used poor judgment."

"Well, matters of the heart tend to do that to people."

I'm standing right here, she thought as they both glanced at her.

Ranthrop continued, "It was a pleasure to meet you, Lady Mary. I can't imagine what it would be like to bring a child up on your own, but you have outdone yourself. She is a remarkable woman. Did you know that she saved my life on our journey?"

"No, I didn't." Mary put a hand to her heart.

"'Tis true. You should be very proud."

Mary smiled thoughtfully. "I am. Thank you."

"Well then. I bid you good-bye."

"Good-bye," Mary said wistfully.

Ranthrop nodded to Valerie before he made his way from the party. She watched him go, hearing his footsteps crunch against the grass and dried leaves. Words bubbled up within her, refusing to burst forth.

Mary whispered loudly, "Valerie!" She felt her mother's hand on the small of her back, shoving her forward.

"I…" She glanced over her shoulder as her mother shoved again. The shove popped the bubble, and she called out, "Ranthrop!"

He stopped halfway to Franci's greenhouse and turned around. She walked to meet him on shaky legs.

"Yes?"

She needed an excuse, but she didn't have one other than the part of her that didn't want him to leave. She looked back at the party. The only one who seemed to pay them any attention was her mother. The rest were busy eating or dancing.

"You didn't get to enjoy much of our feast. Do people dance at your feasts?"

"Oh, yes. Sometimes all night."

"Would you like to dance…before you go?"

"Yes, I would love to."

He offered his arm out to her, and she placed her hand through it without thinking. It wasn't until he led her to the dance area that the stately sight they made had her feeling self-conscious. Apparently, anyone who'd seen Reggie and Franci kissing must have gotten over the shock because all eyes seemed to be on her and Ranthrop now.

As his hand found her waist, she spotted Ricky, who gave her a thumbs up. It was enough for her to forget everyone else for the moment. Why should she care what anyone thought? Other people from Blinney Lane had been in the book. And her mother, as shocking as it was, didn't seem to object to Ranthrop's presence.

Her mother. It dawned on her then. Ranthrop had asked her mother for permission to marry her. He'd made a point to tell Mary that she had saved him.

"You know, you don't owe me anything," she said as he moved them in time with the music.

"What do you mean?"

"I mean for saving you. Is that why you asked my mother if you could marry me? It makes sense now," she added, more for her own benefit.

"Not at all. I told you I craved adventure after the war. I realized you were the adventure I needed."

What adventure? Certainly, he didn't plan on making more treks to Terradoon. She was probably the first woman who had ever given him a run for his money. She'd seen how her charm wore off. She was a shiny new object for men because they thought she was different. Once her glimmer was gone, they moved on to new adventures. She was a five-minute girl, like a pit stop. Ranthrop was still stuck in his first five minutes. Marriage? She wasn't convinced.

"You have enough adventure left at your keep. Two, in fact, were waiting for you when we got back."

"The wenches? I haven't touched any since I met you!" She glowered at him, and his defensive look muted. "They caught me by surprise. I did what I could to send them on their way. I had no thought of them after the time I'd just spent with you."

She did her best to keep her feet moving during the debate. "Why did you have them there in the first place?"

His face looked pained as he squeezed her hand. "There was a hole in me for the longest time, during and after the war. They were just bodies, Valerie, women who were eager to please returning warriors who had no wives or women of their own awaiting them at home. But in the morning light, they would be gone and my burdens would soon return. I grew bored of them, knowing they would never pacify the nagging inside of me. Why, one of my last orders to Varmeer was to clear them out of my keep. If he hasn't, I'll throttle him."

"Leave Varmeer alone. He's devoted to you."

"Unfortunately, for me."

He spun her, and she rolled her eyes. "So what was your plan? Get rid of all your wenches and replace them with just one? If they couldn't…fill your nagging hole, what makes you think that I will?"

"I need a woman like you to rule my lands with me."

A woman *like* her—not specifically her. Not good enough.

"You rule your lands just fine by yourself."

"I need a woman who can help me make sound judgments."

"My judgments are poor."

She tripped on her feet when he stopped dancing and grasped her by the arms. "Damn it! Varmeer says I need to be more eloquent, but I cannot! I don't know how!" She froze from his sudden outburst. He cursed under his breath before looking back at her. "It's like the story you told me of your dragons. I have been walking around all these years with a dying heart. But I'm damned, you see, because not just any dragon will do. I have seen the other half of my heart and without it, I'm as good as dead because I know the rest of my life will be a void. There's only one dragon with the power to keep my heart alive, and it's you. My heart needs your heart and yours alone."

She blinked at the tears in her eyes. Her lower lip trembled, and her voice was soft as she spoke. "That was almost eloquent."

Ranthrop exhaled, pulling her in close. She felt his breath on her cheek as his hand stroked the back of her hair.

"Oh, my lady, you once asked me not to go. Tell me what I need to do to hear you say it again, and I'll never leave your side."

Valerie pulled her head back, swiping at her eyes. She sniffled, her other hand pressed to his chest. "You don't belong here, and I can't stand the sight of you in polo shirts. Take me with you."

The horror of worry on his face shifted to disbelief. She smiled at his endearing stupidity, threaded her arms around his neck, and murmured, "Aren't you going to kiss me?"

His forehead rested on hers, and he sighed a sound of relief. "I'm going to kiss you forever."

She held tight to him as their lips met, still afraid he would disappear because his presence defied the laws of nature. His arms circled around her and when their lips parted, he peppered her cheeks with kisses until her face hurt from smiling so wide.

Ranthrop reached around her legs in a quick movement and swept her into his arms. She threw her arms around his neck, her heart fluttering at the feel of weightlessness, laughing as he spun them around. When he stopped, he carried her back into the midst of the party.

"Good folk of Blinney! I am honored to announce that Lady Valerie has accepted my proposal of marriage."

She heard collective gasps and looked at the faces of her friends. She located her mother, who wove her hands together and smiled.

"You are looking at the future Lady Groslivo who I will be proud to have rule the Southlands by my side for all my days. We extend an invitation to you all to join us very soon for a wedding feast at Groslivo Keep so you may see where we will spend many happy years to come."

"Groslivo Keep?" Mary squeaked. Her eyes rolled back in her head as she fainted.

Ranthrop called down with loud curiosity, "Mother? Mother!" Valerie squirmed from his hold down to the ground. "Does this happen often?" he asked her.

Valerie gave him a reassuring pat on the chest and flashed a smile before rushing to check on her mother. "I think she likes you."

Lightning Source UK Ltd.
Milton Keynes UK
UKHW041858120419
340971UK00002B/51/P

9 781948 540438